THE SASKIAD

BOOKS BY BRIAN HALL

BRIAN

HALL

HOUGHTON MIFFLIN COMPANY

THE

SASKIAD

BOSTON   NEW YORK   1997

For information about this and other Houghton Mifflin trade and reference
books and multimedia products, visit The Bookstore at Houghton Mifflin
on the World Wide Web at http://www.hmco.com/trade/.

Library of Congress Cataloging-in-Publication Data

Hall, Brian, date.
The Saskiad / Brian Hall.
p.   cm.
ISBN 0-395-82754-X
I. Title.
PS3558.A363S27   1997   813'.54 — dc20   96-25841   CIP

Book design and decorations by Anne Chalmers
Type: Electra (Linotype-Hell), Lithos (Adobe)

Printed in the United States of America

QUM   10 9 8 7 6 5 4 3 2 1

"Ithaca" in *The Complete Poems of Cavafy*, copyright © 1961 and
renewed 1989 by Rae Dalven, reprinted by permission of
Harcourt Brace & Company.

FOR PAMELA

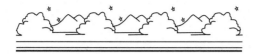

PART 1

JANE

When you start on your journey to Ithaca,
then pray that the road is long,
full of adventure, full of knowledge.
Do not fear the Lestrygonians
and the Cyclopes and the angry Poseidon.
You will never meet such as these on your path,
if your thoughts remain lofty, if a fine
emotion touches your body and your spirit.
You will never meet the Lestrygonians,
the Cyclopes and the fierce Poseidon,
if you do not carry them within your soul,
if your soul does not raise them up before you.

— Cavafy, "Ithaca"

1

THIS IS WHERE she is now: a Greek island, low and away, last of all on the water toward the dark. Ithaca lies between two ridges at the head of a long crooked bay. No automobiles desecrate the silent streets. The modern world has been rubbed out like a mistake. The great stone clock tower on the eastern slope chimes the hour, its triad of gongs shimmering in the gelatinous air.

The sun is motionless, huge. How deliciously she can feel the heat on her arms! She peels off her clothes, and her skin is golden like the sun. Her arms and legs glide, buttery at the joints. She can feel quite distinctly the dirt under her bare feet. She glides between the clapboard houses with their wraparound porches, their nested gables and towers. Beautiful homes like carved chests containing fine things: all the people she does not know.

But here is an incongruity amid classical Ithacan order and repose. Her own house: the swaybacked porch, the three floors of mismatched windows, the white paint so indecently peeled that only splotches remain like lichen on the rotting shingles. Rising from the shallow roof is a belvedere, a small room with windows all around. A Captain's room.

There is nothing she wants so much as to get up into that room. She would be able to judge the weather up there. She would pace undisturbed, lost in thought, unaware how much her men admired and loved her.

She bounds onto the porch and tries the door. Locked. She grips the knob and pulls, confident of the swelling strength in her hands. But the door holds firm, indifferent to it.

2

As always, she wakes early, thinking, thinking. The new girl will be in school today. She saw her sitting in the Vice Principal's office. The new girl!

She listens. Quiet.

The sky is empty of stars. She turns on the light by her bed. Blind blackness presses against her window. How frightening! But when she turns out the light, her faithful stars have come out to cheer her: Orion in the northwest, and directly overhead the Big Dipper, which travelers call the Wagon because it wheels, never stopping, never sinking into the wash of the ocean. A supernova blazes in late-setting Boötes, the Herdsman, who herded Odysseus home. And the Moon, her planet, is a wind-filled sail racing along the ecliptic, waxing, always waxing, toward some fullness, some completion she can hardly wait for, but cannot foresee.

Could it have something to do with the new girl? She is so beautiful.

The stars are fading. She is the only one to keep a safe eye on the cunning dark, to help bleed this blind black to gray. No one else thinks of these things. Perhaps the new girl will. The beautiful new girl.

3

When she catches the first glimmer of the lake, she slips quietly down and pulls on rubber boots in the back hall. Outside is the sodden snow of a Tylerian January.

In the barn Marilyn lumbers, steaming, to her feet, the back up first on splayed legs, the udder swaying hugely. Saskia dumps a scoop of pellets in the trough and shovels muck into the bin, then squats to rub the furry udder, coaxing the coo into letting down. Marilyn never lies in her own muck. She is a good coo with a clean udder, a pleasure to rub. Saskia works white ointment into the rear teats, and the udder veins bulge, the teats swell. She fires into the bucket a long sequence of pump-action double-barreled blasting. She has the strongest hands of anyone in her grade. At the Ithacan Carnival last summer she pushed the dial on the grip machine up to "Bone-crusher." Afterward, Marilyn is rewarded with a pile of hay and a hug as wide as two arms can reach. Saskia delights in the hot bristle against her cheek. When Saskia was little, an earlier coo pushed her against the wall, making her cry. Thomas ran to rescue her, his brown robe flapping. He lifted her a mile high and kissed her.

In the coop, the chickens mince around her feet like bathers crossing hot sand. She leaves three eggs on the sideboard in the kitchen and pours a saucer of milk for Gorgon, who sidles her fat black body up to the dish with a grunt-like purr. It is a Discipline to love Gorgon, who bites and claws, and squats furtively in corners to do her business along the baseboards. Saskia once wrote and illus-trated a reader for the crew that started, "Fat cat, black cat! What cat? That cat!" Pirates threatened, but Gorgon eventually saved the day. A rather pathetic fallacy.

Back upstairs, Saskia picks a skirt and shawl for school. No need for a shower. The caramel smell of Marilyn in her hair is better than any soap. There's a flush of aqua along the eastern ridge. Time to raise the crew. Barring a rescue by the new girl — swinging down on a rope with a Tarzan yell? — the best part of her day is over.

4

Across the hall, her boatswain is still asleep, damn her eyes! "Get up, you scoundrel! The wind freshening, and a falling glass — no telling what the day will bring!" A lazy dog, yes. But she's damn comely. A hoogily thing. "Come on, Mim, it's almost seven." Saskia rummages through the pile of stuffed animals.

"I'm up!" Mim bubbles up, animals tumbling. "Where's horsey?"

Saskia picks it off the floor. Good God, what the Admiralty sends her. On the lower deck she rouses the rest of the crew — Austin, Shannon, Quinny — to the usual accompaniment of grumbling. Poor devils, it must be hell to be pressed into this service. Weevily food, never enough sleep. And where does it end? Beheaded by a cannonball or sent shrieking under the surgeon's knife. "Don't blame me," she always tells them when they cry. "Blame Boney." They straggle off to the latrine. (Or is that the loo? Perhaps the ship has no such thing. Simply off the side? Not on *this* ship.) Quinny takes his sheet with him. "Your hygiene!" she bellows after them. "I'll be checking!"

Tall, capable Lauren is in the kitchen brewing coffee which, like the Captain, she thinks of as soon as her eyes open. She is monumental in her nightgown, her ton of hair unbound. Saskia reports to her back: "Quinny wet his bed again."

Lauren's shoulders sigh. "You stripped it?"

"He does it himself now."

"Well at least he's doing *something*." She turns to face Saskia, her eyes still cushioned with sleep. "How old is he, anyway?"

"Seven."

"Ridiculous!" She bangs closed the freezer door on her fancy Ithacan coffee. "Get him to make the bed up himself, too. If he's going to do that like a *baby* —"

"I'm working on that."

"How did he get to be seven years old?"

Saskia assumes that's a rhetorical question. "It's not a big deal."

"Teach him to do the laundry. Then he can wet his bed all he wants."

"It's no big *deal*." You really shouldn't bother Lauren before she has had her coffee.

"Don't be a martyr, Saskia. Nobody likes a martyr." The coffee machine lets out a Bronx cheer. Lauren fills a mug. Hurry up and drink it, you crabby old thing! She sips, smacking at the heat. "If you want to be Quinny's servant, go right ahead. *I'm* getting dressed." As if getting dressed is the way not to be Quinny's servant. Lauren sips again and closes her eyes appreciatively. What is it about coffee? The Captain fights a battle in a gale off a lee shore and never changes expression. But give him a cup of the real thing after a month of burnt-bread swill at sea, and the sparkle in his eyes is a lovely sight.

"You're a good girl, Saskia," Lauren says, seeming to reconsider.

"Woof!" she says testily.

Lauren shrugs. "All right, you're not a good girl." She goes up to dress.

Saskia scrambles eggs for the crew and sets out Marilyn's milk along with tots of fresh-squeezed rum. Shannon and Austin are sent back to wash their hands. Austin bops Quinny and Quinny blubbers. In the Judgment Book, Austin has eight demerits, Mim three, Shannon two, and Quinny twenty-six. When you reach ten demerits you clean out the latrines or swab the deck, or when it's hot you fan Saskia and Marco with wicker platters and feed them peeled grapes. But Quinny is under a different system. Discipline, in Quinny's case, has proven counterproductive, no matter what Lauren says.

Saskia fills lunch boxes, checks book bags and clothing, tucks a wad of tissue paper in Quinny's back pocket. She wipes his slobbery chin. Lauren reappears in her greenhouse clothes to dispense regal kisses.

The bus jolts down the last treacherous slope and nearly takes out the fence by Lauren's field as the driver, a real toby, backs and fills in the turnaround.

"Morning, Chief." (His daily witticism is to call her Chief.)

"Morning, Toby."

They rattle through the bedraggled Tylerian landscape under dirt-soup skies, picking up dregs and pigs. Saskia sits in the front to keep a safe eye on the Toby, and Quinny huddles next to her for protection. Austin and Shannon sit in the back and holler for the short cut, an especially mogully "seasonal" road — basically a streambed — the Toby will take now and then when he fancies himself a nice guy. The back of the bus whips on that road, sending barns flying. Mim always sits over the rear wheel casing. The seat is saved for her, because everybody likes her and not even the dregs hide it. Two pigs who get on near town sit with her, and they are as quiet and good and neat as she is, although not so furry. The three of them hold their books on their laps and gaze at each other with long-lashed eyes. Saskia wonders what they talk about. When they laugh, they sound like forest mammals, laughing knowingly about mammally things.

The oldest barns get off at the high school. Tyler Junior is next. "You can't come with me, Quinny." He may start blubbering. "I'll be on the bus this afternoon."

"Have a nice day, Chief!"

Her last seconds of freedom are the time it takes her to walk up the concrete path, through the fortified quadruple doors, each with its one baleful eye of netted glass, into the tiled gloom, the bang of lockers, the shouting and pushing and sneering and blubbering. Count off! Baa-aa-aa!

5

The new girl's name is Jane Sing. Ms. Plebetsky calls it out in English and directs the class to welcome her.

Sing! The new girl nods, acknowledging the praise. She is tall and slender, with skin as brown as Saskia's brown eyes and yards of black hair as straight and glossy as an ironed horse's tail. She turns back toward the Plebe, so that her face is away from Saskia, the hair a satin veil between them. Can Saskia make her pull the veil aside? She bores with her eyes into the back of the new girl's head. Calling Jane Sing. The hum of her heart, the glowing ring of a glass as she rubs her finger on the rim. Sinnnggg . . . Sinnnggg . . . Turn Sing. Turn Jane Sing.

Jane Sing turns. Her eyes run quickly over the faces, glittering as they search for Saskia, and when they find her they pause, they light like blackbirds on their rightful perch, home.

In gym her locker is far away among the afterthoughts, beyond the next grade's Y's and Z's. Hurriedly putting on her uniform, Saskia tries to see Jane Sing through the crush of pigs, but by the time she pushes down to the end, Jane is already dressed, her hair pulled behind her in a ponytail, showing her chocolate wafer ears, which Saskia stares at. Jane looks up. Saskia panics and hurries past.

Her arms and legs glow in the bright gym lights. Her round brown knees are a blur between the shorts and the socks, she handles the ball well. She runs at Saskia bouncing the ball, Saskia watches her beautiful legs, her willowy arms feinting right and left, she watches her flit past and jump for a basket.

"Sheez louise, Saskia! What are you *doing?* Quit daydreaming!"

Back in the locker room Saskia pretends to read notices on the bulletin board while Jane undresses a few feet away. Walking to the shower in her underclothes, Jane passes Saskia with another sidelong glance, as if to say, "When will you have the courage? Only ask me."

Saskia wraps a towel tightly over her underwear. Her skin is not dark or beautiful. Yellowish, it looks terrible when sweaty, pale and buttery, like something grown in the cellar. Jane's bra and undies hang over a hook outside a stall. They are edged with a pretty scalloped pattern. The bra is a yoke of patches. Of course willows don't have breasts. Saskia can imagine Jane's torso in the shower, the lines of it as straight and pure as her limbs. In her own stall, she bares herself and immediately covers herself again with steam clouds. When Saskia is bare, she is really bare. After two years of mooniness she still has practically no body hair. Even on the triangle there's only a few scraggly hairs like a revolting bunch of insect antennas. The hair on her head is cobwebby. With their inimitable charm, dregs run up and blow on it, as though she were a dandelion gone to seed. Mim is furry and mammally. Jane Sing is a gazelle. Lauren has silky hair all down her floor-length legs. But there is something reptilian about Saskia, something lizardy. Hairless skin, watchful eyes that don't blink.

And she has breasts. No willow, but a stumpy lumpy apple tree. "Cross-your-heart bra!" the dregs yell. "Over the shoulder boulder holder!" Saskia has read books in which heroines long for breasts, in which they bare their fronts to the moonlight to make them grow. But that cannot be right. No real person would be happy to see the first mushy stirrings of the pink blobs, the swelling in the flesh around them like some dreadful allergic reaction. And yet here they come. Udders! Soon they will be swaying hugely and getting in the way. And there is nothing you can do about it, not a thing.

6

Ms. Rosenblatt spells it on the board, and there is an *h* hanging on the end: Singh. But you still pronounce it Sing. The *h* is hanging breathless, Saskia thinks. That's a pun. In her notebook she writes, "Saskia Sing."

"Jane's family comes originally from India," Ms. Rosenblatt is saying with a phony wide-eyed expression. "That's a very long way away!"

Jane Sing keeps her eyes straight ahead. Saskia would be embarrassed, too. The Blatt always talks as if this were the first grade: "Ooh, a vewwy wong way away!" She hovers next to the world map with her pool cue. "Does anyone know where India is?"

"Beautiful place, India," Marco grunts.

"So you've said."

"They're all idolaters. They worship cows." He snorts.

"I worship cows, too."

"No you don't." He gives her a noogie. "You *milk* cows, Aiyaruk. That's not the same." How nice it is to have friends who know everything about you from the first moment! There are no disappointments, no embarrassing discoveries.

"No one has a guess?" The Blatt is wilting. Saskia raises her hand. "Yes, Saskia?"

"India is that thing hanging down below Cathay."

"Cathay?"

"China, stupido," Marco whispers.

"China. It's that thing hanging below, there." Like an udder with only one teat. Perhaps that's why they worship cows.

"Yes, very good, Saskia."

"'Yes, very good, Saskia,'" simpers Marco. "The old cow doesn't even know what Cathay is."

"Are all the women in India as beautiful as Jane?"

"All the maidens are. Their flesh is hard. For a penny, they'll allow a man to pinch them as hard as he can. But there is nothing to pinch."

"I guess not." If anyone pinched Saskia, they would get something, all right.

"They all go around naked. Because it's amazingly hot."

"And they're hard and brown?"

"Like mahogany. Even their breasts."

"Jane doesn't have those."

"She will."

Not swaying hugely, but as much a part of the clean lines as the curve of the hips, the curve of the grain in the wood. "It sounds beautiful, that way."

"Oh it is, my lass." Marco gazes at Jane for a long moment. "A man could lose his mind altogether over a maiden like that."

Marco is kind of a sex fiend.

But here comes the Blatt, down the row with handouts. "We have to hurry through this unit if we're going to get to Rome by March," she says querulously. The handout is a list of dates and headings. Heroic age . . . Periclean Athens . . . greatest artistic flowering . . . cradle of Western civilization, blah blah. Only the Blatt could make Greek history dull. Saskia writes in her notebook: "Rome by March! We March on Rome! Beware the Ides of March!" She wishes she had a lean and hungry look. That is partly what makes Jane so beautiful: a lurking hunger. For what? For a friend, of course.

She tunes out the Blatt. Counting syllables on her fingers, she writes a haiku:

> Lovely limber limbs
> Skip past to make a basket —
> The coach yells at me

7

In the tiled gloom, on the way to her bus, Saskia has a last chance. Jane Sing is at her locker. Saskia has thought of so many things to say — advice, something friendly, something special between the two of them, something Jane alone would understand and know was meant for her alone. But Saskia suddenly realizes how impossible they all are. Dumb, barnish ideas.

Jane is arranging things in her locker, intent. She does not see Saskia. She will not glance coolly and say, "Are you ready now, at last?" and turn with Saskia, to walk out into the sunshine with her. She is too tall, too beautiful. She comes from India. Saskia is going to walk past her without a word, hating herself.

"Hey scuz, look out!" Someone shoves her. Her books skitter off the ends of her chasing fingers and fall. Laughter. A pair of dregs splits and passes to either side, happily surveying the scatter. "Pretty clumsy, scuz!" And they are gone in the crowd before she can do anything except stare dumbfounded, think of anything except running and hiding. In front of Jane Sing! She gathers her stuff in the gloom, down among the scissoring legs. Her poor rumpled books! Two stupid dregs, their heads torn off, stuffed into garbage bags, their brainless laughter drained into horror and fear and begging for forgiveness as the bags are thrown into the back of the truck and cackling she pulls the lever that brings down the hydraulic crusher, so lonngg . . . ! Her eyes bulge. She can't believe it, she is going to cry right here.

"Fucking idiots," Jane Sing says from high above.

F— Even that word is all right, cradled in her lovely voice. What is it, that voice? Smooth-sided, spoken out of a cedar box. The page with the haiku is in Saskia's hand, ripped at the bottom. It is coming, she has no time . . . "This is for you," she says with her awful squeak, like something getting stepped on. She thrusts the page. "My name is Saskia." Jane Sing's mouth begins to open and Saskia glimpses a pink tongue pointed like a felt-tip marker. But she runs away. She hides in the opium den, barely making it into a stall before the lightning cracks across her forehead, her eyes tumble out, and the rain pours.

8

In the dark time, propped up in bed beneath her lamp, she labors over her autobiography, which begins:

Like all real people, I go under several names. To the laconic Captain, I am simply "Lieutenant," and proud to bear that humble title under his wise command. Marco calls me Aiyaruk, which means "Bright Moon" in the Tartar tongue. By Odysseus' side I am Saskion Monogeneia. Lastly, the Novamundians, with their typical lack of imagination, call me Saskia White.

My personal color is white, for the obvious reason. Thus, my planet is the Moon and my metal is silver. My armorial bearing is sable, a baston sinister, argent, between a crescent, argent, and sol, or.

The sable background is the night, held at bay by the silver light her eyes shine on it. The baston sinister signifies bastardy. The crescent on the left is herself, while the sol on the right is the one whom she would follow, if only she found one worthy: the Captain to her faithful Lieutenancy, the perfection of gold to which near-perfect silver aspires.

Lauren and I have a farm in Novamundus. Ours is a goodly land, fertile and yielding to the plow. It lies on the western shore of mighty Cayuga Lake, along both sides of fast-flowing White Creek. The farm is now known by the name White-on-the-Water, although it was not always thus.

Actually, Saskia is the only one who calls it White-on-the-Water. She loves geographical names, and English ones seem especially delicious, like sandwiches: Stratford-upon-Avon; Stourport-on-Severn. Lauren calls White-on-the-Water simply "The Place," or if she is feeling eloquent, "The Old Place."

Lauren is Plant-master at White-on-the-Water and her store of wisdom in this matter is great. With the help of silent spells and incantations she causes wondrous things to grow. I am the Animal Keeper. I tend to Marilyn and I encourage the chickens in their laying of eggs. In summer I cut Marilyn's timothy with my personal scimitar. Lowly jobs, some would say, sneering. But I do them willingly and well.

Marilyn and the chickens are at White-on-the-Water only for milk and eggs. Saskia knows the Novamundian practice: chasing the chicken, swinging it like a noisemaker to stop its noise. Or hoisting the coo by the hind leg at the end of the fifth milking year, the wave of blood splashing from the throat into the trough. Lauren and Saskia don't allow any of that barbarity at White-on-the-Water. The chickens mince and dither until they keel over from tiny heart attacks. Marilyn will experience a sudden massive stroke in her meadow on a sunny spring day and collapse in a patch of clover so lush and loving it will lower her gently to the ground. Such care is ordained. If you do not treat the things around you with the proper respect, they will not be good to you. You will not have earned their goodness.

9

Down, she floats down, deeper, pulling down with her the precious consciousness, a trapped bubble, that she is going down. She monitors her breathing and the slow dissolution of blankets, the confusion of place. Koan: I am in two places at once. This is what it is like. Remember.

A Greek island. No people, no cars. The clock tower chimes the gelatinous hour. She peels off her clothes, feeling the delicious heat. She walks between the beautiful houses, and her own house is there, itself and not itself, the Captain's room rising from the roof. She bounds onto the porch. The door is locked.

But she is getting better. She remembers the crucial fact: she brought a key. It lies solidly on her palm. She turns the key in the lock, and the door opens. How laughably easy! The inside of the house is exactly as she knows it. She climbs the stairs, passing Lauren's room and the crew's quarters and continuing up until she emerges in the top hall, her cabin to one side, Mim's berth to the other. There are no more stairs. The attic is nothing but a crawl space, reachable by means of a folding ladder bolted to a panel in the ceiling. But that is no way to get to a Captain's room.

Looking down, she realizes she is still naked. Strange that she could have forgotten that. The thought of her loose in the house naked, her bare flank rubbing against the bristly wallpaper, makes her feel buttery all over, as if she could shrug off her arms and legs as painlessly as kicking off shoes. She opens the door to her cabin. She is standing on the threshold of an enormous room. Thrones backed against the walls are upholstered in rich cloths and furs: brocade, damask, vair. Saskia runs her fingers over the cloths and along the polished curves of the mahogany. She sits in the thrones one by one, luxuriating in the touch of rough and smooth.

A bard is strumming a lyre and singing of heroic deeds. Men sit at long tables, feasting noisily. Saskia joins them. Nothing could be more right or proper. She has bathed and been anointed with olive oil, she wears a tunic as sheer and soft as the skin of an onion, shining as the sun shines. One of the men spies her and calls out in greeting, "Help yourself to the food and welcome, and after you have tasted dinner, we will ask you who among women you are." A maidservant brings water for her to wash her hands in, pouring it from a golden pitcher into a silver basin. A grave housekeeper brings in the bread and serves it to her, adding good things, generous with her provisions. Saskia puts her hand to the good things that lie ready before her.

This is how it has always been and always will be. The maidservant will always pour from a golden pitcher to a silver basin. The housekeeper will always be grave, and generous with her provisions. Odysseus has complained that young people fail often to act properly when custom demands a thing. "For always, the younger people are careless," he has said. But not all. Saskia strives always to do the proper thing, as you could never have hoped for in a young person. So she puts her hand to the good things that lie ready before her as she has done countless times before in exactly this way, so exactly this way that each instance is not a repetition of an occurrence but the same occurrence returned to, like a dream. She can no more do something different than she can change what she has already done. In this unbreakable web of the done, there is a small, still space into which Saskia fits perfectly.

When she has put away her desire for eating and drinking, the man who spoke to her before says, "Come now, recite us the tale of your sorrows, and tell us this too, tell us truly, so that we may know it: What woman are you and whence? Where is your city? Your parents?"

The men are turned to her, waiting. They would wait forever if necessary, with their goblets empty at their elbows. They would wait, deathless, their grave warriors' eyes turned toward the space into which she fits perfectly. She stands, hooking her thumbs in her copper belt and tossing back a thick mane of hair. "See, I will accurately answer all that you ask me." The warriors catch each other's eyes, nodding approval. As you could never have hoped for in a young person. She begins: "Like all real people, I go under several names . . ."

10

Today is the day on which Saskia and Jane will become best friends. In the tiled gloom, Saskia proposes to herself a test: she gave Jane the haiku at her locker, so that is their special place now. If Jane is at her locker now, that means she is waiting for Saskia.

She pushes through the fire door and scans the crowd. Of course if Jane is not there, it doesn't necessarily mean anything. Her math class might have run over. She might be hurrying there at this very moment, glancing anxiously at her watch, praying that Saskia has waited for her. Of course Saskia would wait!

But Jane is already there. She is peering into a notebook and twiddling the lock. One leg is lifted, the foot flat against the inner thigh of the other leg, which is locked back, curved like a bow. Saskia catches her breath. She has never seen anything so graceful. Storks stand that way, resting for a moment on their long migrations. So do nomads, like the mysterious Masai who go on safaris with Denys Finch-Hatton, or the Australian Aborigines that Bligh saw from his open boat, after the mutiny. The Masai run for hundreds of miles across the African desert, no one knows why or where. The Aborigines cross and recross their outback, recognizing no boundaries, singing their magic songs. The lifted leg is like a folded wing. If Saskia tried to stand that way, she would keel over.

Yet she knows she can speak to Jane Sing now. Jane is a veldt roamer, but Jane is also waiting for her. The Masai allowed Finch-Hatton to travel with them. Jane must have loved the haiku. "Hi!" It feels so easy all of a sudden.

"Hello." She takes the leg down and opens the locker.

"My name is Saskia."

"I remember."

Of course she remembers, stupido. "What were you looking at in your notebook?"

"My locker combination."

Jane is so tall she can see right onto the top shelf of her locker. "You shouldn't write it there. The dregs look for them in notebooks and steal your stuff."

"Who?"

"The dregs. The boys."

"It hasn't happened to me before."

"Dregs in India probably aren't like the stupid dregs here."

"I've never been to school in India," Jane says coolly. Saskia can feel her face heating up. Did she offend Jane Sing? "I mustn't be late for class," Jane says, turning.

Saskia turns with her. "We're in the same one."

"That's true."

Jane Sing sounds marvelously mature, doesn't she? *I remember. That's true.* It suits her smooth-sided voice, flowing out of its cedar box. She is from Vastamundus, even if not from India. (Saskia doesn't understand that, the Blatt said she was.) Saskia doesn't say judicious things like "That's true," and it shows what a small-town barn she is. "Have you gotten to know anyone yet?"

"Not yet."

They pass under the big clock. "The V.P. designed the schedule," Saskia says, "and it's the most cunning thing you ever saw. Some classes are forty-eight minutes, some are fifty-one. Lunch is twenty-nine! It's all carefully planned to confuse you so they can pile on the demerits and get slave labor in the afternoons. English starts at nine-thirteen! How can any self-respecting class start at nine-thirteen?"

You're babbling. Stop babbling.

"The V.P. is the Vice Principal?"

"Yeah. The Very Putrid. The Vicious Pupil-hater. The Virtually Pandemic." Saskia once spent an enjoyable afternoon with a dictionary, making a list. "The Vitally Polluted. The Vitriolic Pusball." Jane glances sidelong at Saskia, who shrugs, adding, "There's a rumor going around that he's the Antichrist." How big are his shoes? Saskia never thought to look.

"And what about the Principal?"

She asks questions so reasonably! She merely wants information, like a mature person: Ah yes, and what about . . . ? Do tell me about . . .

"That's the P. The Pusillanimous. Did you see him your first day here? I saw you in the V.P.'s office." The folksen she was sitting with must have been her moor.

"Just for a second."

"Yeah, you hardly ever see him. It's pretty sad, actually. He's got leprosy."

"He — what?"

"We see him once a year, when he gives a speech at the opening assembly. They prop him up behind this podium that's mainly there to hide his hideous deformities. You can't understand a word he says. They say that's not uncommon with lepers. They keep his office dark and they incense it to hide the smell."

Jane Sing turns her gazelle eyes full and wide on Saskia. She bites her lip. "You're joking." The bell rings.

"Oh, shit," Saskia tosses off as calmly as she can. "Come on!" They run the last straightaway to English and slide in just as the Plebe is swinging the door shut.

On the way to French Saskia says, "Actually, I think he's just shy or something."

"The Principal, you mean."

Note how they are already on the same wavelength. "He's pretty old. I was sent to his office once when the V.P. was out on a rampage rifling lockers and mugging students and so on, and he sat the whole time behind his desk leaning way back and holding his hands out in front of him like he was trying to ward me off." Mumble mumble shouldn't mumble try to mumble and those two old white palms up and out saying noo please go away noo don't come nearer! Saskia felt like a leper.

"So where should I write my locker combination?"

~~~~~~

Advice! Jane Sing wants advice! "Don't write it anywhere. Just remember it."

"Numbers don't stay in my head."

"You need a trick, that's all. What's your combination?" Jane hesitates. No, this cannot be right, they cannot have secrets from each other. "Mine is twenty, nine, one. The trick is, if you switch the nine and the one, you get nineteen, and nineteen is one less than twenty."

Jane Sing looks in her notebook. She hesitated because she couldn't remember it, not because she doesn't trust Saskia. She was waiting for her at the locker, it is their locker now, she trusts her. "Twenty-one, three, twelve."

"That's easy! They're all multiples of three."

"I'm not good at math."

"That's not math, that's just numbers." Jane shakes her head impatiently. "OK, twenty-one minus three squared is twelve. Even better, the whole thing's a palindrome."

"I said I'm not good at math!"

Will you just *stop* showing off? I'm not showing off, I'm trying to be helpful. Jane doesn't think so, she'll decide you're a drip and you'll only deserve it.

But at lunch magnanimous Jane sits with showoff Saskia, anyway. A long silence drags by. Don't babble. Don't be a drip.

Three dregs at the next table have stolen a smaller dreg's cap and are keeping it away from him, braying as he pleads with them tearfully to give it back. Yah! Yah! A shout in your ear. A rubber band aimed at your eye. A thumbtack on your seat. Saskia shrinks, hoping they won't notice her. She wishes dregs would all disappear. Nothing bloody, nothing mean. Just a quiet, genderwide ceasing-to-exist. "What rawholes," she finally says, cowardly quiet.

"What?"

Saskia takes a roll of shredded wheat stuffed with vermilion sliced almonds and chartreuse cottage cheese out of her lunch bag. "I said, 'What rawholes.' Those dregs."

"What's *that*?"

"What?"

"That!"

"This? It's a millet roll with tamarind seeds and camel's milk. I make them myself." Saskia takes a dainty bite. "They eat this all over the Mongolian Empire. Camel's milk keeps better in the desert than coo's milk. Higher fat content. You want to try some?" Jane just stares at it. Saskia holds it out. "Go ahead. I've got plenty."

After looking it over slowly, Jane nibbles one end. "It's cottage cheese."

"Yeah, it's similar. You like it?" Jane doesn't answer. "Well, it's not for everybody."

The next class is Technology. "Mr. Brandt is a big dumb lug," Saskia explains to Jane. Actually, he's the only teacher she sort of likes. He spot-welds metal bands around his biceps and pops them off as he points the way to Muscle Beach. His coffee floats a rainbow sheen, which proves it's really high-grade machine oil. "We're in the middle of a unit, so he probably wants you to double up with someone. You can do my project with me, everybody else is just making candlesticks."

"What are you making?"

"A sextant." The Captain lost his overboard in the horse latitudes and he has a birthday coming up.

Sure enough, after attendance Mr. Brandt comes over and raises the question of Jane's project. "She can work with me," Saskia says instantly.

"OK by me," he says, boring meditatively into an ear with a parsnip-sized pinkie. He doesn't give a hoot about projects as long as you watch him pop armbands. "OK by you?" he asks Jane.

Of course she wants to work with Saskia. She loved the haiku, she was at her locker, she asked for information on principals and locker combinations. Saskia bores a hole in her cheek. Yes. Yes.

"Sure. Sounds like fun."

Saskia's heartwarmth erupts and spreads. Suddenly, Jane Sing giggles. "Big dumb lug," she says, after Mr. Brandt has lumbered off.

The tall dark willow from Vastamundus giggles with the stumpy apple tree from hicksville. Not believable, after all. Yet Jane's coffee eyes sparkle unmistakably. She has found a friend, Saskia whispers to herself. Me! She shivers and hugs herself, she is so very big blooming warm from her stomach lungs heart out to the tips of her fingers and toes HAPPY.

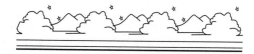

PART 2

JANE AND
LAUREN

Then pray that the road is long.
That the summer mornings are many,
that you will enter ports seen for the first time
with such pleasure, with such joy!
Stop at Phoenician markets,
and purchase fine merchandise,
mother-of-pearl and corals, amber and ebony,
and pleasurable perfumes of all kinds,
buy as many pleasurable perfumes as you can;
visit hosts of Egyptian cities,
to learn and learn from those who have knowledge.

— Cavafy, "Ithaca"

1

Lauren is sitting cross-legged on her meditating pillow in front of a houseplant. She has had a long day, you can tell from the lines in her forehead. Her mud-caked work boots are on newspaper in the corner. Dirt is worked into the creases of her deep-tanned hands.

She is attaining peace. Her lips and eyelids are slightly parted, so that the strong straight teeth and opaque eye-whites gleam through slits. Her hands rest palm-up on her knees, thumbs and middle fingers forming egg-shaped holes, receptors of energy. She is probably pondering a koan like one hand clapping, or a tree falling in the forest when no one is around to hear it. What Saskia would like to know is, if you don't ponder these problems, are they then not problems?

The plant is a magnificent bat-wing begonia, taller than Saskia, its leaves glowing veinily in the purple evening light. Three sprays of frosted red flowers stick out yellow tongues. Lauren's plants and vegetables fetch good prices at the Farmers' Market because she meditates with them, praising them. In return she says they take her out of herself into their alien lives, their calm and undemanding rootedness. "Plants are natural Taoists," she has told Saskia. "People chase illusions. Plants *are*."

"Mm?" she murmurs now, sensing Saskia's presence.

"Dinner's ready."

White-on-the-Water's communal dinners are a daily ritual, a holdover from when the farm was a commune. If you don't want to come to dinner, Lauren gets on your case for being too individualistic, not vegetable enough. The commune existed back when Saskia was young and Thomas was here, along with many others who have since gone away. Several people worked on the farm then, not just Lauren, and Saskia remembers the chaotic plantings, the crop failures. She also remembers endless talking, poetry readings, vans in the field, people on their way to India or just back from it, folksens and barns walking around buck naked. There were prayer wheels, huts, a guru name Truth. People had names the guru gave them: Laughter, Grass, Star. Lauren was Striding Tree.

At first the commune was called Wonderland, and those were the days of hemp and LSD, endless talks and buck nakedness. Then it was renamed Godhead and drugs were banned. Women covered themselves and talking stopped, though the dances went on, sometimes all night. The guru went to live in a tower the commune built for him on top of a geodesic dome.

Amazingly enough, although she was only four when it ended, Saskia remembers all this. Well, not exactly. She does remember, though, looking at some old photos and having one out of ten questions answered by Lauren. Those grudging answers go back so far, they have become indistinguishable from Saskia's own memories.

Upstairs the twins are a mound of giggles under Mim's covers in the dark and Mim is stalking them, growling. "Wash your hands, everybody, and get to dinner. On the double." Complaints, resentful looks. Crews can be like that, you can't worry overmuch about it. Quinny is on the lower deck, kneeling in a circle with his dinosaurs. "Dinney time, Quinner. Let's get the others."

"Can we tell Austin and — ?"

"I already told them."

"I want to tell Austin and — !"

"Don't whine, Quinny, I already told them. Let's go tell Jo."

She takes his hand and he trips along docilely. "You're slobbering, Quinny." She hasn't got any paper. It's all over his chin, what a mess. She takes him into the bathroom and washes him up. They go out the back door and across the drive to Jo's trailer, a slope-shouldered aluminum hulk huddling sullenly in the weeds. Patches of blue light shift around the curtains. Blatter blatter. Through the door Saskia calls, "Jo?"

"What?"

("Let me say it!" Quinny whispers.)

"What is it?" The blatter quiets.

("Go ahead, go on," Saskia urges.)

"It's dinner, Jo!" Quinny trumpets, on tiptoes. "It's time for dinner!"

"All right."

"Let's get Bill now," Saskia says. She raps on the door of Bluffaroo Bill's trailer. "Dinner!"

"I'm working!"

"Well it's dinner all the same!"

Silence. Typical that he doesn't answer, that he hasn't even got the consideration. "So are you coming or what?"

"I'm coming, I'm coming! Christ!"

"He's coming, he's coming!" Saskia says to Quinny as they head back to the house. She and Marco have been practicing their impersonations. She assumes the retracted and pained expression of Bluffaroo's eyes, the hunch of his shoulders, as if the damp-breathing face of the world were too close, its comradely arm too heavy. "Christ!"

"Not rawhole enough," Marco says. "Look more persecuted."

So here they all come, padding over the troughs and crests of the warped boards of the common room, into the dining room and around the two-ton oak table beneath the spidery brass chandelier with the fake candle-flame bulbs, half of which have been burned out for about a century now. Dinner is brown rice with toasted almonds, scallions, and raisins; fried eggplant with a garlic-potato sauce (an ancient Greek recipe); home-baked beans; a cuke salad with fresh tarragon, straight from the greenhouse. A tasty ribsticking meal for these short and cold Tylerian winter days. Saskia is by miles and miles — let's face it, light-years — the best cook at White-on-the-Water.

Not that anybody notices. Only Lauren, seating herself calmly at the head, utters an automatic "Looks good." The crew is too busy giggling and shoving. "Cut it out," Saskia says. "Austin —"

"What?"

"Stop it."

Gravely she sets the good things before them, generous with her provisions. Bill is jutting out his ultra-trimmed beard and looking around him like the whole world and everybody in it is a major letdown. That's a habit of his. He probably keeps his beard ultra-trimmed because he's trying to compensate for his body, which is "going to seed," as they say. He has that sort of lard-butt body type that makes men look high-waisted and elbowy. "Boy, *somebody's* hungry."

He groans histrionically. "Could I please eat in peace?"

What did she say? "Gee, you're pretty crabby today."

"I'm just in the middle of something, I want to get back to it." Fork fork. His arms are inflating even as Saskia watches.

"You ought to get more exercise."

"Excuse me? Look who's talking! That thing with all the glare up in the sky, that's the sun, you know. In case you were wondering." Hyuck hyuck. Fork fork.

"Bill, you're going to choke on something," Lauren says.

"Et tu, Brute?"

"Just slow down! You're making me lose my appetite."

"This is pretty good, Sas," Bluffaroo says, food pouched in both cheeks. She hates it when he calls her Sas. He has never once called her Saskia. Must be too much work, getting all those syllables out. "Can I tell you, though."

"No."

"If you want to keep the eggplant from getting soggy, you need hotter oil."

"They're soggy because you piled twenty onto your plate at once, Pig of the Universe." It's true. Saskia's three slices are perfectly crispy.

"You're getting ruder every day," Lauren says.

"What about him? I don't insult his cooking!" Which, you may believe, is a token of amazing self-restraint. Whenever it's Bluffaroo's turn to cook, there isn't a pot left east of the Mississippi without a black crust at the bottom. He'll do something Bluffarooish like decide halfway through that maybe he should make his own gourmet doodah croutons for the salad. He tells everyone he's making something that will bury the store-bought croutons under an avalanche of Bluffarooish superiority. But in the meantime, crushing herbs in the pestle, holding open his doodah gourmet cookbook with pudgy fingers, he forgets the casserole in the oven, and since his flesh-blob of a nose is apparently too small to smell anything, it's always Lauren or Saskia who calls from the common room, or down from the second floor, "Is something burning?" Then he has to cook something else in a hurry, so dinner is doodah croutons and boiled soybean franks, and then Lauren has only five minutes to eat because she's going to her waiting job down in Ithaca. She is so hard-working and all Bluffaroo has to do is make her dinner on time, and he screws it up.

So why do they let him cook? Lauren cites empowerment. He's supposed to be learning by doing. But he isn't getting better, Saskia says. You can bring that up during crit/self-crit, Lauren says. That's another communal thing that Lauren tries to get going between Bill, Jo, Saskia, and herself. It's always a disaster. Criticism: Bill, your cooking stinks. Self-criticism: Maybe I should be more patient about Bill's lousy cooking.

"I've figured out how to get into that new section," Bluffaroo is saying to Lauren. "I moved Sam's jump into the gorge before the scene with Rudolph and the transvestite, so now I can open immediately with the discovery of Sam's body under the Cayuga Street bridge. I've got to call the coroner, find out how much they bloat up. Sas, could you pass the salt?"

"You don't need any more salt. Austin!"

"What?"

"Stop it."

"Stop what?"

"I saw you do that."

"You must have forgotten to salt the beans."

"No, everything is salted exactly right."

The patented eye roll. Lord, give him patience. "Please give me the salt."

Saskia hands it to him. "It's just going to make you even more uptight."

"Say what?"

"It'll raise your blood pressure."

"Thanks, you do that just fine." Hyuck hyuck.

Then there is Jo. She has already finished and is sitting quietly, stone-faced. Is she thinking about anything? Saskia tries to calculate the line of her gaze. She seems to be staring at a patch of table between Austin's plate and Mim's glass. If you waved your hand in front of her eyes, would she blink? Jo never eats much, and when she's done she smokes. Not hemp even, but tobacco. She is thin and looks a lot older than she is, which is twenty-eight. She has a lower lip that sort of droops. She looks out of the side of her eyes at people, that lower lip drooping in wonder and dislike, as if to say, "Who the hell are you? Why don't you drop dead?" Perhaps it's an expression she learned for her job, as a cashier in one of Huge Red's cafeterias. Austin can make a perfect Jo face. It's basically his halibut face, without all the mouthing.

Sometimes Jo and Bluffaroo will team up. Bluffaroo will talk about the fifty-two ways the place could be fixed up and Jo will say Wouldn't That Be Nice, with a snort that means it will happen when hell freezes over. The two of them look like circled wagons, defending themselves from the Native Americans. Eventually, though, one of them will decide to yank the rug out from under the other and go solo. "Why don't you just do it yourself," Jo will suddenly say, "instead of pissing and moaning?" Saskia wishes Lauren would say: "You don't like it here? Fine. Live somewhere else." It's not like they pay rent or anything. But Lauren sits through it all calmly, ignoring them as though they were children. And she tells Saskia not to be a martyr.

"Thanks for dinner," Jo says to no one in particular and heads back somnambulently to the blue light. Yes, master. Bill smears a napkin around his lips. "Merci pour zee meal, ma'amzelle."

He's smiling. This must be a little joke. The stubble at the edges of his beard twitches. "Try not to be such a jerk," Saskia says.

Lauren sighs. "Sometimes I feel like throttling both of you."

The crew is straining to bolt, and Saskia releases them even though none of the plates are empty, and Shannon's is nearly full. They stampede toward the stairs, Austin leading: "Last one up is a turd-bucket!" Saskia regards the puddled food dejectedly. Sometimes she just doesn't have the energy. Quinny has remained behind. Obviously, the turdbucket. "Guess what?" he says to Lauren. He has such a high voice. They say boy sopranos turn into basses. Hard to imagine.

Lauren was about to get up. "What?" Quinny hesitates, blank-faced. "Well, what?" Lauren never has enough patience with Quinny. You'd think she'd know better.

Quinny leans close. He cups his hands and whispers confidentially, "I told Jo to come to dinner!"

Lauren pats his head. "I don't know what we'd do without you."

Saskia is cleaning up. "Why don't I help," Lauren says.

"No, it's my turn." That's the system. You clean up after your own dinner.

"You've been a martyr all week," Lauren says coolly, knowing just where the sore spot is.

But it's self-protection, Saskia pleads silently. If we cleaned up after each other, everyone would be in the kitchen all night after a Bluffaroo fest, scouring lava out of pans. I'm not a martyr, I'm not. Lauren has done her disappearing act. Some communal dinner, Saskia thinks, tipping scraps into the compost bucket. A real mess. Ha ha ha.

2

I was born twelve summers ago, on the Fourth of July. It was said by the people of Wonderland that the loud noises occasioned by the explosives the Novamundians take childlike pleasure in setting off in traditional celebration of their National Day caused beautiful young Lauren, who was big with child, to go into labor. Wonderland was in an uproar, and hemp had dulled the wits of those whom Lauren needed. Only resourceful Thomas acted quickly. He bundled groaning Lauren into Betsy and raced up the rough dirt roads.

Betsy is a Ford pickup, vintage 1965, a good year. Back in the commune days she was psychedelic, with a rainbow across her hood, doves and paisleys in attendance, and the word "Wondermobile" in balloon letters on her sides. She was indeed a wonder to look at, aglow in the Ithacan sunlight, but Tylerian townies would break her side mirror or let air out of her tires. After Thomas and the guru left, and the commune withered away, she was repainted. Saskia cried at first to see her disappearing under swaths of tomato red, but eventually she conceded that Betsy looked dignified in one color. A lady. Betsy was older now, and it was right and proper for her to have put away childish things. Now she is lamed with a bad hip that makes her list to the right, and toothy with rust from years of splashing through road salt. Her headlights look upon the muddy roads and smelly ditches of this bedraggled world with a tolerant, long-suffering expression. Surely she has seen everything by now. Twice, probably.

Eager for knowledge, I was determined to come out on the back seat and see what the fuss was about. Thomas coaxed Betsy to ever greater exertions. She flew the last mile, taking short cuts across meadows and streams. Amazed witnesses later said they had never seen a truck so nimble.

Thomas took good care of Betsy, washing her and tuning her up, listening to every knock and clatter. Now she drives best for Lauren and Saskia, Lauren coaxing gently on pedal and stick, Saskia patting the dashboard. Bluffaroo is rough, and Betsy tries to buck him out of the cab. She hates Jo so much she stops in the middle of the nearest intersection and floods.

When Betsy screeched to a halt at the hospital, Lauren was holding me on her stomach and I was looking curiously out the window. The doctors ran out and stood around us, astounded. There was nothing for them to do but cut our cord and give me a bath. I was a small babe, weighing only four pounds, but healthy and vital withal. I stayed in the hospital for a week. Of this period I remember little.

I got my Novamundian surname from Lauren. Thomas chose "Saskia." Thomas had a great love for the paintings of Rembrandt van Rijn, and Rembrandt's wife was named Saskia. Nobody except Thomas and Rembrandt knows what Saskia means!

Names are fraught with meaning. Lauren is so named because of laurel, the beautiful tree that honors men with her touch on their crowns, as Lauren deigns to kiss her shorter boyfriends' heads. "Bill" brings "bilious" to mind, and "belly." "Thomas" makes her think of "tomcat." But he had a dog. Etymologically, anyway, "Thomas" means "twin." Significance?

And what about "Saskia"? Being mysterious is nice, but only if you yourself know the secret. Does "Saskia" mean "secret"? Lauren swears up and down she doesn't know. It was Lauren who told Saskia about Thomas's love of Rembrandt, after Saskia had been pestering her for information. Saskia found a book about Rembrandt in the great Ithacan library. It had nothing in the text about the meaning of "Saskia," but there were some nice portraits of people in dark rooms lit by embers. The person standing for the portrait could simply take one step back and they would be swallowed up in the gloom. Now you see me, now you

Rembrandt would look up from his easel and say angrily, "Will you stop fooling around?"

Thomas, of course, is not Novamundian but Phaiakian. The Phaiakians are "the people of the long oar," great seafarers, near the gods in origin. Thomas is blond with wine-blue eyes. The word "Phaiakians" means "The Shining Ones."

Saskia puts down her autobiography and looks for the millionth time at the map of Phaiakia that hangs over her bed: two large islands amid a cloud of smaller ones, and largest of all, a peninsula jutting north, curving eastward like a green mitten with fingers and thumb gently grasping the sea. You can tell it is a wise and good land merely from the cradling shape of it, a land fit for its people. One of the astronomers profiled in her star book was a Phaiakian. He lived in a castle on a green island and looked out of a tower and discovered more stars than any man before him. Near the gods.

She turns off the bedside lamp. In the blackness of predawn, her own stars are like a Rembrandt painting, and like Thomas, too. The Wagon (which farmers call the Plow, for the circle of the seasons and the work that never ceases), the supernova in Boötes, the eternally waxing Moon: their reassuring glow keeps her company for a while, but then fades away into the dark.

3

After some experimentation, the two girls discover that they are the same height only when Saskia stands on her toes on two textbooks on a stairstep above Jane. "How tall *are* you?" Jane asks, so openly marveling that it's a darn good thing Saskia isn't sensitive about her height.

"That's classified information." Saskia has not gotten taller by a nanometer in two years. All of her growth vectors are horizontal. This explains why, for all their difference in height, Jane weighs only five pounds more than Saskia. Saskia's breasts are ballast, like the balloonist's bags filled with sand. If she could only cut the rope and sling them off, yelling "Bombs away!"

Jane Sing is double-jointed all over. Where other people put hands on their hips, she turns her wrists impossibly and seats them in the middle of her back. She curls one leg several times around the other and collapses her ankles outward so that she's standing on the sides of her feet. Everything about her is vertical: she pushes up the metal bracelets on her arms, they slide back down. Through the long drop from ears to shoulders dangle earrings that jiggle and flash like aspen leaves. And her hair! She has a way of tilting her head when she talks that causes the long black curtain to tassel forward over her shoulders. She throws each side back by dropping a shoulder and sweeping the hair with a flick of her wrist and a toss of her head, pursing her lips in a way that means, "You might be dying of jealousy, but really it's rather a nuisance having such long hair."

She lived in Boston for two years, and before that in England. The Blatt's Indian hypothesis is true to the extent that her parents were born in a town that used to be in India, although now it's in Pakistan. England apparently explains the smooth-sided cedar-box voice. "You've never heard an English accent before?"

Saskia hangs her head. Small-town barn. "I've read English books," she offers. The Captain speaks with a smooth-sided voice? That cannot be right. Perhaps his years at sea roughened it. The salt air corroded his cedar box. The Captain definitely has a gravelly voice. That is why he harrumphs all the time, to rearrange the gravel and have time to ponder, ponder.

Jane is already thirteen, which, of course, is exciting. But Saskia actually kind of likes being twelve. Twelve is a practical number, graciously divisible, a tool kit. Math would be an even more wonderful discipline if we had two extra fingers so that we counted in base twelve. Thirteen, on the other hand, is a prime number. Primes are intractable. You can't mess with them, they go their own ways. Secretly, Saskia worries about turning thirteen this summer. If she has got mooniness and breasts already, what will happen when she's a teenager? God, she'll get moony every other day, her breasts will balloon into medicine balls.

Since Jane turned thirteen last September, why isn't she in the next grade?

It's a sore subject. "I've been moved around so much, I got behind," Jane says crossly. During those years in England, she went to half a dozen different schools. "I would get fed up with one and have to try another."

Saskia understands the feeling, but she never knew you could switch schools. She thought schools were like obnoxious households: they were simply the beds you had to lie in. "How many different schools did your town have?"

She can tell from Jane's face that it's a dumb question. "These were boarding schools."

Perhaps because Jane is older, she smokes cigarettes. She sneaks four or five a day in a stall in the opium den, just like the tough pigs. In class she chews on the ends of her ballpoint pens or sucks on her hair. "I'm oral," she tells Saskia.

"It's really not good for you," Saskia offers hesitantly, meaning the smoking, and not knowing if that's a barnish thing to say or even more folksen than smoking.

Jane is not scornful. She actually seems to take Saskia's opinions seriously. "I know. But I'm hooked. I'm terrible!" At least she is not as hooked as Jo, for whom the butt is as permanent a part of her face as her mouth is. Saskia has imagined that if you slid the cigarette out from between Jo's lips, it would turn out to be a cotter pin and Jo's jaw would fall off. Jane has also smoked hemp, as she has casually mentioned a couple of times. Fortunately, none of that has materialized yet in Saskia's presence. Let's face it, hemp makes you kind of stupid. Lauren and Bluffaroo pass a joint around sometimes after dinner, and the next thing you know they're giggling because one of them knocked a glass over, hyuck hyuck.

But the first time Jane comes to White-on-the-Water is right after school, so Lauren is in her plant-master mode. Saskia is proud of her as she turns, tall, capable, from the stretch and bend of aphid spraying (naturally, something natural, a vegetable soap), to say hello. Bluffaroo and Jo are nowhere to be seen. "Both trailers are off limits," Saskia explains. "Major leprosy colonies." The soap dissolves the soft-bodied aphids, like sulfuric acid.

Saskia brings down Lauren's sewing basket, and out of it come bolts of brilliant damask, sumptuous brocade, cloth-of-gold. The bolts are laid out on the kitchen's scarred wooden table and arranged in a manner pleasing to the eye. The spice jars in the rack over the stove yield galingale, spikenard, cubeb. The clamor of the market — the sellers hawking wares, the caged chickens squawking, the wooden wheels rumbling over the stones — is nearly deafening. A score of languages are spoken within earshot, every color of skin can be seen. The Wanderer herself is a striking pale gold. She reads off the words chalked on the shoulders of the jugs beneath a table: "Date wine. Rice wine. Ai, and palm wine, too!" She rocks out the stained bung and breathes deeply of the heady fumes. "I haven't had so much as a horn of decent palm wine in months!"

It has been a long journey for the Wanderer, from Kubilai Khan's capital through jungles and deserts, from one wretched village to the next. But here at last is a fine town, bustling with sellers of rich goods in every street. The Wanderer lingers in the striped shade of this awning because the merchant is comely, with a lively eye. Judging from her duskiness, this town must be south of Cathay. Ai, but it is good to look upon such a maiden after so many months of sleeping under the stars, wrapped in one's cloak against the mountain frost!

"As-salaam aleikum," the maiden says, bowing her head gracefully.

The Saracen tongue? The maiden must be a worshiper of Mahomet. But not wearing the veil. A tart? Curiouser and curiouser. "Aleikum as-salaam," the Wanderer responds.

The merchant maiden continues in the trade language of the area. "I think you'll find these cloths to be of very high quality, sir." Where has this golden Wanderer come from, the dark maid must be wondering. What lonely roads has she walked and what evil things seen? The pain of the world is in her eyes. Alas, it is the lot of the Wanderer to leave a trail of broken hearts.

With a connoisseur's touch, she runs her fingers over the cloths. She slides the silk tinglingly along her arms. She rubs the coarse buckram against her cheeks. "Mmm. That's fine fustian." The ripple of twill, the ridge of wale, the tickling grassy yield of nap. Soon the merchant maid is picking up the bolts after the Wanderer and holding them to her own cheeks.

"And what might you be buying, good sir?" the maiden asks at length.

"Some of everything, perhaps." The Wanderer smiles charmingly. "Or nothing, perhaps. I might buy you out, or I might leave you with all your goods and not a bezant of mine." One must keep them guessing or they will steal you blind. Marco taught her that.

The maiden's eyes flash — a fiery one! — as she counters, slim dark arms on hips, "You'll find no better wares than these in all of Arianmariandishdashdale."

The Wanderer falters. Arian— ? She pushes away the thought that it is an improbable name. Southern India, perhaps. Some of the names there are absurdly long. But the people of India go naked, and this maiden, alas, is modestly attired. "I meant no offense." What are a few bezants compared with such beauty? "On my soul, I will buy it all!" If Marco were here he would be bouncing a palm off his forehead and bellowing, "Stop! Stop!" Marco is a trader first, a practical man, ever despairing of his impetuous disciple. "My name is Aiyaruk. What is yours, pray?" The dark maiden hesitates. "You do not trust me with it?"

"I'm thinking. My name is Al-Embroidia Al-Fastansia Al-Marammjibwa!"

Well! Quite a name. Aiyaruk must admit it is impressive. But perhaps too impressive. Perhaps it is rather pretentious, *non?*

The maiden rushes on, "And I am the daughter of the queen!"

"No you're not." There are no queens in the Khan's empire. Everyone knows that.

"I am too. You must obey me."

Things have taken a wholly improper turn. Aiyaruk draws herself to her full height: "I am a disciple of the far-famed Marco Polo. I obey no one but my master." The maiden also draws herself up, and Aiyaruk finds herself farther below than ever. Unfair to take advantage of Aiyaruk's size! Uncalled for! Aiyaruk's voice drips with sarcasm: "And anyway, what is the daughter of the queen doing selling wares in the streets of Arianmarianwhatever?"

"I'm standing in for my slave. He had to go to the bathroom."

A brazen lie! And yet . . . there *has* been a slave underfoot for the last minute or so. Insolently fingering the bolts of cloth and asking impudent questions, he looks an unhealthy young dreg, besnotted and beslobbered. "This must be your slave," she exclaims, grabbing the boy roughly by the arm.

"Yes, that's him. Hand him over."

"The daughter of the queen, and all you can afford is this disgusting thing?" The slave is whining. Aiyaruk boxes his ears and he runs away wailing.

"That wasn't really my slave," the maiden says haughtily. "My slave is still in the bathroom."

Aiyaruk sniffs. "You're just embarrassed to admit it."

"Why is Quinny so upset?"

Lauren is standing in the doorway, a hand cupping the head pressed gooily into her hip. Saskia and Jane trade a glance. They understand each other without a word or a wink. "I don't know," Saskia says, puzzled.

"I don't either," adds Jane. They shrug.

Lauren is exasperated. "I don't understand half the time what his problem is. I want you to include him in what you're doing, Saskia. You're good with him."

"Sure."

"You're a good girl."

Saskia winces. "As-salaam yoorwelkum."

"Hm?"

"Never *mind.*"

"Well excuse me, Miss Temper."

Go stick your head in the compost heap. "Come here, Quinny." He transfers his clutch readily to her. He never blames anyone, he only wails for comfort and accepts it from any quarter. Saskia will be nice to him for a while.

"You girls will have to get this stuff off the table," Lauren says. "Dinner will be early. I'm working down at the café tonight."

"Yeah, yeah, OK."

Lauren heads out to the greenhouse. Jo calls this "mowing the grass for dinner," and breaks into her wheezing laugh. Jane offers a handful of cubebs to Quinny, assuring him they're sweet. He spits them out, coughing and sneezing. "As-salaam howdyoulikem?" Jane asks, and she and Saskia have a very nice laugh together.

4

Lauren works hard. Spring, summer, and fall she's at it all day in the field and greenhouse. In winter she still has the greenhouse, and her waiting job in Ithaca, and at the winter solstice there are the Scotch pines to cut and sell on top of everything else. "You get the whole summer off from school," she says to Saskia. "What about me?" Saskia hangs her head. "I need some time for myself."

That's only fair. After dinner she disappears up to her room to meditate, and after meditating she climbs into her brass bed — as high as a table, as wide as the barn door, as massive and firm as Earth herself — and reads, mostly books about meditation. "I am at the beginning of the greatest journey," she has said to Saskia. "I am only now learning what it is I truly want."

In the ample bosom of that brass bed she sleeps soundly. She never wakes when Mim has a nightmare or Quinny starts blubbering and has to be taken to the bathroom. The bed was the first piece of furniture Lauren and Thomas bought for the house, Lauren said. They found it at an estate sale for a dead giant, and it took six men to lift it into Betsy. They had to take out the door frame to get the bed into the bedroom. Then they didn't put pads underneath it, and over the years the feet dug deeply into the softwood planks.

Once every couple of months Lauren goes to a meditation retreat for three or four days and that is when Saskia really appreciates how hard she works the rest of the time, because Saskia is almost run off her feet following the farming instructions she leaves behind. The astrology group meetings aren't as bad, because they last only a day. The members get together on a farm on the next lake over, to cast horoscopes, or something like that, and talk about their swami, who died two years ago. This is not Truth, the Godhead guru, but someone later, named Baba Yogi. Lauren has his picture by her bed: he looks pretty gentle, actually kind of simple-minded, with milk-blue eyes and a triangle of white hair on his lower lip. Saskia never saw him in real life. She couldn't go to the astrology group because she had the crew to take care of. The group is now publishing eight volumes of aphorisms that the leader left behind, scribbled on little pieces of paper. Lauren says they are gentle and profound and above all playful, in a saintly, all-knowing, bodhisattva-ish way.

When Lauren is reading in bed instead of meditating it's all right to come in and say good night. Saskia loves the way she looks at these moments, so hoogily in a cone of lamplight, her ton of hair unbound, her pillows piled around her. She has a wide face with almond eyes and cheeks so well defined they look glued on. It's not a mobile face. In fact it's rather mask-like, which is why you have to be so careful with her. Whether that mask is inborn or learned Saskia doesn't know, she has no other relatives to compare it with. Lauren never talks about her family. It's as though she never had one, as though she sprang out of someone's head fully formed.

Her reading glasses are as big and round as two full Moons, and the eyes behind each seem as calm as the Sea of Tranquillity. The book she is holding might be *Being Peace* or *Be Here Now*. Saskia will linger at the door, and Lauren will look up and slowly, deliberately close the book on a finger and lower it to her lap. In the evening after meditating or for days after a retreat Lauren does everything this way, one thing at a time, with a concentration so steady and slow it seems to ooze from her like molasses to coat the object of her attention.

It often seems that Lauren's present is not instantaneous but infinite, leaving no room for past or future. Years ago there was a pendulum wall clock in the kitchen with an uneven tick that sounded like a peg-legged captain limping. When Lauren first looked at it each morning, she would reach up and move the minute hand backward or forward five, ten minutes. That was Lauren's power, young Saskia imagined: the very fabric of time slid tinglingly past faster or slower as Lauren oozed faster or slower along the infinite line of her present. The clock had to be adjusted to fit the day Lauren was making.

Sometimes after Lauren lowers her book and gazes at Saskia, instead of saying good night she will ask if Saskia wants to brush her hair. Mim's hair is thick, burnt umber, pert, hey-you-guys hair. Jane's hair is elegant, gleaming, ruler-straight, obsidian. But Lauren's hair, one must concede, sweeps all before it. As long as Jane's, as bushy as Mim's, and of a color indescribable even for Saskia, who knows all the color words. It might crudely be called auburn, but it has claims on copper and bronze and a faintly pink rust, and it hints in some lights at things more exotic, like cinnabar and peach. When you sink your hand into it you imagine you will draw it back out swirled in hues like an Easter egg.

Lauren puts down her book, rises regally from her brass bed to put on an Indian robe and settle into a chair. She gathers the mass like a pile of autumn leaves and deposits it in back, where it hangs almost to the floor. A tapestry of hair, before which you ought to bow down and worship. The first touch! It feels like wool, like a light electric current. Saskia pats it down and it bounces back, she clumps it in her hands, she fluffs it, she runs her hands through it, her fingers parted like fork tines. She reaches in deeper, finds her way elbow-deep to

Lauren's large head and massages her scalp and temples. Lauren sighs. "Why don't we do this every night?" Why don't they? Only Lauren can answer that.

Lauren's hairbrush fits coolly into Saskia's hand. She brushes back from Lauren's forehead. Lauren says, "Harder." As Saskia brushes farther back she steps away from the chair and lifts the hair so that it becomes a costly fabric on a loom that Saskia must stretch herself across. Fine silver threads are woven into it. Lauren wants Saskia to pull them out. The hair grows silkier in her hands, a deep shine developing. "You're strong," Lauren says. Saskia proudly brushes harder.

When Lauren climbs back into bed, Saskia would like nothing better than to climb in with her. Not to be with Lauren — that would be babyish — but to swaddle herself in that buffed, miraculous hair, wind herself in it like a caterpillar in its cocoon. She might wake up a butterfly. They say good night. Lauren turns out her light and falls into the dreamless sleep of the well-brushed.

How painful to compare Saskia's hair! Its color is also indescribable. It was once your garden-variety blond, nothing to write home about, but respectable. Then, around the time the mushy pink blobs came, it began to darken, the way cheap varnish darkens and clouds. Saskia ruefully calls it "blondish."

"Reminiscent of blond," Jane says kindly.

"An allusion to blond," Saskia says.

"Blond*esque*," Jane says, inspired.

But the color is the least of her problems. It has of course not escaped Saskia's notice in her wide reading that heroines — that is, genuinely intelligent, valiant, resourceful ones like Joan of Arc, not repulsive, sickly sweet, goody two-shoes ones like Little Dorrit — are few and far between. And among the few that exist, one trait is constant. They might be tall or short, beautiful or plain, but they always have thick hair. Thick hair is the mark of character, of spunk. It is the enhancement of beauty, or the solid compensation for plainness. What can it mean when you are both plain *and* thin-haired? Will you never be the heroine of your own story?

Lauren has two friends. One of them heads another ex-commune, with a water hole everyone goes swimming in during the summer. The other is a dancer and teaches at an alternative school in sunny Ithaca. All three of them are tall and beautiful. They form an equilateral triangle: perfect, no weak spots. All three have abundant hair, the ticket into the club. Lauren braids her hair into a rope that would dock an ocean liner, and the three of them stride out, laughing, for an evening on the town. Men drool after them slavishly. Goddesses, with goddesses' rights, they use men according to their pleasure. "Chew 'em up," Saskia says. "And spit 'em out!" Jane crows.

Saskia locks herself in the bathroom and drapes a towel over her wispy blondesque head. Studying herself in the mirror, saying, "Oh yes blah blah blah," she practices ducking her forehead to make the ends of the towel slip forward over her shoulders, then flipping the two ends back with a nonchalant motion of her hands. It feels so good she could cry.

5

Thus am I half Phaiakian and half Novamundian: a daughter of both worlds, belonging in neither. The ways of the Novamundians seem dull and crude to me and yet I would not be at home in Phaiakia, either, because I do not speak Phaiakian. Thomas spoke Phaiakian to me when I was young, and I knew it and spoke to him in it, but I remember it no longer. I remember only that the words were gentle and soft and of a rare beauty.

Liquid sounds that floated in the middle of the mouth, not deigning to touch brute teeth, tongue, or lips. There were words that dissolved in the air like mist, words that gurgled like water going down a drain. The sentences tipped back and forth like wavelets, rocking you to sleep. A sea language.

Phaiakian has somehow faded away from Saskia, leaving behind an outline of a memory of a feeling about them, a hollow glow indicating something that she once held and carelessly lost. She once read a fantasy book in which there was talk of an Old Speech, a magical language that had been forgotten for eons by the race of men. In this Old Speech, all things had been called by their True Names, and if one knew the True Name of a thing, then one knew the thing itself, one knew its nature. Bits of the Old Speech were remembered by certain wizards, wise and good men. Saskia hopes someday to find the Master who will not teach her so much as remind her of what she once has known, who will lead her back to her true lost self.

Whenever the Saskiad is sung by the bard in the feasting halls, it is interrupted at this point by the listeners, who demand to know: How did Thomas the Phaiakian meet Lauren the Novamundian?

Therefore will I explain: When Lauren was just entering folksenhood, she came as a disciple to Huge Red, the famed citadel of higher learning that looks down from its promontory onto sunny Ithaca. She sat at the feet of the Masters and learned many things: she read the Great Books and learned the esoteric Greek System. She was quick, a delight to her Masters, and was soon to be awarded the cap and the Latin scroll that signifies an Adept.

Baccalaurei in Artibus. Ars Magisterium. Words of grandeur and power. But thanks to Tyler Junior, Saskia has only a smattering of Latin. The languages taught at Junior are Spanish (Ms. Birnbaum) and French (Mr. Hooper). In other words, none of the important languages, like Latin, Greek, Phaiakian, Mongol, Turkish, or Persian. Saskia was going to take Spanish, since the Captain is fluent in it (he was a Spanish prisoner of war for two years), but at the time when she had to make the final decision he happened to be a fugitive in Boney's France — a wonderful adventure in which he was hidden in a Loire château by a French nobleman with a *très belle* daughter-in-law, who of course fell in love with him, as any woman must. And so the Captain was learning French, and it seemed appropriate that his Lieutenant would learn it with him. Unfortunately, the Cap-

tain became fluent within thirty pages, leaving his Lieutenant behind, and the *très belle* daughter-in-law, in the person of Mim,
seemed to know no French at all. But it was too late: Saskia was stuck
reading crushingly boring schoolbook stuff about a couple of drips
named Didier and Marie. Monsieur Oopair is a rabbity man with
red-rimmed pop eyes and halitosis who picks the remains of his
breakfast out of his beard, examining each particle and then eating it.
Dégoûtant!

Only Jane has kept the situation from being a total loss by taking
French herself. Not that she is in Saskia's class. Jane already had two
years of French in merry olde England, so she's with the ninth graders and still better than anybody else. She has a lovely French accent.
The French nobleman's daughter-in-law is now chocolate-colored,
and the Captain could not be more pleased.

Jane was taught Latin in England, too.

"It's not fair!" Saskia wailed.

"Shit, I hated Latin," Jane said. "What good is it to anybody? All I
can remember is *semper ubi sub ubi.*"

"That's what the pope's speech is called, right?"

"I don't think so. It means, 'Always wear underwear.'"

But those were troubled times. Novamundus was at war. The
disciples knew it was an unjust war, but no one would listen to
them!

A great battle between the disciples and the Ithacan centurions
swept Huge Red. Lauren was captain of a brigade of disciples.
When she lost a bloody skirmish — a valiant rearguard action in-
volving swordplay on a footbridge suspended dizzyingly above a
gorge — the centurions exiled her from Huge Red. The only
choice left to her was to join the colony of Novamundian exiles in
India, a land in the East famed for the wisdom of its Masters.

After much wandering through deserts and jungles, over mountains and across mighty rivers, the exile Lauren came at last to the
court of the wisest Master of all wide India and found her rightful
place at his feet. Soon Lauren was his favorite disciple.

Then it came to pass with the passing of days that a new disciple knocked at the gate of the court of the wisest Master of all wide India. He had eyes of the clearest blue and hair like the sand of the Phaiakian dunes. He was a seafarer, an adventurer, a man who had traveled much in the realms of gold, and he had come at last to learn the Wisdom of men who knew nothing of the sea, who ate not their food with salt, nor knew of ships. His shield was azure, oar upright, or. He carried that oar on his muscled shoulder and the gatekeeper of the court of the Master asked, "Why do you carry on your shoulder a winnowing fan?"

He planted his oar in the Earth and said, "I have found my resting place."

Thus it was that Thomas the Phaiakian entered the court of the Master. And thus it was that there he found his home in Lauren, who is not a traveler nor a seafarer, but a woman of the earth, a tiller of the soil. And they did love each other in the court of the Master amid great rejoicing, and she did return from her exile, bringing Thomas with her to Wonderland, as the prophecies had foretold. And so loved were Thomas and Lauren by their Master, the wisest of all Masters in all wide India, famed for the wisdom of its Masters, that the Master came to Novamundus with the young couple and lived also at Wonderland as their guru, Truth, and took only them and their circle as his disciples.

6

"So wait a minute," Jane says, bemusedly tracing the pink floral pattern on her bedroom wallpaper with a sepia finger. "Who are Mim's parents, then?"

"Jo is her moor, too." Saskia is lying on Jane's bed. The tufts of the white bedspread are deliciously nubbly against her arms.

"But that makes Jo *everybody's* mother."

"That's the whole problem. Mim was the first. When Jo got pregnant with her, she was only seventeen and the far was some guy named Mack or Mick or Max who was only eighteen and they had to get married."

Jane flops over onto her stomach and grimaces down at Saskia, her hair forming a tent around the two of them. "*That* old story! How depressing!"

"This guy Mack or Max or whatever hadn't finished high school and had some lousy job like garbage man or chimney sweep. They lived in someone's attic and wore burlap sacks and ate cat food. Then the twins came along." Saskia imagines the far, a greasy motorcycle dreg, looking through the glass in the maternity ward and counting his fingers, horror-stricken. "After that they were really poor. Lauren told me Mack or Mick had some sort of operation so they wouldn't have any more kids."

"He must have got his tubes tied."

"Yeah, whatever. But they must have done it wrong, because Jo got pregnant again."

Jane nods wisely. "That happens sometimes. And that one was Quinny?"

"Exactly. So Mack or Mick just took off. While Jo was pregnant. He couldn't handle it." Saskia sits up, emerging from the tent of Jane's hair into her bright bedroom.

"He was history," Jane says. Her narrow face is wedged between her hands, her legs are lifted from the knee, her bare feet happily tapping teaspoon ankles together.

"He was outta there," Saskia says, admiring Jane.

"He said, 'Eat my dust, Jo.'" The girls laugh.

Saskia wriggles around on the spread, feeling the nubbles under her bare arms and feet. "I guess it's not so funny, though," she adds, for form's sake. "Lauren says Jo was desperate."

"So Lauren took them in."

"Yeah."

"What a good person she is."

"What a martyr."

"I don't blame Mack for taking off. Jo is such a sourpuss."

"She smokes like a proverbial factory."

"She looks almost retarded."

"But how could Mack leave Mim? I mean, really! She's so beautiful."

"She *is* beautiful," Jane confirms. Her hand is balled under her chin, a confirmatory pose.

"He must have been a schmuck," Saskia says. That's one of Bluffaroo's words, along with half-pint, small fry, hotshot. Saskia has been called them all.

"No wonder Austin and Shannon look like Jo," Jane says.

The twins are tall for their age and gangling like Jo. They have her thin face and pointy chin, the same sidelong, hooded eyes. Quinny, on the other hand, is short and moon-faced. "I guess Quinny takes after Mack or Mick. And who knows where Mim came from. Maybe Jo found her in a rush basket in the river."

"Ugly people often have beautiful children, and vice versa," Jane observes. "Ever notice that?"

Like me, Saskia thinks. Is that what she means? Tall Lauren of the floor-length hair and muscular Thomas of the wine-blue eyes: they mate like gods and what do they get? A lizard. "Yeah, I guess."

"So do any of them think of Jo as their mother?"

"I don't know. I guess."

"They all sleep in the big house."

"That's the way the commune used to work. The idea was the barns were all together and the folksens took care of them all together. It had something to do with Native Americans."

"So Bill is Jo's boyfriend?"

"No."

"I thought they lived in the same trailer."

"Bill lives in the one nearer the house."

"How long has he been there?"

"A few months. A year, I guess."

"So why is he there?"

"That's what I want to know."

"But doesn't he do anything?"

"He calls himself a writer. That's what he's supposedly doing in his trailer all day."

"That's cool! I've never met a writer before."

"Bluffaroo isn't a *real* writer. He's always talking about some series of novels he's supposedly working on. You'd think his trailer was the cave of the Eleusinian Mysteries, the way he carries on about staying out of it." Bill refers to it as his Work. He says it like that: capitalized, lapidary. Saskia has his epitaph all figured out: A Jerk, He Worked. She can't wait until it's needed. "I just think it's really pretentious to talk about writing a series of novels when I don't think he's even written the first one." Something to do with making Ithaca into another Alexandria. Ithaca is Greek and Alexandria is Egyptian, stupido. Bluffaroo says it will be a "tetrahedron" of novels. What is a pyramid of novels? The pyramids aren't even *in* Alexandria, stupido.

No one has ever seen anything by Bluffaroo except a few lousy haiku. He calls them "moment essences" and uses no capitals, not even for his name. (Hey Bluffaroo, I think it's already been done.) He types them on little rectangles of special doodah green rag-paper he buys at an Ithacan art supply store and thumbtacks them to the bulletin board in the kitchen. He uses four tacks for each haiku and pile-drives them into the board so deep that only he, with his superlong fingernails, can pry them out again. Later, he remounts them on more special doodah rag-paper (blue) and sews them into numbered volumes which he puts in the common room on a shelf labeled "moment essences of william hobart owens."

w.h.o.?

Here is Bluffaroo in the lyric vein:

> nature is shameless
> her clouds litter the skylake
> silk veils flung away

Or:

> harlequin moon bows
> low, hat doffed, sly by the wings —
> the last curtain call

Hunh?

"Actually, the books aren't bad-looking," Saskia says to Jane. "Pretty blues and greens, good sewing job. He missed his calling."

Saskia once asked Bluffaroo to make a volume of her own haiku, which, let's face it, are better, and he told her to make it herself. Then he tried to weasel into her good graces by saying he would show her, but when he read one of her haiku, you could see him struggling to make the connection: I am the haiku writer here. I didn't write this. Haiku. Not by me. Haiku. Not by me. Does not compute. "That's really quite good. May I suggest —"

"No, you can't."

"Look, if you want help, you can't take that bratty tone." She whipped out her bazooka-sized flamethrower and blasted his shelf of collected haiku, turning it into a glorious roaring sheet of flame reaching from floor to ceiling.

"There's something just plain wrong with Bill," Saskia says.

"You think so?" Jane asks.

"Don't *you* think so?"

"Shit, I don't know."

"He pretends to be mellow, but actually he's really tense. Haven't you noticed that?"

"I only saw him for about a minute."

"It's like he's telling himself, 'Be mellow, Bill. Just be mellow now.' But then he jumps down your throat. You didn't notice that?"

"Maybe you're right. Maybe he's a little jumpy."

"Exactly! Bluffaroo is exceptionally jumpy."

"It's a little spooky, in fact."

"I just don't like the cut of his jib." As the Captain would say.

Damme, the service doesn't need men of his kidney! "He looks like the kind of guy who might go on a rampage."

"You mean like the V.P.?"

"Worse. He's probably got an enormous arsenal in his trailer and that's why no one is allowed in. He's not working on books at all, he's taking apart and oiling an M-whatever or an AK-something-or-other and a so-and-so bolt-action repeater. One of these days he'll kick open the door with an army boot and come out in camouflage gear, armed to the teeth, and he'll shoot anything that moves. And afterward people will say, Gee, we didn't really know him, he seemed mellow, he just stayed in his trailer all day."

"Fuckin' A," Jane says. The two girls collaborate on a shocked silence. Jane's hand is barely half an inch away from Saskia's. Then Jane says, "Those trailers are so *depressing*. And all the junk in the yard makes the place look like one of those backwoods places in the movies where the couple from the city are afraid to go up to it after their car breaks down. A dog attacks them and the hicks on the porch just watch."

"We don't have a dog," Saskia objects, a little hurt. But she can remember a dog at Wonderland, many years ago. A sleek, black and white bitch who ran so fluidly and fast she was like a swallow skimming over the meadows. She flushed birds, herded bugs with her nose, and flopped down like a dropped marionette when you scolded her, turning toward you a bright face with lolling tongue and eyes arched in innocent surprise. She was Thomas's dog and she left with him. Saskia has always wanted to get another one, but Lauren has always refused. "You don't want one."

"No, *you* don't want one."

"You only think you want one."

"No, *you* only think I only think I want one. You're Lauren. I'm Saskia."

"Don't be obnoxious."

Jane jumps up from the bed. "I need a cigarette in the worst way! Let's go to the cemetery." She pulls Saskia up. "If I smoke in here my mother has a conniption." She goes into her closet and rummages among her shoes. "I even have to hide the pack because she fucking pokes around in here." Jane shakes a pack down out of the toe of a cobalt pump. Smart hiding place, since Jane has about five hundred shoes. The girls put on their jackets, Jane slipping the pack into a pocket. "We're going out!" she yells as they go through the front door. No answer. "We tried." They head down the driveway.

"Jane!"

"Shit," Jane says under her breath. "Don't look back."

Too late. Stupid Saskia has turned. Jane's mother is beckoning from a window. "Jane!"

Jane whips around. "What?!"

"Where are you girls going?"

"I *said* we're going out!"

"Where?"

"For a *walk!*"

"Well don't be gone long, honey, I have to drive Saskia home soon."

Jane turns and takes Saskia's arm, propels her toward the street. "Christ, a fucking interrogation all the time."

Saskia liked that "honey." How pretty! Like honey-colored hair, which Saskia has always thought must be beautiful, although she has never seen it in real life.

They walk out of Tyler's only suburban development and down the county road past the aqua water tower to what passes for the town center: gas station, greasy spoon, funeral home, four churches. ("My dad marveled at how much lower house prices were here than in Ithaca," Jane said. "Has he figured out why yet?" Saskia said.) The cemetery is behind the oldest church, the one with the stubby Doric columns. The girls sit on the dead grass of the frozen ground behind an obelisk that is tilting because of some tree roots. It's typical Tylerian weather, gloomy and cold, windy, not doing anything in particular at the moment but basically taunting, "I can rain, sleet, or snow anytime I want to, just remember that, scuz." Saskia huddles. No wonder she never goes outside.

Jane has a cigarette in her mouth. With one hand she flicks open a pack of matches, folds one down, catches it under her thumb against the emery strip, snaps it. She ducks her head and grimaces as she cups the flame, then tosses her hair back and points her chin and the cigarette straight up as she puffs life into it.

"Ahh, that's good," she says. "*That's* good." Her long legs are drawn up, her knees under her chin. So lovely. "The first time I made out with a boy was in a cemetery."

Saskia feels her face, despite the weather, getting hot.

7

Naked and limber, she stops on the stairs. A commotion is coming from the kitchen: shouts, squawks. She turns toward it, gliding down.

The sunlight is fierce. Merchants' awnings stretch the length of the crowded street. Chickens and slaves run underfoot. This is her city, her home. She walks the streets, knowing the way. She greets old friends at every turn. "Aiyaruk!" they call out, delighted. "Where have you been?"

Today is the day on which the Khan's emissaries come, and the city has turned out to greet them. She makes her way through the crush of bodies to the Square of Martyrs. The emissaries wear robes of white and sit astride white horses, splendidly caparisoned. They come only once a year, to choose the maidens who will be brought to the imperial city of Khan-balik. She stands among the others quietly, not pressing herself forward as some do, nor calling out shamelessly. She is wearing a jerkin of camlet, sturdy leathern boots, a belt of copper with an amber clasp.

The emissaries pass on their steeds, impassively reviewing the maidens. Then they catch sight of her. Startled, they murmur among themselves, stroking their long beards. The chief among them motions her forward. The crowd parts. He leans down as if to help her onto a horse. Ignoring his outstretched hand, she grasps the steed's mane and vaults easily onto its back. The emissaries look at each other and nod. They ride out of the city.

This is the custom: each maiden has been judged, and awarded marks according to whether her features are well formed and in harmony with her person. Each has also been observed, to make sure that she sleeps sweetly without snoring, that she does not give off an unpleasant odor, that she is a virgin. (The last is tested with a robin's egg and handkerchief, and virginal blood is known by this virtue: it will not wash out. The test is sure. Let this be a warning to the heedless young.)

Only maidens awarded ten marks are taken to Khan-balik. Some years, one or two are awarded eleven. There have been rumors of a twelve, every decade or so. Now the excited news flies forward from village to village, from signal fire to signal fire, reaching the imperial city long before the emissaries and their charges: among this year's maidens is one who has been awarded thirteen marks.

In the great city of Khan-balik, in the Great Khan's palace, in the antechamber to the bedroom of the Great Khan himself, she stands with five other maidens, and this is the custom: for the next three days and nights they will serve the Great Khan, ministering to all his needs. He will use them according to his pleasure. The other maidens are dressed in elaborate finery. They babble emptily among themselves. "Will he like me?" they ask each other. "Is my hair all right?" "Did you see blahblah last night, it was so funny!"

When the door to the bedroom opens, they rush in, each vying to reach the Khan's bed first, and like a clutch of chicks they jump on it, while she stands off to the side. They hit each other with his pillows before settling down to a game of Truth or Death. Suddenly the Great Khan is standing by the door, splendidly attired in beaten gold. The five maidens run squealing to him. He carries them to the bed and puts them under the covers. He strokes and kisses them one by one, according to his pleasure. One by one they fall asleep.

Gazing at the sleeping maidens, the Great Khan heaves a deep sigh. He gets up from the bed and comes to her where she is standing. He looks at her for a long time. His robe of gold is a wonder to behold. He stretches out his hand and drops it on her shoulder. His voice is octaves deep, but kind, so kind: "So you are the maiden of whom I have heard so much." She answers nothing. His hand is warm.

"Come," he says, turning her toward the door. "I have much to show you."

8

Jane's bedroom is eerily tidy, even down to the furniture, all in white uniforms with gold trim, like admirals on parade. There is nothing on the walls but two framed pictures of French villages. Where are the drawings, banners, maps, mobiles, drums, weapons, star charts, periodic tables, medals of valor, coats of arms, cryptograms, scalps, totems, declarations, anathemas, emergency supplies for a long siege, clues to treasure buried elsewhere in the house?

"My parents don't allow messes," Jane says.

"So this is basically a motel room."

Jane laughs. "Just show me where to check out!"

On the floor is carpeting, as pink and bushy as troll's hair. Go out the door and it continues in royal blue down the hall and even covers the stairs like knee padding and goes on, kelly green, into the living room, spreading into all the corners, obsessively, the same way Saskia has to spread peanut butter on bread so that the crew won't make a fuss. Outside, the house is canary. Two trees the size of coat racks rise, collared and guy-wired, from pitcher's mounds of cedar chips, and around them nothing but more carpeting, winter beige, shorter than the troll's hair indoors but spread just as obsessively into the corners. Beyond lies the street, in the middle of which a gargantuan mirror creates an amazing trompe l'oeil effect: one would almost believe that there really is another house and lawn across the street, identical in every detail to this one.

Everything in the Sing household works. Imagine! When you turn a knob on the stove, the gas poops on right away. Go ahead, flick any switch in the house: the lights light, the garbage disposal growls, the television's mesmerant dragon eye sleepily bats its lid and focuses on you, glaring in its wakened rage. There is something exhilarating about this. Sing-things are dependable in a way Saskia never imagined possible. You don't have to talk to them, praise them, pray to them to get them to behave.

But there is also something disconcerting about it, isn't there? Everything at White-on-the-Water has personality. As the fan over the stove picks up speed, you have to edge the dial back or it will clatter against its cage and break a blade. The oven door closes so obediently only when it's cold; as it warms, it slowly sneaks open until it's furiously trying to bake the ceiling. That's why there is a broom handle in the corner, in case you were wondering. You slide it through the handle on the oven door and wedge it in the radiator. Betsy's passenger door opens only from the outside, but when you roll down the window to reach the handle you'd better push the glass down as you crank, or it will hang for a second before dropping with a screech of panic into the depths of the door, whence it can be extricated only by taking the panel off. These are the contracts between people and things. You respect things' idiosyncracies and they, in turn, will faithfully work for you, in their own ways, year after year.

The Sings had an electric can opener — fascinating in itself, as it mumbled around cans like a chipmunk parting the seams of a peanut shell — and one day it woke up. Saskia was actually present at the moment of waking. The opener balked at the corners of a squarish can and disdainfully let it drop to the counter. "What's wrong with this thing?" Mrs. Sing complained, rapping it on the head. After studying it, Saskia saw that it wanted, in fact, only the smallest encouragement: as each corner came under the blade she gently lifted the bottom of the can and around it went. So exciting, this sudden blossoming of self-awareness! And so little to ask, this scrap of attention from the people for whom the opener worked so hard! A few days later the can opener was gone, and a new one stood on the counter. Saskia was shocked. What comfortless world was this, unbound by contracts, populated by automatons?

At first surprised by Saskia's outrage, Jane came to agree with her. The treatment of Sing-things matched anyway, she said, what had always "bugged the shit out of her" concerning her own position in the Sing house. "It's like I don't really exist," she says, sitting on Saskia's bed, a rumpled platform of sheets and blankets over plywood propped on cinder blocks. "As long as I'm not in some kind of trouble, they ignore me. It's all Peter this, Peter that. It's some Indian thing. The boy is a god, and the girl is nothing."

Saskia saw Peter briefly at a meal. A tall dreg with a smooth face, pudgy around his thick-lipped mouth, he is lighter skinned than Jane, a beamer — a joy boy — whereas darker Jane broods. "My dad drives him wherever he wants to go, to look at buildings. He took two days off from work to go with him to some whizbang architect school he's thinking about going to next year, whereas he would hardly even take a measly lunch break to go with me to court."

"Court?"

"Some piddling thing about trespassing. Did you know that in India parents have to bribe suitors to take their daughters off their hands? What kind of fucked-up way of doing things is that? I think I'm worth a few camels."

Mr. Sing is a meaty man, prosciutto-colored, with about ten pounds of beard. When Saskia first saw him, she thought he was recovering from two black eyes and only later realized that the alarming dark rings in the deep pits on either side of his nose were permanent. He will start a conversation with someone three rooms away by foghorning, "Jaa-AYN!," "Pe-EETER!," or "Smii-IITAA!" Everyone bends over backward to accommodate him. Mrs. Sing is bird-like. Her voice chirps tunefully, hopping around on the lightest and tiniest of feet. In profile her nose is almost a perfect quarter-circle, and Saskia finds herself staring at it, thinking of trigonometric functions.

"You get your color from your dad," Saskia tells Jane. Saskia is intrigued by the world of family resemblances: the mix-and-match principle, the total-gene-dominance principle, the what-in-hell-happened principle. "But your basic build is like your mother's. Especially your neck." When Mrs. Sing chirps, her chin goes up and her head waggles on its long supple stalk in time with her music. "Whereas Peter has your mother's color and your dad's build."

"Peter is going to be fat," Jane says with profound satisfaction.

Alas, the Sings don't wear those colorful togas the Wonderland communards used to bring back from India. Mr. Sing heads off to Huge Red's Nutrition Department in a rumpled tweed suit and tie, an umbrella tucked fussily under his arm, and Mrs. Sing wears pantsuits. But the food is intriguingly odd. Mrs. Sing buys two-foot-long airy loaves of bread that are softer than pillows. The slices stick tenaciously to the roof of your mouth like rubber patches. Square and white, they seem woven, ripping straight one way but not the other. "How do they do that?" Saskia wonders out loud, tearing three slices in succession.

"Stop that," Mrs. Sing warbles, lightly slapping Saskia's hand. This, like the death-squad disappearing of the can opener, is a stunner. Lauren never touches Saskia.

Mrs. Sing's corn is acrid, foot-smelling. Biscuits explode from a tube you whack on the head of the nearest long-suffering Sing-thing. At table, the girls tap the biscuits against their plates to make the weevils crawl out, until Mr. Sing growls at them to act their age. Saskia loves the TV dinners: everything tucked so hoogily into its little compartment, like spices on a merchant's table. The most amazing thing is the rice, which is even whiter than the woven bread, as shiny as cartilage. "Are you full?" Mrs. Sing chirps at Saskia. How could she not be, from swallowing this packing material? In the kitchen Saskia sees the box, which promises "perfect rice, every time." Is this Indian, then, this urge to control run wild? If so, it's as exotic as Saskia could wish for.

9

At Wonderland, I was a happy child, running with the other children and excelling at games. My laugh was like a clear bell. In summer, I turned nut brown from the sun.

In case you don't believe it, she has photographs: there she is, her naked brown little self, arm slung over the shoulder of another naked boy or girl, the two of them dirty, grinning insolently, staring up into the camera as if the snap of the shutter were no more than their due.

This was the Thomas Age of Wonderland, when the sun always shone and everything we put our hands to prospered.

She spreads the photos out on her cabin floor and stares at the myriad faces. She can remember a few names, a Blossom here, a Shiva there. Who are these children squatting with her in a fort in the tall timothy? Only the black and white puppy is familiar, bounding into the frame with bent ears poised like chopsticks.

People came and went, but Thomas and his dog, Lauren, the guru, and I were always there. We were the faithful.

All the faces are gone now, either one by one, taking tents or vans with them — how terribly mobile these people were! — or in the final mass exodus, when the guru came down from his tower amid the wailings of his people, the gnashing of teeth and rending of garments, the fire-blue flashes of pure Shakta energy. He left, urging all to accompany him, and Lauren came behind in righteous anger, dispersing those who lingered.

The guru is a confusing element. There is only one photo from the Wonderland period that includes him: a fuzzy dark shot of all the disciples crowded on the front porch. He is standing near the middle, an imposing figure, tall, pale, and bald. Yet a photo Lauren has from the court in India shows him as a slight, swarthy man. Since he knew how to change base metals into gold, perhaps like Proteus he could also change his appearance.

The fuzzy dark shot, by the way, also contains a rare glimpse of Thomas: as the favorite disciple, he is sitting next to the guru, wearing a brown robe, his beautiful hands forward on the arm rests of his chair, his light hair tousled. Those beautiful hands used to rest on Saskia's blanket when he came in to kiss her good night.

Thomas worked in the garden with Lauren. He sailed in the bay, in a fine boat he made himself. He meditated with the guru and learned much wisdom from him.

After the guru ascended the tower, though he was still at Wonderland (now styled "Godhead"), we never saw him. Only Thomas went up, to take him his simple fare of brown rice. The guru sat alone and meditated for many months. Up in the tower the stars blazed so clearly, he could see every one, and he learned them all. When he had learned the last one, he came down from his tower and left us.

By then, Thomas, too, was gone. Why? How? All Lauren will say, her face closed down, is, "He had to go. He had no choice."

It came to pass with the passing of days that Thomas's time with us came to an end. He did not wish it thus. But when the call came, he was ready. He took up his oar and put it back onto his muscled shoulder and walked out through the gate of Godhead, whistling to his dog, who came running like the wind. He lifted the dog into the boat that he had made, raised a sail and dipped the oar, and the bow of the boat lifted and the wake creamed behind, and the boat disappeared up the lake. He did not turn to look back. Across the water of the lake, the dog howled until it could be heard no more.

Like the guru, the boat is problematical. Along one wall of the barn, almost lost in the tall weeds, an old wooden boat lies upside down. The mast is gone and the bottom staved in. Lauren has never volunteered anything to Saskia about the boat, and when

Saskia asked, she said she couldn't remember how it got there. Is it Thomas's boat? If so, why is it in the weeds, when Thomas left in it? And if not, then whose boat is it?

Once or twice a year a postcard comes in the mail, with stamps from exotic lands, and Lauren reads the brief text and looks for a few long seconds at the picture on the other side before handing it curtly to Saskia, saying, "From Thomas." Does she seem distracted as she returns to the bills? Saskia keeps the cards safe under her bed, in a box next to the photos. There are ten, dating as far back as six years ago, but she has a feeling some came before that, although Lauren denies having any. The latest arrived four months ago. Several of the pictures are of ports. One is a glacier. Another, a flock of crimson birds. No Rembrandts. Thomas's handwriting is large and forceful, with looping g's, p's, y's. The exclamation points are huge and flared at the top, like oars upright. He writes in English. The ten texts, in order, are:

1. Lauren and my Saskia: Although I haven't written lately, I think of you often. I miss you both! Keep the faith. Love, Thomas.
2. A busy time, but I'm happy. Except of course that I miss you! Thomas.
3. Thomas is writing this, on a stormy day with high seas, cups rolling on the floor. He is sending his love to Lauren and Saskia.
4. Narrow scrape — brave men! I am well, and can feel that you are, too. Love Thomas.
5. Missing you! Thomas.
6. My Saskia and Lauren: I do think of you often. Please forgive my infrequent cards. I am fine, but very busy. I will write again soon, and at much greater length. Love, Thomas.
7. Thinking of you! Love, Thomas.
8. Missing you! Love, Thomas. p.s. Happy Birthday for my Saskia! I wish I were there to celebrate with you, but I am needed here. Much love, Thomas.

9. Missing you. Thomas.
10. Thinking of you! Thomas.

The last two do not say "love," but neither do numbers two and five, so one may reasonably conclude that the omission does not mean anything. The obverse of number four is a photo of two men, neither of them Thomas, in a horseshoe-shaped inflatable boat in a rough swell, backed up against a wall of metal plates riveted together. They are flung around, hanging on tight. Something near them in the water is sending up a plume of spray. A sea monster? Angry Poseidon?

Thomas did once send a photo of himself. He is standing in his own boat, much bigger than the boat he had at Wonderland. The hood of his parka is down, his arms crossed. He is not smiling, but he seems filled with joy. His faithful black and white dog is by his legs. Unlike his master, the dog is smiling, eyes arched in innocent surprise. The bent ears have learned to stand up. The photo is turning orange.

Saskia pictures Thomas plying the seas in his Phaiakian boat. His dog has gray in her muzzle now, and if she had to run, she would be slower. He is steering with the oar in the water behind him. He sings Phaiakian folksongs in the dark of night while navigating by the stars, his voice the only sound on the flat sea. He is content, having no choice.

"What does he do now?" she asked Lauren.

"Something very important, I'm sure."

"But what?"

"If he wants us to know, he'll write about it."

"Aren't you curious?"

"Truth and Baba Yogi taught us to let go of curiosity. It's unhealthy, a striving."

Saskia gave up.

After Thomas left, Saskia and Lauren were all alone. Lauren brooded, meditated, brooded. The farm went untouched for a year. The house would run out of food. Saskia remembers a period — two days? two weeks? — of mayonnaise sandwiches, mayonnaise on rice. Then Lauren started giving Saskia chores. Saskia was proud to be trusted. Soon Lauren was treating her like an equal. Lauren did her work, Saskia did hers. It was just the two of them in the big decaying farmhouse by the water. The tower, the dome, the huts were torn down, the wood burned in the wood stove. The trailers were desolate, like boats beached along the drive, breaking up in the surf. But this quiet, this solitude, was all right. There were books to read, left behind by long-gone communards, in corner shelves and closet tops and boxes under beds. The dry pages of the cheap paperbacks would split, powdering the air with the smell of graham crackers. The leather bindings of the old tomes would smear her hands with cinnamon powder, which she would dab on her forehead as a mark of wisdom. Reading, reading, Saskia let her skin lighten to yellow. The blond in her hair drained to the tips and dripped off, leaving mousy brown. The chunky muscles in her legs dissolved. Like a lizard, she stayed out of the sun.

Now when she lays out those old photographs and looks at, say, the circle of long-gone children squatting in the tall timothy, she picks out the insolent and dirty short one with the half-dome forehead and sees only a stranger among strangers.

10

When Jane gets permission for an overnight at White-on-the-Water, Saskia volunteers out of turn to cook the communal dinner. "Fire up the athanor!" she shouts. "Get down the crucibles! Let the transmutations begin!" Jane doesn't know the first thing about cooking, but she is disarmingly cheerful, as usual, about admitting her ignorance. (I've got to learn how to do that, Saskia tells herself, never learning.) "That's because at Sing Sing your moor does everything," she says, backing her head out of a steam cloud. Outside in the village street the peasants see the steam pluming from the cellar windows and whisper, "The professor is at her experiments again!" They back away, crossing themselves. "This is called the Red Work," Saskia explains, flushed from the heat. "If we were only making silver, it would be called the White Work. Cakes and cookies and so on. Do you know what the only edible stone is?"

"Sugar?"

"Salt." She taps a shaker over the pot. "It just might be the Philosopher's Stone." After all, it goes into everything, and we know that the Philosopher's Stone, though infinitely precious, lies everywhere, unrecognized. It is the Quintessence, summoned forth out of the spirits of mercury and sulfur, and in its turn it can spiritualize metals, generating that to which they aspire, *l'essence de l'essence*: gold.

One of the Disciplines of the Wise is the trance in which the essences of nature are not only perceived but felt, physically. Saskia will sit for an hour in the grass down by the shore, pondering a koan until she enters that space wherein silence and stillness press against her like solid walls. The heart of the Discipline is watching: delving with the reptilian eyes that don't blink. One takes the tree in and it shimmers like liquid within, shedding its dross to become the Essence of Tree. By taking the world within yourself, you dissolve into the world. This, doubtless, is the culmination of that buttery feeling she summons when she undresses in her cabin and rubs herself against rough and smooth.

Of course the dinner is a resounding success, the murmurs of appreciation at the table so heartfelt one looks forward to them crescendoing after the dessert into a standing ovation, ecstatic cries of *encore!* calling the girls from the kitchen for bow after bow. But instead Bill mumbles, "Thanks much," pats his midriff with a pale hand, and takes his hemp pouch out of his breast pocket. By the time Saskia and Jane have cleaned up — another novelty for Jane — the sounds from the dining room are a somnolent drone, borne into the kitchen on billows of sweetish air. And after the crew has been frogmarched through a toothbrushing and strapped into their beds for the night, the kitchen is a mess again. "Raided!" Saskia peeks into the dining room: "Hemp haze. Hard to see." Bill and Lauren are nuzzling. Yugh.

Jane comes to look. She figured out a while ago that Bill was Lauren's boyfriend. "Wow, they're really going at it." Saskia turns away. "Where's Jo?"

"She doesn't smoke hemp. She probably realizes she can't afford the brain damage." Jane is looking intently through the door. "Let's go back upstairs," Saskia says.

"In a sec."

Saskia is certainly not going to clean up the mess. Lauren and Bill will leave it, too, and the food will dry and stick to the plates and they'll have a hard time cleaning it tomorrow. Tough noogies. "They're heading up," Jane says, coming away from the door. She swivels her hips and smiles, twitching her eyebrows.

"Yeah, whatever."

"God, Lauren is so beautiful. She could do better than Bill."

"No kidding."

"So are we going upstairs too?"

"I just remembered I have to check something in the barn. Let's do that first." Bill huffs and puffs so loud you can hear him all the way up on the top floor, it's disgusting.

When they do go up a while later, all is safely quiet. Lauren is reading a book in bed. "Good night, Lauren!"

"Good night, girls. Sweet dreams."

Up in Saskia's room, Jane's eyes are sparkling. "So what happened to Bill?"

"He must be back in his trailer." Post-puff.

"She boots him? After they do it?"

"Lauren never lets him sleep up here, if that's what you mean."

"Wow!"

"Well would you? He probably twitches all night." Think of that ultra-trimmed beard poking into you, those disgusting long fingernails. On second thought, Saskia doesn't want to think about it.

"Lauren hasn't ever let any of her boyfriends sleep with her. She says she can't sleep with someone else in her bed." At least Kevin argued with her. Boy, the fights they had! Bluffaroo just takes whatever morsels are thrown to him.

"What an Amazon!"

"She is not!"

"No, I think it's great!" Jane closes the door. "Now *I* want to get stoned." She goes to her jean jacket where it's hanging among the Tartar spears and takes out a pouch.

"You mean now?" Saskia squeaks. "Here?"

"I'm in the mood in the worst way."

"I . . ." What can she say? "I've never done it before."

"I figured that. It's easy." Jane dangles the pouch like a mouse held by its tail. "This is a nickel bag."

"I know *that*."

"All right, then."

Saskia looks on in dread as Jane labors over her desk, shaking out shavings, pinching the paper into a groove and licking the edge with her felt-tipped tongue. She holds up a sliver almost as neat as the ones Bill makes, which are so uniformly neat they look like something you would buy in a Family Pak. "I don't want to try it," Saskia blurts out. She backpedals: "I mean . . ."

"Don't worry," Jane says, putting a match to it and puffing it into life. "There's nothing to it." She holds it out to Saskia. Saskia just stares at it. Jane has insisted it's not moronizing, you just have to be inside it to see that. "Look, how do you know you don't want to unless you try?"

Words of reason. Jane is so good to her, so patient. She puts up with all of Saskia's barnish timidities, her slowpoking. How can Saskia disappoint her? "It makes you giggle," Saskia says unhappily.

"If you don't like it, just don't do it again. It's not like you don't have a choice afterward." Well, that's true. Saskia prides herself on her willpower. "Come on, girl," Jane says gently. She puffs again to make sure it is still lit and places it in Saskia's hand.

Saskia's heart aches at the thought of Jane's goodness. Surely she would do anything to please Jane. Suddenly she wants to be enfolded in the long arms of this older, wiser girl. Jane would kiss the top of her head and smooth down her wispy hair. What Saskia fears most is becoming a different person, the way Odysseus' men changed when they ate the honey-sweet lotus and forgot their way home; the way Lauren changes from the capable woman who keeps Bluffaroo in his place to the silly thing that nuzzles him and lets him scuttle into her bed. To change! That is not the way to be right-acting, to be trustworthy and constant such as one would never expect in a young person. You change, and you find you don't fit your space anymore. Where would you be then but falling, forgotten?

One must have the constancy of *things*. When she was little, Saskia had a blue-jean book bag with an olive canvas strap. She took it with her into sunny Ithaca and filled it with books from the great library. It was a good book bag, capacious and sturdy. After a while it got a rip in the bottom and Saskia put it away, intending to mend it before she used it again, so the rip wouldn't get bigger. But somehow — she was so young and thoughtless! — somehow she forgot about it. The book bag just went completely out of her head. For a couple of years she brought books home in a knapsack. And then one day, for no better reason than when she forgot, she remembered. It was such an old memory by then. Was it a true one? She remembered where she had put the book bag, but the place was in her own room. Surely it could not have lain there all that time, unnoticed. But she moved aside this and that, and there it was, exactly as she had left it, folded up, with the rip in the bottom. It had waited there patiently all that time for Saskia to come and fix it. Saskia had betrayed it, and yet it had waited for her. It didn't even blame her. It was ready to be her book bag again, capacious and sturdy as ever. Holding it in her arms, she cried.

Funny. She is crying now, too. "I can't," she sobs miserably, holding the stupid thing in her lap. "I just can't!"

Jane is silent. Saskia doesn't dare look up at her. She can picture the disappointment and disgust in her eyes. God, she knew she would blow it, she just knew it.

"It's all right," Jane is saying. "Look!" She is crumbling the joint in her hand. The curls of hemp shake out between her fingers. "I won't smoke either. I'll go on the wagon."

"Don't do that —"

"No, I've been thinking about it anyway. I've been smoking too much." Wiping her eyes, Saskia looks around for a tissue. "I've been terrible," Jane laughs.

And Saskia laughs with her, flooded with relief. "Where are the darn tissues?"

"Here."

Saskia honks, and laughs again. She is beginning to feel that cool calm you feel after you have been a baby and made a complete fool out of yourself. When you can't sink any lower.

"I'll be a reformed drug addict," Jane says. "How about that?"

Actually, that sounds kind of neat. A reformed drug addict! Dark circles under your eyes, the pain of the world in them. To have been there and back.

"Are you OK?" Jane asks. There is no wavering in her face, no doubt. She could quit anytime she wanted to. And she would quit for Saskia's sake. Won't Saskia walk that road for Jane? How else to share what she knows? Then they could quit together. They could suffer and be strong together. They could write haiku about it.

Deep down, Saskia believes she can overcome anything. The barns' ridicule at school doesn't hurt her because she wills it not to hurt. She could smoke a pack of cigarettes every day for a year and then quit, cold turkey. How can she prove she is superior to this hemp business, this stuff that Bill and even Lauren are weak enough to need, if she doesn't try it and then spurn it? The poor joint lies broken in Jane's hand. "I want to try it after all," Saskia says humbly.

"All right!" Jane sweeps together the crumbs and rolls another. "OK, first you take a deep drag." She lights it and sucks on it as if she were inhaling all the air in the room. She holds herself stiffly, chest out. "Thn hld t n." Wisps of smoke curl dragon-like from her flared nostrils as she hands the joint to Saskia. "Tzi-zi." Saskia turns it in her hands. A little stick of pencil shavings. Pathetic really, once you look at it. She feels the strength in her, the imperviousness. She inhales.

Far away, through the hacking and the pain, Jane is patting her on the back. If she could just get her lungs out onto the floor, she could douse them with water. "You've got virgin lungs, girl." Not anymore! On Saskia's second try the cough erupts again, but less painfully, and on the third she manages to hold her breath for a few seconds. The stuff scrapes around in there, sanding down edges. "There you go! Not so bad, is it?"

"Hm" is all Saskia can say, wide-eyed, holding it in. It tastes like a vacuum cleaner bag. She can see sparks whirling like stars in her deflowered chest, leaving cancerous black holes as they bury themselves in the defenseless membranes. But she feels nothing else. She feels none of the slow tide of warmth, the soothing nonchalance that Jane has described. Willpower. As in her controlled dreaming, she simply says to herself, "I am here. I am Saskia." Thus does she hold on to herself.

The joint goes back and forth, and she continues to feel nothing. This is immensely reassuring. "Don't worry," Jane says. "Sometimes you don't until the second or third time. It varies. I'm pretty fucked up, anyway. This is superbo stuff. But it's expensive! Where do Bill and Lauren get theirs?"

"Bluffaroo grows his own." Down in the hold, in a windowless room, he has trays, banks of lights, timers. His hemp is as doodah as his croutons. It, too, is held up and explicated, its superiority characterized in excruciating detail. "There's some trick about getting male and female plants together and then frustrating the females."

"That makes the oils build up. Probably like that congested feeling you get when you're interrupted."

"Hm?"

"You know, doing the dirty deed."

"Oh, yeah."

"Do you think he'd sell to us?"

"I can't see Bluffaroo being that helpful."

"Maybe we could just take some." Jane's color is high, her espresso eyes glitter, *espressivo*. Her pointy pink tongue is much in evidence as she talks enthusiastically. She is more beautiful than ever. Saskia wonders why she never before noticed just precisely how beautiful Jane is.

Time for bed. Saskia turns to say something to Jane, but Jane is naked, just like that, rummaging in her overnight bag for her nightgown. Saskia looks away. She has to go to the bathroom to change into her own gown. She stands for a moment at Mim's door to listen. Once when Mim walked in her sleep, she actually went downstairs. What a spooky sound that was, the creak of the old stairs in the blackness! It took all of Saskia's courage to get out of bed and follow. "Mim, what are you doing?" But she kept walking without answering. In the darkness of the common room the bat-wing begonia was terrifying, a crouched form ready to flap those leathery wings and lumber aloft, moaning for blood. Mim went right out the front door and down the porch steps. She stopped in the gravel turnaround. She just stood there, with her arms at her sides, staring at nothing, a ghost in the moonlight. "Mim, what are you doing out of bed?" Saskia asked, hugging herself.

"Out of bed?" Mim's eyes pointed straight ahead.

"What are you doing down here?"

"Down here?"

Saskia took her arm. "Let's go back up."

"Out of bed?"

It was one of Saskia's nightmares come to life, her horrible sneaking suspicion that everybody else in the world is really a robot, that one day when she eavesdrops, say, on Lauren and Bill, she will hear them conversing in dead, flat tones, not bothering to sound human now that the only human is not present. She turned Mim toward the house, nearly fainting with terror that the younger girl would say, "Out of bed? (click) Out of bed? (click) Out of bed?"

The girls smoke a second joint between the sheets. "Damme," Saskia growls in her Lieutenant's voice, regarding the joint judiciously. "Damme! A fine cigar, this! It draws well!" Jane laughs and laughs.

Saskia has never had anyone in her bed before. What could Lauren be bitching about? There is just enough room for the two girls to lie comfortably, touching flanks. She is so happy she would like to shout something around the world, or jump sky high. "Look at this." She turns off the light.

Jane giggles. "What are those?"

"My stars."

Jane snaps the light back on and stands on the bed to peer at the ceiling. "You can hardly see them when the light's on."

The ad in the mail-order catalogue showed the glow-in-the-dark stars sprinkled randomly across some stupid dreg's ceiling. Saskia stood on a ladder with a star chart crooked in one arm and marked each position with a pencil before sticking a single star. Her ceiling is astronomically accurate: a spring evening in the north temperate zone, circa 9 P.M.

Jane slips under the covers again and huddles against Saskia. "It's cold out there."

"There's some culture where they believe that every person's soul is tied by a thread to a star," Saskia says. "When a star falls, the thread is broken, and the person dies."

"You know the strangest things," Jane murmurs.

"Which star would you choose to be your soul-star?"

"Haven't the faintest. Which one is least likely to fall?"

"None of them really fall. Shooting stars are actually meteors."

They smoke the last of the joint. Long minutes of silence go by.

Then Jane says, "Listen!"

"What?"

"Don't you hear it?"

Saskia listens. "No." Then she does. Far away. A barely audible flutter. Slowly growing, coming nearer, a steady determined murmur. *King, king, wong-king.*

"Geese!" Jane whispers.

A haunting cry like a lonely spirit passing over the house in the night. *King, king, king, wong-king.* Somewhere up in the darkness a mysterious V points north, heading north. Who knows where? Reedy new-melted ponds set in snowfields, places they remember from last year, the goose at the point leading the way by celestial navigation. The calls are fading now as the geese leave Tylerian air space. *King-king.* They don't care about the girls, nor even know that they exist.

Jane sighs. "God, I love that sound! I used to imagine they were talking to me. 'Come on, girl! Fly!' In England I used to imagine I'd wandered all my life. I'd pretend I never had a fucking family. I would look at the houses I passed and think, 'How can people lock themselves up in those cages when the world is so unexplored? The same bed every night? How boring! What's over that hill? What's over the next?' God! The thought that I might just walk over the hill and then over the next one, and the next, never turning back. No one would know who I was. God. I loved the thought of that."

Saskia thinks of Thomas, walking inland with his oar on his shoulder. He walked until no one knew him or his people, until he was so much a stranger in a strange land that the man at the gate mistook his oar for a winnowing fan. What would Saskia's "oar" be? How would she know she had truly escaped? Would she carry a mixing bowl, until someone asked why her war drum was uncovered? Would she carry a school paper, until someone asked why she wrote such terribly long and dull haiku?

But Saskia does not want to leave rainy Tyler. She wants to wake up and find that Tyler has left her, that it has been supplanted by a world in which the houses are carved cedar boxes with open doors and Captain's rooms and uncluttered vistas, a world like the ones pictured on the herb tea boxes, all green fields and blue skies, a world called Ithacan Sunburst.

Saskia doesn't want to talk anymore. The silence between the girls drifts on, growing deeper. The stars have gone out. Normally Saskia would turn on her lamp again to recharge them, but she doesn't want Jane to guess that she is afraid of the dark. Her myriad failings rise up vividly before her: her ugliness, her weirdness, her timidity. What on earth does bold, beautiful Jane see in her?

11

Naked, she glides up the stairs. Damme, she will make it this time. She mounts the quarterdeck and opens the door of her cabin. She is wearing fine broadcloth breeches and a cutaway coat with two rows of brass buttons. She would so dearly love to have the brass gilded, but on a Lieutenant's share of prize money, it just is not possible. The Captain's scope and hat lie on her desk. A cup of his beloved coffee steams. The Captain's room is on the poop deck above. How to get up there? She surveys her cabin. There couldn't be a way up that she has never noticed before.

And yet there is. Memory pours in, filling her like a glass. Yes! There *has* always been a door between the bed and the bookshelf! How strange that she never opened it before! She opens it. Steep wooden stairs going up. She climbs. I'm coming! She rises into a small space with windows all around, a space soaked with golden light. She can see in all directions over the trees and rooftops of sunny Ithaca, miles north up the mighty blue bay. And the tall Captain is standing there, erect, his back to her, his beautiful, sensitive hands on the wheel. "Captain!" She snaps to attention.

But he does not turn around. His hands grip the wheel, urging it left and right. "Please forgive me, sir. I . . ." What excuse can she proffer? There is no excuse. She leans forward to see his face: gaunt, black with anger. Still not looking at her, he opens his mouth to say something, but his face curdles into a scowl and he stops himself.

She admires this in him, this iron British reserve. She herself is so blabby, always putting her foot in her mouth, always bragging embarrassingly. You can read Saskia like a book. But the Captain brutally suppresses his emotions, and there is something wonderful about the tortured look that spreads over his face as he says nothing, harrumphs, and turns away. She hangs her head. "I betrayed you. I'm sorry."

He pulls the wheel savagely, with all his strength, and the ship lurches. Loose from its foundations, it lumbers forward with an octaves-deep sound of groaning and grinding. It rolls over one Ithacan house, and another, leaving splinters in its wake. With a final huge and wretched sigh, it tips over the embankment and slides into the water.

The Captain turns from the window. "I . . . I . . . ," she stutters, on her knees, barefoot, penitent. She awaits the well-deserved stroke. But his dark scowl crumbles. His eyes disappear into squints, his chin trembles. He begins to weep. He does not turn away, he simply stands there with his arms at his sides, weeping piteously. She takes him in her arms and fetches tissues out of her pocket to wipe his slobbery chin. She keeps repeating how sorry she is, yet she knows she will never make up for her betrayal. The ship rocks gently on the water.

12

Elementary school was tolerable. None of Saskia's teachers knew what to do with her, so they were relieved just to let her work on her own projects, somewhere in the back of the room, or better, out of sight and mind in the library. No one had told Saskia that barns undergo a mysterious and sinister transformation during the summer after sixth grade. On Saskia's first day at Tyler Junior, someone in the crowded hall called, "Hey, White!" and when she looked around to see who it was, three dregs covered their faces and howled, "Aarrggh! What a dog! Arf, arf, arf!" Barns had broken out of their cocoons and unfolded leathery wings. For some unfathomable reason, sticking to yourself and not bothering anyone was no longer an option. The smallest things you did — a word you used, the way you looked at the bottom of your shoe — were immensely important to other barns. Fully half of them were outright lunatics, devoting great amounts of their time, energy, and ingenuity to making your life miserable.

Saskia wore the clothes she had always worn: nubby wool tights, ankle-length skirts, one cardigan over another, sturdy work shoes. The barns had a field day. Someone wrote "Saskia Witch" on her locker. "Just ignore them," Lauren said. But Saskia couldn't. She would walk up to a snorting dreg and stare balefully at him. Then she would inform him he had just been cursed to the seventh generation.

And the teachers! They were crazy, too. Paranoid. They wouldn't let Saskia work on her own projects, because they were sure she was trying to pull a fast one. They would even take her books away. "I'm sorry, I thought this was a school," she would say, but they never got the bitter irony. Like all paranoiacs, they were illogically, maddeningly rigid. They would begin, "I understand" or "I'm sorry," but what followed was a recorded message. Saskia wanted to scream and charge at them, stick them with pins to puncture their eerie robotic demeanors.

Even social studies was a problem. Saskia's first report was on ancient Egypt, and frankly, she outdid herself. The text was twenty-eight pages. There were drawings of clothes and tools; a series illustrating embalming, step by step; a foldout map of the Nile valley in six colors with a key. Saskia learned some authentic Egyptian writing from an Ithacan library book and wrote a whole page as Queen Shasakhiya of the Fourth Dynasty, outlining her glorious accomplishments. The report came back, and the only marks the Blatt had made were for misspellings. The comments were on the back: "Very enjoyable. Well integrated pictures. Good vocabulary! All in all, extremely well done. Sorry it was so late. D."

In other classes, things got downright ugly. When the Plebe, during the American poetry unit, ordered her inmates to show their creativity by copying from the textbook three poems they liked and pasting magazine pictures to accompany them, Saskia rebelled, wrote her own haiku, and drew the Plebe in jackboots, wielding a riding crop. The last haiku read: .

We've learned so much here,
Copying poems word for word.
Thank you, Kommandant!

Not content with merely giving it an F, the Plebe ripped it up. After that, Saskia wouldn't stop barking "Jawohl!" and goose-stepping around the room until the Plebe caught her arm and actually slapped her (which, by the way, is against the law in this state). Saskia tried to slap her back but missed and, humiliatingly, burst into tears. She was sent to the V.P., who with his flushed bull neck straining at the collar of his polo shirt called her, with his usual self-control, a little snot and a spoiled little brat. Saskia sat quietly and looked at the football trophies on his wall, hoping he would disburden himself of her by, say, drop-kicking her out of school. But though she was snotty, she hadn't blown anything up, or been caught smoking, so her parole was held up.

Then Jane came. Linking up with Saskia was the worst thing she could have done, tactically speaking. Saskia's name is on all the bathroom walls. She is the kiss of death.

"What's a 'scag'?" Jane asks Saskia, bristling.

"It's sort of like a 'scuz,'" Saskia replies. "Only crustier, I think."

The same dregs who yell "Cross-your-heart bra!" at Saskia started to follow Jane with cries of "Tim-berrrr!" and "See Jane Sing! Sing, Jane, Sing!" They stopped only after Jane held one down by the throat and belted him, giving him the heaves and making him cry. "God, this place sucks," Jane says. Saskia struggles not to look pleased. There is little chance now that Jane will make other friends.

The girls are called "lesbos." In every class they sit together, until they are separated. After that they pass notes, which the barns in between can't read because Jane's are in Latin and Saskia's are in Egyptian. The barns pass them anyway, because everyone knows Jane belted a dreg. When a teacher gets dramatic about the girls' behavior, they roll their eyes and croon "Onnh!" to each other in mock intimidation. "Tough guy!" "Dem's fightin' words!" Jane is impregnable, an old hand at this sort of thing. But Saskia is seen as the leader, and after a joint meeting with the V.P. Saskia signs her notes "Saskia 'Disruptive Influence' White" and Jane, "Jane 'Simon Says' Sing." They escape together to the stalls of the opium dens, where Jane smokes cigarettes, Saskia essaying a hit or two, and they plan their campaigns. They slip into the woods during recess to share hemp. They skip school once, planning to forge sick notes, but the school calls their homes and Jane is grounded for a week. "Why weren't you grounded?" she asks Saskia.

"Lauren said she could understand my feelings but skipping only made things worse. So I promised I wouldn't do it again."

"Shit, Lauren is great!"

Especially after the skipping episode, hemping in the woods is risky. Saskia tells Jane she wouldn't mind getting booted out of school, but Jane says her parents told her if she got booted one more time they were going to find a school with searchlights on towers and slavering German shepherds.

Of course sunny Ithaca, with its alternative school, has the answer to all their problems. Saskia saw the school one afternoon when Lauren and she went to see Lauren's goddess-friend who teaches there. There were students *actually hanging around after school.* They were dressed in long skirts and scarves. They were chatting in a friendly manner with bearded teachers. A girl went by in bare feet and she was wearing red-and-blue-corded ankle bracelets. She had oil paint on her clothes. Everyone had names like Matteo, Garland, Haven.

If Saskia lived in sunny Ithaca, she would leave her carved cedar box each morning to climb through oak and maple woods to the shining school on the hill. There would be no bells, no big clock. There would be a board for notes. "I'm in room 7," Saskia would write. "Anyone interested in trig can meet me there."

She would joust intellectually with the other scholars, honing her dialectical skills in debate: Who was wiser, Aristotle or Plato? Can there be beauty without truth? Which is more fundamental, fire or water? "Here's a better idea, Bob," she would say, and show a teacher how to organize his course. She would work prodigiously, memorizing enormous tables of Latin verb conjugations. She would take off her steel-rimmed glasses and pinch the bridge of her nose in scholarly fatigue. She would stay late, and when night fell she would ascend to the observatory and work for hours in the utter quiet, in the soft red light, arcing the telescope from star to star. Like Mim, she would get straight A's.

But there is a catch. The alternative school is public. You have to live in the district. "So have your parents figured it out yet?" Saskia asks Jane. She means the lower house prices in rainy Tyler.

13

Jewels are her eyes
And satin her raven hair,
Nor blemish has she.

Endless is the love
She dips from me like water
Into her cupped hands.

Now ponder — can you
Guess of whom I speak? She is
Here, if you but look.

14

Being thirteen, Jane can talk about private things, but Saskia will get embarrassed and clam up. Smoking hemp helps, so the weekend afternoons in Saskia's bed are important opportunities to be guarded jealously. The subject is inexhaustible. Even the briefest selection would have to include:

1) BREASTS

Jane would like a pair.

"You're kidding!" Saskia bursts out.

"It's not fair," Jane complains. "I'm older than you."

No matter how "ex" ex-hippies are, they still strip at the drop of a hat, so Saskia has seen naked folksens her whole life, but for some reason she still hasn't gotten used to it. Lauren is six feet tall. At night when she lets down her floor-length hair, she is Junoesque, a column fluted with the folds of her nightgown, a magnificent upward sweep of Woman. But remove that gown and you see that the classical line is broken. Lauren's breasts are not small. They are flattened along the top where they sag against her chest muscles, and they bulge out poutingly lower down. As she emerges siren-like from the water hole, they dip and collide with each other. Saskia, in her demure one-piece, quails, embarrassed for her. They are the only part of the female anatomy quite as painful to glimpse as men's things.

"But Lauren is in her thirties," Jane points out. "And she never wore a bra." The role that bras play in eventual boob sag is discussed. Jane cleaves to the old line that years of bralessness cause the breast muscles to stretch and weaken. Saskia read a magazine article in which the opposite was asserted. Bras, it said, allow the breast muscles to atrophy.

So what is a person to do? Bind them, perhaps, thus obviating the dilemma. "I could wrap a towel around myself every day," Saskia says. Slide a rod through a twist and rotate it, winch-like. Perhaps as it squeezed her, it would make her taller, too.

2) MOONINESS

Not having had a bout yet, Jane is dying of curiosity. "My mother refuses to discuss it. Whereas I know Dad has given fucking Peter a few man-to-mans." Saskia can see Mr. Sing in the leatherized den, his meaty arm around Peter's shoulder, talking and gesticulating obscenely while his son nods and brays. Meanwhile, Mrs. Sing in the gleaming kitchen waggles her head and chirps "No!" as she lightly slaps Jane's hand.

If Jane's moor is reluctant to talk about it, Lauren seemed oddly eager. She argued that mooniness was something women should be proud of. Women were in touch with the cycles of life, while men were cut off, oblivious. Every bout of mooniness was like spring, a renewed contact with the powers of regeneration, the turning wheel underlying being and becoming, the mystic female link with blah blah blah.

Saskia wasn't buying. She was struck only by the lunar connection. "Although my clock isn't quite right," she confesses to Jane. "I run fast." Aye, a precocious Moon! the Sun might say, clapping her proudly on the shoulder.

Lauren's speech was only the beginning. She was dead set on holding a show-and-tell. "Women's shame and ignorance of their own bodies is slave mentality, a result of male-dominated society." Lauren was the only person in the world Saskia could be sort of undressed with, when, say, trying on thrift store clothes. But when Lauren sat on her bedroom rug facing Saskia with her floor-length legs spread and told Saskia to do the same, Saskia wanted to run away. "The female body is a beautiful thing," Lauren scolded. Saskia spread her legs, and hung her head. Following Lauren step by step, in a daze, she felt around some outer things, touched some inner things, named a couple of things. There was room in her for only one other emotion, throbbing painfully at the edges of her vast embarrassment: envy at Lauren's perfectly bushy triangle. Lauren had to smooth the curls to either side to show Saskia what she was talking about.

The crowning humiliation came when the first bout arrived shortly afterward, as if Lauren had ordered it for Saskia from a catalogue. "Western life is so empty of ritual, so soulless," Lauren said. This was by way of explanation for her brainstorm: the mensis meal, which was something like a birthday party except that the guest of honor hid upstairs, refusing to come down until Lauren shamed her

into it by reminding her how much work she had put into the prepa-
rations. And so, among the red candles, the tomato soup and the
beets, while the crew looked on with goggle eyes, Saskia was formally
inducted into Womanhood, wishing all the while that the Earth, with
which she, as a woman, was supposed to have such affinity, would
open up beneath her feet and swallow her.

3) A CERTAIN OTHER M WORD

Jane calls it "the dirty deed," and it takes Saskia so very long to catch
on. Even then she cannot believe it of Jane, not really. It belongs to
another world, light-years distant. Could Jane be so far from Saskia
that she would have a part in it?

Jane draws well, and since she is not allowed to hang her sketches
in Sing Sing, her large brilliant butterflies and her bare-legged girls
astride Arabian horses have added to the luxuriant chaos on Saskia's
walls. In her own bedroom, she removes a drawer from her dresser
and takes from the space beneath it a sketchbook, which she holds on
her lap, turning to Saskia. "You show me everything you do, right?"

"Of course."

"Absolutely everything?"

Saskia nods.

Jane hands the sketchbook to her. "If you want to look," she says
with uncharacteristic shyness. "These are my secret drawings."

Secret! How Saskia loves that word. Treasure maps? Codes? No.
Naked dregs and pigs. Saskia glances away.

"You think they're awful!"

"No —"

"You're turning red!"

"No!" Saskia looks back at the drawings. She turns the pages. "No,
I like them," she says weakly. She frowns judiciously, focusing on a
point a few feet beyond the book. They are only kissing and hugging,
really. No big deal. "Nice," she says.

When the sketchbook is back in its hiding place, Jane says, "Don't
you ever?"

"Ever?"

"Do it?" Then, accusingly: "You don't, do you?"

Do it? How? She doesn't want to know how. God, what would her men think? Marco, the Captain, and Odysseus are with her always. Would they stand in a circle and watch her? How was it? they would ask at the end, gazing at her intently. Nice? "Do it? Sure," Saskia says. But a little later, not looking at Jane, she says, "No."

"Never?"

Must she spell it out? "Never," she confesses miserably. She feels as if she should shout it so that Jane, on the other side of a widening chasm, might hear it. What? Jane would call back, her voice faint in the rising wind. I said "Never!" Saskia would yell, and the word would be lost, swallowed in the abyss between them.

"I don't know what's wrong with me," Jane says. "I think of it all the time."

4) DREGS' THINGS

Hemp does work wonders. On the first warm day of Tylerian spring, in the post-daffodil, pre-apple-blossom period when the ponds in the dirt roads are at their deepest, Saskia and Jane lie on a warm rock by the lake, looking up at those cumulus clouds flung away by Bluf-faroo's shameless nature, and run through every name they can think of. "Dick," Saskia is suggesting, her head propped on a root, her legs crossed.

"A kid's word. Don't you think?"

"OK. Dink?"

"Come on, even worse."

"Well I don't know . . ."

"Prick," Jane takes over.

Saskia winces. "It's ugly."

"Sharp, like pricking your finger."

"There's not enough vowel sound. All the really ugly words are like that."

"Like what?"

"Like . . . you know . . . like shit, or whatever."

"Shit. Bitch. Tits. Clit. You're right!"

"What else?" Saskia asks.

"How about penis?"

"How about it?"

They giggle. "Well . . . ," Jane says, "you always want to say *peee*nis. Sounds whiny."

"Sounds shrimpy."

"Like a mosquito flying into your ear. Pee-*EEEE*-nis." They laugh. "Then there's always phallus."

"Oh, always." More laughter. "It's too academic."

"It should go next to a diagram. 'Pictured at right is the human phallus . . .'"

"It could be a Roman general."

"Punctillius Phallus. Phallus Maximus."

They are laughing hard now, rolling on the slab. Saskia jumps up and declaims over the water, "Friends, Romans, phalluses, lend me your ears!" This leads to "Four score and seven phalluses ago," "Don't shoot until you see the whites of their phalluses," "Shoot if you must this old gray phallus," and "Give me liberty or give me a phallus."

"So what else?" Saskia gasps.

"Cock," Jane says.

That one, for some reason, does pack a punch. Saskia takes a hit off the joint, blushing.

"It's a tough-guy word," Jane says. "The leather-jacket guys by the stone wall never say 'Suck my penis,' they say 'Suck my cock.'"

God. Suck my . . . God. Don't be such a barn. Cock, cock, cock. Suck my . . .

"Hog," Jane says.

Saskia splutters.

"I heard a guy call his that once. 'My hog is cold,' he said."

"That's sooo disgusting!"

"Yes, you think of something . . . I don't know, something *snuffling* around —" And for minutes afterward, the girls simply howl.

5) *IT*. HOME BASE, ALL THE WAY, WHATEVER YOU WANT TO CALL IT

Once you begin on this matter of sex, there is no turning back. Vistas open only on other vistas, depths are plumbed only to reveal depths beneath them. Each revelation is like a door bursting open, letting in an icy blast. Vastamundus! In all its terror and mystery, Vastamundus waits for Saskia. A limitless frozen lake fanned by leathery wings, it is unimaginably, hugely *out there*. Jane must eventually speak of her personal encounter with sex, with the *real thing*, dreg and all. One listens to such a thing only in the safest of places: miles under the covers of one's own bed.

In one of Jane's schools in Boston there was a dreg, pale and blond with a smooth, angelic face. He was always hanging around the pigs but saying nothing, serenely staring at them with his cloud-gray eyes and listening to their talk. They were used to him and they talked about all sorts of things as if a dreg weren't there. One day he came up to Jane and said, "Let's go into the woods together."

She had heard about this, about him going into the woods. "What for?"

"We could have some sex."

She laughed. "Forget it."

He said he had done it with some of the other pigs. He named them. They had gone to a certain place — Jane knew the spot — and they had taken their clothes off. They had lain in the leaves. "It's beautiful," he said. "It's love."

"Fuck off."

But the next day when she saw him she said, "All right, let's do it." She had thought about how she could say "Fuck off," but was she so cool? She had kissed a dreg or two. Once she was sharing a blanket with a dreg while watching TV in his room, and he was massaging her bare foot, and he undid his pants and held her foot against his thing while they both continued to watch *Monty Python* with great intensity. But that was all. She had liked the way this angel dreg had asked, so earnestly. No braying. "It's love," he had said, unblinking.

After class they walked to the place in the woods and made a pile of leaves. "Now you take your clothes off," he said.

"You take your clothes off first," Jane countered.

"That's not how it's done."

"Forget it, then."

"Maybe we could take them off together," he said.

Jane watched him, going no further than he went. But eventually he took off everything, and so did she. Just standing there in the clearing with him, both of them naked, she felt it: what she felt when beginning to do the Deed, a drop in her center of gravity. They lay next to each other in the leaves, which were prickly against her back and legs. At this point, Saskia stops listening. That is hemp's special protection: tuning out becomes easy, as one's own thoughts grow irresistible. Saskia pictures the scene vividly, stuck at that moment of lying down. Saskia is with the angel dreg, feeling the "letting down" in her abdomen, a pleasant settling-down-to-business, as if someone were stroking her there, getting her enzymes to flow. The dreg is blindingly white, like a slat of sunlight through curtains. She can see nothing but his slim outline as he lies with her in the leaves. The leaves tickle her back and rub like a bristle brush along her legs. She snuggles down into the leaves. The white small dreg snuggles down after her. She reaches up and gathers him like a doll into her arms. She kisses him, and he kisses back, his mouth surprisingly big and warm. This image and the feeling that comes with it are repeated over and over, as Jane talks in the distance.

Jane pokes her. "So have you ever held one?"

"What?"

"Are you listening? I can't believe it, you're not listening!"

"Yes I was."

"What was I saying, then?"

"You asked if I ever held one."

"One what?"

Saskia rewinds her tape. "A dreg's thing." Held a dreg's thing? Jane held the angel dreg's thing in the pile of leaves?

"So have you?"

"Sure."

"When?"

"Now and then."

"You're lying!"

"I am not!"

"I dare you to touch one!"

Dare?! You dare to dare me, dusky dryad? Guards! Bring me a dreg's thing, with all speed! The girls bound out of bed and into the hall. Saskia feels wrapped in cotton. "Quinny!" she hears herself call. "Quinny, come here!" She sees her hand grab the banister, the stairs run up eagerly under her feet. They find him in the crew's quarters. "Let's go!" He reaches up from his circle of dinosaurs, the little fool. They run him back up the stairs so fast he trips, so they half lift, half drag him up the last steps and into the cabin.

Jane shuts the door. "Off with your pants, Quinny," Saskia says. He looks at her blankly. "Come on, off with your pants." Saskia unsnaps them. Quinny whines, "Noo." He bends and presses the waistband to himself with his forearms. Saskia reaches for the zipper and he doubles over. Insolence! "Jane —" she motions. Jane grabs Quinny from behind and pulls his arms back, straightening him out against her knee. Saskia hauls down his pants and underwear. They catch on his shoes. His thing is pointed like a crayon and hooked, crouching protectively over his bag. Hook and bag are shamelessly hairless, as white as the angel dreg in the leaves, with blue shadowed in the depths. Ugly, like a blind worm, like something grown in the cellar. Saskia cups her hand and drops it over the bag and hook as you would trap a moth on the wall. The bag is warm and soft in her hand. The hook is rubber tubing with something firmer, like clay, inside. Saskia squeezes it between her fingers so Jane can see. "Ow!" Quinny says, and goes from blubbers to frightened wails.

"How does it feel?" Jane asks. The bag is tightening, shrinking away from her, becoming a wrinkled walnut. Saskia squeezes it harder. "Ow!" She takes Jane's free hand and pulls it down. Their two hands are side by side, one yellow and one mahogany against Quinny's white thighs. "It feels like all the others," Saskia says. "Don't you think?" With great concentration, the girls take turns rubbing it and pulling on it, but eventually Jane says, "I guess he's not old enough," and Saskia pushes him away with a disgusted sound. "Ugh. Of course not."

Quinny runs for the door. But he is hobbled by the pants around his shoes and so he falls on hands and knees. His thing gives a little squirt. "He's pissing!" Jane shrieks, laughing. Saskia can't resist giving his smooth white bottom a nice smack, and he howls and squirts again, a real stream. Then she gives him another smack — the smack of a delicious kiss on the hand-shaped red mark.

15

For years the whole house was mine. On Saturday mornings, Lauren would back Betsy up to the storage shed and we would stack crates full of good things in Betsy's bed. The Sun would rise, shaking his mane, as we drove down to the bustling Farmers' Market in sunny Ithaca.

That was the best day of the week. The old jousting field just outside Ithaca was covered with stalls and tents. The striped awnings snapped in the breezes coming off the lake. Lauren and Saskia would fold out a table next to Betsy and arrange their inviting wares. The buyers came from all over Vastamundus, drawn by the far-flung fame of Huge Red. They would descend from the glass and stone buildings on the hill to wander among the stalls, inspecting the wares and murmuring outlandishly. Listening to them, Saskia knew that one day she would go up the hill to Huge Red and learn those languages. Then, when she was running her own stall someday, she would greet every wanderer flawlessly in the right language. Soon they would buy only from her.

When I entered school, the teachers marveled at my ability. They soon realized they had nothing to teach me. My love of solitude by then was so great that I found the presence of barns disturbing. I rebuffed, perhaps unkindly, the efforts of others to make friends with me.

In my seventh summer an abandoned moor with four young barns came to our door, seeking succor. Lauren and I discussed the matter at length and decided to take pity on them. The moor was undeserving. Our charity was for the barns' sake.

From the first day, Melanie was as sweet and adorable as always, though for a long while she stuttered. The twins bullied the youngest, two-year-old Quentin. Barns, like wolves, will always gang up on the weakest member. They have no moral sense. Saskia has always sympathized with the weak and the outcast, such as one could never have hoped for in a young person. Using sympathetic magic, she cured M-M-Melanie of her stuttering by renaming her Mim, and she gave young Quentin strength by renaming him Tarquin, after the Etruscan warrior kings.

She knocked herself out for the crew. Because of them, she could no longer go to the Farmers' Market on Saturdays, but she never reproached them for that. All weekend, and under her lamp at night, she pondered how to help them. She drew up lessons in math, English, and culture. They sat before her in a two-by-two grid. She administered tests, corrected their answers, gave out grades, and pasted color-coded stars on their foreheads. She devised treasure hunts, with hidden clues leading to other clues, or to maps in code. The clues were clever:

> It hangs on a wall,
> You see in but can't go in —
> But Alice did once.

Birthdays were like Midsummer's Eve, when the Lord of Misrule reigns, and to everyone's delight the last becomes first. Saskia would dress like a lowly serving wench and cook a seven-course meal for the birthday barn, and hand him or her a menu in floral script, saying, "For your delectation," bowing humbly. Between courses she would ask sir or madam if the joint was to their liking.

Most importantly, she gave them what all barns need: magic. On their first day of school she would don a cloak, wave her hands impressively around their heads and shoulders, and explain that she had woven a protective spell around them. She would tell them on a summer evening as they went to bed to look out for the fairy-of-the-lake that night, and as twilight deepened she would slip outside in a white sheet and sparkling silver veil and dance in the high grass beneath their window.

Under my firm yet kindly command, the crew slowly came away from the brink of mutiny to which their previous captain had goaded them. It became a joy to me to hear once again the laughter of a happy crew as they danced the hornpipe or set to work with a will.

Sometimes, coming back in Betsy from the great Ithacan library, Saskia would suddenly feel like the absolute last place on earth she wanted to go was back to Tyler and the crew, back to the same troubles and duties. She would feel so old and tired. Lauren would drive up the hill out of Ithaca, north through the town of Ulysses, skirting the towns of Hector and Ovid. And set amidst them all, unaccountably, was the sore thumb: Tyler. Not a Greek or Trojan warrior, nor a poet, but a president no one ever heard of — "What number was he?" — who became president only because the real president had died, who was thrown out of his own party and called "His Accidency." And Saskia's town was not even really named after him, but after a postmaster who lived at a lonely crossing next to a cornfield in the nineteenth century.

She would stick her head out the window of the speeding truck and let the wind flap in her ears. *Fuppituh-fuppituh-fuppituh.* The hoofbeats of a Mongolian horseman. He was just out of sight, in the next dimension. All he saw as he galloped were the limitless steppes. But he could hear Betsy's engine, so he worked his steed into a lather, giving chase to this phantom growling through the endless grass. "Aiyaruk!" he shouted. He wore his black hair in thick greased braids. *Fuppituh-fuppituh-fuppituh.* Stop! she wanted to tell Lauren. She would look back to catch a glimpse, but as she looked the sound would stop. He was like a dim star that you can only see out of the corner of your eye. "Aiyaruk!" Lauren drove on mercilessly. He would rein in his exhausted horse and raise his arm in farewell. The phantom growl would fade in the fitful wind.

One day he will catch her. Stretched to the utmost from the back of his steed, he will tear the fabric of space and pluck her through Betsy's window. They will gallop together through the sea of grass under the limitless skies, not moving themselves, but turning the Earth beneath their horses' hooves like a ball.

16

Jane is spending every weekend at White-on-the-Water. "My parents approve of you," she tells Saskia with a derisive laugh. "They say you're responsible, 'unlike the hooligans I usually hang around with,' bitch bitch."

"But I *am* responsible," Saskia protests.

"Not the way they mean," Jane says with satisfaction.

These weekends together, light-years from school and Sing Sing, are paradise. By Friday evening, the girls are done with all the homework that is not too stupid or too demeaning to do, and after that they are as free as geese. Jane is a fount of ideas for Adventure. Under her direction (with Saskia as Technical Adviser) the girls shanghai the crew for a session of slave buying in the tented courts of Khan-balik. The slaves, hobbled, are led from their cage to the auction block, where the two bidders feel their muscles and examine their teeth. Saskia bids astronomically on the heavy-haired Babylonian maiden, while the degenerate Etruscan is galed down for a pittance.

With the first tolerably sunny days of spring — even Tyler gets some occasional sun, mainly to remind you of what you're missing — come a move outside and the inauguration of the Khanate wars, to which the meadows and woods around White-on-the-Water are admirably suited. Aiyaruk is a giantess. She was born the daughter of Kaidu Khan, in Samarkand, in the heart of Grim Tartary. When it came time for her to marry, she told her father she would wed the man who could vanquish her in a trial of strength. Since Aiyaruk was beautiful and charming, men came from all over to make trial with her. The pact was this: if the youth could vanquish Aiyaruk, then he should have her to wife, but if Aiyaruk should vanquish the youth, then he must forfeit to her a hundred horses. The contest of strength was arm wrestling. Aiyaruk amassed more than ten thousand horses, and never married.

There is not much known about Aiyaruk's adversary. She seems happy simply to be on a horse with weapons in hand, surrounded by her fanatically loyal soldiers. There was some trouble over her name. The Technical Adviser drew up a list of possibilities: Ogodai Khan, Chagatai Khan, Mongu Khan, Batu Khan, Hulagu Khan. The Director wanted Al-Embroidia Al-Fastansia Al-Marammjibwa Khan. Impossible, said the Technical Adviser. Why? demanded the Director. Because it has to sound Mongolian, that's why, not like a tablecloth pattern. There was a small fight. But they settled eventually on the Dark Khan. The Director liked the mystery of it. The Technical Adviser liked the accuracy.

As extras, the crew are bounced from role to role according to need: slave, concubine, herald, cannon fodder. Their lines are easy: "What, ho!," "Yes, my liege?," and "I fear I breathe my last." The gages are thrown, the mediations scorned, the anathemas pronounced. Aiyaruk beats her breast and intones, "I will not live or rule if I do not wreak a revenge on the Dark Khan of which the whole world will speak!" She and her army draw up in battle array in front of the barn, while the Dark Khan arrays hard by White Creek. The standards snap smartly in the sharp wind. The Maid of Samarkand, resplendent in white armor, flies the feared ensign of sable, illumined by crescent and sol. The Dark Khan, stunning in cochineal, flies gules, lion passant, or. ("Singh" means "lion" in some language.) The war drums begin to beat and both sides charge, setting arrows to the string. None can doubt then that they are mortal enemies. Ash branches make fine bows, and lethal arrows when finned with cardboard. The best material for spears are lengths of bamboo, painstakingly sharpened on the concrete floor of Betsy's garage and hardened in the eyes of the stove. The metal shields are circular, ridged concentrically. Sunlight gleams from the copper tops of the helmets.

Mim and Austin distinguish themselves by their bravery. Shannon is cautious, but stout withal. Quinny is hopeless. He runs the wrong way. An arrow whizzes by him and he collapses, blubbering. He says his helmet hurts. He drops his spear. All prisoners, following the Tartar custom, are castrated and enslaved. Another custom is that neither Aiyaruk nor the Dark Khan can be made a prisoner. If one is captured by the other, she is honored for her prowess. She gives her parole that she will not escape until the ransom is paid, so no restraints are necessary. The two drink claret in the captor's tent and speak admiringly to each other in clipped understatement.

One weekend, Jane has to go with her family to Niagara Falls. "Maybe I can send them over in a barrel," she says. That weekend, Saskia finds the crew impossible to handle. They don't want to go on a treasure hunt, they don't want a story read to them. They want only to be warriors. "It's raining, anyway," Saskia points out. Then they want to be slaves. "When is Jane coming over?" they keep asking, until Saskia is ready to stick them in the oven and serve them for dinner. Well why shouldn't they prefer Jane, since Jane doesn't keep the Judgment Book or herd them to school in the mornings? It only makes sense and Saskia doesn't care in the least. Her job is not to be liked by her crew, but to have her orders obeyed. When Jane comes the next weekend, the crew crowds around her, pressing on her the banner of the lion passant and saying, "Let's go." Even the sun has come out again to welcome well-loved Jane, and everyone heads for the meadow.

17

"Saskia, let's talk." When the hairbrushing goes on for a while, it sometimes puts Lauren in the mood. This is when Saskia might get a Thomas tale, if she plays her cards right. "You're twelve years old."

"Correct."

"I understand this is a rough time."

"Doesn't seem so bad."

"I had a rough time too at your age. Everybody does. Your body is changing, your interests are changing. You're feeling a lot of new things you don't understand. You need to act out, I know that."

"Mm."

"You're a very private girl, Saskia. You never tell me what's bothering you. I'm always here to listen. You don't have to tell me. It's all right to be private." There is a pause. Saskia fluffs Lauren's hair. "But when you don't tell me anything, I don't find out about problems until somebody else tells me. That's not being considerate. Are you listening?"

"Sure."

Lauren's voice focuses a little. "That's embarrassing for me."

"Who said something to you?"

"I got a call from the school."

"What about?"

"About your behavior, what else?"

"I figured that. What *about* my behavior?"

Lauren turns in her chair and looks resentfully at Saskia. "Don't be like that, I'm talking to you like an adult." She turns back. Saskia brushes. "I count on you. You have to be more responsible than other girls your age."

"I am."

"Well that's what I count on."

"So what about my behavior?" Or is this twenty questions?

Lauren continues in a lighter tone: "I'm so glad you've found a friend. We're so isolated out here. I had a close friend when I was your age and it was very important to me."

A difficult age, yes. We've already established that.

"Jane seems like a good friend."

"Yeah."

"She's very pretty."

Saskia counts to ten. "But what about my behavior?"

"It was the Vice Principal who called."

"He's a rawhole —"

"Please, Saskia! Don't use those words! They really grate on me! There's a perfectly good English word —"

"OK, he's an asshole."

"Whether he is or not, you and Jane are treading on thin ice. That's what he told me."

"You still haven't said what I've supposedly been doing."

"Smoking reefer."

Saskia doesn't answer. She kind of thought nobody knew that.

"Is this something Jane got you to do?"

"No."

"I see some wildness there. The pretty ones can get away with things."

"What's the big deal? You smoke it all the time."

"You're too young to handle it wisely."

"Not like you."

"Yes. Not like me. And I don't smoke it 'all the time.' And anyway, if you get into trouble at school, what am I supposed to do? Have you thought about that? Have you taken a single minute to think about me, about everyone else here? Or are you only thinking about yourself?"

"I won't smoke in school anymore."

Lauren's eyes move over her face like searchlights. "You promise?"

"Of course I promise."

"Well that's something, anyway." Her eyelids descend to half-mast, her cheeks bunch into hard buns. This is the look that comes over her when she is getting her way. She runs a hand through her hair, suggesting puzzlement at the interrupted brushing. Saskia resumes. "It would be much better if you stopped completely."

Saskia knows Lauren's strategies. That switch back to her normal tone, in which she sounds like she is speaking to you from the fourth dimension, means she's achieved what she really wanted. "I don't see why, if you do it, I can't do it."

"How much do you smoke?"

"Maybe one joint a day? Max."

"Hm." Lauren is quitting the field. Her ensign is argent, a laurel, vert. It shows to best effect when flapping in full retreat. "That's one too many. But I suppose it could be worse. I don't appreciate Jane getting you into it."

"I tried it before Jane did."

"Yes, it's good to protect your friend. I protected my friend, too. Friends are more important at your age than parents, aren't they? No responsibilities, just fun and games."

Just bugle sounds, fading.

18

Saskia is instantly awake, her heart pounding. She turns on the lamp and sits up, holding the covers to her chin. When the sound comes again, she almost jumps out of her skin. Fingers rattling like twigs, tapping on the black square of her window. A murmur, a moan for blood. "Saskia!" She presses herself back against the wall. Oh no oh no. The moan comes again. "Saskia! Open the fucking window!"

Jane? Windows are horrible things at night. You approach, and all you see in them is yourself coming fearfully nearer, your face a smudge, your eyes empty sockets. Will a claw grab your hand as you lift the sash? "Saskia!" Only speed can save you. She runs toward the ghost running toward her in the glass and throws up the sash. "For chrissake I thought you'd never open it!" In the long grass below, Jane is standing in the moonlight. "Get down here, girl!"

"What's the matter?"

"Just get down here!"

Saskia closes the window. Go out? Into the dark? She puts on her Lieutenant's slippers and robe. She ventures out to the top of the stairs. She goes back to get her spear from the weapon rack behind her door, and sallies down. Jane has come around to the front porch steps. "What's the matter?" Jane beckons. Saskia steps out on the porch. The night air is cool. "Let's go inside."

"No, this way," Jane says. Saskia hesitates. "Saskia, come on!" Saskia closes the front door and goes down the steps. "What's that?"

"My spear."

"Oh . . . fine. Keep an eye out." Jane heads up the driveway and Saskia follows. "I thought I was going to wake up the whole fucking house."

"Why didn't you just come in and get me?"

"What, aren't the doors locked?"

"Why would the doors be locked?"

Jane snorts. "I suppose it figures."

The girls head up the dirt road. Trees block out the moonlight. Saskia balances the spear in her hand. "So where are we going?"

"Just a short way."

"How did you get here?"

"I drove." Past the first switchback they come to a car.

"You drove *this?*"

"Sure." Jane climbs into the back seat and slides over. "Come into my lair, my pretty, heh heh."

Saskia gets in. Jane leans into the front seat and punches in a little doorknobby thing on the dashboard. She slips in a tape and her favorite group comes out of two grilled areas under the back window. Saskia looks around at the burgundy interior, feels the leatherette armrest. "Gee, this isn't so bad —"

"So the fucking school called my fucking mother."

"Oh . . . Yeah, they called Lauren, too —"

Jane punches the seat in front of her. "I'm fucking grounded again! I can't believe it. I'm so ripshit!"

The knob on the dashboard pops, and Jane holds it to the joint in her mouth. "It's a lighter!" Saskia exclaims before she can stop herself. What a rube! Her editor doesn't work well at night.

Jane passes the joint and on a stream of spent smoke says, "It was the fucking Vice Principal."

"That's what Lauren said."

"He dies." Jane says it matter-of-factly, and a thrill trickles down Saskia's neck. Jane brandishes the spear. "He gets this between the shoulder blades. I have to put my foot on his back to rip it out of him. I clean his lungs off it with paper towels."

"Dis-guusting!"

"A lesson to traitors." Jane tokes and smolders, especially beautiful. "Grounded!" she mutters. "I'll show them fucking grounded. I'll drive all the way to Canada if I want to. I'll write them a postcard from Canada saying kiss my ass, signed 'Your grounded daughter.' Ha!"

"How long?"

"Two weeks! It's all so fucking hypocritical! Suddenly it's this big deal, like it's this huge surprise. They're just ripshit because I got caught and it makes them look bad, their daughter the derelict. So what did Lauren say? Let me guess, she said she could relate and you need your space and there's no problem."

"I promised I wouldn't smoke in school again."

"And she believed you?"

"I *won't* smoke in school again. I gave my parole."

"But that's it?"

"She can't ground me." Saskia giggles at the idea. "I'm here all the time anyway."

"Two fucking weeks! I'll die cooped up that long! You know my mother said something about you and me maybe not spending so much time together."

"I thought she approved of me."

"She does, but she says I'm corrupting you. How's that for loyalty? 'That nice girl' blah blah blah. My own fucking mother!"

"So is she going to keep us apart or something?"

"I'd like to see her try. I'll fucking show her you and me. I'll drive here every night for the next two weeks. We'll sneak you into my room. They'll find out we've been fucking living together. Nobody tells me what to do about my friends, nobody."

The joint shrinks to a confetti speck and a second is lit. Jane's face slowly unknots. By the time Saskia asks about the driving, Jane is calm enough to explain. The Sings lived in a row house in Boston and there were cars everywhere. There was no danger of her parents suspecting even if they heard the engine. The Boston drives were just joyrides, when the Moon was up and her parents were being more-than-usual rawholes. Once she drove to Walden Pond and walked barefoot on the shore. She listened to the frogs and trees like old Henry David. Another time she drove to her school and broke a window. In Tyler the garage is only big enough for one car, so the second is parked on the sloping driveway. You put the car in neutral, take off the emergency brake, and roll right into the street, silent as you please.

Saskia is filled with admiration. The two girls are slumped together companionably, passing the second joint back and forth. The pauses between sentences have grown deep. This is the right moment, the right place. "This is so hoogily," she says.

"What does 'hoogily' mean, anyway?"

"You know."

"I mean what exactly does it mean?"

Saskia ponders. "It means . . . I don't know, just hoogily. Us being together in here is hoogily. It wouldn't be hoogily if only one of us was here."

"So it's like, um, snug?"

"As the proverbial bug."

"In the proverbial rug."

"Maybe it comes from the word 'hug.' Hugs are hoogily."

A long silence.

Jane stubs out the speck of the second joint, a quick and nervous movement. She frowns to herself. She turns in the seat and slips her arms around Saskia. "Like this, you mean."

"Um . . . yeah."

"This is hoogily," Jane says, still frowning.

"Yeah." Saskia can hardly speak, she is blushing so madly. She does not move a muscle. Her present is stretching, flowing in both directions toward infinity. Jane kisses her cheek. A sweet, chaste kiss. Her eyelids flutter against Saskia's temples like butterfly wings. "You are . . . so . . . small!" she whispers in her ear.

"I know that," Saskia says ruefully.

"I *like* that. You're not gawky like me. You're a package." She squeezes Saskia, as if trying to make her even smaller. "We have to swear to be best friends forever."

"Yeah."

"But we have to swear it. We have to swear to have total trust in each other, that we'll never hide anything from each other no matter how personal or embarrassing." Just as Saskia's men know Saskia. But they know everything at once, from the first moment. Who knows what secrets about Saskia might disgust Jane, might ruin everything? But with Jane's arms around her, she says yes, she will swear.

But how to do it? They ponder the problem.

They put their right hands together, palm to palm, and knuckle their bowed foreheads. They swear on everything they hold dear. They swear on the powers of the Moon and stars, of coats of arms and books of wisdom. But Jane says it is not enough. This is the most important moment of their lives. Everything will be different after this night. She opens the door. "We have to go outside."

The girls stand together in the dirt road. No wind. The waxing Moon is somewhere behind the trees, sinking. Saskia can hardly see Jane, though she is only a foot away. Where is her spear? "We have to take off our clothes."

"You think?"

"It's the only way. We have to stand naked before God."

Naked before God . . . It sounds wonderfully solemn. But naked before *Jane?*

Jane is taking off her clothes. "We have to run through the woods naked. We have to let the trees know us."

"It's cold . . ."

"Not if you run. Come on!"

Hesitantly, Saskia parts her robe and shrugs it off. But what to do with it? Jane is dropping her things right in the dirt, even kicking them away. No, not her loyal Lieutenant's robe. Saskia folds it and places it gently on the trunk of the car. Stay there, now. You wait for me. She is cold in her flannel nightgown. This is enough, surely. Saskia does not have to glance away from Jane this time, she cannot even see Jane in the darkness, only a flash of teeth as a hand tugs at her nightgown. Her voice is good-natured: "Come on, scaredy-cat!" Saskia gulps down air. No, no. I won't. She pulls the nightgown up over her head and holds it away from her. Take it. The night air is all over her, lips as big as cushions, mouthing her warmth. She is dissolving into the night air. Jane puts the gown next to the robe. "And the slippers, girl," she says softly. Saskia eases them off. The pebbles of the road are painful against her feet. She is covered in goosebumps. What has she always known? She is not naked, before Jane or God, nothing wonderful or solemn. She is only plucked.

"Let's go!" Jane takes her hand and pulls her down into the ditch lining the road. Saskia bottoms out and lurches up the other side. The woods close in overhead. She stumbles along, her feet smarting on the pine needles and cones. She stubs her toes on something and almost falls. Jane drops her hand. "Wait! Wait!" Saskia cries. She can't see Jane ahead of her, she can hardly see the ground. She has no spear, no hair. She blunders on, terrified. She can hear Jane running ahead through the leaves. "Come on!" Jane calls. *"Please wait!"* Saskia almost shrieks it. "I'm right here," Jane says, as Saskia runs into her. "Let's go!" She grabs Saskia's hand again and runs off in a new direction. The ground rises and dips, Jane pulls her this way and that between the trees, they scrape through a bush and another, they half fall down a slope into a leafy bowl. There are leaves all over her, paper-thin shells against her skin, crumbs of dirt on her stomach, something touching every part of her as if she fell into the mouth of the world, every inch of her skin howling. Clambering out of the bowl, she puts her free hand on something slimy, and the howl becomes a wail. Yugh, I can't. "Just go, stupido," Marco growls. "Don't let go of her hand." "I'm trying not to —" "Well don't, then. Go!" "I'm going, I'm going!" Through more bushes and leaves. Across a fallen tree. Dirt caked on her thighs, wetness running down her knees. On and on, deeper and deeper into the woods, until they couldn't possibly find their way back. Her skin is drawing in, shrinking to a wizened lump like a dried apple. They are miles in now, beyond all help or hope of discovery. They will lie in the leaves and freeze to death.

A clearing. A steep stony slope rises in front of them and Jane starts up it. She drops Saskia's hand to scrabble in the sand and Saskia chases her frantically up the slope, the sand and pebbles giving way under her feet so liberally it's like trying to run up a down escalator. She pushes with her legs, she grabs with her hands and sinks to her elbows, she flails upward, pebbles and sand cascading around her, tickling, scouring off the dirt, soaking up the wet. She reaches the top feeling as bristly as a porcupine, every quill standing out and vibrating. The flat top is a narrow band. She is back on the road. Jane is a bar of darker dark swinging a pendulum of hair, bobbing away from her. "Come on!" Saskia catches up with her on the far side of a curve. Miraculously, the car is there, and Jane next to it, picking her clothes up out of the dirt.

Now a strange thing happens. During the seconds it takes Saskia to shrug on her nightgown and robe, the terror she felt in the woods drains out of her and filling her to replace it is elation. She is no longer cold. Even the darkness is not dark. Her soles burn, a toe is stinging, she can feel the grit beneath her clothes, the scrapes on her sides swelling hive-like, throbbing, yet she dances around the car, whirling with her arms straight out, the stars visible between the trees overhead spinning around her. Her spear is in her hand. She thought she loved Jane. But she had no idea what love was. Her love is so great now it bursts out of her and floods the woods, the whole nighttime world, with warming cold and darkness visible.

It cannot end here, she realizes. No, not now, not this short of some glorious culmination. Something else must happen to carry her over the top. Something exactly right. She takes Jane's hands in hers and shines her silver light into Jane's midnight eyes. "The last thing," she says. "We have to worship Marilyn."

The barn is always warmer than the night. The girls light their candles. Shadows dip and sway like udders. Marilyn steams like a furnace doused with water. You can hear the gurgle of the green fuel in her chambers. She gives out a grunt and her head lifts, swivels toward the girls and regards them wonderingly with bulging dragon eyes in which the candle flames jiggle. "It's all right," Saskia says.

"*Pouhhf*," says the coo, blowing veldt air on Saskia and rolling her eyes. The girls pat her on the hip knobs, slide their feet under her flanks and wriggle their toes. With a groan and a long-suffering look, Marilyn lumbers up. Jane and Saskia sit side by side on the milking stool and stroke her toasty udder, tingling with white hairs. Reluctantly, knowing it is not the usual time, Marilyn lets down. The veins bulge, the hoses swell. She looks at the girls apologetically as if to say, "Well, dears, you asked for it." Saskia leans forward and presses her cheek into the bristle as she rollingly squeezes. Jane is sitting behind her, her arms along her arms, holding her hands. "Good girl," Saskia murmurs into the octaves-deep gurgling. The bucket plashes and foams.

Afterward, Marilyn eats her grass with her legs tucked demurely under. She will expect to be milked regularly at 2 A.M. from now on. Coos are consummate ritualists. They are to be worshiped because they fit into their spaces more securely than any other of God's creatures. The girls put the pail of milk on the barn floor and place the candles on either side. They kneel.

"Marilyn," Saskia intones, "we worship thee."

"Marilyn," Jane repeats, "we worship thee."

"We ask you —"

"We ask you —"

"— in the name of the great and holy coo of vast and wise India —"

"— in the name of the great and holy coo of vast and wise India —"

"— to grant us an eternal bond of love —"

"— to grant us an eternal bond of love —"

"— stronger than anything or anybody —"

"— stronger than anything or anybody —"

"— anywhere."

"— anywhere."

Saskia ponders. Marilyn lets out a loud *pouff.*

"We seal this prayer to you —"

"We seal this prayer to you —"

"— on pain of death and eternal damnation —"

"— on pain of death and eternal damnation —"

"— by drinking of your holy milk."

"— by drinking of your holy milk."

"So promised, and done as promised, on this the Lord's day —"

"So promised, and done as promised, on this the Lord's day —"

"— the third of May, in the year one, anno bovinus Marilyni."

"— the third of May, in the year one, anno bovinus Marilyni."

Marilyn rolls her tongue far out along the trough, reaching for grass. Saskia dips a ladle into the bucket and hands it to Jane, who gazes steadily into her eyes as she drinks. Saskia dips the ladle again and drinks herself. Then she dips it a third time and pours the milk onto the floor. "So is it done," she says. The girls blow out the candles.

They walk up to the house in holy silence and part without a word. Saskia crawls back into bed. She can see herself riding in the car with Jane, laboring up the switchbacks to the county road, arrowing through dark fields, rolling between the rows of uniformed houses standing at attention, cutting the engine and coasting up the driveway, creeping to her room so quietly ankle-deep in troll's hair, slipping into her bed. Saskia is in two places at once. She is flank to flank with Jane. Sleeping together each night, naked before God and each other, they will show Sing Sing that grounding Jane is simply irrelevant.

19

Saskia is in the Captain's room. Beneath her spreads all Ithaca. On the water of the bay rides an open boat, oars tossing up the sea spray. It hits the shore so fast it rides up onto the land. The oarsmen lift out food and casks of red wine, bronze tripods, cauldrons. They lift out something wrapped in a coverlet and set it gently on the sand.

A man, asleep. All that is visible is his curly red hair. The oarsmen drag their boat to the water and row back up the bay. The man lies on his native ground, asleep in the deepest, sweetest sleep, a sleep most like death. Home at last, at long last, home again. He looks defenseless, curled up under the coverlet on the shore of the big bay, and Saskia wants to go down and protect him, she wants to move his tripods and cauldrons behind some trees so no one will rob him while he sleeps.

But girls are playing down there. Naked girls who have finished the laundry are throwing a ball. She knows what is going to happen. So she makes it happen. She causes one of the girls to throw the ball too far. The tallest one tries to catch it. She runs reaching out, her black hair streaming behind her, but the ball skitters off the ends of her chasing fingers and falls, bounces, rolls.

It rolls near the man, and the dark tall naked girl chases it. And she in the Captain's room remembers finally, completely, where she is. She is sprawled on her stomach on her bed in her Captain's cabin.

Everything below happens because of her. The very first time she did it, as she does it now, in the web of the done. She presses her face into the warm yielding glass. The dark girl reaches for the ball where it lies near the man. The split-second nexus —

Wake! she commands.

The man wakes.

Stop!

The girl stops.

The man rolls onto an elbow and looks up at the mahogany girl. His reddish beard is thickly curled. His face is blunt, cunning, strong. They gaze at each other as she holds them for a long moment. His first view of home: the girl who has been waiting for him without knowing it. The bed is bristly, shivering warm against her stomach.

Now!

The man throws off his coverlet. He too is naked, his body compact as an oak barrel. He lunges forward and clasps the girl's legs. "I am at your knees, O Queen." The girl bows, touching his hair. She bends lower to kiss the top of his head, his cheek. The hide against her stomach stirs. The man slides his strong hands up the flanks of the girl and pulls her to the ground in front of him and the stirring hide is drawing back along her abdomen like an undertow pulling the water taut as he grasps her dark ankles and pulls her long legs around him, and he covers her, and she enfolds him, and he is home, and he is hers, and the water rushes forward carrying her along the top of the cresting wave for a long breathless instant until she is curled under, pounded down into the surf and left at last in the shallows like a thrown stone, the water rippling deliciously away.

20

The years went 'round in their seasons. The apples and pears swelled on the branches and were duly harvested. Each spring came, with rain and more rain, and the lengthening of days. I grew slowly in Wisdom.

But something was missing. The winters were not as cold, the colors were not as bright. Perhaps as I grew in Wisdom, I understood better how lonely it is at the top. The crew filled the ship with "the patter of little feet," but it was not enough.

Saskia tried twice to make friends in Tyler Junior. But neither time worked out. The atmosphere was too poisoned. Saskia was the kiss of death. The pigs she tried to make friends with turned out to be the worst of all. They waited until her defenses were down and then socked it to her. Her secrets were broadcast. One of the pigs who betrayed her fell down an elevator shaft (everyone blamed everyone else). The other was hit by a school bus and trapped underneath. The driver made it worse by backing up. Dis-guusting! Then Saskia saw the new girl in the V.P.'s office.

And it came to pass with the passing of days that a new girl knocked at the gates of Tyler Junior. Her shield was gules, lion passant, or. "Say the password, friend, and enter," smirked the leprotic gatekeeper.

The new girl answered calmly, "Friend."

The gatekeeper's smile froze. His nose fell off. The people cheered. The gates swung wide.

Those are the last words of Saskia's autobiography. (Actually, Saskia sort of borrowed that password trick from *The Lord of the Rings*, but probably no one will notice.) Each time she's done a rewrite, she has faltered here. What could she add? There was both too little to say and far too much. Something else had begun with Jane's arrival. Now she writes without hesitation, filling the rest of the page:

Epilogue:

Thus it was that Jane Sing and Saskia White, after many trials, found each other at last. And thus it was that they swore to each other, on the most solemn of vows, a bond of eternal love. The two halves of the soul had come together as one. Together, whole in each other, Jane Sing and Saskia White lived for many years, until the Last Days and the destruction of Novamundus.

Jane Sing and Saskia White lived happily ever after! That is the line on which you close the book.

21

8 May

Lauren and my Saskia:

Missing you, and thinking: I find myself with unexpected resources. How about a summer trip? I will pay all expenses. This is the best idea I've had in years. Say yes. It has been too long.

Love, Thomas

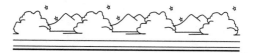

PART 3

THOMAS
AND JANE

Always keep Ithaca fixed in your mind.
To arrive there is your ultimate goal.
But do not hurry the voyage at all.
It is better to let it last for long years;
and even to anchor at the isle when you are old,
rich with all that you have gained on the way,
not expecting that Ithaca will offer you riches.

— Cavafy, "Ithaca"

1

JANE HAS BEEN on planes before, so she lets Saskia sit by the window. Besides, it's Saskia's birthday. The ground falls out from beneath them. Saskia turns speechless from her vista to look at the tube she is sitting in, tilted skyward like a telescope. "This is the Captain speaking . . ." This is a Captain's room she never could have imagined.

The plane barely levels off before it starts descending again. A runway shows up at the last possible second. Inside the terminal a uniformed folksen asks, "You girls need any help?" Jane declines. Saskia trips along at the end of her arm. Without Jane, she would never get out of this sea of people, this endless spidering of corridors. The second airplane, like houses in dreams, is bigger inside than outside. They take off in dusk and the City spreads below them like a switchboard jammed with calls. They fly over a distinct edge, into nothingness. "We're over water now," Jane says.

"We've left Novamundus?"

"I think we go up the coast for a bit."

The airplane meals are as hoogily as TV dinners, each item snug as a bug. Afterward, a flowered panel at the front of the room is flipped around and they watch a movie about captains and starships. Then everyone is supposed to sleep. Of course the girls don't. They whisper together in the dark, over the hush of the air conditioning. "How are we going to recognize him?" Jane asks. Sand-dune hair, wine-blue eyes, beautiful hands. "I can't believe we're going to meet him! Aren't you excited?"

"Sure." But she isn't really. There have been too many new things since leaving Ithaca to think ahead. And to what? She remembers a man lifting her a mile high to save her from a coo. Kissing her good night with his hands on the blanket. She can't picture him in an airport, standing in a crowd like any other folksen, waiting for her.

The serving wenches slide up the porthole lids and reveal that dawn has come early. Folksens rub their eyes and line up with toothbrushes. The women stand in the aisles and brush their hair. It's like the old commune days, everyone doing their private business in public. All that's missing are a few folksens walking around naked, scratching themselves.

A woman heading up the aisle says to a man sitting in front of the girls, "Sleep well?" and he answers, "Yes, very well!" A moment passes before Saskia realizes that the two spoke in Phaiakian. And that she understood it. She feels a rush of alarming warmth fill her chest. Her memories are real! There really is a man waiting for her at the airport. He will have an oar on his shoulder and she will have a haiku in her hands. He will put a hand on her head and call her into existence, saying, "My Saskia." He will tell her what her name means.

The plane dips and the seat belt sign dings on. "This is our final approach . . ." She is suddenly so nervous she feels like she might throw up. Out of her mouth will come basketfuls of butterflies.

2

"'Too long,'" Lauren quoted, handing the card to Saskia and applying herself vigorously to the envelopes with the windows. "He's certainly right about that." For the first time in eight years, Thomas had put on a return address: a poste restante. On the other side was a picture of puffins. Lauren twitched the card out of Saskia's hand. "I mean, what does he expect of me?" She read the card again, turned to the picture, then back, and read it a third time. "After all this time. How can I? He must know I can't."

Saskia looked at the puffins. Lauren twitched the card out of her hand again. She held it a millimeter away from her nose, as if she were smelling it. "This is just like him," she said meditatively. Did she mean the words or the smell? She went back to the bills. Saskia just stood there, holding the card. Lauren rapped her kind of hard on the head. "Hello?"

"He wants to see us?"

"No," Lauren said, smiling her meanest smile. "He wants to see you."

Later, brushing Lauren's hair, Saskia coaxed more out of her. "He knows I can't leave the farm, so it was safe to invite me."

"How does he know you still run a farm?"

"He knows."

Saskia hates it when Lauren answers like that. Is she talking about mystical knowledge, or has she been secretly communicating with him all these years, or is she just shrugging off the question? "So what are we going to do?"

"We can't do anything that I can see."

"We have to do something!" He had been forced to leave. He had had no choice. Now the terrible compulsion had lifted.

"Oh yeah? Who died and left you in charge? I'm not doing anything. He doesn't want to see me."

Saskia brushed for a while. "Well why don't I go?"

"Right! A brilliant idea!"

"Why not?"

"Why can't he come here? Why is he making offers he knows I can't accept? He can stay here as long as he wants! You and he can have a great time together and then we can make another appointment for when you're twenty." Lauren held out her hand for the brush. "Thank you."

"But what if he can't come here?"

"We can save him the airfare and send him a photograph."

"But what about —"

"Saskia." Lauren turned in her chair. "Going away for the summer is out of the question. I'm going to sleep now, good night."

Well, the battle was long, and it got dirtier and dirtier. Lauren had the weight, but she didn't have the staying power. As Saskia's teachers knew to their sorrow, if Saskia did not want to drop a subject, then it simply could not be dropped. Lauren was aggrieved, then furious, finally exhausted. By the end they were barely speaking to each other. "Do whatever the fuck you want," Lauren said. She quit the field.

Saskia was magnanimous in victory. She knew Lauren didn't actually care whether Saskia *qua* Saskia was around or not. What she was worried about was all the work she would have to do, and Saskia could take care of that. She had been safeguarding her knowledge from the crew, to prevent any erosion of her authority, but when you came right down to it, Mim was eleven, and perfectly reliable. You can't make gold without melting metal.

Under Saskia's gentle tutelage Mim picked up the barn work quickly. But her real responsibility would be the crew. Could she handle it? Saskia stressed the need for maintaining hygiene and discipline. Mim stared at her with wide eyes, nodding. Saskia worried she would be a pushover. "You'll use the Judgment Book, right?"

"Sure," Mim chirped.

Looking at those adorable hey-you-guys eyes, Saskia would feel despair. What would she find when she came back? Austin and Shannon flying around with leathery wings, Quinny in an unmarked grave under the ash tree, and Mim back to stuttering and crying, gaunt and hollow-eyed like something Edward Gorey would draw over the caption, "M is for Mim, left by her Master."

There had been the minuscule possibility, as Lauren said, of a better arrangement, of Thomas coming to White-on-the-Water. But when Saskia wrote him a short, hesitant letter — other than the tersest expression of the business at hand, she had no idea what to write, so she wrote nothing — he wrote back and said No, they had to come to him, what he had in mind was a hiking trip that would end at a place where he had to be in August, and he was paying for the plane tickets, so what was the problem? By the time his letter arrived, Lauren was no longer the problem. She was sulking, refusing to discuss anything, insisting Saskia could do whatever the you-know-what she wanted. What Saskia wanted, of course, was to bring Jane. This required delicate handling. Jane's parents were dubious. "Who is this man?" asked Mr. Sing in the muffled bellow he reserved for normal conversation. "Is he responsible?"

Jane was disgusted. "They don't give a shit, but unless they butt their noses into everything, they're afraid it will look like they don't care about me."

"How about if Thomas wrote you a letter?" Saskia asked Mr. Sing.

He pondered, handling his beard. "All right. I'll talk to your mother, too."

Yikes! Saskia assumed that would be the end of that. "A trip with Thomas?" Lauren would say innocently. "Oh, is he out of the mental hospital?"

But Lauren told Mr. Sing that she could see no objection to Jane's going, that it would be, she was sure, a valuable and educational trip for the two girls. Saskia was astounded. Had she grossly misjudged Lauren? Lauren was angry, she had lost, but she would not be petty or unfair. Would Saskia have found it in herself to be so noble? She suspected not, and hung her head. Later, she apologized to Lauren, truly contrite. She even admitted she had been an obnoxious brat.

"You were, kind of," Lauren said. "But I also looked deep into myself, and at the center I found selfishness."

Where's the tape recorder when you need it? After that, things were better between Lauren and Saskia.

In the meantime, Saskia had written again to Thomas, asking if it was all right to bring Jane along and mentioning the Sings' concerns. A letter bounced right back: "Fine. The more the merrier. As for your friend's parents: tell them this is a well-organized trip, about a dozen families traveling together, staying in hostels, cooking common meals, a real family affair, perfectly safe, etc, etc. If it's a money thing, tell them I can pay for her. Since Lauren isn't coming."

The Sings agreed, but said they would pay for Jane's flight. "They don't want to look cheap," Jane sneered.

Weeks had passed with the fights and the letters, and school was ending. There was barely enough time to get Saskia a passport. Meanwhile, she tiptoed around Lauren. She cooked glorious meals out of turn. She tried not to point out to Bluffaroo what a jerk he was. On Lauren's own birthday she made a banner that stretched all the way across the common room and blew up balloons until her cheeks ached. The birthday haiku read:

> A simple message:
> Thanks for putting up with me.
> Signed, Obnoxious Brat.

At night she brushed Lauren's hair with extra assiduousness, and on one of the last nights, Lauren sighed and said, "I'll miss you."

Saskia brushed harder, her heart full. "Should I . . . Should I, you know, say anything to Thomas?"

Lauren was silent for so long Saskia started to wonder if she'd heard the question. Finally, she said, "I can't think of anything."

The passport came, and suddenly it was time to go. The Sings brought Jane to White-on-the-Water, where she would spend the last night. They said goodbye. Mrs. Sing was tearful. "Boy, if I could turn on the faucet the way she can," Jane said after they left, "I'd never get grounded." Mim put the crew to bed that night. Everything went well, but maybe that was because Saskia was hovering just outside the door. Jane and Saskia crawled into bed and got stoned. "I'm going to be thirteen tomorrow," Saskia said, awed by the thought.

"Welcome to the club, my pretty, heh heh." The girls kissed a little. Chaste, sweet kisses. When Saskia fell asleep, she had a dream. She was walking with her pack on her back down the dirt road toward White-on-the-Water. She had seen the world and was returning home, full of adventure, full of knowledge. As she came up on the porch she saw the thick cobwebs, the shuttered windows. The door creaked open. Mrs. Sing stood there, dressed in an Indian toga. "Welcome home, honey," she said. She led Saskia into the gloomy, decrepit hall and opened the door into the common room. Quinny was in there, standing naked in a bathtub. He shrieked and tried unsuccessfully to hide behind a shower curtain. Mrs. Sing slapped Saskia's wrist. "Better not go in there!" She closed the door and led Saskia up the rotting stairs. She opened the door to the crew's quarters. Bill was in there, standing naked in a bathtub. He shrieked and tried unsuccessfully to hide behind a shower curtain. Mrs. Sing slapped Saskia's wrist. "Better not go in there!" She led Saskia to Lauren's room and opened the door. The brass bed, as high as a table, as wide as the barn door, as massive as Earth herself. The inner sanctum, the cave of the Eleusinian Mysteries. Thomas and Lauren naked on the high brass bed, doing you-know-what. "Come in!" Thomas said. "The more the merrier!" Saskia crawled between them. They hugged her. It felt delicious. She was the cheese in the sandwich.

She woke up. Still dark. She turned on her lamp and got out her autobiography, which she hadn't looked at in weeks. She read it straight through. It was unbelievably barnish. Stupid and embarrassing. She went downstairs to the common room, not even bothering to turn on the lights. She wasn't nearly so afraid of the dark as she used to be, not since the night she and Jane ran through the woods. She burned her embarrassingly immature autobiography in the fireplace.

3

Dateline:
1:08 A.M., July 6, Anno Neo-Thomasus 1. København, Phaiakia.

We are truly near the "realms of endless day," as it is past midnight but only dusky. The Phaiakians call this time of year "the light nights," and it is a season of revelry. There is so much to put down, I will endeavor to get it all before sleep overtakes me. Yesterday — can it be only yesterday? it seems a lifetime ago! — Jane and I escaped from Novamundus. Our flight was without incident. København was our port of call, and we arrived in a timely manner.

Customs took a long time. Phaiakian was spoken all around. We went through a door and all the waiting people were on the other side. I was nervous! Would Thomas look as I had remembered him? Would he recognize me after so many years? But Thomas knew what to do. He was holding a big sign that said "Saskia and Jane!" on it. He was exactly the way I remembered him. We had a "touching reunion." He carried both of our packs. We got on a red bus to go into the city.

The city is very beautiful. We saw it wandered. Boats like shoes, rocking. rest of day is blur. So prety!! We

The sign over the heads of the people caught Saskia's eye, not because of the names on it, but because it ended with an oar upright. "That's him," she said to Jane, marveling at the calm sound of her voice. A stranger was in the way, so she could only see the beautiful hands held high, gripping the bottom of the oar. She came up to the railing and tried to say "Thomas," but what came out was her patented squeak. The oar came down, and from behind the stranger now you don't see me, now you Thomas was standing there. "Saskia," he said. Perhaps "Saskia" means "scimitar." With that one word he divided the world, like the Gordian Knot. The Post-Thomas Age ended, and the Neo-Thomas Age began. He did not put his hand on her head. What a barnish idea! He dropped the oar and lifted her up, pack and all, right over the railing, and held her, eye to eye. "My Saskia," he said slowly, breathing deep, deluging her brown eyes with his wine-blue ones. She fell into that sea with a soft plop and was swirled, sucked under. Should the embarrassing truth be told? Saskia failed the Captain, who would turn away from a long-lost friend with a manly comment on the weather. But Saskia is a girl, and she drowned in Charybdis. She tried to gulp down air, but water rolled into her mouth. Thomas swirled her tighter and tighter in his arms while she gulped for air and choked on water. He had come to stand above her and speak a word to her. His sinewy hands were on the blanket and he was leaning over to kiss her.

Thomas's voice found her in the depths. "Where is Jane?" Saskia covered her eyes. She heard Thomas say something to Jane. She could feel his voice groaning in his chest. How could she have forgotten how deep it was? He let her slide down until her feet touched linoleum firmum. She turned her eyes away from Jane.

They took a bus into the city. "Are you hungry?" Thomas asked. They said no. "Tired? You want to take a nap?" No. "We'll get rid of the packs first." They changed buses in the city center and rode out again. The Phaiakians were a tall and handsome people. The soft liquid sound of their language flowed over Saskia's head. She watched canals go by, filled with boats. They got off near warehouses. Thomas led them through a chain-link fence, along a train track cushioned in a bed of asphalt. Cranes swung netted loads. They walked along a quay. Each boat was tied to one of those squat bulgy things. Saskia ought to have known the word, but she didn't. "Bollard," Thomas said, stretching his palm out toward it, calling it into existence.

Saskia looked for his boat. There was one shaped like a fat wooden shoe with an upturned toe, a cabin the size of an outhouse and some radio stuff on top. But they walked past it. At the end of the quay was a long building. Through a screen door they could hear babble, glasses chinking. "Starting early," Thomas said. He led them up wooden stairs and down a long hall. Old dark wood and an oily stink: a shadowy, cobwebby place, lit by a bare lightbulb every ten steps. Thomas opened a door on the right. "Home!" Two bunks in a small dark room, a small dark galley beyond. Even the ceilings were made of wood, narrow slats behind chitonous varnish. Thomas slung the packs on the bunks. "We'll be here for three days. I think it will be cozy, don't you?"

"Yeah," Saskia said, and meant it.

"Where's the bathroom?" Jane asked.

"Top of the stairs." He opened a cupboard. "Take some paper."

Since they weren't tired, Thomas took them back into the city, but everything was like a blurred background, moving too fast, with Thomas bright and motionless in the center. When he told her to notice something she turned her head in that direction, but her mind was like the black and white puppy she remembered who, when you pointed, would try waggingly to please by sniffing the end of your finger. Looking at Thomas, she would try to convince herself that he was really there, that if she crossed the space between them she would in fact bump into him.

They had dinner in a veggie café on a small street. "Can I smoke in here?" Jane asked, looking around at the ashtrayless tables.

"I'd rather you didn't," Thomas said. "But it's a pleasant evening outside. Saskia might want a smoke, too." He looked at Saskia with questioning eyes.

"No thanks."

"I'll be right back," Jane said, and went out.

"I don't smoke," Saskia assured Thomas.

That wasn't a lie, she didn't smoke cigarettes. They could see Jane through the window, leaning against a wall, a leg up, fingers of a hand wedged in a pants pocket. She looked right and left as she smoked, checking things out.

"Does she smoke a lot?" Thomas asked.

"Hardly ever," Saskia said loyally.

"Smoking shortens your breath. It becomes a problem on a long hike." He looked at Saskia. "I have a prediction," he said in an appealingly firm tone. "Jane will give up smoking on this trip." Jane returned, threading between the small round tables. "How was it?" Thomas asked. "Nice?"

"Just what I needed."

"Glad to hear it."

Saskia could see that Jane was impressed. Thomas did not like smoking, but his tone had been respectful throughout, thoroughly unfolksenlike.

Menus had arrived. "You're still a vegetarian?" he asked Saskia.

"Yes."

"Good." Saskia blushed with pleasure. "I hope you don't mind, Jane," he said politely. "No meat on this trip."

"No problem," Jane said. She had gotten used to it at White-on-the-Water. Thomas passed the girls' orders to the waiter in Phaiakian, but it was clearly not necessary. "Almost everyone speaks English here," Thomas explained. Of course. The Phaiakians were near the gods. They probably understood all the languages of the world.

"And how is Lauren?" Thomas asked.

"OK," Saskia said.

"Still farming?"

"Just the field by the turnaround."

"You still have a cow?"

"Marilyn."

"Dog?"

"Cat."

Thomas grimaced. "How can you have a farm without a dog?"

"That's what I say!"

"Did Lauren ever get a real glass greenhouse up?"

"Yeah."

"Good for her. Somebody helped?"

"No. Well . . . a guy named Bill helped a little."

"A boyfriend."

"No."

"A husband."

"No!"

"Is he living there?"

"In one of the trailers. He's living with this woman named Jo." Saskia caught Jane's eye, and they understood each other without a word or wink.

"Jo Flynn?"

"You know Jo?"

"Sure. Jo is at Godhead?" Thomas seemed to take a while to digest this. If Saskia had known that Thomas knew Jo, she never would have fibbed about her and Bill living together. Anyone who knew Jo would find it hard to believe she was living with anybody. "That means the three kids are at Godhead, too? What are their names, Melanie, Shannon . . . one other."

"Two others. Austin and Quinny."

"Austin, that's it. And Quinny?" Thomas thought about that for a second. "'Quinny'!" He frowned. "What kind of name is that?"

Saskia blushed again. "His real name is Quentin."

"He's the youngest."

"Yeah."

"What's he like?"

Saskia shrugged. "Fine." She didn't want to get onto Quinny at the moment.

"So is Lauren still doing what the planets tell her to do?"

"I guess."

"And Mars told her not to come? Or Venus, I suppose. Mars is bullish and Venus is bearish and that means reunions are in the shithouse."

"She can't leave the farm."

"That's only an excuse."

"Um . . ."

"Never mind." His hand brushed out what he had said. "I'm sorry she didn't come."

"She really wanted to!"

"No." He smiled. "In fact, I'm surprised she let you come."

Saskia didn't answer. The only reply that occurred to her was "So am I," but that seemed rude. Whether it was rude to Lauren or to Thomas, she didn't know.

"She didn't send a letter, either," he mused. "I wonder why not. She was hurt, I would assume. Angry, maybe?"

"Maybe."

"Because I haven't written once a week like a good boy since I left? If she knew what's been going on these years, she would understand." He flipped out his napkin like a matador flashing his cape before the enraged bull and tucked it into his collar. The food had arrived. "Were you hurt, too?" he asked, inspecting his plate. "That I didn't write?"

"You did write."

He laughed charmingly, boyishly. "I should have written more."

That was all Saskia had wanted to hear. If Lauren knew, he had said, she would understand. Folksens were picky, demanding to know, but Saskia could understand and forgive without knowing. And forgiving him, she felt she could be more open. "It's not the fact you didn't write much that made her, you know, hurt, or whatever. I think it was because she couldn't write to you. You never sent an address."

Thomas didn't answer immediately. He furrowed his patch of brown rice, turning it with his fork, sowing it with salt. "Did she happen to mention to you that when I left she told me never to write?"

"No."

"So you've only got half the story, then. She told me she never wanted to see me again. She told me if I came on the property she'd have me arrested."

"Wow!" Jane said. "Why?"

"You'll have to ask her that."

"She never says anything," Saskia said. "It's really annoying."

"Perhaps she's ashamed," Thomas said. "I could have sent addresses regardless, sure. But why put myself through the humiliation? I knew she wouldn't write, and I was right, because she didn't write this time. I had hoped you were old enough by now to write on your own and come on your own, and I was right about that, too." He forked rice and bean curd into his mouth. Saskia nibbled without much interest. "That's the only reason I waited so long. Until you were old enough that she would let you come on your own." He attacked his vegetables.

By the time they were done, he seemed to have forgotten about Lauren. He unscrewed a thermos he had brought along and poured coffee into the cap. "My only vice. Bad habit. Though not as bad as smoking." He looked at Jane with twinkling eyes.

Later, walking back to the wharf, he asked about the girls' lives in Novamundus. He asked good questions, and he actually listened to their answers. "It's been hard for me," he said, "wondering how my Saskia was doing." He had had to go. He had had no choice. Lauren would have had him arrested. Amazing! "From Thomas," she always said, banishing the postcard to Saskia's realm. "You keep it." But then why did she let the girls come?

Now, in the bunk with sleeping Jane, Saskia cannot remember what she said to Thomas. As she talked about herself, she looked at him, drinking him in over and over, but he was like lemonade, only increasing her thirst. The oddest thing is that now she can't remember what he looks like. She sees a man's outline out of which blazes the concept "Thomas," filling the street or these little rooms with utter Thomasness.

She struggles over this, her first journal entry. She is having trouble getting the tone right. When she burned the autobiography she resolved to purge herself of barnishness, of affectation. Her writing seemed to her of a piece with her inability to admit ignorance, her need to show off all the time. Take the case of Odysseus' bow. Circumspect Penelope brought it down from her chamber and announced in the feasting hall that she would marry the suitor who could string the bow and send an arrow through the twelve axes. Odysseus' bow was so strong that none of the arrogant suitors could string it, even after heating the wood and rubbing it with melted fat. Yet Telemachos — yes, young Telemachos, despised by the suitors as a mere boy — could have strung the bow. He stood up for all to see and felt the strength swell within him as he bent the bow to the stringing point, but the disguised Odysseus secretly signaled him to stop, since that wasn't part of the plan. So what did Telemachos do? In front of all the suitors who made merciless fun of him he put aside the bow unstrung and said, "Shame on me. I must be a weakling, or else I am still young."

Saskia longed for that peculiar sort of strength. To be able, when the need arose, to let the foul waters of derision wash over her. She needed to practice it, as she practiced her controlled dreaming, as a Discipline of the Wise. A journal seemed a step in that direction: to put life down as it really was, right when it happened. The nitty-gritty, the brass tacks. That meant whenever Saskia said something really boneheaded it would go right into the journal, unperfumed. She would read it every night as a lesson in humility.

Through the closed door she can hear Thomas moving around in the galley. Pacing, hands clasped behind his back? Jane was fading fast and he insisted they go to bed. Big days ahead. He would sleep in the galley. The girls said they wanted to sleep in the same bunk, anyway, so Thomas could sleep in the other bunk. When he saw them together under the blanket he was moved to speak in Phaiakian. "*Hvor hyggeligt!*"

Jane laughed. "So that's where it comes from!"

He said good night and turned to go. "Aren't you going to kiss me good night?" Saskia asked tremulously.

He paused. "If you want. I didn't know . . ."

"You don't have to," she said, being a martyr.

"I'd love to." He leaned over Saskia, breathing the dark nighttime and morning smell of coffee. He kissed her good night and his cheek was lightly bristly, like the wallpaper in her dreams.

Now he paces the deck while Jane sleeps, and Saskia struggles with her new style. A good thing she is filled with such energy!

She writes "blur" and the world blurs.

But . . .

Where is his boat?

Where . . . is his dog?

So prety!! We

4

The girls spend three days in Thomas's wake, hurrying after him through the lovely city by the harbor. On the crowded sidewalks, Saskia is lost among this skyscraping people as in a primeval forest. But no one sneers at her shortness, perhaps because she is always with Thomas, and Thomas, she realizes as she slowly takes him in more clearly, is not quite as towering as other Phaiakians. A sneer at her would be a sneer at him, and surely no one would want to face Thomas's wrath. One look at his muscled arms, swinging as he strides in his seven-league boots, would convince anyone of that.

The day skies are a trembling blue, the night skies a deeper blue, the wind fresh and thrilling. Saskia admires the Phaiakians' balanced boats, their cunningly shaped and lofty towers. Surely there are alchemists and astronomers still thriving in this city of copper and brick, down in vaulted cellars or up in aeries. Thomas takes the girls to the Adepts' own stronghold, the inner sanctum, which the Phaiakians call the Round Tower. It wears a runic inscription on its brow like a mark of wisdom, a dab of cinnamon book-bark: the words "Doctrinam et" above a sword, then "dirige" and something in Hebrew, then "in" and a heart and a crown, and at the bottom "1642" divided in the middle by a big "C" with the number 4 nestled inside it.

"What does it mean?" Saskia asks, awestruck.

"'Direct truth and justice, O God, into the heart of Christian the Fourth.'"

"He must have been a very wise king."

"Christian the Fourth? Not particularly. He lost half the kingdom conducting ill-advised wars and emptied the treasury by building monuments like this one. But he was popular. Fools like that always are."

Inside the tower they mount a spiral of steps, up which Thomas says the wife of Peter the Great once rode in a coach-and-four, madly lashing on her steeds. Going that fast, she probably missed the exhibition on the top floor, which you get to by ducking through a low door.

"Tycho!" Saskia exclaims.

"Bingo!" Jane echoes, laughing. "Tango!"

"No, Tycho Brahe!" He is the Phaiakian astronomer mentioned in Saskia's star book. And here in the Round Tower is a whole exhibit devoted to him, with reproductions of his instruments, a topographical model of the island on which he worked, even a life-size ground plan of part of his castle-observatory, marked out on the floor with black tape. Saskia pores over everything. She steps meditatively from room to room of the castle, drinking in the silence, the somber light. "Let's go," Jane says, walking right through a wall. Saskia steps to a lead-latticed window and peers out across the windy moors of the lonely green isle to the wine-blue sea. 'Twill be a fine night for gazing. If the sextant hasn't been finished, she'll know the reason why.

Jane and Thomas have wandered off somewhere. Saskia heads regretfully for the exit. By the door a Phaiakian is selling books. Most are thin pamphlety things, but Saskia notices one real tome, a hardback, dust-jacketless, dusty, with a crackling binding. It's in English: a biography of Tycho. She asks how much it costs, and the man scratches his head. "I don't even know where this came from," he says, turning the book in his hands. "It's the only copy I have."

If there's one thing Saskia knows, it's that you absolutely do not blow the chance to buy a Mysterious Book That Comes From Who Knows Where. She haggles, speaking the trade language of the area. The man lets her have it for fifty Phaiakian crowns. Thrilled, she tucks the book under her arm and goes out to find Thomas and Jane.

When they stop later at a café, to rest their feet and fill up Thomas's thermos, she takes out the tome and reads a little. The typeface is old-fashioned. There is tissue paper between the engraving of Tycho and the title page. The Latin quotes are not translated. Yes, it is that wise a book.

Tycho was a student at the medieval university across the road from the Round Tower. He would have clambered down from his cold garret and hurried across the muddy road to the runic tower with his hand on his mortarboard, a ruff at his neck, his black gown flapping. He was hurrying to avoid the hostile townies with whom he would have to cross swords, if he met any, and for that purpose he carried a rapier on his belt. Home and family were far away across the Sound, in Scania. He was Saskia's age, thirteen. On the tower roof was an observatory. Tycho would map stars and pace undisturbed, lost in thought, even when the road below was pestilential, when the whole city was being sucked under by the plague. He would look out over the head of the drowning town and wait, guarding the flame of wisdom.

Thomas has been saying her name. "I was just the same," he says, smiling on her. "Lost in books. But we're going now."

They pass the tower again on the way to the harbor. An ancient seat of wisdom, out of whose venerable bricks knowledge oozes to coat you like molasses. But the modern world is fallen, graceless. After buying the book Saskia found Jane and Thomas on the tower roof, where the observatory used to be. The telescopes had been replaced by machines with orangutan faces into which you dropped a coin for a minute of magnified city viewing. The machines were so debased they didn't even tilt skyward.

5

Each morning the opposite bunk is empty, unslept in. Thomas says he does not want to disturb the girls, so he sleeps in the galley. But where? Under the table? He makes breakfast, flipping soymilk pancakes into the air. Off they go, free as geese! The whole city is theirs. In the evenings they have dinner back in Thomas's rooms, hyggelig around the wooden table which fills half the galley. Thomas cooks expertly and fast, reaching for his ingredients in the tiny cupboards without looking. In fifteen minutes the food is ready, and somehow the pots are already clean.

"How long have you lived here?" Jane asks.

"I got here two days before you did."

"Where were you before that?"

"Here and there."

Where is his boat, his dog?

When they are done eating, Thomas whisks away the dishes and they are clean almost before they get to the sink. Blink twice and you would think dinner never happened. A pot of coffee bubbles on the stove.

"So why do you like Rembrandt so much?" Saskia asks.

"Excuse me?"

"I was wondering what it is about Rembrandt that makes you like his stuff."

"How did we get onto Rembrandt?"

"I was just . . . Since Lauren was telling me how — you know, you named me after Rembrandt's wife, or whatever. I was just wondering."

"Oh, right. Rembrandt." Thomas scrapes his chair back, crosses his arms. "Well, he's a great painter. Don't you think so?"

"Sure."

"There you go!" He gets up to pour the coffee. "I hope you like your name," he adds, looking concerned.

"I do!" Saskia says. Does it mean "seeker"? Saskia informs Jane that Rembrandt was the greatest of all the painters of Thomas's people.

"How lucky for us if he were," Thomas says. "Unfortunately, he was Dutch." Saskia wonders if hiding under the table is an option. Perhaps "Saskia" means "stupid."

The last dinner in Thomas's galley is the best of all. "After this it will be camp food," he says, removing the frontal lobe of a cauliflower and setting it next to the hazelnut-potato log on Jane's plate. After dinner he unrolls a map and weights it with compass and thermos. "We are here," he points to the city, a black patch on the eastern edge of Phaiakia. "Tomorrow we'll take a train." His finger travels north along the coast. It crosses the straits to Scania, where

Tycho was born, and moves north again, through hundreds of leagues of flat green country, farther and farther north. Saskia exchanges a look with Jane. "To here," Thomas says. His finger has cut through mountains to a long western coast and is pointing to something tiny among a jumble of islands and glaciers. "From here, we hike. We hike for a month through the most stunningly beautiful country on earth." His finger moves still farther north, over mountains and valleys, past glaciers, along dotted ferry lines connecting islands. Watching that finger, Saskia feels a prickling in her scalp. Thomas has to stand up to hold on to his own finger, as it moves inexorably north. Leaning across, he taps a point beyond the edge of the table, where the map hangs down. "Here." Inside the Circle. The land of feasters and sun worshipers, joyful people who live a thousand years: Hyperborea.

"What's there?" Jane asks. A tower. A tower rising from the middle of a vast sea. Childe Saskia to the Round Tower came!

"A river," Thomas says. "A wild river, a living thing. An artery for this whole area" — his hand caresses the map — "flowing down to the sea with water just melted from the snowfields, crystal clear ice-cold ichor."

"Ichor?" Jane asks.

"The blood of the gods," Saskia explains.

"Wow!" Jane says.

"Sounds good?"

"Sounds great!"

"We're going to swim in the river," Saskia murmurs, struck with fear and wonder. They will swim up the artery to the snowfields of Hyperborea and be cleansed of their dross, they will shiver into the essences of themselves. And at the end of this umbilicus will they find the omphalos?

"Not swim," Thomas is saying. "Something more important. We are going to save the river."

6

Dateline:

12:55 A.M., July 10, Anno Neo-Thomasus 1. On a train, north of Scania.

I am lying in a bunk let down from the wall on two chains. Jane is asleep. Thomas is in another compartment, with some guy with huge hiking boots from Australia. Jane and I have a small washbasin with a wooden cover that you can raise and hook to the wall. You step on a lever and the water comes out lukewarm. There are two luggage racks just above my head, and there are metal hooks for hanging coats or what-have-you. The window is slightly open and cool air is coming in. The landscape is quite flat and everywhere there are fields of grain. When we pass a road crossing, the dinging of the crossing bells gets louder and flashes by, and then the pitch drops because of the Doppler Effect.

Hm. This is going to take forever at this rate. You're supposed to cover the here and now, but perhaps you're also supposed to pick and choose a little.

Other Phaiakians will be gathering with us in Hyperborea. What could be more natural for the water-loving Phaiakians than to save a beautiful river, to keep it forever wild and free? Phaiakian is coming back to me. We say "Godnat" and "Sov godt," which mean "Good night" and "Sleep well," and "Goddag" and "Godmorgen" and "Ha' det godt." You don't pronounce three quarters of the consonants, instead you sort of slide around them juicily.

She stares out the window for a while, watching the farmhouses go past. The night is so light, a tractor is moving across one of the fields.

> Unable to sleep
> a farmer finds needful work
> through the twilit night.

Saskia has heard that some people simply stop sleeping. Will that happen to her, whose sleep has always been the lightest tissue, a cobweb across her face that the smallest sound would tear? Of course Tycho didn't sleep at night, because he had his work to do. But what did he do all summer, when the sky was too light for stargazing? Come to think of it, Phaiakia is a pretty strange place for an astronomer, with its twilit summers. He probably pasted stars on his ceiling to tide him over until autumn. He probably lay in his bed and wished he was an Arab, down where the nights are ink black and the desert air thin. Look at all the stars with Arabic names, and not a single Phaiakian one. Tycho became a great astronomer against all the odds. Sort of like if Saskia were to become a great basketball player.

She really ought to sleep. She turns out the light and stares at the ceiling. When they crossed in the ferry from Phaiakia to Scania, she stood at the railing, and Hamlet's castle brooded on her right, with clouds scudding appropriately over it. Far away in the south, rising from the water, she could make out the ghostly low curve of the island of Ven. "Ven" means "friend" in Phaiakian. That was Tycho's island, which the wise Phaiakian king Frederick II gave him, throwing all the island peasants in as part of the deal, because there Tycho would not be disturbed by the gapes of the curious, the autograph hunters, the paparazzi. Just the stupid peasants, who never understood what he was talking about. There he built his castle, dubbing it Uraniborg, after the muse of astronomy.

"What are you looking at?" Jane asked, pulling hard on her cigarette.

"That island."

"I found a slot machine down by the snack bar."

She gazes at Jane, who is lying on her side in her long robin's-egg blue nightgown, her hands flat-palmed between her drawn-up legs, her hair every which way. How that girl can sleep! Sleep, Jane, sleep. They lost twenty crowns at the slot machine.

The sky is growing lighter. If she is going to get any sleep, it has to be now. Saskia is thirteen. An actual teenager. Time passes and folksenhood keeps rolling in like a storm cloud, whether you want it to or not. Jane had her first bout of mooniness in May and she danced around happily, the strange wild girl! Both thirteen, both moony. Thus they grow more like each other every day. What has Saskia done to further close the gap? You will never believe it. She looks at the ceiling, so turned in on herself that not even her men are around to ask her how it is going. Yes. Saskia does the Deed. A swirling out like a reverse Charybdis, out to the extremity and then slowly back in, drawing her into the calm center, the eye, the aye, the I, where she gently sinks beneath a film of sleep.

7

A line of white stones marks the Circle, but the train does not even slow down: they are in Hyperborea. The tracks run through bleak tundra, along the edges of silent lakes, slowly higher into stony uplands. Suddenly the land falls away and the train has somehow gotten itself thousands of feet up the steep flank of a mountain, and it crowds back against the slope like a cat not knowing how to get down. Far below is a crooked bay like mighty Cayuga, but Ithacaless. "That, ladies, is a fjord," Thomas says. Moaning through tunnels and whining on the exposed curves, the train works its way downward and pulls at last into the end station with an endearing gasp of relief.

They stay in the town only long enough for Thomas to buy supplies. The houses are wooden boxes painted red, white, ocher, perched on short stilts. Seaweed spots the stones beneath them like droppings. At the edges of the town either a mountain rears straight up or salt water stretches level away. Along the pebbly shores, fish hang in wooden cages, so dried out they look like shucked-off snake skins. "People pay good money for this," Thomas says, tapping one. "You'll never guess what for." Voodoo rites? Self-flagellation? "They eat it."

"Dis-guusting!"

But something does not compute. The Hyperboreans are always joyfully feasting —

"These were fabulously rich fishing grounds for five hundred years. And now it's mostly gone, because of overfishing." He gestures toward the rows of empty cages, the beached and rusting boats. "These people ignore the evidence. They say it's because of the seals. Too many seals, they say, because the damn environmentalists think seals are cute. So they want to kill the seals. That's the solution to everything up here, kill something, kill more, kill everything."

Saskia watches the large townspeople move clumsily through the streets, their pale hammy hands dangling uncleverly. She listens to them speak to each other, unsmiling and dour, in a guttural sort of Phaiakian, not liquid like a pure running river but stony, clotted with consonants, like the hard land rising up, like the concrete dam they want to build on the river of ichor. Saskia understands hardly a word of it.

Who are these people? Where are the happy Hyperboreans?

This is where Thomas, Jane, and Saskia were supposed to meet the other river-loving Phaiakians. The dozen families who would travel together, cook big meals, make it a real family affair. Unfortunately, it seems the girls flew in late, and now the others have already hiked out. Thomas assures them it's OK, they have plenty of time. "We'll probably beat them there."

"This is much better," Jane assures Saskia. "What kind of wanderers move in herds, anyway?"

"I guess." But it seems a small band for a quest through a land of dam builders and seal killers.

After the errands are done they catch a bus and get off at the edge of town. The last zippers are zipped, the last straps strapped. "Everybody ready?" They shrug on their packs and leave the road, ascending a grassy slope. The girls are leaping with excitement. They're off! Wanderers! The sedentary world can eat their dust! Over the hill! Over the next hill, and the next! Who knows where they will sleep? Who cares?

In the chartreuse light under birch trees, they follow a stony stream. There is no path. Thomas will be using a contour map and compass. "This isn't the Appalachian Trail," he calls back to them, pumping skyward. "Here, when you want to get somewhere you pick a point on the horizon and head for it." Picking a point is easy. A few hundred feet above the road the trees shrink to bushes and thin away. Nothing beyond but sedge and wildflowers, and you can see miles, across fjords and islands to the open sea and the edge of the world, where the map hangs off the table.

It was evening already when they left the road, so Thomas is taking them only as far as the first decent campsite. He climbs up to examine some ground, and beckons. "Home!" Aye, a goodly spot, with a fine view south toward mountains crowding one behind another like competitive siblings. They can see a village below. A short first day, and a good thing, she concedes as she slings off her pack and almost falls on top of it. She has developed an ache between her shoulder blades, and a tender place on her foot turns out to be a blister. Jane, meanwhile, hops from rock to rock, care- and blister-free.

There won't be a campfire, Thomas says. He points out that there isn't any wood, and peat fires are all smoke, and anyway, even if there were wood, it doesn't get dark, so a fire just cleans the landscape of its natural organic material and adds to the greenhouse effect for no good reason.

But no songs, no stories around the fire? "The sun is our camp-fire," he says, gathering it into a sweep of his arm. "You need a bigger one?" Can't argue with that.

With his pack open next to him he removes, without looking, his stove, fuel, rice, vegetables, nuts. Dinner is ready. They sit at the top of the steep slope with their steaming cups, their canteen water. "Anybody else want coffee?" No. "Good. Bad habit." This time the girls chorus it: "But not as bad as smoking!"

Thomas scrutinizes the village below while he eats. "These people look on vegetarians as freaks. Down there, they're gnawing on rein-deer legs, or the last few fish they've been able to scour out of the fjords. See this green pepper? Three dollars. These leeks look like fossilized bamboo, and they're eight dollars a pound. They don't grow anything up here but potatoes. Everything else is hacked off passing animals."

They put Thomas's tents up. He insisted on two. "You girls need someplace you can get away from me. I don't let anyone get a word in edgewise." And yet he wrote so little. Lauren had told him not to! Why?

Thomas's watch says almost midnight, but that is meaningless. The sun will not even touch the horizon. In this perfect world the dark has been banished. The three of them gaze at Hyperborea for a long time, Saskia and Jane holding hands, Thomas cupping his coffee. The village below them is silent. Are the villagers asleep? But the people here are silent even when awake.

Who *are* these people? Meat eaters, seal killers, dam builders . . .

Suddenly, awfully, Saskia knows. The *Odyssey* describes a place where one herdsman, driving his flocks in, may hail another who is driving his flocks out. A place, in other words, where it never gets dark. Towering cliffs rise out of harbors that give out to the sea through narrow entrances. Obviously, fjords. The people are cannibals, given to wasteful, joyless eating. They killed Odysseus' men, dropping boulders from their cliffs onto the wooden boats and spearing the men like fish.

A shiver crawls across Saskia's neck. These people are Laistrygones.

Of course! The photograph that Thomas sent years ago, the plume of water spouting up next to the inflatable boat of struggling Phaiakians: a Laistrygonian boulder! But why are they in Hyperborea, overfishing, damming rivers? What joyless ice age are they planning to bring to this sunny, smiling land? And what have they done with the Hyperboreans? Saskia looks down on that silent village, biding its time. As though reading her thoughts, Jane shudders.

She is suppressing a yawn. "Looks like bedtime," Thomas says. Saskia is not tired, but Jane's eyelids are drifting down. Her last view of Thomas, as she zips shut their flap: gazing out over his beloved

land. In his hands, his fortifying coffee. At his feet, the camp of his
mortal enemies.

8

They hike through Paradise, toward the river they will save. Is it
correct to say "morning" when there is no night? Is it correct to say
"day"? Midsummer's Day in Tyler is a measly fifteen hours. In Hyperborea, it lasts two and a half months. A magical time during
which koans become commonplace: Lizard Saskia turns out to be a
stronger hiker than Wanderer Jane. Truly shall the last be first.

The sky over Hyperborea is God's own clock, with the sun for its
hour hand sweeping around the points of the compass. Lie on your
back and look at His time: north, midnight; south, noon. After a
period of precarious sleep, Saskia unzips the tent flap and crawls out
to find Thomas already up, studying a map and yawing the compass.
Sometimes he is off gathering mint or mushrooms while his pot of
coffee waits on the stove. Saskia makes her way down to a stream to
wash her face, skipping back up over the white stones bedded down
in the spongy grass. They camp above the trees, in bowls of wildflowers and heather strewn with lichen-covered boulders, with silent
lakes at their centers, lakes so clean you can drink out of them, and as
you lower yourself to the water you can see fifty feet along the stony
bottoms. God made all the other countries first, Thomas said. When
he made Hyperborea, all he had left were stones. Curious that Paradise turns out to be not a lush garden but a land of stones. The last
shall be first.

The utter quiet of the mornings, if mornings they can be called,
often cloudy, perhaps softly raining, mist moving over the face of the
water. Thomas cups his coffee, silent, and Saskia listens to the silence, rapt, cradling her own cup. She tried a sip of coffee yesterday,
two sips today. The gag reflex is already abating.

It rains frequently in Paradise, but Saskia finds she doesn't mind. When you put on your poncho the rain seems convincingly outside, except on your face, where it is actually rather pleasant, like tears of happiness rolling down your cheeks. And then, too, your feet may be wet, but how nice to know that the worst rain can do is make your feet wet, and that you can, after all, ignore it. You can be a good trouper, after all. And the best thing: the pleasure of setting up your tent and pulling out your sleeping bag, still faithfully dry after hours of being carried through the rain, and putting it in the dry insides of the protective tent. For dinner they crowd into Thomas's tent, and Thomas sits cross-legged in the door of the inner shell and prepares dinner on a crescent of grass beneath the fly, while the rain patters ineffectually and Jane and Saskia cuddle inside, warming their feet in the depths of down bags. "What would *mesdames* prefer for dinner?" Thomas asks. "Rice with vegetables or *riz avec légumes?*"

Saskia says, "Oh, I do so feel like *riz avec légumes ce soir,* don't you, Jane?" and Jane replies, "Yes, rather!"

"*Mesdames* have made a superb choice," Thomas says, handing in the steaming cups.

One morning Thomas puts his head into the girls' tent and says they won't go anywhere until the fog lifts. "Too many cliffs around here for comfort. We'll wait it out. You're both invited to breakfast at my place in ten minutes. Formal attire."

The fog does not lift. They spend the day in Thomas's tent, planning their route, reading, talking. Thomas mends some of his clothes, with needle and lengths of thread that look too short but always end up being exactly the right length for the job. He gracefully ties off ends so minute he might be knotting the antennas of insects. "An overlong thread, we call that a 'lazy sailor,'" he says. "The earth had to put energy into making this thread. If you waste it, you show you don't care about the earth. When enough people waste enough thread, they think they need a new hydroelectric dam." The thoughtless and heedless. Laistrygones! "Every day you are tested a hundred times: are you going to help this planet or hurt it? People wince when

you say that, but it should be a comforting thought. It means everything you do matters."

Saskia goes out into the fog to do private business, and the tents
seem so fragile and small from a few yards away. The mountain is
huge, the fog huger. No road or help for miles. All you have are two
shells of nylon, looking like mismatched socks on the stony slope. But
you are done with your business, you hurry back through the wet
grass and dive through the flap, and magically the huge mountain
and fog disappear. You are no longer far away from anything, you are
here, the only place that matters, where Thomas and Jane are, and a
tent that can hold you and Thomas and Jane is big enough for all
your needs.

Still, one must admit that the sunny periods are better. In the rain
you turn inward, monitoring the degree to which you are being a
good trouper. In the sun you open like a flower and notice what is
around you. As the air warms, the girls strip down to T-shirts. Saskia
wears a ridiculous baggy pair of shorts, much too big for her, whereas
Jane is gorgeous in svelte jean cutoffs. All day the sun warms them,
rotating to reach every spot. Then in the evening it yellows to become their campfire, and a curving bay below is their ring of stones.
Sitting around it after dinner, the girls ask for a Thomas tale.

He muses, eyes half closed, his right hand gently grasping the air in
front of him, gathering there a phantom to mold in his palm. He is
thinking of something that happened when he still had his ship, he
says. Would they like to hear about that?

His boat! What a relief to hear him mention it! What was the boat
called?

A ship, technically. *Lila.*

A beautiful name! Did it have a crew?

Yes, brave lads all.

"What does 'Lila' mean?"

He shrugs. "I don't know if it means anything. I just liked the
sound of it."

Yes, Lila, a liquid sound. And the dog? But she doesn't ask.

Thomas's eyes close and he breathes in the heady fumes of his coffee as the Priestess at Delphi inhaled the earth's exhalations that put on her the oracular spell. The story begins:

Thomas had outfitted a punitive expedition. In his gallant boat *Lila* he sailed from Phaiakia a thousand leagues, to the cold waters frequented by the giants of the deep. "Do you girls know much about whaling?" he asks.

"Um . . . ," says Saskia, stalling. Marco talks about some people who feed salted tuna to a whale, to intoxicate it. Then a man can climb onto the whale's head and pound in a harpoon with a mallet.

"You're not supposed to kill whales, I know that," Jane says.

"Precisely," Thomas says.

"I knew *that*," Saskia says.

Because whales are endangered, Thomas says. There once were millions, sporting in the deep, kings of their watery Paradise, owing fealty only to the guardians of Paradise, the Hyperboreans. Until Man came: Man with his iron harpoons and wooden mallets. Man, in his rapaciousness, his insane bloodlust, slaughtered the whales without quarter.

And of all Men, the worst were the Laistrygones. It was a Laistrygon who invented a harpoon fired from a cannon and tipped with a grenade. It was a Laistrygon who invented the factory ship, which allowed whalers to roam the seas at will, processing their victims far from any port or station.

The Phaiakians fought the whalers on the seas and in the courts. They could not stop the killing, but they got courts to pass laws that at least restricted it somewhat. Except that there was a pirate ship. It was run, of course, by a Laistrygon, and manned by a ruthless crew made up of the dregs of humanity, men who would slit your throat and roll you overboard as soon as give you the time of day. The pirate ship ignored all restrictions. It killed everything it encountered: under-sized whales, breeding females, species of whale that were not supposed to be killed at all.

Indignation mounts, a pleasant pressure behind Saskia's face. "That is really wrong," she says.

Thomas's mission: to locate the pirate ship and stop its ghastly slaughter of the whales.

"Hey!" Jane exclaims. "Are you with Greenpeace?"

Who? How does Jane know all this stuff?

"I've occasionally shared information with Greenpeace."

"Wow!" Jane says. "That's so cool! Greenpeace is fabulous!"

Thomas shrugs. "They get most of the press." His hand makes an apologetic motion. "They're a bit too cautious for my taste."

"So what did you do?"

There were rumors in the roughest bars of the seediest ports as to the whereabouts of the pirate. One-eyed John had heard tell from Pegleg Pete — arrgh, but blow me a man is thirsty . . . Thomas bought rounds. When he knew what he needed, he sailed. And when his lieutenant spotted a fat ship in whale waters, Thomas clapped a telescope to his eye and saw on the prow the name he had been looking for: *Green.*

A cruel joke! The ship had chosen, mockingly, the symbol of the good guys. The green of fertile Phaiakia, the green of cautious Greenpeace, the slow miraculous greening of human conscience. And now here was the *Green*, diabolically slaughtering whales.

When *Lila* found it, a thousand miles from any shore, the *Green* was mercilessly chasing a pod of sperm whales. The sperm whale brain is the largest and most complex brain that has ever existed on Earth. What might such a brain know, what could it tell us? The whales were exhausted, and the *Green* was closing in for the kill.

"Sperm whales aren't very fast," Thomas explains. "The ship rides up behind and the gunner fires the harpoon down into its back. The grenade explodes, blowing its guts out through its mouth." He sips from his cup, letting the horror seep into the girls like rancid oil.

Thomas's strategy? On board *Lila* were three inflatable speedboats, called Zodiacs: *Cetus I, Cetus II, Cetus III.* They were lowered into the water, two men in each. Thomas crouched by the motor in *Cetus I.* His lieutenant stood forward, feet planted apart, holding a bullhorn. The three Zodiacs raced to the rescue, bounding through the waves like dolphins. They rushed under the harpoon in the bow of the *Green* and roared out in front, water creaming to either side and boiling in their sterns. With a last burst of speed, they beat the big ship to the sides of the exhausted struggling whales. "Attention, *Green*," the lieutenant barked through the bullhorn. "You are in violation of rulings by the International Whaling Commission . . ."

"Hooray!" Saskia and Jane cheer, high-fiving.

Thomas takes another slow sip from his coffee. "If only things were that easy."

"Oh," the girls wilt.

No, things are not that easy. The Zodiac strategy is contingent on a crucial assumption: that the whalers will not risk human lives in firing on a whale. Is that warranted? These are Laistrygones, after all. They speared Odysseus' men like fish. "I was covering the whale closest to the *Green*," Thomas says. "The harpoon was pointed at us. Our whale was a pregnant female —"

"Oh no!"

The *Green* was so close, Thomas could clearly see the Laistrygon at the harpoon. He was hugely fat. He ate environmentalists for breakfast. Encased in the gray-yellow fat of the bloated head was a brain the size of a walnut. "Attention!" barked again the brave lieutenant, feet planted, Zodiac bobbing in the swell.

"I thought at first the gunner was squinting," Thomas says. "But then I realized he was smiling." Thomas imitates the smile, like something you might see on a primordial slime mold, if a slime mold smiled. "I thought: The bastard is going to fire. And just as I thought it, that's what he did."

"No!" the girls plead.

Yes. The Laistrygon with the walnut-sized brain fired at the sleek back of the creature with the largest brain on Earth.

"What happened?"

They had no time to react. The harpoon hurtled toward them as a rising swell carried the Zodiac up into its path. There was an explosion and Thomas was thrown clear. He felt the steering oar slip out of his hands. As he went under he saw the bullhorn sinking out of sight, turning lazily end over end, still barking "Attention, attention . . ."

He was under for long seconds, but at last he struggled to the surface and spat bitter water. "It felt like someone had put a plumber's helper to my ear and tried to unclog my skull."

The water was bitter with the taste of blood. Blood was running into Thomas's eyes. The Laistrygon had hit the whale.

"The pregnant whale!" Jane and Saskia wail.

She was rolling in her death throes. *Cetus I* was deflated, a scrap of rubber pinned to the whale by the harpoon. Thomas struggled in the heavy seas, stripping off the clothes that weighed him down. *Cetus II* now bobbed before him, hands reaching down. They lifted him up out of the sea and gave him a piece of cloth to wrap himself in. He saw the dead whale being dragged up the slipway of the *Green*, "*Cetus*" nailed to its stomach like a tag identifying the corpse. He pondered deeply in his great-hearted spirit.

Thomas flings out the dregs of his coffee. Bitter taste in her mouth, like her own blood. "What did you do?"

Thomas shrugs. "We left."

"But didn't you do something? Didn't you get back at them?"

"*Lila* was low on fuel, we couldn't keep following them." Thomas is angry. "Anyway, I was hurt."

Not all of the blood belonged to the whale. Thomas lifts his shirt. Across the whole of his muscled stomach lies a closed furrow fringed with knotted pink skin. "Wow!" Jane says.

"The harpoon line snapped down like a knife."

So the fat smiling slime mold wasn't challenged to a duel and reduced to a pitiful wreck, begging for mercy? He didn't fall with satisfying irony in front of his own harpoon to be pierced, exploded disgustingly? This is not a good story.

9

The straps stopped hurting Saskia's shoulders after Thomas had her tighten the pack's belt. "You've got the perfect build for hiking," he said. "Your hips hold the load." Poor Jane, on the other hand. Her belt slips down her straight flank and squeezes shut an artery, making her left leg go numb.

As they hike along breezy ridges or descend slopes toward trees and ferry slips beyond, Thomas stretches out his hand and names the plants and flowers. Wintergreen, primrose, wood anemones. The juniper bush, whose berries the Laistrygones pluck for flavoring a blood-based sauce they eat with dead birds. The dandelions are the size of chrysanthemums, and hovering around them are bumblebees as big as pompoms. Thomas shows the girls how they can swing from trunk to trunk down a steep grove of birches, catching themselves from falling at the last second with a hand flung out to another trunk. Down to gentler slopes, where the rowan trees grow, their berries lightening to a buttery yellow. Thomas says the berries will blush crimson, and will last well into the winter, faithfully providing food for the birds.

Waiting for the ferry, they buy provisions. Thomas is cautiously polite with the Laistrygon behind the counter, who frowns, and Thomas must repeat a sentence louder. All the vegetables are in two boxes at the back, beyond the tiers of pâté, bacon, and blood sausage, the tubs of mutilated fish. Thomas scowls, looking through the few neglected carrots and onions, while the Laistrygon eyes him warily. Most of the landings have waiting rooms and bathrooms with hot water, so after restocking they clean up, washing their hair in the sinks. This is easy for Saskia, but Jane must work at it laboriously, length by length, her slender brown back arched over the white sink, dripping water on her pants.

At a post office, Thomas insists the girls write postcards home. "They'll be waiting to hear from you."

"Not my parents," Jane says. "Out of sight, out of mind."

"They'll be surprised, then. Happy to hear how much fun you're having."

"Not my parents."

"Let me put it this way. It will reflect badly on me if you don't write home."

From the wire rack, Saskia picks a snowy-peak/blue-fjord card for the crew and Lauren. Jane chooses one showing a line of hogs snuffling grotesquely in a trough. "I always send my parents ugly cards," she explains.

Thomas reminds them that they are supposed to be on a group trip. No point in telling them the plans changed, it wasn't anyone's fault.

"Then we better make sure our accounts match," experienced Jane says. "How many people have we got?"

"Twenty-five," Thomas says. "The organizer is a Swede named Lars. He has a webbed scar on his left thigh from a shark attack. The cook is a gnarly old salt named Peder. He wears a funny hat, has a quick temper, and can do a back flip, but only when he's been drinking and everyone begs for it. There is a red-haired boy with green eyes named Øyvind. His name means 'island wind.'"

"That's beautiful," Saskia says.

"You both think he's dreamy."

"Come on," Jane giggles. "'Dreamy'?"

"Intense. A rebel. With bedroom eyes."

"This is fun," Jane says, scribbling.

"Don't forget to say you miss them."

"Sure, while I'm lying."

Saskia adds a P.S.: "If the crew is not following Mim's orders, when I get back heads will roll! I have spoken." She contemplates a P.P.S. for Lauren: "Why did you tell him he could never come back? Why didn't you tell me?" But she doesn't write it. In a way, Lauren did tell her, all those years when she said with her face shut down, "He had to go. He had no choice." Lauren stood at the gate with a flaming sword. Why?

At the other end of the ferry ride they head up again, back through rowans and birches, up to Prussian blue harebells and apricot hawkweed. On the higher slopes they see reindeer. How could Laistrygones gnaw on the legs of these gentle creatures, antlers haloed with fur? They hike past a mountain lake of glowing cobalt. "Beautiful, isn't it?" Thomas says. The girls breathe yes. "It's that color because

it's dead. One third of the lakes up here are too acidic to support life."
The girls shudder and move on.

The blisters of the first days are gone. During lunch Saskia takes off her boots and proudly feels the horny pads that used to be her feet. She rubs them against Jane's bare leg, saying, "I'm horny! Get it?" and blushes at her boldness. As afternoon wears on toward evening the sun slides farther and farther north, a brass gong shimmering over the water. They stop to camp. While Thomas cooks, Saskia and Jane lie out in the heather, boots off, their feet luxuriating in a long exhalation, and watch the sun that barely seems to move in the sky. "Like in my dreams," Saskia says.

The deep gold of sunset has always been transitory. You have always been able to see it change from moment to moment, and in a few moments it is snuffed out. Now here you are, in a land where the sunsets linger hour after hour, where the sun is a wily king who refuses each evening to die at his appointed time. The present moment stretches out to infinity, coated in amber. "Eternity was manifest in the Light of the Day," Saskia quotes. "Thomas Traherne."

"Heaven is a place where nothing ever happens," Jane quotes. "David Byrne."

10

When Thomas tells a story his eyes become star sapphires, twinkling almost spookily. Perhaps they are the sort of jewel from whose depths one can read prophecy. Deep in the thousand planes of reflected light are the thousand possible futures and pasts, and he looks into his own eyes, breathing coffee, to select the true tale from among the myriad false. "This is my earliest memory," he says one evening.

"What did you look like?"

He hesitates. Like all good-looking people, he has probably never thought much about what he looks like. His hair is corn-silk fine, lightly curly like Saskia's but still blond, as Saskia's was before it clouded from embarrassment over her mooniness. He doesn't obsessively trim the edges of his beard like Bluffaroo, whose thicker black beard ends in revolting areas of tiny nibs sprinkled over irritated skin. His gentle, ginger growth just disappears into the collar of his wool shirt, where it gracefully expires. His chest, the girls know, is hairless. Jane has said that Saskia and Thomas look alike, and though Thomas distinctly reddens, freckling, in the sun while Saskia browns, one must admit that their body types are similar. The chunky muscles reappearing on Saskia as she hikes are reflected in the fine hard delineations of his torso, the multilayering of strops and branching arteries that make up his arms and legs. No wonder Saskia is so ugly. She was supposed to be a man. There must have been a mistake at the blastula stage. Somebody pushed the wrong button and breasts were encoded. Poor Tycho was even uglier! When he was twenty he was drawn into a disputation with another Adept over a subtle mathematical point. Words were exchanged, young blood grew hot. A duel was the only way to keep their good names. They met in darkness, rapiers glinted, and Tycho's nose was sliced off. For the rest of his life he wore a prosthesis made of gold and silver, and whenever it became wobbly he would fetch out of his pocket a box of glue and meditatively rub his bridge.

"I wasn't very big," Thomas is saying. "We were living on the mainland —"

It juts north, so it is called Jutland. "Did you live in a house?"

"Yes."

"What did it look like?"

"It was small."

Perhaps they were poor. Perhaps Thomas had to go to work young, assume responsibilities. Each morning he milked the ko before trudging off to a sixteen-hour shift at the meatpacking plant, earning five dollars a week watching kos being hoisted by the hind legs. There he grew to hate the slaughter of any animal. "Have you always been a vegetarian?"

"In fact, I'm the third generation. My father's parents became vegetarians in the twenties. Part of a back-to-nature movement. My father converted my mother. This incident concerns my father —"

"What did he do?"

Thomas looks at her patiently. Stop interrupting or he will clam up.

"He was a minister. He came from a long line of ministers." Thomas pauses. He is wondering: Is she going to ask something else? Or will she finally shut up?

She shuts up.

"My father was a minister and my mother was a minister's wife. An intelligent and active woman, but women back then didn't have much choice, as you girls probably know."

Yes, they were subordinate to their men. Not like now, when Lauren owns White-on-the-Water and runs the business herself and boots her men out of bed as soon as she gets what she let them scuttle in for. Not like now, when a manly man like Thomas nonetheless has sensitive and gentle hands, and expects the girls to be strong and responsible, and listens seriously to what they say. "Anyway," he is saying, "it's hardly a story, just an early image, really. I remember a beautiful evening, the sun sinking slowly down, everything getting yellow and quiet. I was playing outside by myself."

The cherub Thomas *would* play by himself. He must have had few friends, he was too responsible and mature for other barns. Poor Tycho never had any friends either. The other aristocratic drengs (that's the real word, by the way, not "dregs," just as "ko" is the real word for "coo") were all drinking, cavorting, and gaming while Tycho was working hard at his astronomy studies, putting the pleasures of heaven above those of the earth. "My father came out our front door and down the steps."

Saskia's grandfather! Perhaps he was a stern patriarch, stiff in his minister's black cassock and white ruff, with a shaven upper lip and an unforgiving beard jutting out, Jutland style.

The minister did not have a suitcase or clothes bag, Thomas says.

He wore a light jacket, which he was buttoning up. As he crossed the grass to his son, playing innocently in the yellow light, he smiled and as he passed he laid his hand for a moment on the crown of Thomas's head. "I can still feel that," Thomas says, touching the top of his head. "That light touch."

Perhaps not so stern, then. A genial man, quick to laugh, walking with a slight waddle, endearingly clownish in his ruff. Wherever he went, meat eating fell off and vegetarianism blossomed.

"It was so strange," Thomas says, gazing into his own eyes, separating truth from falsity. "There was nothing abnormal about his behavior, he didn't have any luggage. And yet I knew. Somehow I knew that something was wrong. When he went to the car instead of the bicycle, I realized that he was leaving us. He was going to leave us forever."

The girls catch their breath. Perhaps there had always been something wrong about that geniality, something hollow. When he thought no one was looking, his face went spookily blank. He never quite managed to be "one of the boys," just as Bluffaroo, whenever he tries to ingratiate himself with Saskia, smiles uneasily and fakes interest in what she's doing. "I suddenly saw quite clearly that he would get into that old car and drive off and never come back, never call or write a letter, just vanish off the face of my world as if his purpose there had ended. I started to cry." Young, cherubic Thomas crying, behind today's Thomas's eyes. Through the mystic link of blood, Saskia can feel it, the pressure mounting behind her own eyes.

He was walking toward the car and Thomas ran after him, his fingers jammed in his mouth, crying his heart out and begging him not to go away. He started the car and waved from the window, smiling that hollow smile. Thomas's mother was coming down the front steps to see what the matter was, and she held Thomas back, comforting him, a kindly woman, a baker of pies, a minister's wife, but oblivious to what was happening, while his father waved and drove away, drove out of their lives forever.

"God!" Jane breathes. "That's awful!"

Thomas smiles gently. All around them the mountains and waters are hushed, ashamed that such things happen. The crouching sun is red with anger. Saskia is having a revelation, a sudden widening appreciation of the painfulness of every life, not just her life, the painfulness of Life itself. The limitless frozen lake of Vastamundus is not carnal knowledge — nothing so barnish — but the knowledge of pain, pain woven into the fabric of the world like a net of merciless metal threads. Run your fingers through the fabric and get sliced.

"Ever since then I've wondered where my father was going that day. When I asked him years later, naturally he couldn't remember. And for my part, I can't remember anything about his return, what time it was, what he said. I have just that one image of him leaving."

Saskia is lost. "I don't understand."

"I was wrong. I was sure he was leaving, but I was wrong."

Jane expels air. "What a strange story!" Saskia is silent.

"Childhood is a strange thing," Thomas says. "Facts are nothing, conviction is all. My father did come back. But he had made me think he was leaving, and I never trusted him after that."

11

Lunch in the shelter of an overhanging rock. The biscuits have gotten wet. Thomas hands them out drooping over his fingers. "Gross!" the girls say. But they are kidding. It's nice to be eating even the soggy ones with apples and nuts when you're hungry and hyggelig under a rock on a wet day. While they are lying around afterward, delaying a return to the rain, Thomas's head on his pack, Saskia's on Jane's stomach, Thomas suddenly says, "Lauren hasn't cut her hair, has she?"

"Oh no," Saskia says, horrified.

"How much gray is in it now?"

"None."

"So she has you pull the gray hairs out."

"Yeah."

"You must have to pull a lot."

"Not really. Almost none."

"Mm." Thomas seems to file that away somewhere, noncommittally. He brushes his hand over the top of his head. "That beautiful hair. Everybody loved it. And here I am losing even the little I have. But just imagine how tough it must be to have hair so beautiful that it's considered your most important attribute. Beautiful-haired Lauren: that's how everyone thought of her. And then to have it dry up and turn gray. It would be like losing yourself. She probably colors it."

"No."

"How do you know? She would do it secretly. She would be embarrassed about it."

"If she did, she wouldn't have a gray hair now and then."

"Mm. Good point."

"Thank you." Point Saskia. A merry disputation!

"So you're telling me her hair is still beautiful."

"Yeah."

"Very," Jane puts in sleepily. Consolingly or pityingly, she is gently stroking Saskia's hair.

"Why didn't you bring a photo?"

"We don't have a camera."

"Has she got wrinkles?"

"No."

Thomas traces the lines radiating from the corners of his eyes. "These are good wrinkles. Sun, wind, laughter lines. Surely she has some of those."

"Sure."

"I sense a pattern here. You're only admitting to the good things."

"I just can't remember about wrinkles."

"She always had sweet breath. Like apples."

"Yeah!"

"Comes of being a vegetarian. Not the revolting roadkill breath that meat eaters have, right Jane?"

"Right," Jane murmurs.

"But there was something particular about Lauren. Her sweat smelled as fresh as sap. That's why she was named Tree."

"I thought it was Striding Tree," Saskia says.

"Tree for short. Has she gotten grossly fat?"

"Not at all."

"Pleasingly plump?"

"No."

Thomas sighs. "Are you trying to tell me she's still beautiful?"

"Gorgeous."

"I wish you'd brought a photo. Does she smoke?"

"You mean pot?"

"Yes."

"A little."

"Ah." Thomas processes that. "So she went back to it. I was afraid of that. Such a stupid habit." Saskia and Jane look at each other. "I can sense that neither of you are stupid enough to be into that sort of thing. I'm sure of it."

"We're not," Jane says.

"Not into it, or not sure of it?"

"Both." They haven't, in fact, touched hemp since leaving Nova-mundus. Then again, they haven't had any to touch.

"You know, it rots your brain out from the inside, like a peach. You could think of it as a gradual lobotomy."

"You never smoked?" Jane asks.

"Of course I did. We were all stupid at Wonderland. Did Lauren ever tell you that pot made her stop menstruating?"

"No," Saskia says. Hemping stops mooniness? What a great idea!

"That's why you don't have any siblings. Lauren wanted more, you know. She came from a big family. But instead she grew a mustache. She had to have it burned off with electrolysis."

"But she has periods now."

Thomas shrugs. "Once the commune changed to Godhead, drugs

were out. Even coffee! Meditation was the natural way to God. I suppose her system recovered. Which is why it's depressing she slid back into it."

"She doesn't smoke much at all. It's probably just for old time's sake."

"Sure. Nostalgia for the days when she was sterile."

But a sibling! Saskia would love to have a little brother. His name would be Haven, and the two of them would be so close! Blue-eyed, brilliant, a beautiful boy. He would confide only in her, and she would protect him.

"Pot also lowers men's sperm count. With all the sex going on at Wonderland it's just as well we smoked, or we'd have drowned in kids. When you were born I'll admit I was relieved to see how much you looked like me. Although you would probably rather look like your mother."

"No."

"As they say, 'Mommy's baby; Daddy's, maybe.' Every man's worst fear. Of all the advantages women have over men, the most appalling is that they absolutely know that their children are their own. Even kings couldn't be sure. In some ancient societies, rule didn't pass to the king's son but to his sister's son. Why? Because his sister's son was the only relative he could be certain had some of his own blood."

"I see," Saskia says. Actually, she doesn't.

"Women know what they're about," Thomas muses. "They can make any man a eunuch. If they were capable of parthenogenesis, they would never have anything to do with men. That's one of the reasons I like women. The fact that they don't like men."

"They don't?"

"They're disappointed in us. I like that. It shows they're idealists. Why am I saying 'they'? I mean you. You and Jane. You don't need boys, do you? Do you have a boyfriend?"

"Me?!" Saskia says. "No."

"Of course not. That's what I'm saying. The boys are jerks, aren't they?"

"Yeah."

"How about you, Jane?" He prods her with his toe. "Wake up."

"Unh?"

"Boyfriend. Do you have one?"

"I wish." Jane settles her back more comfortably against the tree root and closes her eyes again.

"Speaking of which, Lauren must have a boyfriend."

"No."

"She's had lots since I left, though. She's between two at the moment."

"No, she hasn't had any."

"I can't believe that."

The first one Saskia remembers is Jeff, who drove the pine-green truck. Then there was Victor, who wore black turtleneck sweaters and had a big mustache, which he waxed. He was always bringing his pale fingers to his face and caressing his mustache while he stared off into the distance. Creepy. Then Kevin, who had long hair and a bushy beard and a hard belly like a Mongol war drum. He had come to put in a new septic system, and he took to mooning after Lauren. He spent so much time in the garden with her, asking the names of plants for the tenth time, that he was fired by the boss of the septic tank company. Apparently, Kevin got fired a lot. A photo left from the Kevin Age shows him turning the flexed muscles of one shoulder toward the camera and laughing through stained, crowded teeth. On the shoulder is a new, raw tattoo: L A U R E N, backed by a rose and clippers, crossed. What a tåbe. Lauren doesn't even grow roses. She says they're so overdeveloped they have a sickly karma. In the photo you can see above the tattoo another one peeking out of the sleeve that says N I C O L E. Here and gone, and all he left was a photo, and all he took of Lauren was a name in a column. *C'est l'amour!* And after Kevin, the Bluffaroo himself. Bluffaroo has solved the problem of getting fired by never having a job in the first place. Saskia told Jane that Bluffaroo had only been around for a year, but that was wishful thinking. Bluffaroo has been at White-on-the-Water for four years, the longest by far of any of the usurpers. Surely there has been some mistake. Some bureaucratic snafu has held up the issuance of Bill's walking papers.

Faced with Thomas's unyielding disbelief, Saskia concedes: "She's had a couple of boyfriends, or whatever . . . But they've been incredible losers."

"Naturally. All successors are, it's a physical law."

"And she hasn't really liked any of them. She hasn't let any of them sleep in her bed."

"The brass bed?"

"Yeah."

"Well, of course not. It's my bed."

"Oh. I thought —"

"If another man falls asleep in it, when he wakes up he finds he doesn't have any genitalia. He's as smooth as a Ken doll."

"Gosh."

"It's the Curse of the Brass Bed. Lauren never told you about that?"

Saskia is speechless. The awful secrets of the inner sanctum. Lauren the High Priestess on the high bed, using men according to her pleasure, her hair wild, something alive, devouring, a maenad. Wow! But Saskia notices something in Thomas's eyes. "You're kidding!"

"And you're gullible. Anyway, Lauren making her groveling boyfriends walk home in the rain. That's just what I've been saying. Women hold all the cards." Beneath Saskia's neck, Jane's stomach is rising and falling regularly. Thomas winks. "Do you think she's dreaming about boyfriends?"

"We were talking late last night."

"She ought to drink coffee."

"We'll teach her." Saskia now drinks a whole cup every morning, nursing it like Thomas, crouched with him around the sun.

12

Dateline:
1:30 A.M., July 22, A.N.T. 1. In Camp, Hyperborea.

We humans must learn to fit into the web of life, not tear it. If we tear it, killing whales, poisoning our environment, then we too will someday fall out of the web.

Consider our lowly gray toilet roll, unpretty to look at. It has no bleach, no perfume. We bury it beneath the turf, in the moistness, where it quickly breaks down and returns its goodness to the soil. Why do people want perfumed rolls? Thomas says it is a sign of sickness that we are disgusted by something natural. Toilets waste precious water because we don't ever want to smell anything. The water hides the smell from our pampered noses.

Truth to tell, the hardest part for Saskia about getting used to the camping life has been doing her business. She accepts that it is her own fault, not that of the perfectly natural things she is leaving in the hole she scraped out with a stick. "You might as well be ashamed of breathing," Thomas says. "Here's an exercise. Say, 'Thomas, I think I'll go take a shit,' without blushing."

"I think I'll go take a shit, or whatever," Saskia murmurs.

"You blushed."

"I can't help it!"

"OK! Be ashamed of your own shit if you want to be. That's your business. But surely you're not ashamed of my shit. I would find that insulting. Say: 'Hey Thomas, I saw you making a nice big shit the other day.' Look, you're blushing even without saying it."

Jane is in stitches. "What's so funny?" Saskia asks her indignantly.

When we are hiking in stony areas, we keep our feet on the stones as much as possible, instead of crushing the grass and flowers. Jane picked some lichen off a rock and Thomas pointed out gently that lichens are the first step on the road from stone to soil, and this land needs all the soil it can get.

"As the signs in the U.S. parks say, 'Take only photos, leave only footprints.' In Tasmania they have an expression I like even better. They tell you to be a 'phantom walker.'"

"You've been in Tasmania, too?" Jane asks.

"I've been in Tasmania twice."

Thomas doesn't even kill mosquitoes or horseflies. All the poor mother mosquito wants is a little blood for her needy eggs.

Saskia and Jane have not yet advanced to that plane, but Thomas is tolerant. "Perhaps it is too much to ask of everybody," he says, a mosquito gorging on his forearm. He doesn't even get welts. Talk about discipline! The horseflies are awful. Half as big as the pompom bees, they come out in force in dry weather. When they land on you they pause to gather strength before tipping forward and jamming a post-hole digger into your flesh. They are slow, but hard to kill. A direct hit only stuns them for a moment. Nonetheless, Jane has worked out an effective routine. She delivers a thunderous slap and the fly falls to the ground, kicking its legs. Before it can recover she stamps on it several times, yelling, "Take that! And that!" She emerges from the frenzy with a flushed face, smiling.

"How was it?" Thomas asks playfully. "Nice?" Even he avoids horsefly bites. He waves the flies away.

"OK, I understand the mother mosquitoes, but what do the fucking flies want?" Jane asks.

"Just a square meal."

"Why can't they be vegetarians?"

"Ah, the zeal of the convert."

Perhaps flies are a test of our goodness, of our reverence of life for life's sake. Well, it's a hard test.

Once at dinner Thomas said, "Consider what your needs are when you want to go to sleep. You need your sleeping bag, so you take it out of the stuff sack. Now you've got this empty stuff sack. What are you going to do with it? You also have to take your clothes off, so you do that. But what are you going to do with your clothes now? They're lying all over the place. You crawl into your sleeping bag. You discover that you would really like to have a pillow. But — wait a minute! You can put your clothes in the stuff sack. Voilà! A pillow!

"Think for a minute about how wonderfully that works. Our needs will mesh, if we only let them. If people learned to love most the things that worked simply and well, this planet would not be in so much trouble."

Perhaps when all the stones have been lichened to soil, when all the mother mosquitoes have blood for their babes, when all the horseflies have gotten a square meal, when all the people learn to love most the things that work simply and well, perhaps then the Laistrygones will disappear, the dams will stop being built, the whales will stop being slaughtered, and Saskia will know what she has been put on earth for.

13

How fortunate that Saskia learned patience from dealing with Lauren. Knowledge comes to those who wait. Thomas did have a dog.

"My father bought a puppy when I was three."

The man was probably trying to buy back the affection of the boy whom he had betrayed. He would have brought it inside, a brown wiggle with a red ribbon, and set it by his wary son. He would have smiled ingratiatingly, the revolting stubble twitching at the edges of his jutting beard. Why don't you like me? he would have asked. "It was becoming clear by then that there wouldn't be any siblings. My parents thought a dog might make me less lonely."

Thomos Monogeneios. Like father, like daughter. His shield is azure, charged with oar upright, or. Responsible, lonely, locked in his room.

Thomas stretched forth his hand and named the dog Lila. A liquid sound, for a sea dog. He and the dog grew up together. They played together, slept together. Lila, a rocking sound, to rock him to sleep. She was his best friend. She thought she was human. When he went off to school, she wanted to go, too. She would watch him do homework and later she would open his school books and hold them down with her front paws, dip her head and drool on the pages. "My parents were not dog people," he says.

Of course not. They were oblivious. Lila always ate the same food Thomas did. The vet pompously said you could not raise a dog a vegetarian. They are carnivores, my boy, he said, placing a plump hand on his fussy waistcoat and peering over his half-moon glasses. But Thomas proved him wrong. "She was a Border collie," Thomas says, eyes closed. "A glossy, black and white dog with coal-black eyes."

"I remember her," Saskia says. "I have photos of her."

"No. You never saw her. She died when I was seventeen."

"How?" Jane asks anxiously. Jane is a dog person. In England her family had a dog that her parents gave to friends when they came to America. She has never forgiven them for that. Boston is no place for a dog, they said, and anyway Peter was allergic. Dog stories make Jane cry even when they have happy endings.

"Old age," Thomas says. "She was fourteen. That's the tragedy of dogs. They're your friends for life, but they only live a dozen years. You feel guilty. It would have been the perfect friendship, but you lived too long." He sighs. "When she died I felt so alone. It was much harder than when my parents died."

How did his parents die? But Saskia is too timid to ask such a thing.

"So how did your parents die?" asks Jane.

"Ohh . . ." Thomas picks lint off a sleeve. "A car accident. When I was twenty."

"Well who was the dog then at White-on-the-Water?" Saskia asks. "She was black and white, too."

"All my dogs have been Border collies."

"What was her name?"

"Lila. All my dogs have been named Lila."

"And all your boats," Jane says.

"Only one boat."

And now no boat, and no dog either. Why? "So where's your boat now?" Saskia asks, taking the plunge.

Thomas grunts. He pitches his dregs, unsmiling. "I'll tell you about that some other time."

14

In *Through the Looking-Glass*, when Alice walks through the wood where things have no names, she puts her arm around the neck of a Fawn. The Fawn lets her do it because it doesn't know it's a Fawn, and Alice doesn't know she's human. When you forget who you are, anything is possible. The Jane Sing and Saskia White who lived in Novamundus are dead. In Hyperborea, they still say "Jane" and "Saskia" to avoid confusion, but in the two sleeping bags zipped together, they are Saskia Sing.

> High against the sky
> he waves, he's found a campsite.
> "Come," he calls. "Come home!"

They joke about things, walking along far behind him, holding hands. "He's so dreamy!" Jane says. They giggle. Together they crow, "What a dreamboat!"

Saskia can tell that Thomas is exactly on her wavelength. When Jane takes the gray roll and walks slim-legged away over the turf, Saskia watches Thomas's eyes follow her until she disappears behind an outcropping. On days when Jane and Saskia are hiking apart, it becomes obvious that Thomas's frequent stops are to wait for Jane, not Saskia. Saskia clambers up to him, but he continues to look down, shading his eyes. "Where did you last see her?" he asks. "How far back was she?" He slings off his pack and sits down. He will wait patiently. Saskia wants to go ahead, and Thomas lets her. "If you get all the way to this point, stop and wait for us." Saskia hikes on, excited at the thought that Thomas is waiting alone for Jane.

Evidence: He is standing with Jane and explaining the life cycle of some ferny thing. He puts his hand on her shoulder. He leaves it there longer than he would with Saskia. He pauses and looks at her, his eyes look deeply and steadily into her eyes while he talks about reproductive cycles. All he would have to do is gently pull her toward him and kiss her. But Jane is looking down and the chance is lost. She kneels to touch the ferny thing and he stands over her, arms akimbo, frustrated.

Yin and yang. Dark and light, willowy and compact, adventuress and adventurer, mercury and sulfur, female and male. Getting a back rub in the tent, Saskia drifts contentedly, imagining . . . She and he would be all alone beneath the brick vaults of Uraniborg, in the alchemical cellar. Alembics and retorts crowd tables and shelves. The furnace roars like a lion. Litharge bubbles. His best student, she lies on a marble slab in the hot cellar while he applies to her back his famous elixir, dispensed by every apothecary in plague-bedeviled Europe: Venice treacle mixed with aloe, myrrh, and saffron, to which is added tincture of corals and solution of pearls. It flows across her back, tingling, gold-lit by the roaring furnace like hairs on the back of a hand. Tycho works the potion deep into her skin, his arms glistening with sweat, bulging with muscles developed from adjusting his huge Augsburg quadrant, his four-cubit sextant. Yet he is gentle handling her, entrancing her with his unguent as witches of old did for each other before riding their wicked brooms to midnight sabbaths. The master is balding and bullet-headed, his nose wobbles. She is not embarrassed to lie naked before him, because he is as ugly as she is.

15

Dateline:
12:45 A.M., July 28, A.N.T. 1. In Camp, Hyperborea.

A river is a wild and beautiful thing. In the spring it flows high and carries nutrients up to the soil all around, like the Nile. In the autumn it's low and all kinds of flowers and plants grow in the exposed river bottom. Insects come and feed on the plants, and birds come to feed on the insects. Fish swim up the river to spawn, and bears and wolverines come to catch the fish. Whales come up as far as they can, and sport in the pools. They surface, blowing oar uprights of steam. They are the geniuses of the place. Reindeer come down from the highlands to lick the minerals and drink the pure water.

Building a dam on a river is like cutting its throat. It bloats up like a corpse, becoming stagnant and smelly. The fish are trapped. The plants die and the animals go away.

So why, you ask, would anyone build a dam? Some people in this world are:
   a) greedy
   b) wasteful
   c) stupid
   d) all of the above

"Everything spoke to primitive man," Thomas said. "You don't cut down a forest when you can feel its soul bleeding, you don't strip-mine when you know it's the skin of your mother you're flaying." He was not looking at them but through them, wrestling with his vision. "The wrong people won history's battle. The Christians were the empty ones, with their creed that said only humans had souls, their greed that could never fill their own emptiness. Primitive peoples didn't lose to the Europeans because of technology, they lost because they tried to understand these blank-eyed invaders. They tried to connect, and they fell into the void."

Thomas says that Masters in India teach you how to enter into the being of other things. In communing with them, you commune with God. God is in a mosquito, and you touch God when you become a mosquito, when you feel yourself flying around, looking for someone to land on. You breathe yourself into things, which is the origin of the word "inspire." So I'm not killing mosquitoes anymore. It is a good Discipline. There was a Native American chief, Thomas says, who said: "What happens to beasts will happen to man. All things are connected. If the great beasts are gone, men would surely die of a great loneliness of spirit." When you come to feel that even insects are your friends, then surely you will never be lonely.

16

A Thomas tale: "Lila was the perfect traveling companion." On long and lonely roads he would sing and she would croon along. While he cooked, she sniffed out onion grass, wild thyme, and sage. "She carried her own pack. She never disagreed with me about when to stop or which way to go. She never complained." She slept in his tent, at his feet. She jumped up growling, hackles raised, at sounds in the night. She was almost shot by a drunken soldier in Burma when he grabbed Thomas by the shirt front and she lunged at him.

"Is this the first Lila?" Jane asks. She is chewing mercilessly on one of Saskia's pens. In order to get out of the downwind spot at story time and to improve her wind on the ascents, she is trying to give up smoking, but she says it's driving her nuts.

"No, I got her when I was eighteen. We took off when I was twenty. I was searching for enlightenment." He strokes quotes in the air around the word. "The sixties."

"Where did you and Lila go?" Saskia asks.

"Easier to say where we didn't go."

"You were in Tasmania," Jane points out.

"Twice," Saskia adds.

"That was our down-under period. We were mainly in the Australian outback."

"Following songlines," Saskia says.

"We did some of that, yes. With a good friend."

An Aborigine, who stood on one leg. *My people have never let a white man come on a Walk,* he would have said in noble tones. *But for you, Thomas, friend . . .* At night under the stars in the desert wastes, around the campfire, he would sing his songline songs and Thomas and Lila would respond with Phaiakian sea chanteys. Thomas would be stirring the campfire with the end of his oar, hardening it in the process. *But Thomas, my friend,* the noble Aborigine would say, *why are you hardening your winnowing fan?*

"This is the Lila I knew," Saskia says.

"No."

"This Lila sounds like she thought she was human, too," Jane says.

"All my Lilas thought they were human."

"I guess we could have guessed that."

"I never treated them like 'dogs.' Chase slobbering after this stick, go eat this crap in your corner, stay off the goddamn furniture. If you bind a child's hands from infancy, it will grow up an idiot: no opposable thumb. Most dogs have been brain-damaged by their owners, who should be held legally responsible."

"Was Lila with you in the ashram?"

"Yes."

He knocked on the gate of the court of the wisest Master of all wide India, an oar on his muscled shoulder and his pack on his back, his faithful companion by his side. Lila flew an oriflamme: her shield was gules, bowl attendant, ermine.

"There was a wise guru at that ashram," Saskia says.

Thomas shrugs. "I thought so at the time."

"He was small, coffee-colored."

"So Lauren still has that photo."

"On the wall."

Thomas grimaces. "I took that picture at a wedding. I was trying to get a shot of him manifesting, but he stopped while I was focusing."

"Manifesting?"

"Vibhuti. A special ash for putting on your forehead and using in rituals." He laughs. "Some of us even ate the stuff. Anything to suck up some of that holiness. In some ashrams the followers drank the guru's urine."

"Gross!" the girls chorus.

"Fortunately our guru wasn't into that particular fetish. Because we certainly would have done it."

"Not you!" Saskia says.

He looks at her, half smiling. "Why don't you think so?"

"You were the favorite."

He chuckles. "Maybe that's why I was the favorite. Maybe I was the one who would smack his lips the loudest."

"But what's manifesting?" Jane asks.

"Creation. Proof of god-like power. His hands would be empty, his arms bared to the shoulder. Nothing up his sleeve, you see. He would put his hand over yours and vibhuti would pour into your palm."

"Wow!"

"Indeed. It bothered me. I didn't want to believe something so material. He would do it with rice, too. It added a whole extra symbolic level to throwing rice on newlyweds."

Saskia is not surprised. If you can make gold from lead, surely you can also make rice from nothing. She wonders if it was real rice he made, or whether if you mold it out of nothing it tastes like nothing, like Mrs. Sing's rice. Perhaps Mrs. Sing just puts her hand over the pot . . . But no, Saskia saw the box. "And he came with you to Wonderland to start the commune, right?"

"Who?"

"The guru."

Thomas looks at her. "Hasn't Lauren explained all this to you?"

"She never says anything, except the guru was named Truth, and I thought he came from India."

"You have no idea what Truth looked like?"

"Lauren showed me a photo with everybody on the porch. It's true he doesn't look like the ashram guru, I always kind of wondered about that. But I thought —"

"What does he look like in the photo?"

"He's the bald guy standing next to you."

"Right. That's Raymond."

"I thought his name was Truth."

Thomas is getting impatient. "That was the name he gave himself, but his real name was Raymond."

"Lauren just said the guru was named Truth and he eventually had the commune build a tower for him to live in. She said you were the only one he allowed to come up and speak to him while he was in the tower, because you were his favorite."

"She said I was Truth's favorite?" He looks amused. "I suppose she was trying to be complimentary. Yes, that was always the holy grail, to be the favorite. Lauren didn't mention that Truth went off the deep end?"

"Um . . . no."

He waves that away. "Misplaced loyalty. Truth was on the wrong path, and on the way to finding that out, he went nuts for a while. Lauren should have let go. She's too loyal."

"So Truth wasn't Indian." Saskia is still trying to negotiate that curve.

"A cab driver from Brooklyn. How did we get on this, anyway?"

"The ashram."

"Didn't you meet Lauren at the ashram?" Jane asks.

"Yes. In fact, that does finally bring us back to Lila. Lauren and I met because of her."

He and Lila were sitting out under the stars, and Thomas was pointing up, saying, Look at the Wagon! Lila leaped up, growling into the darkness. Who's there? Thomas asked, pointing forward the fire-hardened oar. Then Lila, with that unerring dog sense, wagged her tail. Tall, capable Lauren materialized out of the darkness and stroked the sleek coat of the intelligent dog. What a superb dog, she said. And isn't the Plow beautiful tonight?

"Lila died at the ashram," Thomas is saying.

"What happened?" Jane asks, her hands raised protectively to her throat, fearing the worst.

"She was hit by a motorcyclist."

The girls moan.

"I didn't see it. She came to me limping, I had no idea what had happened. She wasn't bleeding. Dogs usually try to go off by themselves if they're in a bad way, but she stuck right by me. I assumed she was all right. I should have known she would stick by me no matter what. She died during the night, at my feet."

"That's so sad," Jane whimpers, rocking.

Thomas is looking away from them, across a valley with a dead cobalt lake in the middle of it. "What about Lauren?" Jane asks.

"What about her?"

"You said you got to know her because of Lila."

"Lauren saw the incident. Unfortunately, Lila ran away from her. It took her until the next day to find out who the 'owner' was. She came to tell me, but it was too late." Wrapped in a colorful toga, hesitating at the door of his prayer hut. You don't know me, she says, hanging back, circumspect, but — I know you, he says. You are Striding Tree, rooted in the ground yet not immobile. The Wagon you call the Plow, although it never sinks into the earth. She steps into the hut, the bright day at her back. And you are Thomas, always yourself, pure Thomasness. The Plow you call the Wagon, although it circles, going nowhere. She reaches out a hand. I . . .

Tears are spilling down Jane's cheeks. Dog stories do it every time. Thomas is looking at her. "Aren't you going to finish your coffee?"

"I still don't like it," Jane boohoos.

"What a waste!" He grimaces down into the black liquid. He is about to toss it out. But instead he drains the cup and grinds the dregs between his teeth.

17

They follow a wide river valley for miles into the backcountry, through pine trees with rosy jigsaw bark, walking in eye-bathing shadow on a sea of needles, the sunlight tapping their shoulders. Thomas picks up a stick and discards it, picks up another, hefts it, keeps it.

"What's that for?"

"You'll see."

They zigzag up until the trees thin out. The mountain starts to play a favorite mountain trick, saying, Here's my summit; ha ha, that was only my shoulder; no, my real summit is up here; whoops! fooled you again; now this time I'm serious . . . They climb up by a mossy waterfall out of tundra completely, into a stony wasteland, where they find snow, first in streaks, then swaths, finally fields. Water rills from the lower ends, pooling, overspilling, muttering single-mindedly toward the river. Snowy peaks rise another thousand feet. Thomas tells the girls to wait and crosses a steep snowfield, testing for firmness ahead of him with the stick that he knew, mage-like, he would need. He calls the girls across after. The snow is wet and coarse like the salt the trucks spew on Tylerian roads, rusting Betsy and murdering trees. When they stop for a rest on a rock there is nothing but snow, silence, empty sky.

And evening on them already. Where could they camp up here? "There's a hut," Thomas predicts, decanting steaming coffee from his thermos, swirling it, nosing it. "Just over this pass." Minutes later it comes into view, a wooden box tied down with guy wires. The door is unlocked. Inside, hyggelig bunks are built into the walls, a table sits beneath the window. They sling off their packs. Thomas looks left and right, gathering disapproval. "The last people here were røvhuler." He crawls on the floor, picking up bits of paper, empty food cans. His eyebrows collide over his nose. "They probably didn't pay, either." He peers through the slot in the box where you're supposed to leave money for each night. "If we run into them . . ." A satisfying image: they round a corner and there the røvhuler are, throwing bottles over their shoulders to shatter on the rocks and later cut the feet of itinerant reindeer. Thomas leaps on them, his mage's staff blazing in his hands. He strikes right and left . . .

After dinner he spreads out the map and frowns at the sepia contour lines. "We have to cross this peninsula, and we'll be above five hundred meters the whole way. There is only one way to get down the other side and it's steep. Here." His finger taps the spot. "If this good weather breaks, the cloud cover will come down to three hundred meters and it might not budge for days. That would get us into some trouble." He considers, sliding his finger down cul-de-sacs, stroking the dark patches of thousand-foot cliffs. "Therefore, I want to be off this plateau by the end of the day after tomorrow. It will be harder hiking than what we've done so far. But I know you girls can handle it." Saskia and Jane trade a solemn glance. Aye, men, it's a dangerous mission. I want volunteers. Me, sir! No, me! "We go to sleep immediately. Breakfast at five."

The girls brush their teeth in the cold blue outside. The sun has floated behind a ridge. It will sink tonight, for a few minutes. Technically speaking, Midsummer's Day is over. The thought pangs in Saskia's chest. "Can't we have a story?" she asks, once they're all in their bags.

"We have to go to sleep."

"Just a short one?"

He sighs. "What do you want to hear about?"

She throws caution to the winds. "Tell us about Wonderland. Lauren never wants to talk about it! Like it never existed! Tell us about when we were all there together. Tell us about Truth!"

"You don't want to hear about Truth."

"I don't even know how we — Since you and Lauren met at the ashram, how did we end up at White-on-the-Water?"

Thomas is lying on his back with a hand behind his head, the other on his chest. He has less hair under his arms than Lauren does.

THOMAS AND JANE

169

THOMAS AND JANE

"It was time to start our own commune. Lauren's family had a lot of land."

"They did?"

"They still do."

"You're kidding."

"Lauren has never told you about that, either?"

"No."

"You Whites are the second largest landowners in the county, after the lumber company. You didn't know that?"

"No."

He makes a disgruntled sound. "Inexcusable that she hasn't told you these things."

"Maybe she's ashamed." But why be ashamed of owning land? Maybe because Native Americans didn't own any.

"There happened to be twenty-five acres by the lake with a house and barn the family had owned since the glaciers retreated, but no one had been living there for years. They signed it over to Lauren on condition that she fix up the house, which, among other problems, had a three-foot hole in the roof. The cellar was a pond. It even had fish in it. We used to feed them from the stairs. The moisture had warped all the floorboards in the common room." The waves! Saskia remembers a toy frigate she pushed from trough to crest, the spray flying back from the bowsprit. "The foundations were rotted out. It rained the whole first winter, and every time the wind was up we lay in bed waiting for the house to unmoor itself and ski down the slope into the lake. Giving Lauren the house killed two birds with one stone: it got both the house and Lauren out of the family's hair. They were embarrassed to have her back from India."

"Why?"

"Pregnant by a man she wasn't married to and wasn't going to marry, smoking dope, dropping acid, into yoga, tantric meditation, ayurvedic healing, Buddhist mindfulness, Taoist groundedness, levitation, all the latest chi-extending, karma-raising disciplines trucked in from Katmandu or Rangoon or whatever ashram our newest arrivals were coming from. Nothing could have been more obnoxious to the White clan. They're pillars of the community, a goddamn colonnade. They think meditation should be illegal, like heroin, although their wives are all Valium addicts. Every one of Lauren's six brothers is a corporate lawyer. Her father looks like Chairman of the Board for World Domination, Inc. He suffered my presence only once, when Lauren signed the papers for the house."

Lauren has brothers?

A man sits at the oak table under the spidery chandelier by a pile of envelopes, keys a calculator, scratches paper with a gold pen. Saskia is barely tall enough to see the tabletop. He has been here before. He holds each paper down on the table with the palm of his hand as though it might try to scuttle away.

I know how to multiply, she says.

What's two times three?

Six.

What's four times one hundred?

Four, eight, twelve, sixteen . . . She pulls at her lip, hot-faced. That's a lot of fours.

Four hundred, he says, still scratching on his paper.

John, Lauren calls. Is she bothering you?

"But Truth . . . ," Saskia says.

"What about him?"

"He was important, wasn't he? He was the master of the commune."

"He was also out of his mind."

Saskia is still trying to get used to this idea. He sat in a tower and learned all the stars! "What made him . . . you know, go off the deep end?"

Thomas is silent for a moment. "To be fair, everyone was a bit crazy at Wonderland. Partly from the drugs, partly from the constant navel-gazing. People were breaking each other's personalities down for the sake of big-sounding concepts they didn't understand. They claimed there was no such thing as sexual or material possessiveness and drove themselves crazy trying to believe it. 'I saw the best minds of my generation destroyed by madness,' et cetera, et cetera."

"What?"

"Nothing. A poem." Thomas breaks off.

Saskia waits. She has learned to sense when people will go on if you just keep quiet. Eventually, he says, "Funny, I haven't thought about the commune for years. It started off so well. We fixed up the house, we had our friends with us, we started the garden. Paradise on earth, it was going to be, with God right on the premises. Or his ambassador, anyway. A model for a new world."

"But Truth . . . ," Saskia says. The snake in the grass. The false prophet.

"You want to hear about Truth," he says restlessly, sighing. "All right, let's see if I can remember." He strokes his ginger underchin. "Let's see if I can get the order right. At the very beginning he gave everyone new names." Adam naming the beasts. "It was a control thing. He was creating his followers anew." Except Thomas. The favorite, he was allowed to keep his name. "Then he started worrying about who was sleeping together. The happiest couples bothered him the most. He would call in the male and tell him to break it off, that a sexual relationship was impeding attainment of at-onement. Couples dreaded getting that summons. But when he told them to stop, they stopped." Did he tell Thomas and Lauren to stop? They were the happiest couple at Wonderland. Is that why Lauren made Thomas go away? "Then his pleasures got more refined. Instead of calling in the male, he would call in the female. He'd have sex with her. Then he'd call in the male, with the female still in his hut, and tell him to break it off. This the man would do. Then in the group meetings he would humiliate both of them, telling the others that they were soiled, untouchable. Then, let's see . . . Oh yes, then he decided all the women had to wear sacks, so that he wouldn't be distracted by them. Then he told everyone to burn their books, because emanations from the books were giving him headaches. Then he started hitting people. A sudden roundhouse, if someone got on his nerves. Then some long, severe beatings, usually in the group meetings. After that he went into silence. Everyone had to communicate with him in sign language. Shortly after that, he climbed into his tower."

"And you brought him his rice. What was he like then?"

"To tell you the truth, I don't remember that period very well. It was an upsetting time."

Paradise in ruins. Lauren telling Thomas to leave, on orders of the crazy guru. As Thomas said, she was too loyal. But he's crazy! Thomas would have argued. I know, I take him his rice. It's very upsetting. No, she would have said overloyally, you must go. You have no choice. And he went, and Lauren, imitating her beloved guru, went into silence.

"But why did everyone let Truth do all this?"

"In a way, they made him do it. Everyone looked to him for answers. Everything he did was Teaching. When he gave them new names they smiled in idiotic bliss, they rocked and held their toes like newborn babies. If he named a girl Ugly, she took it as needed chastisement. Truth was teaching her to let go. If he broke up a couple and had sex with the woman, they said Truth was breaking old habits of thought, possessiveness was bad energy. Why did he beat them? The fact is, they wanted him to. They would come to his hut on the morning after a beating, their faces black and blue, and ask for more. All those people sucking at him, eating away at him. He must have felt like he was giving them his body and his blood, and they only wanted more. As he got more and more outrageous, I think he was unconsciously pleading with them not to listen to him, just to leave him alone. And everyone nodded and said, 'Yes? Yes?' and inched closer. It must have been a pretty heavy scene for poor crazy Raymond."

"Heavy scene," Jane echoes.

"Sixties talk." Thomas smiles bitterly. "Those old words really do taste rotten in the mouth."

"And what's Raymond doing now?"

"Raymond is dead. He killed himself."

There is a long silence.

"You got me talking longer than I meant to. It's late. Good night."

"Good night," the girls say, subdued.

Jane rearranges herself and Saskia takes hold of her hand. They snuggle, trying to salvage vestiges of coziness after this bedtime story. In a few minutes, through the slackening of Jane's fingers, Saskia can tell she has fallen asleep. She lifts her head. Thomas is lying in the same position. His blue eyes are wide open, staring up. They slide down to look at her. "Go to sleep now."

She snuggles against Jane and closes her eyes. Sleep is approximately a million miles away. Too many things to think about. Why did Thomas let the guru do those things? Why did he let Lauren force him to leave? The guru was evil, but he got away with everything, just like the slime-mold harpooner. And yet, he did kill himself. Perhaps Thomas tossed him a revolver with a single bullet in it and said, "There is only one thing for a gentleman to do, Truth." But with Truth dead, why did Thomas leave? Or had Thomas already left and Truth tried to take Lauren but she wouldn't let him into Thomas's brass bed, so he killed himself? Or perhaps Truth was perfectly sane until he tried to take Lauren away from Thomas, but their love was so strong he couldn't do it and his unrequited love for beautiful Lauren drove him crazy?

Saskia opens her eyes. Thomas is lying in the same position, his eyes still open. As this is the first time they have all slept in the same room, it is Saskia's golden opportunity to figure something out, something she and Jane have wondered about. Namely, whether Thomas ever actually sleeps or not. When Saskia writes in her journal at night, she can hear him in his tent, obviously not sleeping. Reading, sewing, writing, map-poring. Often she hears a rustling, followed by the sound of polishing. He has unpacked his stove and is giving it the deep brassy shine she admires while watching him cook. Sometimes she hears him leave the tent and walk somewhere. Private business? Maybe. But she has the funny idea that he is walking out of earshot and doing calisthenics. She imagines him out on the tundra doing a hundred pushups, or sprinting to the top of a nearby peak. When she wakes the next morning, he is already (or still?) up, outside drinking coffee, even in the rain. "Good morning," he says, before she thinks she has made a sound, and through the tent wall he gives her a weather report and advice on which clothes to put on. He knows the contents of her pack as well as she does. His eyes slide down to meet hers again. "Go to sleep," he says gently.

She is determined to stay awake as long as he does. Two can play this game. She closes her eyes and thinks through all the stars she knows. She thinks through all the constellations. She relives her excitement when she discovered the supernova in Cassiopeia and pointed it out to Tycho, who kissed her, he was so happy. She thinks of mapping stars with Tycho and imagines the huge star charts they make together, on which each star is fixed in its declination and right ascension to the nearest second, amazing everyone with their rigor and accuracy. She opens her eyes to look at him. Blue eyes still open. "Go to sleep," he says gently, quietly.

She closes her eyes and thinks of Marco's adventures. She runs through them chapter by chapter, naming the names of people, stuffs, precious metals, wines, furs, spices. She arm-wrestles men and amasses horses. She bangs their hands down so hard she breaks the table and it falls on the jugs of palm wine stored beneath. She opens her eyes to look into his still blue eyes. "Go to sleep," he says gently, quietly, softly.

She closes her eyes and thinks of alchemical symbols, of the seven planets, the seven metals, the seven times seventy-seven steps to the Philosopher's Stone. She thinks of Odysseus on Circe's isle, his men all turned to swine, and he on his unknowing way to Circe's hut. Hermes Trismegistus appears to him and grants him that which all Wise desire, the Philosopher's Stone, the elixir of life, which Odysseus drinks, and he goes in to Circe and is impervious to her witch's brew and manfully draws his sharp sword and rushes at her and overpowers her and they mount the holy stairs to share the bed of love. Then Hermes tells him he must leave her, he has no choice, and he lashes together mages' staffs to make a raft and puts out on the wine-blue sea, keeping a safe eye on the Pleiades and late-setting Boötes, and on his left hand the Bear. But angry Poseidon smashes the raft and the steering oar slips from his hands and he is ducked for a long time before he finally comes back to the surface and spits out the bitter water. Leukothea the sea nymph appears and gives him a magic veil which buoys him as he ties it to his chest and he rides on the veil two nights and two days until an island lies ahead like a shield on the misty face of the water. But the coast is all jagged rock teeth mantled in spray and he is carried up on a great wave and dashed against the white cliffs and beaten mercilessly by the pounding water and almost deprived of his homecoming but he is strong and pulls clear of the surf where it sucks at the land and finds his way at last to the mouth of a river where no rocks are and he sinks exhausted, crusted with stiff salt, on the sand, until she comes down from the observatory and finds him, and the first winged words she addresses to him are "My friend!" because this island is called Ven, which means "friend" in Phaiakian. And she wraps his nakedness in mist and leads him by the hand to the center of seagirt Ven where stands the glorious palace of Alchemist, her master, who receives the worthy Odysseus as is right and proper, calling in the grave housekeeper to set before them the Philosopher's Stone, generous with her provisions, and they put their hands to the Good Thing that lies before them and their dross falls away and they shiver into the essences of themselves and take on immortality like a shining raiment.

"Time to get up."

The air on her cheek is frigid. She opens her eyes. Thomas is sitting at the table, dressed, lighting his stove.

"Wake Jane up. We'll eat and go."

The sky is orchid. They pick through stones in the dingy light, working slowly downhill, into darker and colder shade. Lichen and moss return. Beautiful tiny mauve flowers crowd in the cup of an outcropping, frost on their feathery leaves. They come out into a broader valley, into sunlight. "Aahh!" the girls say. "That feels great!"

"No rest here."

A thick layer of rust and olive sphagnum springs under their feet. The river is low and they find a place where they can cross from stone to stone. The rest of the morning is spent trudging along the valley and up the opposite side. They have lunch by a pile of wooden poles with sharpened ends. "What are those?" Jane asks.

"The Sami bring them up. When it's time to gather the reindeer in the autumn, they build temporary fences across entire valleys."

"Who are the Sami?" Saskia asks.

"You've probably heard of them as Lapps. They were the original inhabitants of this land. It's called Lapland, in fact."

Saskia absorbs that for a while. "And they're allowed to herd reindeer?"

"They own the reindeer. They let their herds out into the mountains in the spring and collect them again after the first snow comes. It's the traditional way, and if you're going to keep animals at all, it's the best way. The reindeer roam free most of the year, have a natural sex life, natural birth."

"What do Lapps look like?"

"Northern. Broad faces, not much body hair. They wear colorful clothes, mostly red, with yellow and blue woven into bands." Red, yellow, and blue: a man's color words. Do their eyes really work that way, projecting on their brains a world of primary colors? "They weave the bands on a hand loom, an ingenious thing you can tie to a tree like a miniature hammock and work with your fingers."

"That's neat!"

"They're amazing people. They've been more or less pushed aside by the present population. You see them now and then along roadsides, in camps of tepees. In the winter they live inland, where they keep their herds."

Locally, then, the Hyperboreans are called Lapps, or Sami. "Why did they let themselves get pushed out?" Saskia asks, aggrieved.

"I don't think they had much choice."

Just as Thomas had no choice. It was written: Paradise would be violated, Man would fall. In the post-Lappsarian world, the Hyper-boreans hover on the edge of the rapacious society that has sup-planted them, aliens in their own land. You might glimpse one out of the corner of your eye, a flash of carmine, azure, xanthic, standing on a stork leg, ready to fly. If you turned to look, he would be gone.

The afternoon hike is very long. After the cold morning, the sun is hot, and in this treeless landscape there is no escaping it. Bright in the eyes, metallic on the skin. White rocks and snow so blinding it hurts. They take a break. "That was it?" the girls ask when Thomas gets up.

"Can't trust the weather." He casts a safe eye at the cloudless sky. They continue around the shoulder of a ridge and drop again, into another treeless valley even wider than the first. The girls keep think-ing that surely they are going to stop, they have gone so far today, but Thomas keeps them moving along the river, over the humps of buried and exposed boulders that fell a zillion years ago from the cliffs above. When he finally allows them to stop, the girls collapse in the grass. "I thought you were in better shape by now," he says, disappointed.

Later, Saskia examines her tanned skin. She darkened easily when she was young, but she is kind of surprised it still works. Her hair, too, is turning blond again for the first time in years, and she has a boy's muscles now. Saskia for once gets into good shape and she looks more wrong than ever. With the light hair and dark skin, she must look like a photographic negative. Reversed light, reversed gender. Oh brother.

"Definitely no story tonight," Thomas says. "We didn't get as far as I'd hoped we would."

"We went farther than we've ever gone before," Jane challenges.

"Yes, and we'll go even farther tomorrow."

Jane, in the tent, is cross. "He's a real slave driver."

Was yesterday long and hard? They had no idea how easy it was.

The valley is enormous. It seems to get bigger and flatter as they move along it. At least back on the slopes there were always new views. Here there is only a slight rise, mile after mile. And the ground is getting wetter. A cubic foot of sphagnum holds seven gallons of water. Jane and Saskia make ingenious detours, double back, vacillate like cats at the ends of dry spurs. "No time for that!" Thomas says, splashing through. "Let's go!" Saskia makes a misstep, then Jane. Cold press of damp socks. Thomas was right. Eventually the girls walk straight across the sponge, gray cold water welling above their ankles, socks afloat. Toes soften, stick together like melted cheese.

And always, the sun. Cold feet, but everything else burning, bruised by the light. Thomas has turned crimson, and tawny freckles compete for space on his face and arms. His shield is gules, oar upright, powdered tenny. At the first break, he pulls out the suntan lotion. "We're getting fried. Saskia." He motions her to him. He spurts the warm fluid on her arms and legs and rubs it in strong strokes from banana to foam along her skin. "Bend your head." Fingers so strong on her neck and shoulders they hurt. "Jane." The same treatment. He is so terse today, so unsmiling. No time for barnish games, this is serious business. They have a job to do. He knows they can handle it. Saskia swells with pride. Perhaps he lingers a little, rubbing Jane. His hands slide slipperily, almost meditatively up and down her long dark legs. At the tops he rubs up under her loose cutoffs. Jane rocks from the force of his rubbing, her eyes blank. He does himself quickly. "We'd better keep moving."

On and on. Finally out of the marshes. No shade for lunch. The grass is hot and stiff. Their socks dry on a rock in ten minutes. "We're not far enough," Thomas says. "It'll be a long afternoon."

"There isn't a cloud in the sky," Jane says.

"That can change anytime."

They hike on. There is nothing to think about but the next break. A thousand steps, two thousand. Saskia's stride is two feet, that's twenty-six hundred and forty steps a mile. Someone has pounded gravel into her soles. Thomas is getting farther and farther ahead of them before he stops to wait. He seems to have more energy the redder he gets. Is he solar powered? When they straggle up to him, he takes off immediately in his seven-league boots.

"It's not fair," Jane says. "You get to rest!"

He turns. "I'm not resting, I'm waiting. I know precisely where we have to be tonight, and I know precisely how fast we have to go to get there. I don't see exhausted girls, I see plain ordinary tired girls. You're not used to pushing yourselves." He takes off.

"He's right," Saskia says. The Adventure is without and within. You can never know the shape of yourself unless you touch your limits.

"How does he know how strong we are?" Jane complains.

"We can do it."

They plod on, mile after mile. They sweat and smell like tropical grease. Bad news from the map. Not far enough. "This isn't working," Thomas says. "You're going slower and slower."

"No kidding," Jane says.

He ponders. "We'll have dinner early, and a two-hour rest. Then we'll continue until we're done." He takes off again.

"Come on," Saskia says to Jane. Coaxing her makes it easier. Something else to think about. They go a mile. A little steeper now, cliffs coming in closer from either side. "I'm never going to do this again," Jane says. "Never in a million quadrillion years." Another half mile. The oil has sweated all out of them, dripped off the fingertips of their swollen hands. Only salt solution now, magnifying the sun's rays. "This is crazy," Jane says. Her face is flushed, breath short. "He's out of his mind." Another quarter of a mile. He is waiting, fidgeting. She says it directly to him: "You're crazy! You're a slave driver!"

"All right," he barks. "Take off your pack! Saskia, you too!"

Dem's fightin' words? If he had sleeves, would he roll them up, circle, push at their shoulders? Come on, come on. He straps Saskia's pack to his front and hoists Jane's to lie sideways on top of his own pack, where he balances it with an upraised arm. "A measly half mile to go. You ought to be able to do that on your knees." He trudges off with the three packs.

"You have to admit, he's pretty manly," Saskia says.

"I have to admit he's a lunatic."

By the time they clamber up to him the stove is purring. Jane doesn't say a word. She moves off while Thomas makes dinner. She sits on a rock and stares down the valley. He glances at her now and then but doesn't say anything. Hot silent evening. "Dinner!"

Jane takes her time coming over. "I don't want any."

"Sunlight suppresses appetite," Thomas explains. "But you have to eat to rebuild muscle tissue."

"I don't want that stuff." Jane has her fingers wedged in her pockets, pelvis thrust forward, knees locked back, ankles caved outward. If she weren't Jane, you would almost say she was pouting.

"What stuff?"

"That stuff."

Thomas looks down at the cup of rice and vegetables in his hand. "You're insulting my cooking?"

"It's the same thing every night. I'm sick and tired of it."

"Oh. My lady is tired of it. And I'm tired of you. This is a camping trip. There are too many days between stores for me to be dreaming up a fancy recipe every night for finicky Jane. If you'd hiked hard today you'd gladly eat whatever I put in front of you."

"I did hike hard!"

"Bullshit. Just eat it." He thrusts the cup in her hands and turns away.

"I did too hike hard!" she says, higher pitched.

Thomas ignores her. "How much do you want, Saskia?"

"I can't help it if you want us to go too far!"

"You're making it, aren't you?" Thomas yells, turning back. He flings out an arm. "There's the pass! Half a mile! After that it's all downhill! You ought to be proud of yourself, but instead you're having a tantrum."

"Why can't we even just have, I don't know, hot chocolate?"

"If you want luxuries, don't come camping with us."

"You drink coffee, why can't I have hot chocolate?"

"Coffee isn't a luxury."

"I saw some Nestlé's mix in the last store."

"Nestlé's, great. And what about the boycott? You want to help Nestlé's kill Third World babies?"

"I just want something other than water sometimes."

"So what's a few babies, I see."

"Then something else —"

"Why don't you learn to drink coffee? Saskia likes it."

"Well I guess Saskia's just a better camper than I am!" Jane's eyes are brimming.

Thomas shrugs. "You said it, I didn't. If you drank coffee, you wouldn't fall asleep all the time. I've never seen anyone sleep so much, you're some kind of . . . *sloth*, some kind of biological curiosity —"

Jane makes a strangled sound. Her upper lip curls out showing her white teeth, she blindly reaches to put the cup somewhere and drops it near a rock, it hits the ground and pops its contents into the air, tips over and is splattered by the falling food. She runs away through the rocks, her long hair streaming.

Saskia sits silently, hugging herself, her head pulled in, her ears pounding like war drums. "How much do you want?" Thomas says thickly, his face so red you'd think blood might spout from his ears. He plops the cup in front of her and grips his own, squeezing it out of round, forking rice into his mouth, the features of his face all drawn into the middle. He squints at the sun, stands and casts glances around the landscape, sits and eats.

Done in seconds, he glances over at Saskia and looks away. He stands up to pin down the landscape again, then examines his fingernails. "I didn't handle that very well," he says, studying a nail edge.

"She's in love with you."

"Oh?" His eyebrows arch. "Is she?"

"Haven't you noticed?"

He smiles slightly. "I've noticed some loving, young lady, but conspicuously not for me."

"She's got a crush on you."

He thinks about that while he lights the stove again, puts water on.

The sun is gliding, wings out, braking toward a cliff perch. "She talks about you all the time." He grimaces, covering his eyes with a hand. He slowly rubs his face until the grimace is gone. Pink deepens again to crimson. The water is boiling. Instead of making coffee, he pours in more rice.

"How old is Jane?"

"Almost fourteen."

He picks up the fallen cup, washes it clean under a trickle from the canteen. "Leave the food on the ground, the birds will get it." He shakes the cup dry. "Fourteen. Practically an old maid."

"She —"

"Don't say it. Don't say anything." They sit in silence. When the rice is ready he spoons it into Jane's cup, tops it with more vegetables, and walks off, canteen in one hand, cup in the other. Bearing gifts. Saskia watches him approach the distant rock Jane's sitting on, circle to the far side to face her. He puts down the canteen and talks, spreading his hand palm-down, as he does when he is holding down your attention. Even from here, Saskia can see how charming he is. It would be worth having any fight with him for the pleasure of making up. He holds out the cup. Yes. Jane closes the space with a hand, the cup passes. He talks some more. He scrapes at the ground, gathering a palmful of pebbles, and tosses them on top of his head, where they bounce on the corn-silk blond, dust drifting to his shoulders. He laughs, deep barrel sounds. Jane laughs. They walk back toward Saskia, Jane holding the cup, Thomas the canteen. The sun has gone behind the cliff. Shadow. Enormous relief.

After a catnap, Jane still looks exhausted. She hunches next to her pack, her arms squeezed between her knees, silent. But she doesn't complain when Thomas says they should go. He has transferred into his pack everything that could possibly fit and now he settles hers gently on her shoulders. "All downhill after the pass," he promises.

"OK," Jane says dully. The wind picked up during dinner, and as they approach the high point of the saddle it grows stronger until their clothes flap. After half an hour they reach the pass, and the wind is suddenly very strong. A bowl lies below them, and beyond, thousands of feet down, a cerulean fjord. Ranged across the whole sky, an army of clouds is advancing toward them. "There they are," Thomas says. "I was beginning to wonder."

So he knew all along.

The clouds are coming in fast. The air is colder on this side, and the middle of the bowl is snowy. They skirt the snow and descend a slope for a few hundred feet, then pick their way tortuously down a steep chute of loose boulders. Thomas stretches out a hand: "Talus." The rocks shift under their feet. Smaller stones clatter around them. A slab cracks in half just as Thomas steps on it, and he almost falls. They reach the bottom with relief. "From here it's a Sunday stroll." A meadow drops quickly and before long they are in bushes, then short trees. Saskia is dead tired. Light-headed. The fear on the talus took the last energy out of her. She stumbles along, keeping her eyes fixed on Thomas's back. No idea where they are going, just following Thomas, every turn, every step. Mosquitoes in the damp dusk biting. No idea where Jane is. Thomas's back. Roots. A bite, so painful it brings tears to her eyes. She slaps at it weakly. It moves and bites again. Horseflies. The descent goes on and on, one slope after another, down and down. Rubbery legs, painful feet, blister, Thomas's back, bushes, flies. A Sunday stroll.

"We're low enough now," Thomas says. But no campsite here. Under the trees, thick undergrowth of bushes. "As soon as we find a place we'll stop." They go through a ravine. Bushes crowd everywhere. Getting thicker. Thomas breaks through the bushes. Another ravine. Steep sides. Crawling up. Bushes scraping along her skin. Bushes so crowded they must stop and retreat, try another way, retreat again. The clouds are dark, rain coming. Find a place. Lie down. A fly jams its jaws into her thigh. Another ravine. Another.

"Ah." Thomas has stopped. Saskia crowds behind him. Someone else. Jane.

River.

On the other side, a clearing. No bushes. Campsite. Place to lie down. "Stay here," Thomas says. He crashes through the bushes upstream. Saskia leans against Jane and drops her head on her chest. They rock, unsteady on their feet, fainting. Wanderers.

Thomas crashes downstream. "Nothing on this side," he says, returning. "We'll have to cross the river." He looks at the two girls. "It's been a hard day, and you've come through very well. I just want you to know that I am proud of you both. You should be proud of yourselves."

The words fill them with sweetest water. He is beaming down on them. Looking up at him, looking at each other, dirty and tired, they smile with cracked lips. They tested themselves and were not found wanting.

"Take off your packs," Thomas says. He strips. He gets to his blue underwear and keeps right on going. Saskia closes her eyes. A splash. She opens her eyes. He is midriver, up to his waist in the fast icy water, holding his pack above his head, his clothes and boots stacked on top. He deposits them on the far bank and wades back. "The other packs," he motions. He carries both across together, one on each shoulder. "Saskia." He squats in the shallows, his bare back rounded before her. She climbs onto his shoulders.

"Aren't you *cold?*" His skin is like ice.

"Not yet," he says through his teeth. He drops her on the far bank. She throws her arms around his neck and kisses him on the cheek. "Mm," he nods tersely, turning. "Thank you."

He crosses toward Jane, sinking back to his waist in the water. "You have to pay a toll for the ferryman!" Saskia calls to Jane. He rises at the other side, the water sluicing around him. Saskia gapes at his whole beautiful backside, every muscle distinct, drawn tight from the cold, facing Jane. He squats before her, hands in the water to steady himself, head bowed. At her knees, a supplicant. Have pity, O Queen . . . He guides her leg over his shoulder. Jane gasps at the slide of her leg along his icy skin. He stands and turns, sinks back into the water.

"You have to pay the toll!" Saskia cries. "A kiss for the ferryman!"

Jane's hands circle his forehead. She is exhausted but so relieved, so happy. She smiles weakly, beautifully. "What?"

"A kiss for the ferryman!"

Jane kisses the top of Thomas's head.

"Boo! Cheapskate! Cheek, cheek!"

Jane, smiling weakly, beautifully, bends over his head and kisses Thomas's cheek.

"Cheek gets you halfway! Lips for the whole trip!"

Thomas barks out a laugh, stopping in the deep water. "Should I drop you here?" He begins to squat.

"No! No!" Jane shrieks happily, pressing his head into her stomach, lifting her legs. "No, ooaa!" A touch of icy water on her behind.

"On the lips! On the lips!"

"OK!" She leans farther over him and kisses.

"Longer! Longer!" Saskia chants.

Thomas is moving again. Jaw clenched now, he climbs out and sinks to his knees to let Jane step daintily onto dry land. "Towels," he croaks. His whole body is shaking. The girls tear apart the packs and diffidently spread the towels on him like placemats on a table. "Rub!" They shyly rub. "Harder!" They rub furiously, feeling how hard he is. "Better," he says, his words more distinct. The girls hold him tight between them through the tight-wrapped towels, their arms linked. Aftershocks come, shuddering all three. "Much better," he sighs, in an almost normal voice. "Look." He detaches an arm from his swaddling and points up. "Just in time." They look over the trees, back toward the plateau. The pass they passed is hidden in fog and cloud.

18

Dateline:

1:15 A.M. August 5, A.N.T. 1. In Camp, Hyperborea.

Whales swim in family groups. They are very affectionate. The parents are legendarily loyal and fearless. They will defend their young even though it mean death to themselves. The mother's milk, like reindeer milk, is ten times as rich as regular milk.

What's really amazing is, whales have never shown any hostility toward people. When divers or boats are near them in the water they show great care to avoid doing injury, even though they could smash a boat to smithereens with a single slap of a mighty fin. And more than this: sailors know that survivors of shipwrecks, struggling far from land, have sometimes found themselves suddenly buoyed up on the sleek back of a dolphin or whale, and carried gently to the nearest shore.

When Odysseus' raft was destroyed by Poseidon, what did the sea nymph Leukothea give him, which buoyed him and brought him to Phaiakia? A "veil." Clearly, the text here is corrupt, probably owing to a German redaction.

Whales keep turning the other cheek. Some divers of yore called them "great winged angels." They are too good for this sinful world. They keep forgiving us even though we don't deserve it.

Thomas has told the girls tales about the many months he searched in vain for the *Green*. The ship had wounded him in his body and in his pride, and he was determined to find it again and wreak a revenge of which the whole world would speak. But the *Green* was ever more secretive. Many times Thomas sailed forth, and many times the mysterious ship eluded him. Betimes he heard rumors of its passing, or came upon bloated corpses left in its wake. Forced to be patient, he heeded the call of other duties. "It is not desirable to cultivate a respect for the law, so much as for the right," Thomas quotes.

That's old Henry David. "It's the same with Spiderman," Jane points out. "He's always doing what's right, but the police don't like him."

No, the international police did not like *Lila*. While she rode at anchor in the rough Arctic waters, Thomas and two of his men one night cut the wire in a chain-link fence and crept out along the pier of a Laistrygonian station where three whaling ships were moored. The outlaws climbed quietly down into the engine rooms and loosened the bolts on the sea cocks until the water gushed in. *Lila* disappeared into the darkness, now you see me, now you

Behind her, softly, the three whalers sank. Once *Lila* confronted, David to Goliath, a nuke carrier. Once a Spanish destroyer fired a shot across her bow. Once Thomas scaled a billowing smokestack and claimed it for *Lila*, unfurling the pirate's skull and crossbones. Once he saved the lives of adorable furry seal pups by painting them bile green, and as he worked a pod of whales hung near the ice pack, passing and repassing, blowing their approval.

Throughout all the adventures, all the years, Lila was the genius of *Lila*. This was, at last, the Lila whom Saskia once knew, who rode in the bow of Thomas's wooden boat at Wonderland, who left with Thomas when he had to go. This was the Lila who stands crowded against Thomas's legs, smiling, in the orange photograph in the box under Saskia's bed. She grew to dislike the land on which she staggered, never losing her sea legs. She was happiest whenever *Lila* turned cleanly from the pier, stern water drumming, and headed out to the open sea. She stood in the bow, tongue streaming in the sharp salt wind like an oriflamme.

Thomas says we spend billions of dollars shooting radio messages into space searching for alien intelligence, and all the time here on earth we're surrounded by other intelligences, right under our noses.

Some whales sing heartrendingly beautiful songs. Perhaps the songs are telling us something, if we would only listen. Perhaps the whales have been sending messages to us for centuries, wondering if we'll ever answer. Research has shown that whale songs are very complicated. Whales will all sing basically the same song, but each individual makes slight changes, so the song slowly evolves. Researchers think the whales may memorize these songs with the aid of formulas, just as the bards of Homer's time memorized their epics.

"We are the aliens," Thomas said. "The whales were here first. Imagine how horrified we would be if horseflies took over the earth.

We would think, Surely this is not what nature had in mind. To the whales, we are flies." But the saintly whales, like Thomas, don't slap.

Perhaps the whales are singing the greatest epic of all: the Life of Mother Earth. Perhaps they are not singing to us, but *about* us. Perhaps they have been singing now for centuries the part where the heroine is under siege, her household goods eaten up by a horde who claim to love her but who really only want to exploit her.

A song woven together like a net, like fabric on a loom whose purpose is to keep the suitors at bay. When will the whales summon the rescuer? "Nature does make mistakes," Thomas said. "Look at the saber-toothed tiger, which couldn't even close its mouth. Perhaps Man, too, became a monster when his head grew too large to fit through his own mother's birth canal. The first thing each of us does with this instrument we're so proud of" — he tapped his temple — "is rip our mothers' vaginas. Don't you think that's strange?"

Unwisely clever Man harpoons the last whale and hauls its corpse up the slipway of his factory ship, his bloody flensing knives poised. He pauses. What is it? He cocks an ear. What is wrong? He turns, wondering, frightened. *What is it?* He spins around. No! A terrible silence deafens him. He cries aloud, a monstrous huge-headed baby. The song comforted him, cradled him, and he never guessed. He spins, sobbing. He is lost, sinking. The cold silent seas pour into his gaping mouth. If the great beasts are gone . . .

19

Thomas unzips his pack and unrolls a shirt, spreads it out on the grass. "Dear Mom and Dad." He wedges a hand into the tight mass and rocks out a pair of pants, musing. "Two days of steady rain ended today, and we're taking advantage of a sunny afternoon to let our clothes dry. I am learning so much this summer." He checks a sweater for dampness. "How inspiring it is to know people who are so committed to making this world a better place to live exclamation point. If only —"

"Slow down!" Jane says, writing as quickly as her neat script will allow her. "' — know people who are —' What was the rest?"

"Who are so committed to making this world a better place to live exclamation point." He examines the sweater's armpit. "If only there were more people like these dedicated goddamnit."

"'Were . . . more —' What?"

"The material is giving way all along this seam. People like these dedicated men and women. I feel privileged to know them. I'll have to sew this up tonight."

"' — privileged to —'"

"I've grown a lot on this trip and I realize now that I haven't always been the perfect daughter."

"' — realize —' Hey, wait a minute!"

"Trust me."

"They've been a hell of a lot farther away from perfect than I ever was!"

"That's beside the point. Trust me." Jane shakes her head, but writes. He sweeps grit out of his pack. "But as Thomas says, realizing your faults is the first step toward correcting them."

"Why am I kissing their asses?"

"Because parents can never get enough of it. You said you wanted them off your back. Well, pucker up." Jane looks doubtful. "That's the last of it. One sentence. 'As Thomas says —' Come on." Jane shrugs and writes. "I miss you both and Peter too two exclamation points love Jane P.S. I quit smoking three exclamation points."

"Talk about laying it on thick."

"With a trowel. They'll eat it up." Jane examines the finished card. "Let me see." Thomas reads it through and hands it back. "It's good."

"It doesn't sound like me."

"Since when do parents have any idea what their children sound like?" He opens a bag of tempeh and smells it, frowning. "We have to eat this tonight. The whole point is, don't waste your energy fighting battles you can't win." He rips off a length of toilet paper, puts his hand on her head and wipes her nose. "See? Comes right off."

20

Patience.

There comes an evening when Thomas, poring over the map, swivels the legs of a compass only once, twice, before stopping to tap. Perhaps the looming of the end of their quest makes him want to tie up other affairs, clear the slate for the righteous work that will be demanded of them by the river's side. Have you wondered, he asks, what happened to Lila and *Lila?*

"Yeah, sort of," Saskia says.

"I never gave up looking for the *Green.*" Through all those years he searched far and wide, the scar across his stomach tingling. But the oceans are huge. While he painted pups and opened cocks, brooding, the *Green* had successful seasons, psychotically killing everything that moved. One day he got a tip on *Green's* whereabouts. He had gotten dozens of such tips before, and had chased them down only to find nothing. This one was no more or less promising than the others. He dutifully sailed from port, Lila straining forward in the bow. When he arrived at the suggested stretch of sea, he soon found evidence of *Green's* depredations. Some spoor was so fresh that hope quickened in him. Perhaps this time . . .

"Two ships can spend weeks in the same area, only a few miles apart, and never sight each other." His scar was throbbing painfully. They were close, he felt, so close this time.

Lila crisscrossed the sea, day after day, encountering nothing but albatrosses in the troughs, feasting on gruesome flotsam. Thomas's crew began to grow unruly. The old man's obsessed, they said. When off watch, they gathered on the foredeck to whisper darkly. But Thomas was patient. It had been so many years. He had his sextant and his compass and he knew they would not fail him this time. He looked up one day from his charts and his blue eyes sparkled in their depths, separating the true direction from the false. He pointed off the starboard beam: "She is over there."

Lila fixed a new course. Half an hour later the call came down from the crow's nest: "Ship ahoy!" A smudge of vile smoke lay on the horizon. His men were wide-eyed, ashamed they had ever doubted him.

On seeing *Lila*, the *Green* turned and ran. "As it happened, they had filled the last of the lockers the day before. They were heading for port." But the whaler, wallowing low in the water with its cargo of death, was no match for the smaller *Lila*. Thomas opened her throttles and she tore eagerly after her prey. Within an hour she was a quarter mile from her target. This is where he would take out the Zodiacs and —

"No, that's for when they're hunting whales. The *Green* wasn't whaling. Don't interrupt."

What did he have in mind, then? He kept *Lila* close to the bigger ship, but otherwise did nothing. Night came, and in the darkness the *Green* tried to lose him, cutting its lights, changing course, drifting silently. But in the morning *Lila* was still there, an unshakable watchdog. She followed the *Green* all the next day, and that night the maneuvering began once again. Thomas anticipated the moves of the other ship with uncanny precision. As the darkness dissolved, the *Green* found *Lila* still there, mysteriously silent. The ships were so close that Thomas could see the puzzled expression on the face of the unkempt captain of the other ship, and the smirk of the fat, slime-mold harpooner who had injured him so long ago. The harpooner gestured obscenely.

And still Thomas did nothing. On the fourth day the ships were drawing close to the *Green*'s port. Once she was safely in, there would be nothing *Lila* could do about her. What was Thomas thinking of? The crew began to mutter again. Faithless ones! He would tell them when they needed to know, not before. As evening closed in, he called them to his cabin and outlined his plan. They left wide-eyed, once more ashamed.

Darkness fell, and the cat-and-mouse game resumed. The captain of the *Green* and his disgusting harpooner must have been confident. Even if they didn't shake *Lila*, what did it matter? They would be in port the next day, and this nuisance over. "They had dealt with Greenpeace," Thomas explains. "They expected a certain politeness from eco types, a certain masochism."

As the captain and the harpooner chortled, *Lila* materialized out of the darkness, her lights off, ghostly white in the moonless night, a thousand tons of enraged retribution, her engines full speed ahead. The *Green* had no time to react. *Lila* struck the pirate amidships and stove in her side.

"Hooray!" the girls yell, high-fiving.

"You see," Thomas says, "I had reinforced *Lila*'s bow with several tons of concrete for just this occasion."

His little surprise. Now he reversed the engines and pulled clear. He turned *Lila* toward the open sea, picking up speed, and turned again, back toward the *Green*, still accelerating. The renegade captain was trying desperately to get his fat, wallowing ship out of the way. Thomas aimed for the same spot, exultation rising in his breast as *Lila* churned madly toward the long-sought target. He let out a Tarzan yell. There was a tremendous shriek of tortured metal. He was thrown off his feet. *Lila*'s bow rose up, then subsided slowly with a sickening popping and grinding sound. Thomas staggered forward along the shuddering deck. In the whaler's midsection *Lila* had torn a twenty-foot gash, its edges knotted with ripped steel. Her nose had reared to bury itself completely in the hull of the other ship and then she had settled, as the steel teeth of the gash punched through her bottom. In the darkness and confusion, through the shouts, Thomas could hear the engines of the whaler whining. The other captain was trying to pull free. Not so fast, buddy!

"Actually," Thomas says, "I wanted to disengage also."

He threw *Lila*'s engines into reverse. But she would not budge.

She had come to grips with her adversary and would not let go. The ships were sinking, locked in their fatal embrace. Horns were sounding, lifeboats were being swung out. The sea poured into the *Green*'s engine room and her turbines went silent. Her lights, which had come on briefly, went out again. Thomas tried again to back *Lila* out of the *Green*'s hull, but to no avail. As the whaler listed it began to push *Lila*'s nose under. Thomas's men were calling to him.

But where was Lila?

"Not again!" Jane covers her ears.

He had left her safe in a cabin aft, but in the confusion before the collision as the crew beat to quarters she had gotten out, eager to help. Now she was nowhere on the deck. Thomas raced below. Water was pouring into the forward hold, and it forced him back. He retreated, waist-deep, tangled in floating clothes, battered against bulkheads. From cabin to cabin he searched frantically, sometimes swimming. A terrible thought occurred to him: Could she have been standing in the bow when the ships collided? Water was swirling around his chest even at midships. He climbed the companion ladder with the water rising after him and called on the open deck, "Lila!" Honks, shouts, groans of the lifeboat cables. "Lila!"

Lila was awash to the conning tower. He backed toward the stern, shouting himself hoarse. "For God's sake, sir!" his crew called from a lifeboat. "Jump clear!"

Without Lila? Never! *Lila*'s lights went out as her engine room was inundated. The deck lurched and canted down forty-five degrees. Thomas lost his footing and slid into the water. He clambered back up to the taffrail. Suddenly, *Lila* upended. Her stern lifted high out of the water, and for a long, odd moment she hesitated. Then sighing, releasing air to the surface in cauldron-sized bubbles, with Thomas astride the peak of her stern, she sank like a stone. Water closed on Thomas's ankles as he jumped and the whirlpool sucked him down, but he kicked up and away. He surfaced at last, gasping, spitting bitter water. His crew lifted him, listless, into a lifeboat. From there he watched unblinking, unresponding, the water boil with casks and lines, boxes, buoys.

No Lila.

"A terrible price to pay," Thomas says quietly.

But the *Green* had been sent to a watery grave. And so clumsy and heavy was she with her cargo of death that her own greedily sucking whirlpool swamped the lifeboats of the Laistrygones. They bobbed momentarily in the boiling water, crying raucously like sea gulls before, one by one, they were sucked under, deprived of their homecoming. The last to go was the harpooner, whose fat kept him longer afloat. He twirled like a beach ball, terror gasping from his gaping mouth, then only his eyes, until . . . glub, glub. Die, evildoers, die! Lilaless, lonely Thomas watched it all, pondering deeply in his blameless spirit. *Die!*

But no. "I had waited until we were just outside port so that there would be no casualties," Thomas explains. "Both crews were picked up the following morning."

"You mean the harpooner got away?" Saskia is incredulous.

"And a damn good thing, too. If we had killed a single person, no matter how much he deserved it, we would have done incalculable damage to our cause. In politics a thousand whales aren't worth one human life, as absurd as that is. Of course, no one cares about the death of one dog." Except for Lilaless lonely Thomas, grave in silent remembrance, and the girls, struck dumb by the tears in his eyes, patting his empty hands.

21

At high noon of an August day Thomas, Jane, and Saskia gaze from a ridge down on a teal river rippling muscularly in the sunlight. Rock walls crowd together at the upper end of the valley into a narrow gorge out of which the river froths. At the lower end, two fenced-in areas of torn-up earth face each other across the water: the collar. The leash is the puckered gash that must be a new road winding up out of the valley toward some Laistrygonian settlement. Along a flat area in midvalley spreads an encampment of dome tents like colorful mushrooms with banners above them stretched between planted pikes: the Good Guys.

Jane and Saskia raise their hands high and let out Tarzan yells. Ai, but it feels good to come down from the highlands and wastes, to be back among one's people! For there is no question that these are their people. The tent dwellers greet them with smiles. Through open flaps Saskia sees them sprawled on sleeping bags, playing cards or reading, holding babes to the breast. Bandannas cover the dulled hair of the womenfolk. Bearded men under a striped awning cook vegetables and soy products.

Saskia strides, proud of her strong legs, her nonchalant dirtiness. She wonders how she might gracefully let everyone know how far she has hiked, how many tests she has lately passed with flying colors. Thomas leads them past the far edge of the camp and continues on to a grassy mound, on top of which he throws down his pack. "Home!"

"I wonder if our group is here," Saskia says.

"Who?"

"The people we were supposed to hike with."

Thomas fits the three tubes together at the top of his tent and flexes them into an arch. He pulls at his beard and surveys the scene, frowning slightly. "They don't exist."

"What do you mean?"

"Just what I said." He picks up his tent by the top arch and places it here and there in the grass, looking for the flattest place to stake it. "Frankly, I was surprised you girls were expecting to meet them when you landed. It was a story to tell Jane's parents, so they'd let her come. I thought the hint was clear enough in my letter." Saskia blushes. He gave her a hint and she missed it? "What I wrote was" — he gazes inward and summons it up — "'As for your friend's parents, tell them this is a well-organized trip, about a dozen families traveling together, et cetera, et cetera.' I thought that would be clear enough."

"You lied!" Jane says.

"Not at all." His eyes twinkle. "I never lie. I told *you* to lie, and you did."

"I love it! Let me make sure I've got it right. As long as I say 'Tell them' . . ." Thomas explains the fine points while Saskia finishes the tent.

"Bent!" Over Jane's shoulder Thomas has spotted someone. A brush-haired beefy man turns, questioning. "Bent!" Thomas gestures. The man hesitates, then walks toward them with a rolling gait. "Bent used to work for me," Thomas says to the girls. "Good man." Thomas's lieutenant, perhaps, who stood in the Zodiac with the megaphone. He looks the part: honest face, frank blue eyes. Much bigger than his captain, whom he would follow anywhere with doggish devotion.

"Thomas," Bent says gravely as he comes up to them.

"Bent, this is my daughter, Saskia, and her friend, Jane. From the States."

Saskia shakes his huge paw. One of Bent's eyebrows is raised. "Daughter?" He looks from Thomas to Saskia.

"You see the resemblance," Thomas says.

"As a matter of fact, I do. And . . . Jane." He takes her hand, looking at Thomas again for guidance. "Daughter's friend?"

"That's right."

"Pleased to meet you," Jane says.

"Bent," Thomas says briskly, getting down to business, "I want to talk to you about the plans for this action."

"They're all set."

"I'm sure they are. But what about contingencies? Have you got a flexible thinker on the committee?" His voice is impatient in the face of Bent's brick-headed overconfidence in Plan A.

"Thomas —"

"Is McBride here?"

Bent sighs. The captain is back, and work will be harder. Brains will have to think again. "Yes."

"Let's go talk to him." Thomas turns the bigger man toward the other tents. To the girls he says, "Take a look around. I'll meet you here for dinner at eight."

The two men walk off together, Thomas urging on Bent, whose

awkward rolling gait slows him down. Has he been wounded? A cannonball, an artificial leg? "Let's explore," Jane says.

They wander barefoot through the camp. People are eating now, sitting cross-legged with elbows high, spooning into eager mouths. A woman speaks in a strange tongue, showing her white-blond son wildflowers growing in a rash next to their tent. The boy's eyes fasten on the girls as they walk jauntily by, arm in arm. "Hello there," Jane says to him, and he quickly looks back at the flowers. They pass other boys, but none of them bray or throw spitballs. None of the girls or women have on face lard. Two girls glimpsed in their orange tent are surely not talking about what was on last night, but are debating, instead, the manifold problems of the world. Perhaps there is a bulletin board somewhere: "Anyone who wants to discuss saving the whales, meet me in tent #8." They scrutinize the banners. One is a rainbow with doves attendant. Another is vert, charged with dam, sable, encircled by gules, a baston sinister, gules. The biggest banner faces downriver, toward the construction site: "NO to the Langelva Dam!"

"It's in English," Saskia says, disappointed.

"The international language," Jane shrugs. She wants to go see the construction site, but Saskia is not so sure.

"Maybe we're not supposed to go down there."

"Come on, girl! What have we been hiking for a month for?" Jane gets her way, of course, and they head downriver. Saskia looks anxiously at the enclosures as they approach. Might an alarm go off? What if they are captured? Surely the protesters' position will be weakened if Jane and Saskia are taken as hostages. They will be known forever after as The Girls Who Ruined Everything.

But as they draw nearer to the site, it becomes obvious that there isn't anyone there. The chain-link fence is ten feet high and topped with barbed wire. Jane calls Saskia's attention to the way the fence goes a few yards into the river and is connected to the fence on the other side by close strands of barbed wire above and below the water. "That would be pretty nasty to get through," Jane says. She has done her share of foiling the best-laid fences.

The girls grip the cold steel wire. Saskia expected to see Cyclopean blocks of cement waiting to be rolled on logs into place, but most of the enclosure is empty. The grass has been churned under by deep-treaded tires and the ground everywhere is glutinous mud. Several trailers and port-a-johns squat in the filth. Big rolls of plastic hulk on wooden platforms. Blue tarps cover angular humps. Piles of long nubbly steel rods lie along the fence. "How do they make a dam out of this stuff?" Saskia wonders.

"Those are reinforcing rods. I'll bet I could —" Jane starts climbing the fence, hooking her long toes and fingers through the diamond holes.

"Maybe you shouldn't do that."

She has already reached the top and is studying the barbed wire. "I could probably get through this."

"Please don't!"

Jane climbs good-naturedly down. The girls decide to wash their hair, and since they have to take their shirts off, they go a long way upriver. They heat the water on Thomas's stove and pour it over each other's head a few yards from the bank, as Thomas showed them, so that the soil will leach out the soap. Anyway, they use a special natural soap Thomas bought, which smells like a candle and is lousy for working up a lather, but he explained that was the whole point. They walk back feeling fresh and clean. Thomas is waiting for them at the tents. "What are you doing with my stove? I thought someone had stolen it."

"We went to wash our hair," Saskia says.

"You don't need the stove for that."

"But the water is cold."

"Welcome to nature. Give it to me, I need to start dinner."

Watching Thomas cook, Saskia decides he is angry about something. Perhaps his subordinates at the council meeting were being brick-headed. She goes off to sit with Jane by the river. The white-blond boy is there, filling a pot. "He's real cute," Jane says, bouncing her heels. The boy runs away with the pot, sloshing water.

"You embarrassed him."

"I don't think he understands English." Jane stretches luxuriously and drops her arm over Saskia's shoulder. Saskia holds on to her fingers. "You know, we haven't seen boys in ages."

"Who cares?"

Jane shrugs. "They're not completely useless."

The girls laugh, Saskia blushing. *She uses them according to her pleasure.* Thomas is calling them to dinner.

While they eat he gets into a better mood and starts to talk again. He tells them about all the havoc the dam will wreak, how much of the valley will drown, what valuable things will be lost forever. "There is a marsh two miles upriver which is important to migrating birds. It will be under a hundred and fifty feet of water. The reindeer come through this valley in large numbers every spring because it's the only easy passage to the lower country for miles." The girls eat their rice, trying to look glum, or maybe outraged. But since they are going to save the river, Saskia wonders aloud, why get depressed? "Because it's not at all certain we *are* going to save the river. Not if the cowards on the protest committee get their way." He is cleaning up now, scrubbing the cups furiously with dirt, not elaborating.

"So what's their way?" Jane asks at last.

Thomas flings the rinse water down at his feet. "Sitting in front of bulldozers and chanting doggerel. Polishing their passive resistance like a trophy for the mantelpiece. Their way has a hell of a lot more to do with feeling good about themselves than getting anything done. I know this kind of people. They've never been here before, they don't know anything about this valley. They come like kids to Camp Protest, they sit in the road holding hands until the police come and carry them to the van, and they sing songs while the van drives them to jail, where they refuse to pay a fine so they spend one night in jail singing more songs and holding hands, and then they go home feeling like saints. And when the dam is built right on schedule they don't notice, because they're somewhere else, sitting in the road and singing songs."

"What are you going to do?"

"Right now, I haven't a clue." He shakes his head, in disbelief that he hasn't a clue. "I know one of the organizers here, a man named McBride who used to have the stomach for some direct action. But I couldn't talk any sense into him." He presses his lips together and pulls at his beard, actually ripping out a few hairs. "To think we came all the way up here to find this bunch of idiots running the show . . ."

The committee! Of course! Not Thomas's subordinates, but something like the Admiralty: a bunch of stupid old men from noble families, inbred, blundering around the oceans losing ships and men, not listening to the infinitely smarter Captain, whom they look down on as a man of low birth. The Captain eventually gets around them, but he must do so resourcefully, speaking honeyed words, full of blandishments. And here the girls have been, stupidly disturbing Thomas, adding to his tension rather than helping to relieve it. "Should we leave you alone?" Saskia asks. "We could go take a walk."

Thomas's eyebrows arch. "Have I been bad company?"

"I just thought maybe you needed time to think —"

He waves her words away. "No —" He delves into his pack. "In fact, I have a surprise." He removes something wrapped in paper and hands it to the girls. "To celebrate our arrival." A bottle of champagne.

"This is great!" Jane says, cradling it in her lap.

"When did you get it?" Saskia asks.

"Before you flew in." He takes the bottle down to the river to nestle it between submerged rocks. He looks up at the sky, which has clouded over during the last hour. "This should be a happy night. Party in my tent in one hour. Formal attire."

Good thing the girls washed their hair! In their tent, they agonize over what to wear. "I can't look good in any of this!" Jane wails.

"How about your jeans?"

"They're dirty!" She pulls on her khaki pants, which perhaps are marginally cleaner than her jeans. "I'll bet he's got something spotless in that pack somewhere. Like a tuxedo."

"Can you believe he carried that bottle all the way and never told us?"

Jane is slipping on her coral earrings. "Girl, at this point I'd believe anything."

He doesn't have on a tuxedo, but his wool shirt and cotton pants are somehow clean, and his tent is festively festooned with red tape, which he commandeered, he explains, from surveyor's stakes he uprooted along the dam road. The champagne sits in the cooking pot, packed in snow.

Jane beams. "This is so . . . !" She can't think of a word romantic enough for it.

"*Mesdames*," Thomas says gallantly, handing out the camping cups. "*Voulez-vous de champagne?*"

The cork pops under his hand. "Music to my ears," Jane sighs.

Thomas pours a round. "We have to make a toast," Saskia says.

"To a month of good company," Thomas says.

"Hear, hear!" the girls say, and the three cups clack. Saskia sits in the triangle, one knee touching Jane, the other touching Thomas, and wonders if she has ever in her whole life been happier. They could not have known it at the time, of course, but on the night Jane and Saskia ran in the woods, the reason they couldn't bring their feelings to completion was that Thomas was not there. Now he has come like a key into a lock and opened them all to a happiness they never could have imagined. Everything has been leading up to this night of bliss in the hyggelig tent by the river of ichor at the navel of the world. Knee to knee to knee they sit, laughing over the adventures they have had: the Round Tower, the ferries, the fog, the flies. The champagne bristles against her tongue, and Thomas pours again.

Saskia sips and talks and laughs and radiates love like a dwarf star, and after a while the bottle is empty and she is light-headed, the perfect amount. Jane is so beautiful with that extra sparkle in her eyes, Saskia wants so much to . . . Jane unfolds her long legs and excuses herself. She zips open the flap and crawls out. Saskia notices it's getting dark. Jane climbed the fence in her bare feet and touched the barbed wire. How bold she is! Where is she going to do her business? Is she there by now? Maybe she is undoing her pants. "Jane is hot to trot," Saskia says. Thomas smiles. Night is back, and the stars are back, and her Moon is sailing again along the ecliptic, waxing, always waxing. The fawn will remember it is a fawn and run away. "Jane really wants to . . . you know."

"No, I don't know."

"She wants to —" Saskia can't say it. "With you. In the worst way, she says. Her exact words."

He laughs, a pained abrupt sound, as he did when carrying them across the other river. "Tell me, what do you and Jane do in that tent?"

"Us? Nothing."

"How old did you say Jane was?"

"Almost fourteen."

He laughs again. "Practically an old maid."

They have uttered these words before. They are in the web of the done, speaking what is right and proper. "She's done it before." The angel dreg in the leaves, holding his thing, laughing about it so boldly. "She's done it lots of times." The same bed every night? she said. How boring! I think of it all the time, she said.

Thomas is smiling. "So what you're saying is, why be a martyr?"

Brown eye to blue eye, he and Saskia drink each other in. "Nobody likes a martyr," Saskia points out.

Jane comes back. Saskia says she also needs to go do business. Which is true. She crawls out and walks away from the camp. While she squats behind a boulder she feels a drop of rain. So nature will help. She walks back to the other tent. The girls' packs are lying on the grass. She quietly loads them into the tent and crawls in after. She opens her pack and rearranges it, putting the tarp at the bottom. There is just enough room for one sleeping bag between the packs. She crawls into the bag. It is fairly dark now.

Murmur of talk in the other tent. Saskia is a Moon maid, dedicated to Wisdom. Her body is no longer hers to give. Like Tycho, she must forgo the pleasures of this world to contemplate the eternal verities of the starry realm. Their voices are hushed. Then comes silence. A kiss? Jane's voice: "What happened to Saskia?"

Thomas murmurs. Silence again.

Jane giggles. "Maybe I should go."

Saskia hears silly slow Jane coming out of the tent. "What are you doing in there?" Jane asks at the flap.

Saskia pulls herself out of a deep sleep. "Hunh?"

"It's raining out here." Jane unzips the netting. "Why are the packs in the tent?"

"Couldn't find the tarp," Saskia mutters. She turns in the bag, sinking into sleep again.

"But we have to get the packs out. I'm getting wet."

Saskia is breathing regularly, sound asleep.

"Saskia!"

Saskia is so deeply asleep she doesn't hear.

"Saskia, wake up!"

Saskia is roused, annoyed this time. "Let me sleep!"

Caught between Thomas and Saskia, Jane hesitates at the flap. "Saskia" means "Scylla" and Thomas is her twin. We'll get you, my pretty, heh heh!

Jane is gone. Saskia hears the zip of the flap of the other tent.

Murmuring.

Silence.

Rustle.

Saskia pulls her T-shirt up over her head. Long hair catching in the collar. Toss. White patches with a pretty scalloped pattern along the edge. And look: not mushy pink blobs, no, chocolate kisses, the first swelling. Curve of the grain in the wood. Turning her on the warm slab. Off with her soiled pants! *Semper ubi sub ubi. Sed non semper!* Ahh. At your knees, O Queen. A man could lose his mind. Turning her. Rubbing in leg-long grunting his elixir of henbane and mandrake root putting her in a trance of earthly delights and broomstick rides to midnight sabbaths among the black trees. Golden hair on the backs of strong hands turning her. Deep in her bag her eyes are closed, she is naked, she is not alone but flank to flank to flank with them, mid-Deed, so hyggelig.

Rain applauds on the fly.

22

Every day, people disembark from the coastal steamer at the Laistrygonian landing eight miles away and are brought up along the dam road in vans commandeered by the committee. The camp expands to the foot of Thomas's mound, so that his tent is like the castle above the huddled medieval town. A committee member appears on a centrally located stepladder and makes announcements with a lieutenantine megaphone about food, availability of emergency funds, the first aid tent, classes in nonviolent resistance, lost and found, quiet hours at night, activities for the children. A plea is made about private business and a crew of hardy souls forms to clean certain areas. On the fourth day, two port-a-johns are unloaded from a van, which, Thomas points out, use toxic chemicals. All people have to do is hike far enough away from the camp and the river, he says. Some of these people look like they need the exercise, anyway.

While the camp is growing, hoisting new banners, planting new pikes, the fenced enclosure downriver remains ominously silent and empty except for a police car that goes on watch duty by the gate. The two Laistrygones in it do nothing but talk and smoke cigarettes until Saskia tires of looking at them through Thomas's binoculars. On the fifth day the committee announces that the dam builders have craftily postponed the arrival of the heavy equipment in the hope that the protesters will drift away. A collection goes around to supplement the emergency fund. Far from people leaving, more straggle in each day from the steamer or the bus, or on foot out of the hills. The camp population rises to 327, according to the board posted by the committee stepladder.

On "the morning after," as they say, Jane was quiet, but that was no doubt because she was tired, heh heh. They had an early breakfast so that Thomas could return to the committee first thing, to try to talk sense into McBride. After he left, the girls wandered around the camp, but didn't hold hands or talk about anything important. Jane took a nap in the afternoon while Saskia hiked up the river to the marsh and watched some birds poke around in the reeds. She wondered if some of them were geese, migrating south again now that Midsummer's Day was over. There were a few *tweeps*, and one loud *wong-king*.

Jane looked great at dinner. She wore her coral earrings again and sat close to Thomas, as naturally as you please. Afterward the girls went to hear folksongs at a place up the slope where you could see north to the ocean, and since it was a clear evening they saw the sun touch the water and roll along it, gingerly lowering itself in, leaving a haze of rose. Saskia couldn't figure out how Jane knew so many of the songs. When they came down there wasn't any question where Jane would go. Saskia lay awake for a long time in her own tent, not feeling like reading or writing in her journal, unable to sleep. Eventually she wrote some haiku, but none of them were any good.

After the sixth day Thomas stops trying to talk sense into the committee. "If no one else here is interested in doing anything effective, what am I fighting for? I should relax, have a ball at Camp Langelva." They all go looking for cloudberries. Later, Thomas cooks an elaborate lunch. Dessert is a cloudberry torte, and Jane and Saskia try to figure out how he possibly could have made it. He said he should relax, but, lunch over, he is having some trouble. Idiots are closing in on him. He frowns, surveys the crowd of tents below his mound, pulls at his beard. Saskia heads down to the river to fill the canteen, and by the time she returns they are in the tent. She stands around for a while, counting her blessings. Then she takes a long walk.

More days go by. The committee announces that the dam builders have postponed again. Now tent dwellers do start to drift away, leaving grassy patches in the camp. Someone on the stepladder pleads for patience and resolve. Thomas talks about the short attention span of sitters and chanters. "They have homes and jobs to go back to. They're too plugged in. They're part of the problem." The crucial element, he points out, is media coverage. "Television crews don't film protesters sitting on their butts." The man on the stepladder says that delay costs money, and the equipment will come soon. Thomas says something about getting attention, provoking an overreaction. He shakes his head, flinging off cobwebs. He takes Jane into his tent.

Saskia wanders over to a class in satyagraha. She goes limp and floppy when the man pretending to be the policeman picks her up, but she is too ridiculously small. He lifts her like a doll. She envies almost to tears the fat man next to her who sprawls beautifully, as resistant to transportation as a beached whale. The white-blond boy is there, too, with his mother, and he murmurs "Hi" to Saskia as he is being carted away. At the end of class they learn some chants, and Saskia writes a haiku:

> People united
> will never be defeated.
> We shall overcome!

But it's so lousy she rips it up. On the way back the blond boy appears beside her and tries to start a conversation. So he does speak English. His mother is Dutch, he says, his father American. "What's your name?"

Saskia regards him warily. He doesn't look at her, he talks to the passing tents, only sneaking glances when she looks away. Obviously a spy, looking for ammunition. Saskia is so gullible. He will be friendly at first, and Saskia will get blabby and brag about something. Then he'll sock it to her. "Saskia," she says, against her better judgment.

"That's a Dutch name," he says, his face brightening in anticipation of the pleasure of some jab. In Dutch it means "dog," arf arf arf. She tells him she has to be somewhere else and runs away.

The girls still do things together, but never talk about It. They understand each other on that subject without a word or a wink. Unfortunately, it is not always clear what else there is to talk about. Twice they have gone to explore, but ended up by the river, sitting facing in the same direction, silently watching the water flow by. Saskia looks over at her friend and wishes she would say something. But Jane is preoccupied, banging her heels or skipping stones. Saskia explains the phenomenon to herself: Jane is a woman now. Night-time has returned, and a new era has begun. Saskia closed the circuit, to bind them all together. Yet Jane has moved away from her. She has been there and back. They were supposed to do that together, re-member?

Saskia lies alone, small in her cavernous tent at night, and tries to recall what she had in mind. Jane and Thomas would come together like yin and yang, and Saskia would be the eely line between them. The night of bliss would never end. They would all dissolve into each other. But morning came right on schedule and there were still three of them.

OK, grant that. Perhaps they were supposed to crawl through the flaps simultaneously, the same light in all their eyes, and wordlessly join hands and dance. But Thomas was out first, terse, impatient to see the committee, and then Saskia, sitting dumbly, dully, not yet believing that she might have been wrong about something, and finally Jane, pale and tired. OK, grant that. Perhaps Jane, at least, was supposed to hold Saskia's hand, and the True Knowledge of what had happened would flow into Saskia as their hearts beat in unison. But Jane didn't do any such thing. She slept all afternoon, hoarding the True Knowledge for herself. Saskia meanwhile thought she might breathe herself into the migrating birds in the marsh but sat on a rock instead and cried (*tweep tweep*) until she had to blow her nose (*wong-king*).

What happened? What next? Saskia lies alone, small in her cav-ernous tent at night, and ponders deeply.

23

But these troubles are insignificant compared to a problem looming larger every day. Jane and Saskia, to their shame, are as plugged in as the sitters and chanters. Hidden deep in their nomad packs lie tickets for their return flight. Two days before they absolutely have to leave, there is still no sign of dam builders or their equipment. "Let's not go back," Saskia pleads.

"Never?" Thomas says.

"Later."

"There's an organization that might give us some trouble about that."

"Whalers?"

"Interpol."

"For what?"

"Kidnapping."

Saskia broods. "We can get back to København on our own."

"No."

"But you're needed here." If he leaves with them, who will guide the committee with blandishments? If he leaves with them, they will be known, after all, as The Girls Who Ruined Everything.

"Needed?" he responds wryly. "I'm not even wanted."

As it turns out, the situation is even graver than they thought. That afternoon Bent climbs with his rolling gait to the mound-top and tells Thomas he's heard the project is being delayed not by any fear of the protesters but by the heavy-equipment-operators' union.

"That makes more sense," Thomas says. "I couldn't understand why they would suffer a delay for these pantywaists."

"We've got it on good authority, but the committee is telling people it's only a rumor," Bent says in disgust.

"They're scrambling. Look around, the camp is dissolving. A union dispute could put this project into next year. They mention that, and tomorrow this place is a ghost town and McBride and company look like fools."

"They'll only look like bigger fools this way."

Thomas shrugs. "I know McBride, anyway. He's praying the dispute will be resolved quickly and the bulldozers will hurry on up here so he can sit in front of one. Personally, I'd say Langelva's best chance at this point lies with the union."

"I hate to admit it," Bent says gruffly, "but you were right about this."

Thomas is gracious to his huge, dimwitted lieutenant. "Of course I was right."

"So now what?" Saskia asks after Bent leaves.

Thomas pulls at his beard. "The union hasn't left us much to do." The Quest is a mess! "Don't worry, I'll make the best of it."

The following morning Saskia notices tepees on the ridge above the dam. Hyperboreans! How long have they been there, hovering just beyond her peripheral vision? Did Thomas summon them, to help him avert disaster? She points them out, searching his face, but he is skillfully deadpan. He shrugs and reminds her that the Hyperboreans' reindeer migrate through this valley twice a year. "Will they come down and talk some sense into the committee?" she asks, awed at the thought of the wise men riding on white reindeer in stately procession through the camp.

"Not their style."

Of course not. Dedicated to noninterference in the affairs of men as well as nature, they have come simply to watch the battle for their river. Saskia scrutinizes their camp through Thomas's binoculars, but sees no sign of life other than smoke rising from one of the tepees. Perhaps they are burning incense and chanting magic incantations.

She wakes during the last, brief night to hear Thomas leaving his tent. He is climbing the ridge to confer with the Hyperboreans. In the starlight he scales the sheer cliff, adjusting handholds, pumping upward with hard thighs, and after Herculean effort he reaches the summit, striding into the circle of their encampment to say, "See, I have come." The Hyperboreans are amazed. No mortal has ever tread on their Olympian aerie. They pull aside the rug over the door of the smoking tepee and allow him to enter the inner sanctum.

Saskia wakes again. Shouts, running feet. She throws on her clothes and leaves the tent. In the red light of dawn she sees tent dwellers streaming downriver. She hurries after them. Police cars are converging on the enclosure, their lights twitching like cockroach antennas. A fire engine appears on the dam road. People are running every which way. Laistrygones are yelling forehead to forehead with tent dwellers, while other Laistrygones guard a place in the fence where the wire has been cut. Things in the enclosure are burning. Saskia dives into the crowd and squeezes through until she is pressed up hard against the cold wire. Belching piles of tires, panels, file cabinets, boards. It takes her a few moments to recognize the trailers. The port-a-johns are smashed, the rolls of plastic slashed. The fire engine backs up to the river and the pump chatters. As the water swells the hose and spurts from it, playing over the fire, the smoke boils thicker, rolling out sideways before rising majestically through the still morning air to form an enormous oar upright.

24

Thomas is in a good mood as they hike up the west ridge toward the Laistrygonian settlement on the coast. Saskia turns before they drop toward the next valley and takes a last look at the abandoned river, at the mangy camp with its empty mound, the enclosure under a remnant smudge, and on the opposite ridge the silent tepees. Smokeless. Because the torch was passed? Thomas does not glance back. He hikes on, whistling, leaving them all to eat his dust.

Marvelous that he can be in a good mood, considering what happened. Resilience must be a prerequisite of this line of work. Despite your best efforts, the pregnant whale is harpooned, the pure river is left to the mercy of pantywaists and unions. You make the best of it, do what you can in an imperfect world. But you must be able to let it go at last, whistle a retreat, prepare for the next fight.

Well and good, but the girls have yet to learn this lesson. They trail morosely after Thomas. Ahead lies the steamer. In a mere three days they will be back in Novamundus, squeezed into the dry shells of their old lives, with chores and parents and crew, and school counting them off as they file bleating back into the noisome cave. They thought Novamundus had ceased to exist, but their plane tickets prove it has been waiting for them all this time.

As though Hyperborea mourned Thomas's departure, rain begins to fall. Only a mist at first, so that Saskia doesn't bother to put on her poncho, but it gradually intensifies until, before she quite realizes it, she is soaking wet. Wouldn't you know it. By the time they straggle into the Laistrygonian settlement the streets are umber rivers, the drains roar lustily, the rain falls like a curtain on the last act. The one café is not open. A typically gray, shut-up, lifeless Laistrygonian settlement. The steamer leaves in two hours. They stand under a butcher's awning, bloody carcasses hanging at their backs. Thomas puts his arms around the huddling girls and Saskia, cold and wet, luxuriates in her absolute misery. Thomas will become a dream again. He will flatten to two dimensions, a couple of scribbled lines every six months.

He was chosen by the Hyperboreans to do what was necessary, but the renegade McBride betrayed him. "*I'm* in charge here!" McBride bellowed, a step away from grappling and rolling with Thomas in the dirt. "I'll have you arrested, by God!" As McBride waxed wroth, Thomas grew only calmer, his eyes twinkling. Thomas was right, of course. The media came running. A man shouldering a camera panned the smoking pile, another man stepped fastidiously through the muck with a mike. Saskia tried to get his attention, to tell him that Thomas did it, but the røvhul was only interested in committee members. Thomas told her it was just as well, there was nothing to be gained by pointing fingers. The committee and the Laistrygones — see how they work in concert! — had nothing on him. He had been helped by some brave lads who had gathered around him in the previous days, and he owed it to them to keep the details secret. Unlike sitters and chanters, they were interested in getting things done, not in going to jail.

The media came and so the world would learn of the disgraceful plans for the Langelva Dam. If the committee had had guts and elected Thomas its new leader, leaving McBride to foam impotently, the river would surely have been saved, union or no union. Saskia and Jane would have stayed on in defiance of Interpol, and Thomas would have raised the morale of the tent dwellers to fever pitch. All would have abandoned homes and jobs, unplugged themselves to wait months, if necessary, until the heavy equipment finally lumbered toward the enclosure, churning the mud of the dam road. Then the tent dwellers, lean and tough from their guerrilla lifestyle, would have poured out of the hills yelling Tarzan yells, nocking arrows, descending on the yellow behemoths to overturn and burn them, to castrate and enslave the operators.

But instead the committee banished Thomas. And yet he whistled, rolling his clothes, packing. "We had some fun, anyway. Gave them a little something to think about. We're smart to get out of here before it gets too depressing."

Under the awning, Saskia is so cold. Thomas kisses Jane and she snuggles kittenishly. Could the Quest have been so meaningless? Did they hike for a month to save a river when no one but Thomas really wanted to save it? The dam has been delayed, but meaninglessly, out of nowhere, the action of people who have no part in the story, no interest in saving anything. (Apparently the union was striking to protest job cuts. The union wants to build *more* dams!) No. Stories do not end this way, taking wrong turns on the final page. Saskia mulls over the significance of this obvious fact. There is something she is missing.

"Perhaps there's a waiting room on the quay," Thomas says.

They venture back into the steady rain and pick their way through the sodden streets, past the silent curtained windows. The quay is a hundred yards of concrete behind a warehouse. The only shelter is the cab of a forklift, with room for one. Thomas ties his tarp between the cab and a stack of crates and they stand under it.

The River Quest must have been camouflage, a diversion to hide the True Quest. Which was? Childe Saskia to the Round Tower came . . . To find the book on Tycho? Or perhaps merely to come to Phaiakia? To find her roots?

"Here it comes," Thomas says.

"Thomas" means "twin." With that word sounding in her mind, Saskia realizes what the True Quest has been all this time, hiding at the bottom like a bottle of champagne.

The steamer boils the water, drifts, honks. A lasso snakes through the air and is caught by a man who drops it over a bollard. "You're coming with us, aren't you?" Saskia says to Thomas. "I mean, all the way."

Watching the steamer, he doesn't answer.

"Yes!" Jane chimes in, grabbing his hand with both of hers. "Come with us!"

He still doesn't answer.

"Aren't you curious," Saskia says, "after all these years?" The Quest: Locate Thomas, lure him back.

"You're forgetting Lauren," he says. "She wouldn't allow me in the house."

"We could set up our tents in the meadow, like we've been doing all summer."

"Unrealistic."

Jane pumps his arm as if she can pump approval out of his mouth. "You could stay at my house!" The Quest: Locate Thomas, tempt him with Jane, lure him back.

Thomas is laughing. "Somehow I don't think that's a good idea."

"How about —"

He raises a hand. "Not now."

The girls wilt. Not return now, or merely not discuss now? He unties the tarp. The gangplank touches down. He steps onto it and hands Jane past him. "You could stay in a motel," she pouts over her shoulder. "You could at least meet my parents. Come to Sing Sing for dinner." Dinner and a movie. A date! Thomas with plastered hair, flowers. The Quest: Locate Thomas, lure him home, domesticate him.

"Sing Sing," Thomas echoes. "That's clever."

"I thought of it," Saskia says.

There are no empty berths on the steamer. They bed down for the night on couches in the second-class lounge. Jane sleeps barnacled to Thomas, one long leg over him, her arms tight around his arm, her head under his chin. He lies on his back and stares up. From the other couch Saskia says quietly, "Please come."

He doesn't answer. Why can't he come? He has no home, no job. He is not plugged in, not part of the problem. Now that Jane is asleep, she can say it. "Lauren will let you in the house. She's waiting for you. She's sorry she made you go away."

He looks over at her. "How do you know that?"

"I just know."

He is amused. "No, you don't. You don't know a thing about why I left except what I've told you. When I said Lauren might be ashamed, you said it had never occurred to you. Now here you are telling me what Lauren thinks." Saskia blinks, her face burning. "As it happens, I could go back anytime I wanted to. Lauren wouldn't be a problem. But not for the reasons you think."

"You . . . don't want to go back, then?"

He looks at her firmly. "Go to sleep now."

In the morning, while they are standing at a window watching islands slide by in slanting rain, he says, "Maybe for a few days."

25

And so it comes to pass. When right is on your side, you will surely prevail. Thomas goes on standby for the girls' flight to Novamundus and naturally a seat opens for him. "Should we call Lauren?" Saskia asks.

"Let's surprise her." He charms the girls' neighbor on the plane into switching seats with him so they can all sit together. At 31,000 feet Jane says officiously, "We have to figure out where you're going to stay."

"Don't worry about it. I've got my tent."

"You'll just live in the woods?"

"I've done it before."

"We can come visit you! I'm an expert at taking my parents' car at night." She rattles on about other things they can do. Travel around to the other lakes, hike in the state park, do some camping, heh heh.

The plane lands late in the City, and customs is slow, so they miss their connecting flight. Saskia calls White-on-the-Water to say they'll be arriving on a flight two hours later. "I'll be there," Lauren's voice floats calmly out of the receiver.

"How is everybody?" Saskia asks anxiously.

"Oh . . ." Saskia can picture Lauren's eyes drifting, uncaring. "Fine."

Always so nonchalant, even when Saskia has been away all summer. What did Saskia expect? "I brought you a surprise," she blurts out. She winces. Thomas expressly told her not to mention it. Aye aye, sir, blab blab. What a little idiot!

"A surprise," Lauren echoes. "What sort of surprise?"

"I wasn't supposed to tell you," Saskia says miserably.

There is a pause. "A good surprise, I hope," Lauren says slowly.

"Yeah." Saskia hangs up.

The sun is setting when they take off in the mosquitoey prop plane. City grid breaks up into tentacled sprawl, dissolves to wooded hills. Darkness descends. Drifting beneath them, solitary lights twinkle through tree branches, looking like stars. Saskia stares out the window. Thomas and Lauren. Truth went crazy because he wanted Lauren but couldn't get her away from Thomas. But then after he was crazy he convinced Lauren to force Thomas out, after all. But although he was crazy, he knew what he was doing, because he knew Thomas had to be forced out so that he would go off and save whales and rivers and sink the evil *Green*. And Thomas knew that, too, which was why he let Lauren force him out, but on his way out he tossed a revolver to Truth so that Truth could kill himself, because Truth, after all, was crazy. And Lauren, too loyal to the dead guru, has never let Thomas back all these years, but now that Thomas is coming back, she won't be a problem. But not, apparently, because she is ashamed, even though Thomas said long ago that she was ashamed. Maybe if she thought it through in Phaiakian it would make more sense.

The saffron glow of Ithaca appears, and the dim glimmer of Cayuga's waters. The plane banks over the water. Well anyway, let's see Lauren try to be calm this time! Ha!

Crossing the tarmac, Saskia can see them in the light beyond the windows: Mrs. Sing in a powder-green pantsuit, on tiptoes, craning to see, Mr. Sing bulking large in rumpled worsted. And Lauren, more or less with them but not even looking, instead finishing a paragraph in some book that's probably telling her to live in the present. "Mom! Dad!" Jane waves and runs through the gate, is enveloped in histrionic hugs, protestations of delight.

Saskia and Thomas walk behind. Lauren glances up from the book and smiles thinly at Saskia. She has not noticed Thomas yet. Or perhaps she doesn't recognize him. Does he look so different? "Well here you are," she says, closing her book and reaching out a hand. "Let me take something." She relieves Saskia of a bag. As she lifts it high to her shoulder, she shifts her gaze up to Thomas, and Saskia stands ready to drink in the gasp, the slackening of the knees, the bursting into tears, the throwing of arms around the neck, the begging for forgiveness. But Lauren merely says with the smile holding steady, "And I suppose you're coming with us?"

"I thought I might," he concedes.

"Why not? The more the merrier, right?"

Jane intrudes, dragging her parents behind. "Mom, Dad, this is Thomas —"

Shaking the parental hands, Thomas is the soul of courtesy and rectitude. Mr. Sing grunts something about his hope that Jane wasn't too much to handle, while Mrs. Sing chirps along on the theme of what good care he has taken of the two girls. Thomas speaks judiciously of Jane's fine qualities. Jane stands beaming, nervous. The girls have practiced their stories about the group they traveled with, and are mindful of Thomas's orders not to breathe a word about nights of bliss, which people outside Hyperborea would not understand. "I have dinner waiting," Mrs. Sing is saying.

"Call me tomorrow," Jane says to Saskia, backing up in the wake of her parents, and looking to Thomas, and on to Lauren, and back to Thomas, uncertainly, "Where — ?"

He waves her on. "Call Saskia." She turns and hurries after her parents, skipping. So happy. And in that boundless happiness and fulfillment has she thought of Saskia, has she been properly grateful for what was, after all, Saskia's doing?

Rumbling in Betsy along the dark roads, Saskia sits between Thomas and Lauren, in silence. Lauren coaxes with pedal and stick. "Sweet old girl," Thomas says, running his hand over the hardened dribbles on her outside panel. "When did you paint her?"

"Can't remember," Lauren mutters. "Long time ago."

They drive again in silence. Lauren is so strange. Why is she holding back from him? He is home, after many years. On the other side of Ithaca, Thomas says, "I should have known better than to try to surprise you. Let me guess. It was printed in your horoscope this morning."

"No." Lauren rams the stick into second and Betsy lurches at the start of a hill. "Saskia told me when she called."

"I did not!" Saskia says, panicking. Thomas is frowning. "I didn't!"

"She said there was a surprise," Lauren goes on mercilessly. "What else could it have been?"

"I didn't mean to!" Saskia wails.

"I'm sorry," Lauren says. "I couldn't pretend surprise, you would have seen through it."

"My coming was Saskia's idea," Thomas says. "She pleaded."

"So you didn't want to come."

"I wouldn't be here if I didn't want to come." Silence. Lauren brakes and weaves, a rabbit scoots left out of the lights. "I see you still drive too fast," he says in a friendly way.

Lauren slows. "How long are you staying?"

"I don't know, how long am I staying?"

Another silence. "I'm with someone at the moment," Lauren says.

Saskia winces. She's not sure, but she sort of remembers fibbing about that. "I know," Thomas says.

"I don't know if that's relevant."

"His name is Bill."

"So Saskia told you."

"Yes. The men must be lined up, taking numbers. I have to say, you're more beautiful than ever."

"I wish it were true."

"It is true." He is speaking in his octaves-deep tone. "You know I wouldn't say it if it weren't true." You can hear the truthfulness in his voice, a cantus firmus. Wonder takes him as he looks on her. Lauren is keeping her eyes on the twisting road. Both of her hands are tight on the wheel as she cranes to see out the windshield. "I do have my regrets, you know," he says deeply. "Deep regrets."

"Not as many as I do."

"You're too hard on yourself."

Lauren doesn't say anything. She turns onto the dirt road that snakes down to White-on-the-Water. They sway together in the jouncing cab. Stones tang against the undercarriage. He keeps his eyes on her, boring into her cheek. "I've always wanted you to be happy. You know that."

Lauren sighs again, shifting down. "Yeah." Betsy flops into a rut going around the last curve. White-on-the-Water slides into view. Thomas's voice shifts upward to break the mood. "She needs new shocks."

"Feel free." Lauren pulls past the trailers toward the garage. On the porch, someone is standing in the open door, framed by the yellow light.

Bluffaroo.

26

Quinny latches onto Saskia and follows her around all evening, like a dog. "Jeez, Quinny, I'm glad to see you, too, but . . ."

"So this is Quentin," Thomas says. He pats the boy on the head and sighs. Quinny has that effect on people.

Bluffaroo has cooked the dinner, and it's the best he's ever done. "Did you take lessons or something?" Saskia asks.

"So nice to have you back."

After dinner there is some confusion about procedure and authority vis-à-vis the crew, which Saskia has to clear up. Apparently, Mim was lax about certain things. It will take a few days, but Saskia will have them shipshape again. Austin gets a demerit for saying Saskia should have stayed away. How awful he must feel when she takes out his present! Wrapped and beribboned, a water pistol. (He fills it and shoots Quinny between the eyes. What *could* she have been thinking of?) For Shannon, colored pencils. For Mim, an adorable seal pup, a reminder that you shouldn't club them. For Quinny, a pterodactyl. As they greedily tear the paper, she has to remind them to read the attached haiku.

But this is peripheral. After the crew is in bed, Saskia steps lightly back and forth between her room and the top of the stairs, straining to hear the murmur of talk floating up from the common room. "I haven't seen him in years, Bill," Lauren said after dinner. "We have a lot to catch up on, just between the two of us." So Bluffaroo took his time cleaning in the kitchen, his ear cocked, before finally heading out the door to his trailer, casting glances back as he went. Yes, you should feel fear, Bluffaroo. You should worry as you head back to your lousy haiku and pretentious books. You managed one good meal, but it will not save you. Thomas and Lauren are talking, and Saskia is weaving a spell.

In her travels with Marco, she came to a place in India where maidens were dedicated to idols in the temple, before whom they disported themselves merrily. On occasion it happened that the temple god would be estranged from his goddess, and until the couple were reconciled all affairs of the people would miscarry. To effect a reconciliation, it was the duty of a maiden to sing, dance, and tumble naked before the god and goddess, asking, "Lord, wherefore art thou wroth with thy Lady? Is she not comely? Is she not a delight to the eye?" In her room Saskia keeps catching sight of herself in the mirror. With brown face and limbs shackled to the old yellow torso she looks ridiculous, as if she had crawled on all fours in a puddle of dye. Quailing, she moves closer to the mirror and turns this way and that, forcing her eyes to stay on her reflection. A boy with two genetic mishaps in the chest region. And she so hoped she would come back from the trip an improved model: thirteen, wiser, somehow pretty. Well, she could always have a job in a sideshow. She turns her back on the mirror and twirls, dips, stretches. "Is Lauren not comely?" She points her toes. Making an arch with her arms, she adds, "Is she not a delight to the eye?" They have been talking for three hours. In that time surely you can clear everything up, even to picky Lauren's satisfaction. "If she knew what has been going on all these years, she would understand," Thomas said.

And it comes to pass. Saskia hears the god and goddess ascending the holy stairs. She hears Lauren's laugh, oddly girlish. She hears her say, "I wouldn't have talked about any of that. It was the one thing I could do. I felt like I'd failed you."

"You didn't fail me," comes Thomas's voice. "I was wrong."

"But I didn't see that. I was just afraid." Lauren's voice grows muffled as they move into the bedroom, the inner sanctum. The door clicks shut. Silence.

Sweet sleep comes easily, stealing upon her like the tide rising. Deep in the ocean, she shrugs off her limbs. She caresses the warm current with flippers. Her own kind are all around, mothers legendary for their devotion to their children, males who would die from the harpoon rather than abandon their females. "I am Haven," a young male sings lustily, passing her, "shining in the waters, quick

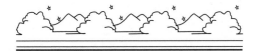

PART 4

THOMAS
AND LAUREN
AND JANE

Ithaca has given you the beautiful voyage.
Without her you would never have taken the road.
But she has nothing more to give you.

— Cavafy, "Ithaca"

1

"PERHAPS it wouldn't have bothered me so much," Thomas is saying tolerantly, "if the man hadn't been a nonentity. In Wonderland days he was one of the lost souls hanging around the area, panhandling for enlightenment, later peddling his own karmic snake oil. He had one trait he could use to advantage: these odd, opaque blue eyes. They seemed so empty, they let him swing both ways. The ultimate worshiper, or God Himself."

A sunny day in September, the fifth in a row. Occasionally poor rainy Tyler gets a Native American summer like this, so clear and warm you want to lie in the grass naked and turn your grossly pale torso as umber as your arms and legs. Saskia has her peasant skirt hiked, her bare feet and legs up in the hot light on the dashboard. Keep that tan! Betsy purrs down the road, bouncing lightly on her toes. When Thomas gave her the new shocks, Saskia stood by and handed him tools.

"His name at Wonderland was Sky. He was always sitting by Truth's right knee. He would have stepped on his mother's face to get there. When Truth went into silence Sky became the interpreter, and he started telling everyone they needed his permission to get an audience. Truth didn't like that and threw him out of the commune."

The snake in the grass, the false favorite. "Then you became the favorite after that?"

"No." Thomas looks over at her. "Perhaps I should correct a misapprehension. I was a favorite of the guru in India, but I was never the favorite here."

"But you took him his rice in his tower, didn't you? You were the only one to see him toward the end."

"Ye-es . . . But that was different."

"How?"

"It's hard to explain. I think by then Truth knew he was on the wrong path, but couldn't get off it. He was having delusions, hearing voices in his head. I was trying to help him." Thomas was better than a favorite, then — a mentor. "But as I was saying about Sky, when he was pitched out of Wonderland he set up his own astrology cabal. That's when he renamed himself Baba Yogi. But he didn't attract many followers until after Godhead fell apart. He was strictly minor league. I can't believe Lauren got involved with him. No — unfortunately, I can believe it. She never really learned the lesson of Godhead. But to think of her sitting at that man's knee, listening to his self-serving drivel. And it's even worse now that the jerk is dead. They're like lost sheep, warming themselves around his photograph. Have you seen the crap they're publishing? Fortune-cookie filler. Deep down, he must have known, he even wrote them on little slips of paper. Lauren is well out of that revolting scene." At a wide stretch in the road, Thomas edges over to let cars pass. "But even if he wasn't a nothing, even if he was another Buddha, Saskia, the point is, the guru-disciple relationship is inherently unhealthy. I'm glad you understand that. The Buddha never proclaimed any truth, because the forms of truth are incommunicable. He proclaimed only the Way. Truth, he taught, can only be reached by each alone, out of his own experience. And his disciples looked at each other and said, 'Ain't that the truth!'" Shaking his head, Thomas reaccelerates to forty.

"The speed limit here is fifty-five," Lauren said the first time Thomas drove to town, turning to look at the line of cars behind.

"Yes, and the SST is destroying the ozone layer," Thomas countered. "But what does that matter as long as some røvhul can have lunch in New York and dinner in London?"

Thomas and Saskia went down to Ithaca this morning to buy lumber, and to look for the pterodactyl Quentin lost yesterday at the

Farmers' Market. Saskia didn't look hard because she knew Thomas would find it, and he did, and now they're driving back up with the rescued animal on the dashboard. Thomas disapproved instantly of the arrangement at Wholeworld whereby Lauren went alone to the Farmers' Market while Saskia stayed home with the crew. "How are they going to learn anything if you keep them at home?"

"Don't you think they'd be in the way at the market?"

"Only if you don't let them help. We used to have a dozen brats from Wonderland down there. They worked in the field, too."

"Yes . . ." Lauren contemplated the undeniable truth of what he was saying. "But Wonderland also went bankrupt every winter. John was in here so regularly bailing us out I had his next mercy mission circled on the calendar."

Thomas laughed. "And he loved it! You said it yourself, the angel of mercy, Christ among the unwashed. Dispensing his blood money. No doubt he took it off the White Corporation taxes."

So on Saturday morning, Saskia came out of the barn after the milking to find Thomas positioning crates in Betsy, Lauren in the storage shed choosing the next to go, and the crew crabwise carrying them in concert from shed to bed. Thomas left a hyggelig space open behind the cab, and he threw in cushions and asked who wanted to ride down in the back, which turned out to be everybody. But Saskia was too mature to care as much as the youngsters, so she sat in the cab between Thomas and Lauren. At the market, Thomas organized the crew in two shifts, so they could spend half their time working and half wandering. "I don't want to be called a slave driver," he said, with a private wink for Saskia. He deliberately put Austin and Quentin together. He put Austin in charge of the money box (Saskia's old job, but she was too mature to be jealous) and told him that he should also keep a safe eye on his little brother Quentin, who might need his older and wiser brother's help now and then. "Now Quentin," he said, squatting, holding the limp boy upright with palms pressed against his shoulders, "you'll be bagging the things people buy. You'll be the last person to handle them before they go out in the world, so it's up to you that they look good. It's important to be gentle." He stared gravely with his sea-blue eyes into Quentin's watery blue ones, and the boy nodded mutely.

Quentin packed the bags as if every tuber, fruit, and stalk were a vial of nitroglycerin. "He's taking too long," Lauren complained.

"It's a beautiful morning, what's the hurry?" Thomas said. "Look at him! That's mindfulness you would die for." From the first day, Thomas had banned the name Quinny. It sounded, he said, like a cross between "quail" and "cringe." No wonder the kid drooled.

Austin sneered at Quentin a couple of times, but managed to go a whole morning without bopping him. Mim piled the summer squash in an inviting pyramid. Shannon wrote the new signs as closing time approached and they lowered their prices. The Captain at long last was back, restoring the age of right rule, when all worked with a will. By the time they were packing up to go, the crew was begging to come the following week. In the cab on the way back Lauren said, "You were right, it worked just fine."

"It gives you a good feeling," Thomas said. "It feels like a family this way."

"So why didn't Lauren learn her lesson?" Saskia asks, playing with the pterodactyl on the dashboard with her toes. "She's not dumb."

"Not at all. Stubborn, maybe."

"Stubborn," Saskia nods.

"Illogical."

"Very."

Thomas expertly estimates Betsy's momentum and cuts the gas partway up a slope so that she coasts to the top, slowing to a crawl before picking up momentum again on the downward side. The idea is to use the brakes as little as possible, since speed lost in braking must be made up with fuel. Stubborn, illogical Lauren gets an irresponsible fourteen miles to the gallon in Betsy, while Thomas gets a worthy nineteen. "I'll tell you something. Lauren was an abused child. Did you know that?"

"No."

"She can't be as strong as people who were raised by loving parents. At Godhead she was no better than the others. When Truth beat her, she came crawling back for more. I tried to get her off that path. But she couldn't follow me, and after I was gone there was Yogi Bear, playing the same old games." Betsy is careening to the bottom of a hill, rocking on her shocks as she shoots around a curve, ducking her head and gulping as she hits the next incline. She coasts to the top, winking, slowing down to the perfect speed for the right-hand turn toward Tyler's only suburban development. "You'll be more patient with Lauren, I hope."

"Sure!" Poor Lauren!

He touches her shoulder, rubs her neck. Utter contentment.

"You know," he said to her in the barn, his arm holding her tight, "you and I are like crystal. Most people are just glass. The world sings a note to them and they can't feel it. But we hum." Saskia loved that image. "But you have to be careful. You have to know when to stop humming, because crystal will shatter."

That was on his first day back, and when they went out of the barn he circled around to the back and waded through the high grass to the place where the old boat lay upside down in the weeds. Tearing tough vines away from the bow until he could get a grip under to lift it, he dragged it into the short grass. He scraped moss away from the stern. Barely visible there, letters of ghostly white: *Lila.*

All my dogs have been named Lila, he had said.

And all your boats, she had said.

A sturdy wooden boat, lovingly made. But not much compared to the metal *Lila*, whale saver, whaler sinker. And not so sturdy, actually. Saskia looked at the staved-in hull, the gray weathered edges of splintered wood. "She'll take some work to fix," Thomas said, rubbing along her sides with his palms, pausing to tap her here and there like the doctor when he says, "Breathe."

"What happened to her?"

"I hit her a couple of times with a sledgehammer. Before I left." Saskia looked at him blankly. "I built her. I didn't like the idea of someone else sailing around in her."

"There she is," he says as Betsy turns into the cul-de-sac. Jane is standing at the end of her street, barefoot, in cutoffs and halter top. Her thimbles are poking through the thin fabric. He leans across to look past Saskia, through the open window. "Going our way?"

2

Still warm nights of September. Saskia takes her sleeping bag and goose-steps through the high grass down to the lake, where she spreads the bag in clover and crawls in, lies on her back and stares into the night sky. The Discipline is to purge yourself of the illusion that you are looking at "sky," at some dumb dome with stars sprinkled on it. If you concentrate hard enough, you can sense the truth: you are stuck like an aphid on a whirling ball, looking out into the immensities of three-dimensional space. Our galaxy is a disk, our sun a minor star near the edge. You can look up out of the disk into the intergalactic void, or you can peer down the length of the disk, past Cygnus, into the heart of the Milky Way, where clusters and double stars swarm thick as cream. Imagine! You are seeing with your own naked eyes the entire length of the galaxy! God sees the galaxy, and the little sun near its edge, and the pinpoint planet circling the sun, and the infinitesimal speck (God rubs Her eye — is the speck real?) lying on her back looking out from the tiny planet. If that doesn't make your problems feel small, Saskia doesn't know what does.

Back when she was afraid of the dark she always brought a flashlight. But it turned out that was exactly why she was afraid. The whole world was black and she was a shining target. Now when she walks away from the house she simply disappears. Her eyes adjust and she can see fine, but no one can see her. How safe she feels! Lauren came down last night, calling to ask some question, arcing her light, and Saskia could have picked her off so easily.

Life would be so much nicer if Earth were located in the heart of the Milky Way. Every night you would have the blazing spectacle of a million stars brighter than Sirius. Saskia always seems to just miss, like the person who falls out of the plane but fortunately there's a haystack, but unfortunately she misses it. Saskia lives in rainy Tyler instead of sunny Ithaca, in Novamundus instead of Hyperborea, out on a spiral arm of the Milky Way instead of in the center. With her eyes adjusted to the grudging starlight we get out here in the boonies, she looks up the slope toward the house. Mim's dormer is dark. What if she has a nightmare? Who will hear her, help her? But Mim is a bigger girl now. She milks Marilyn every other day and gets off the bus at Tyler Junior with Saskia. The crew's window is also dark. Thomas is so good with them. He really makes them want to work, when it's time to sort paper for recycling or clean out the empty trailer. No need for a Judgment Book. One deep frown from him and Austin gets right back in line. When the work is done he engages in manly play. He shoulders them and sprints up and down the stairs while they shriek. He tells them a story, sitting on the couch with Quentin on his lap, Shannon and Austin under each arm. Even Gorgon likes Thomas. When he inserts his hands under her hyper-sensitive stomach and pitches her off his chair, she refrains from ripping his hand to pieces. "How do you do that?" Saskia marvels.

"Mind control," he says, eyes twinkling.

Opposite Mim's, under the other gable, her own window, dark. Her empty room, her empty bed. Saskia feels a pang. Why is Jane still with Thomas, anyway? It's time to put away summer things. Things that were natural in Hyperborea are not natural here in the land of fathers and mothers together under harmonious roofs. Thomas and Lauren's light is on. What are they doing in there? Is Lauren meditating while Thomas does five hundred pushups? Is Thomas tying insect antennas while Lauren reads? Is Thomas telling Lauren a story, filling her twin-moon eyes with childlike wonder? Is Thomas brushing Lauren's hair, pausing to pull a silver strand out of the tapestry? Or are they doing It? *The inner sanctum, the Eleusinian Mysteries.* Are they making siblings?

But no, that is impossible. "None of our problems can be solved,"

Thomas said to Saskia in the barn, "until we deal with overpopulation. There are almost five billion people on this planet, which is about four billion too many — and I'm being generous. Famine is nature's control. We allow deer the dignity of dying off naturally when they exceed their food supply, but we deny it to people. Sending food aid is cruel in the long run. A thousand babies surviving now mean ten thousand babies dying the next time around. We have to start talking about what no one has the courage to talk about, namely, sterilizing people. One child per couple, no exceptions. I was an only child, and it was good enough for me. You're an only child —" He paused, looking at her.

"Good enough for me," she piped up.

"I had a vasectomy after you were born, the smartest thing I ever did. Otherwise, I'd have illegitimate kids all over the planet." Saskia blushed. Aye, nudge nudge, a woman in every port. Say no more!

But — his tubes are tied! Like Mack or Mick. Still, Jo had Quentin. Jane said that happens sometimes. Saskia must be terribly selfish, she would still like a sibling, after all Thomas has said. Maybe if she got some other couple to agree not to have even one, she would be allowed a brother or a sister.

The house is getting brighter. Saskia turns in her bag to see the Moon rising over the eastern ridge. "There you are." Late again! In Hyperborea, Saskia especially missed the Moon. She throws back the top of her bag to bask in the gentle motherly milk light. She certainly would not take her shirt off. If you bare your breasts to the Moon, they will grow. If only she could figure out what the opposite of that might be.

The Moon rises later every night, eternally getting left behind by the sun. When the sun first leaves her, she begins to gain weight, the jilted bride consoling herself by pigging out. By the time the sun is at the farthest point from her, she is a real fatso. But she starts to slim down again as the sun comes nearer, hoping against hope that he will tarry, that he will orbit her. She becomes svelter and svelter, a "little slip of a thing," a strung bow, boyish like a nymph, and like a nymph she then dissolves, now you see me, now you

Then the sun leaves her again and the cycle starts all over. *That* old story! How depressing! Tonight she's in the middle of one of her drastic dieting phases, but she's still fairly blimpy, poor thing. She is haloed by her veil. Her bridal train sparkles all the way across Cayuga's waters. Hope springs eternal.

3

Saskia stands in front of her mirror in the morning and wonders how on earth she can make boys like her better. If she were at a plastic surgeon's, she would unpocket a list that would unroll to the floor and continue out into the reception room.

1. Forehead: reduce by half (add leftover bone to femurs); sand down two hideous chicken pox scars above right eyebrow.
2. Eyebrows: beef up, bushify; insert sweep.
3. Eyes: enlarge; replace shit-brown irises with glowing lapis lazuli ones.
4. Nose: aquilinize.
5. Lips: redden, soften, moisten.
6. Teeth: straighten, with pliers if necessary; close hideous gap between upper right canine and upper right bicuspid.
7. Skin: darken, smoothen, silken; if necessary, resort to skin grafts from one Jane Sing, Tylerian resident.
8. Hair: forget it, start all over again, reorder seedlings from the catalogue; ghastly mistake in shipment.

She can start by washing sweet Marilyn out of her hair. The first time Jane entered the barn at Wholeworld she wrinkled her nose, betraying — so early! — her talents as a siren, her uncanny ability to discern what boys like and don't like. Since Thomas returned, the only soap allowed in the house is the candle-wax soap they used in Hyperborea, and the only shampoo is a liquid version of it, so Saskia crushes greenhouse lavender in a pestle and steeps it in hot oil, lets it sit in a jar for a week and then dribbles it on her head with a dollop of shampoo in the shower. She steps out, her hair smelling like a Greek hillside in the summer sun where manly shepherds drowse. She combs it out while blow-drying it, so it won't frizz into its usual electron cloud, but instead becomes quasi-straight, marginally thicker-looking. A judicious arrangement in the front helps hide the half-dome forehead.

Clothes are a problem. She needs longer, drapier sweaters. She needs svelte dark rust-stitched jeans like Jane's. She needs high-top space-age sneakers, pointy elf boots, cobalt pumps, thigh-high black leather leg huggers. Her brown blunt-nosed bootish shoes make her look like she's on her way to a hoedown. She needs earrings to go in the holes she had bored through her earlobes last week at an Ithacan mall. She needs baubles and bangles she can slide up and down her arms.

But all this requires money. The blow dryer alone blew everything she had saved, plus some she borrowed from Jane, whose allowance is precisely ten times her own. Saskia asked Lauren if she could have a raise, and was turned down flat. You balance the books, you ought to know blah blah bitch moan. It's embarrassing. Most of Saskia's pocket money ever since she met Jane has been Jane's. "Share the wealth" is what Jane says. You have to hand it to her, she is a good-hearted person.

But obviously, Wholeworld needs another source of income. All the other ex-communes in the area seem to have struck it rich by marketing some wholesome outgrowth of hippie culture: natural honeys, yogurts, handmade baskets. So what's left for Wholeworld? Garlic-braiding?

Hair, clothes, money. Things to worry about. Sometimes she is still brushing in front of the mirror, frustrated almost to tears, when the Täbe hits the horn and she has to grab her stuff and run. The crew is on board, well breakfasted by Thomas, looking incuriously at her as she comes up the steps. "Morning, Chief," says the Täbe as she passes with her straight Greek-island hair.

"Morning, Tåbe." Without another word he hauls the door shut and turns up the hill. Oblivious as always.

4

She walks through the gloomy halls with a measured, graceful step. She no longer makes detours to avoid the knots of brayers. Instead she walks by them, head high, eyes forward, unflinching. She does not turn toward whispers or snorts, she merely continues on her way, a half-smile playing over her lips as if to say with worldly tolerance, "Boys will be boys."

She does not hurry to class. When the bell rings she makes no sign of having heard it, she merely continues on her measured way to the door and opens it, unquailing. If the teacher makes noises at her about being late, she shrugs, and apologizes politely, opaquely. The teacher, red-faced, insisting on explanations, looks the fool, not she, who merely acknowledges she is indeed late, but really, is it so important, after all, when this earth will probably not even be here for our grandchildren? Oh, come now. She takes her seat in the back of the class and never raises her hand. She tries not to remember her front-row antics of last year, the arm-waving, the lizardy squeaking about something on the board. She can hardly distinguish one teacher from another. They are shades, moaning about dead things. She writes haiku, or works on The Eye. When called on, she shrugs. Haven't you been listening? they ask. No, she says.

Jane sits in the back, too, and they exchange a slow siren glance. Yes, Jane and Saskia are still friends. They sometimes sit together at lunch. Often Saskia hasn't bothered to bring anything, so Jane gives her something out of her generous Sing Sing pack. "But that's not enough," Jane says. Saskia waves away her concerns.

Jane is soberer now, more prudent. Saskia understands that she is trying to be the Perfect Companion for Thomas. She takes a lot of things seriously. Though she sits in the back, she pays attention. She doesn't raise her hand, but when called on she answers correctly. "It's a waste of energy to fight battles you can't win," she explained to Saskia, as if Saskia hadn't already heard Thomas say it in exactly the same words.

At Sing Sing long-suffering Mrs. Sing cooks a vegetarian alternative for Jane, who lectures the rest of the family about the evils of eating meat. Mr. and Mrs. Sing trade an abashed look as they chomp on their mutton, severing tendons. But they loved her letters from Hyperborea. "You've matured so much," Mr. Sing grunts after Jane does something slyly considerate for him like getting his pipe. "You've become quite a grown-up young lady." He brims with self-satisfaction. Jane curtseys. With a trowel . . . Of course, the Sings have put two and two together. The letters from Hyperborea mentioned Thomas frequently, and now here's Jane, a different girl. "The more time I spend at your place, the more they like it," she laughs to Saskia. "My mother said, 'Thomas really turned you around!' I can't wait till the day we tell them the whole story!" The Sings put two and two together and got three.

Walking half smiling past boys is not enough, though. You have to actually have something to do with them. Saskia has stood at the edges of their knots and listened to their unbelievably stupid conversation. It appears to be driven principally by driveling one-upmanship, toadyism, and sadistic mob instinct. She lets its foulness wash over her. This is good for her. One of them half turns and challenges, fixing her with a BB eye: "What do you want, White?" She stares back at him opaquely for a long silent moment, until he becomes disconcerted. "Just listening," she counters coolly. In fact, they don't bray at her. They turn away, letting her stand there. The Walk is already having its effect.

Or is it The Voice? Saskia has suppressed the squeak. She has found that as long as she forces herself to speak slowly, her voice naturally comes out lower. She has been working lately on a husky edge, although it's rather hard when you don't smoke. She breaks in one day laughing, low and lustrous. One of the boys has been ragging another about something faggoty he did in English class. "Warner didn't even notice," she says throatily. "What a shithead!" OK, so it won't go into her Collected Sayings. But again, though the comment passes unacknowledged, the pack does not turn on her. She stands at the edge, straight-haired, Greek-scented, not rejected.

Her ultimate weapon is The Eye, currently in production. She tests a prototype on one of the better-looking boys, not a ringleader but not a loser-type outcast either, a midlevel brayer named Paul Potyondy. Sitting in class at his four o'clock, she turns it on him. You will look at me, young Paul. You will wonder what is tugging and you will turn. Yes, Master . . . Yes, Master . . . His gaze twitches like a fly in a web. It twitches right, starts back toward the front but stops, drifts back right and farther right. Saskia reels him in mercilessly. His head swivels. He looks at her, frozen, a deer in her headlights. She pours on the juice, radiating him with a lethal dose. He glances away. Too late, my young friend. Your skin cells are ruptured, reddening.

5

It's wasteful to keep your lamp burning at night, so she doesn't write anymore when she can't sleep, but practices entrancing herself with waking dreams, sitting cross-legged on her pillow with thumbs and middle fingers forming egg-shaped holes, beginning with a soft hum of "om" and a koan: How do you wake from a waking dream?

She tunes in like a crystal radio to the non-Novamundian plane. "Friend!" she intones in the prescribed greeting on the Hyperborean frequency. "Friend!" echoes faintly the voice of Tycho, crackling across the ether. She holds out her hand as he stretches forward with his and he splits the fabric of space, grasping her hand and pulling her off the bed through the black window into his world.

He is sartorially correct in doublet, Spanish ruff and slashed sleeves, pointy leather shoes with cork soles. On a gold chain around his neck hangs the Order of the Whale, bestowed on him by the grateful King Frederick II (father of the unwise Christian IV, who would squander his kingdom's money on foolish wars and take it all out on Tycho). He is balding, bullet-headed, not handsome, not tall. He endearingly touches the bridge of his nose to make sure it is still on, before leading her through viridian fields. Ignorant peasants veer away with fearful glances, crossing themselves.

He built Uraniborg at the exact center of the island, in a square enclosure of earthen mounds. As Tycho and Saskia approach, the slavering English mastiffs guarding the gate break into barking, announcing their arrival. Saskia flies her usual sable, baston sinister, et cetera. Tycho flies the arms of Brahe: sable, a pale, argent.

"What's the password?" the lackey calls down.

"It's your lord, you fool!" Tycho growls, adjusting his sword belt meaningfully. The lackey descends bowing and scraping, and murmurs cravenly as he opens the gate. Inside all is classical order and repose: an apple orchard, and in its middle a flower garden, and in the midst of the garden, Uraniborg.

How to describe that magical castle? Think of an illustration of a gentleman's summerhouse-cum-spaceship in a Jules Verne book that Saskia has read. Now take away Victorian froufrou and add dignified Renaissance whimsy. The square central structure is flanked by round towers topped with cones that can be folded back to reveal sextants, azimuthal quadrants, armillary spheres. The windows are crosshatched with diamond quarrels and topped with scrolled capitals. From the roof sprout obelisks and little cupolas, and in the middle there's an octagonal belvedere crowned with a clock tower, and at the top of the tower flutters a weathervane of pure gold: Cetus exhalant. Historians record that Uraniborg was made of unpainted brick and sandstone, but the building crouching muscularly before Saskia ready to spring heavenward is undeniably white, green, and pink. Why? Tycho shrugs: "I liked the look of it."

The door springs open under his hand. They ascend to the second floor, and on to the third, where even Saskia must stoop under the low ceiling. Here are the cramped garrets where the Disciples live. They crouch over their desks, pinching the bridges of their noses in scholarly fatigue. Tycho indicates a narrow staircase in the attic gloom and he and Saskia, hand in hand, mount the holy stairs, rising through the floor into an octagonal space with windows all around, a space soaked with the milky light of a million stars. She can see in all directions at once, across the fields of Ven to the still glow of the ocean waters, stretching boundless to the horizons. "So many stars!" she breathes.

"I was sick and tired of Arabs naming them all."

The crystal-clear air, the blazing stars, the strangely still waters. "The ocean is all ice," she says in awe. "We're at the North Pole! We're at the center of the Circle!"

"The center, yes. But not the North Pole."

She looks again at the fields of snow, the boundless ice, the strange and strangely brilliant stars. "There is no Wagon," she whispers, a shiver snaking down her back. "No Hunter. No Herdsman." She looks at the Lord of the Seagirt Isle. "We are not on Earth."

"No."

"Where?"

"A planet called Hyperbores. It is always night here."

The stars swarm thick as cream. Saskia whispers, "We are at the center of the galaxy."

"Yes." He drops a heavy hand on her shoulder. "I name the stars here." He points to a supernova: "Tycho." To a star haloed by ice crystals in the arctic air: "Mim." To a dying giant of shifting colors: "Lauren." To a double: "Austin and Shannon." To a weak fourth magnitude, guttering: "Quentin." To a white dwarf: "Saskia."

She breathes in self-satisfaction like pure oxygen. "Listen!" He stretches his hand out. "Do you hear it?" No. And then yes. A sound so octaves-deep it is more felt than heard. It feels like Earth as a young girl turning deep in her sleep, deep down in her core, turning to find a more comfortable position. But they are not on Earth. "The crystal spheres," Tycho whispers, his lips unmoving. He stiffens. His eyes roll up into his head. He begins to vibrate. And through his hand now like stone on her shoulder his vibrations enter her. Her eyes roll up in her head. Together at the center of the galaxy Master and Disciple stand frozen, vibrating to the music of the spheres.

"Om." Her eyes unroll. "Om." She is shivering from the cold. "Om." She is sitting cross-legged on her bed.

6

In the basement, the trays of hemp and the doodah lights are gone, and in their place well-oiled wholesome woodworking tools stand ankle-deep in wholesome good-smelling shavings. In the garage, *Lila* stretches upside down across two sawhorses, and Thomas positions the wood that he cut and planed with his own hands and folds it gently along the curve of the hull as Saskia sits and admires the sensuous curve in the grain of the wood.

Thomas and Saskia have taught the crew how to recycle more, but recycling is not really a solution, Thomas says. It's like putting a band-aid on a malignant tumor. Ninety percent of what we use, we should not use. We must "reduce the waste stream." As much as a pure river of ichor is good, so is the waste stream bad, the stinking sewer down which we are all flowing to hell. Wholeworld goes beyond wood-pulp toilet paper to washable cloths. "This combines the best of Christian and Islamic traditions," Thomas says. "Doesn't waste paper as the Christians do, and uses less water than the Muslim method." He puts out one cloth per person, each hanging in a ring in a row by the bowl. "Like napkin rings," Saskia says brightly, fighting down her infidel and unenlightened disgust. Paper towels disappear as well, and tissue paper, and wax paper. Cloths festoon the kitchen, handkerchiefs are made from Lauren's sewing scraps, food is wrapped in a reusable chintz-like material. Thomas decrees a complete embargo on the import of plastic into Wholeworld. Most plastic cannot be recycled, which proves it's evil, and people did fine without it until this century, which also proves it's unnecessary. At the veggie co-op soaps, oils, nut butters, vinegars, herbs, and teas can all be bought in bulk, drained from a spigot into glass jars brought from home, and returned home clinking in bags of netted jute.

For Quentin's birthday Saskia intended to buy him another dinosaur, but it turns out all the dinosaurs in Ithaca are plastic except for some expensive ones in a doodah store in the pedestrian zone that Thomas determines are made of teak, and you can't buy teak because of something about rain forests and the world gene bank. So there she is, dinosaurless. Thomas encourages her to make one for Quentin, pointing out how dependent we are on this prepackaged society where even our birthday cards are written by someone else. He is right, but unfortunately the stegosaurus that Saskia painfully constructs out of wire and clay is kind of a mess. The tail falls off while Quentin is unwrapping it, and Saskia is crushed. Fortunately Thomas saves the day by producing from behind his back a diplodocus, egg-smooth and elegant. He carved it from a limb that fell off one of the apple trees, stained it with walnut juice, and waxed it with beeswax. Everyone oohs and ahhs, Quentin is thrilled, and Saskia's pathetic failure is forgotten.

Lauren already uses natural stuff in the garden, but Thomas extends the ban on death-dealing chemicals throughout Wholeworld. The use of chemical cleaners never mattered much before because only Saskia cleaned things in the house, and even she did it rarely because no matter what she picked, she always found that it hadn't been cleaned since some previous geological era, probably the First Thomas Age. Now in the Second Thomas Age a huge project is under way to swab the decks from stem to stern. Thomas introduces the crew (who await his orders round-eyed, armed with mops and rags) to a cleaning solution made out of water, baking soda, and vinegar. The furniture polish is vegetable oil and lemon juice.

Energy is also part of the waste stream, and in this area Novamundians are particularly egregious sinners. Thomas points out that the refrigerator probably accounts for about eighty-five percent of the electricity consumption at Wholeworld, since they don't have a TV or a stereo or a radio, or a clothes dryer, or a dishwasher, or an iron, or a toaster, or a mixmaster, or a garbage disposal, and all the clocks are the kind you wind. Thomas says that the way to reduce the consumption of the refrigerator is to never hold the door open for more than a few seconds. If the same item is always put in the same place in the refrigerator, then you always know where it is and can get it quickly. Thomas draws a life-size diagram that shows where on which shelf everything should go and tapes it on the refrigerator door. Saskia is amazed at the way you can look at the diagram and then open the door and see everything inside exactly as the diagram promised it would be. It's like Newtonian physics: the diagram is the set of simple laws, and the contents of the refrigerator are the proof that they are correct. She finds this very comforting.

Thomas and Lauren together are a joy to see, the way she listens to him, the way he praises her. When he first inspected the greenhouse he turned at the end to sum up and said, weighing each word like a nugget of gold, "You have done an excellent job here," and Lauren swelled. Saskia watched them in the vegetable field through Thomas's binoculars: Thomas walking meditatively from row to row with Lauren beside him. He pointed, asked questions, then walked on, nodding, as Lauren gave him the information he needed. Then they stood at the edge of the field and it was his turn to speak, and he spoke for a long time, his beautiful hands making gestures that showed her just what he meant, and Lauren listened, really listened, without interrupting, without veering the conversation off in her own stubborn and illogical direction.

At dinner good cheer reigns. Saskia no longer has to discipline the crew. Lauren sits straight-backed and regal at one end and Thomas perches, leaning forward, at the other, and they are the two posts that hold up the harmonious roof. Even Jo wakes from her trance and seems to realize there are other people in the room. The relationship between Thomas and Jo is not the one Saskia would have expected. She kind of pictured him taking one look at Jo — her sour sunless face, her nicotine teeth, her dazed TV eyes — and drawing back in horror, tracing Earth-protective signs in the air. Jo would promptly disappear in a puff of cigarette smoke, her clothes fluttering to the ground in a heap.

But it hasn't turned out that way. Thomas and Jo acknowledge each other's existence. When Jo lights up at the table, Thomas coughs and hacks, flails his hands, and says, "Jesus, Jo!" and she looks at him, holding the elbow of her cigarette arm, and calmly rasps, "Oh go fuck yourself." Jo never smiles, she looks at him with her eyes hooded and dead, but the strangest thing is, Saskia gets the distinct impression that she is having fun. Once, spying from behind a door-jamb, Saskia even saw Thomas take the cigarette out of Jo's mouth and put it in his own. "No," he said, wagging his head, handing the butt back, "I don't get it. It tastes like death."

"That's why I like it, Tom."

"You're too deep for me, Jo."

"You wanna talk about deep, go sit on a carrot."

Perhaps Thomas sees most people as poor victims to win over from the enemy, whereas he sees Jo as the enemy herself. And you have to get to know your enemy. Or maybe he is just fascinated by Jo as the essence of anti-Thomasness.

After dinner comes the storytelling. On the couch in the common room the crew collects under Thomas's arms like Brussels sprouts on the stalk, while Lauren hogs the armchair close by and Saskia pulls up the rocker. His stories begin, "A long time ago, when Mother Earth was still a young girl . . ." They involve wolves and whales, eagles, foxes and ravens, wise animals and gentle people roaming unspoiled forests and sailing unspoiled seas. When spoilers appear, they threaten convincingly for a while, but are ultimately dispatched satisfyingly. Thus fiction for children improves on the reality adults must face: the fat slime-mold harpooner would be smeared all over the end of a tale told to the crew.

"What mankind needs is a new Earth-centered religion," Thomas said in the barn. "But not this warm and fuzzy New Age goddess worship. We need something brutal. A matriarchal spin on the Old Testament eye-for-an-eye: an Earth goddess who says, 'Look pal, if you drink my blood, I'll suck yours right out of your veins. You eat my body, and I'll devour you raw.' We need maenads again to descend periodically on the male principle and tear it to pieces. Power and fear. The devouring womb. That's all men understand."

Tycho argues for an Earth-centered view, too. It's simple to prove that Copernicus is wrong: if the Earth were turning, Tycho says, then a weight dropped from a high tower would land some distance from the base. Since this does not happen, then obviously the Earth does not turn. According to the Tychonic system, the sun, the Moon, and the fixed stars revolve around the Earth, whereas all the other planets revolve around the sun. Copernicus gets all the press, just like Greenpeace, but the Copernican system was no simpler than the Ptolemaic one. The Tychonic system fit the observable facts *better* than the Copernican, because Tycho actually bothered to take measurements, while Copernicus never held a sextant in his life and wouldn't have known his ass from an astrolabe. You probably didn't know that.

When the story ends, Thomas claps his hands. "To bed now! Quick! Goodnight kisses in two minutes!" The crew bolts for the stairs. Thomas and Lauren and Saskia make the final rounds, assuring themselves that everything is shipshape. As Saskia snaps on each light, each room shows itself to be tidy and clean, cobwebless, dustless. Every nook and cranny and alcove and corner sparkles with vegetable oil and smells of lemon juice. In the dining room the chandelier shines like ship's brass and the two-ton table glows oakishly.

An island of sanity in this insane world. Lock the doors! Raise the drawbridge! The castle Wholeworld flies sable, a globe vigilant, azure. Thomas and Lauren and Saskia mount the stairs together. Everyone now is on an early schedule because it makes better use of daylight.

7

"Hey Jeffrey, how was your date last night?" says Bob Roszak.

Jeffrey ducks his head and smiles. He goes, "Huh, huh, huh," bobbing his head.

"Did you get some, Jeffrey? Did you get in her pants?" Phil, Tony, Brad, Marie, and Monica make a sound as rhythmic as cicadas, a group snickering.

Jeffrey shakes his head, smiling. "No, huh, huh."

"But you're such a stud, Jeffrey!" Bob glances around at his entourage, checking for inattention. "All the girls are hot for you." Marie's and Monica's jeans are so tight they get triangle infections. They told Saskia that in the opium den. "Look, Jeffrey, look!" Sue Terwilliger is waddling down the corridor, her short arms buoyed outward by her mercilessly convex body, her little hands like five-pointed stars because the fat between the fingers keeps them sprung apart. "It's Sue Tarantula. She was telling me yesterday how hot she was for you." Fat Sue Terwilliger and retard Jeffrey Watzman, fumbling animalistically in some dark corner. The image stimulates Bob's group to new heights of snickering, a greedy gasping sound of trough-snuffling.

All of this will end, Saskia vows silently. When my people come.

Her infiltration continues. It has turned out to be easier than she ever would have imagined. The fact that the teachers already hated her was a big point in her favor. She merely had to fine-tune the reasons for their hatred and cross that mysterious line beyond which misfitdom suddenly turns cool. A scant week ago she was still hovering barely tolerated at the edges of groups in which a brayer might turn and fire a salvo at her to see if she jumped or ran or, worst of all, said something uncool. Saskia knows well what is not cool: making mysterious hand motions and informing people they are cursed to the seventh generation is not cool. You might say it is the epitome of uncoolness. But she still is not sure what *is* cool. Most of what the certifiably cool people say seems asinine to her. Fortunately, not answering but simply staring opaquely while a half-smile plays over her lips seems to qualify as adequately cool. The tåbes can't tell that Saskia is panicking inwardly, wondering if she's about to blow her cover.

Anyway, a week ago one of the most craven and mean of the toadies decided once again to test if Saskia's position was weak enough so that he could roll forward and crush her under his puny treads, protected by the sixteen-inch guns behind him. "Why are you hanging around, White?" he whined, sliding his eyes to right and left. His name was Marty and he survived by butt-licking the Bob Roszaks and Doug Maxners of this sinful world. "Why don't you buzz off?" He made buzzing sounds and waved in her face. (This illustrates the language problem. Who could possibly guess that something like that might be cool?) And then the amazing thing happened. Dexter Jordan, the coolest guy in Tyler Junior, the guy who lives in the crumbling Queen Anne behind the cemetery all alone with a grandmother nobody ever sees, who runs his own business employing classmates to clean people's houses, who led the Tyler Tigers to crushing victory at the all-county junior high basketball championships, the guy who punched out the hulking psycho Richie Fisch, the guy who is so cool he can utterly ignore Bob Roszak and Doug Maxner, who is so cool he can have Sharon Fells as his girlfriend and wait for her after school even though she wears Eleanor Roosevelt glasses and gets straight A's, the guy who is so cool he could actually *sing the lead* in the spring play last year and still be universally acknowledged as far and away numero uno on the coolness scale, whose singing the lead in the spring play last year led to the Tyler Junior High School chorus having more boys in it this year than it had ever had in its entire history — yes, he, Dexter Jordan, stopped at that moment on his way from triumph A to triumph B and said to Marty, "You leave Saskia alone. She's OK." And then walked on, not looking back, leaving them all staring after him with their mouths open, turning to look at Saskia with their mouths gaping like halibuts, afloat in confusion. After that, the circles opened silently for her.

"Hey Tarantula!" Bob brays. "You want Jeffrey to fuck you, right? Wasn't that what you were telling me the other day?" Sue quickens her waddle and passes, keeping her eyes hard alee. The V.P.'s face swells as he bellows at Saskia and Jane for passing notes, yet he neglects to enclose Bob's neck in his halfback hands and hammer his head against the trophy case. No wonder the Observatory is sending its best agents to this benighted planet.

Saskia is one of them because she is such an amazingly quick learner. A scant week after the Dexter Jordan breakthrough she is already realizing that being accepted in every braying group is not the Way to real coolness. That way Martyness lies. Bob Roszak is beneath Dexter Jordan's contempt, so why shouldn't he be beneath Saskia's? The crucial thing is not to gravitate toward the center but to *become* the center, to exert your own gravitational force. By chasing coolness, we fall ever farther behind it, yet if we stop and turn away, lo, coolness is there.

"I gotta go," Saskia says in a bored tone to Marie and Monica. "See you." She ignores the boys. They call after her, "Later, Saskia!" and she casually raises one listless hand without looking back.

She has borrowed more money from Jane and bought face lard, which she keeps in her locker and applies in the opium den, removing it before she gets on the bus in the afternoon. She watched Monica do a touch-up job and extrapolated the technique. "My old man," Saskia said, stroking black onto the insect antennas rimming the bottom of each eye, "has a conniption if he sees me with this. I have to keep it here because he fucking pokes around in my room."

"Mine's just the same," Monica said, an inch from the mirror, pinkie-probing an eye corner of glittering green. "My mother was normal, she showed me, when I was like ten. But my dad says I look like a hooker, and I'm like, 'Fuck you!' But I didn't say it." Monica laughed. She was always quoting her røvhul dad and giggling as if to say, Come on, folks, there's only so much I can take seriously.

Monica and Marie are both ninth graders. Saskia never misses an opportunity to talk with them in the opium den. Both girls have tumbling masses of just-out-of-bed brown hair. All the face lard and eye goop is perhaps an attempt to give their small pale chinless faces a ghost of a chance of competing with the storm systems swirling around them. "You were so weird last year," Monica says. "I mean, no offense or anything."

"A phase." Saskia shrugs. "You know how it is."

That, by the way, is an excellent all-purpose comment whenever you can't think of anything else to say, because no one ever answers, "No, I don't know how it is." The Captain has a corresponding phrase, which he uses whenever his mind goes blank during trivial high-society balls and meetings with the stupid Admiralty: "Your Excellency is too kind."

Marie has a pocket-sized tape player which she fetches out of her turquoise leatherette purse and puts on the radiator in the den so that they can make up their faces to the head-bashing beat of Satanic Silk, her and Monica's favorite group. The lead singer, Andy Devereux (compared to whom Marie and Monica have crew cuts), just got married to some Hollywood bombshell and Marie is achingly sure the woman is going to stomp on Andy's heart. The cover story of this month's *Pulse* is all about how she still has a thing for Brian De-mondo, the drummer for The Queen's Hangmen, who is currently on trial for beating a fan into a coma.

> I had a girl
> a sex machine
> but she wouldn't shut up
> so I pulled her plug
> now conversation's easy
> she nods at everything I say
> hey hey hey
>   (backup vocals:)
>   You should try it toooo . . . !

Thus Andy. Monica and Marie dance in the area between the stalls and the sinks, doing a kind of front and back jig-step with a wave from butt to shoulder and heads snapping right and left. Their gum snaps, too, as they chew rhythmically, frown, and droop their lips like Jo. "Woah, woah, woah!" Saskia tries imitating it and throws in a couple of leg-lift twirls, courtesy of the Naked Reconciliation Dance. "You're pretty good," Monica nods. She crosses her wrists as if she were handcuffed, bobs her jean-squeezed butt far out behind her, and bites her lip, "Oh, oh, oh!"

Monica is Bob Roszak's girlfriend. Saskia has an uneasy feeling they do some pretty voksen things together. She glimpsed Bob kissing her behind the dumpster and came away with the vivid impression that Monica's shirt was unbuttoned. That image fluoresced in her mind for days. But she knows they haven't done It, because Monica mentioned one day, while teasing her bangs, that Bob wanted her "to go all the way" but she wasn't sure.

"Do you love him?" Marie asked.

"Sure I love him."

"Well that's all that counts."

They all nodded. But Saskia wasn't sure whether Marie's statement constituted a yes or a no vote.

Saskia draws the line at smoking cigarettes or hemp. There was a big debate about this in Infiltration 101 — whether, if the Mission would otherwise be imperiled, it would be acceptable to go so blatantly against the Way. Saskia successfully argued that in nearly all cases you can extricate yourself from the dilemma. To Monica and Marie she says, "Don't you care about what that's doing to your lungs? I smoked like a factory last year and it got so I couldn't walk up the stairs without sounding like I was going to hawk up a hairball."

"Oh gross!"

"Saskia!"

"Not for me, no thanks. I'm on the wagon." She dips a finger into an unguent and rubs black pain-of-the-world under her eyes. Long ago she wondered if refusing to smoke was barnish or more voksen than smoking. Now she doesn't bother to wonder, she *makes* it more voksen. That's what it means to become the center. It's your gravitational field, you make your own rules.

"Yeah," Marie says, sighing on a smoke stream. "You're right, but . . ." She shrugs. "The way I look at it is, life's a bitch and then you die."

"Fair enough, girl," Saskia says.

"I didn't know you smoked last year," Monica says.

"All the time! In the woods."

"Didn't you use to be friends with Jane Sing?"

Saskia hesitates. "Yeah."

"She seems like a real dweeb to me."

Saskia is putting together a Novamundian-Phaiakian dictionary, as an aid for other operatives. "Dweeb" apparently means a person who is not as thoroughly despicable as a "scuz" or a "scag," but who, by virtue of blatantly uncool behavior, is well outside the circle of conceivable acquaintances, in the darkness beyond the penumbra in which "dinks" dimly dwell. "Oh," Saskia says, speaking honeyed words, "Jane's not so bad. She's kind of weird, that's all."

"Kind of," Marie sneers. "She's from another planet."

"She still follows me around. I haven't got the heart to tell her to buzz off." Saskia is finished.

"Let's see," Monica says. She and Marie put their heads together. "It's funny. I never would've thought last year you were pretty. I mean, no offense or anything. You look real nice."

"Yeah," Marie chimes in. "You look real good." They snap their gum as if to add exclamation points. Saskia is planning in her next report to urge clemency for these two.

8

At the point in autumn when the leaves seem to burn on the maple trees, when every night Saskia hears geese *wong-king* south again, there dawns a day when *Lila* is done, a celebratory sunny day, a Sunday, on which Thomas puts down his tools to rest. She sits upright on a sling in the garage, her hull egg-smooth and eco-green, her gunnels and benches refinished, her name in newly white letters across the stern.

Jane and Saskia and the crew and Thomas carry her out into the cool sunshine, Thomas barking orders to watch the bow and lift the stern higher. They struggle with her through the high grass down to the water's edge, where a floating dock that has been in pieces in the barn for years (Saskia always wondered what those pallets were) has been reassembled by Thomas, and while he and Jane wade wincing into the cold water, Saskia and the crew scuttle onto the dock, bending lower until *Lila* touches the surface, lightens, floats. She rocks gently, li-la, li-la. Thomas and Jane run in to change into dry clothes, and then Thomas brings down the rudder under his arm, and after that the mast on his shoulder. Lauren lugs the sails. Thomas takes Lauren on a guided tour of the boat, explaining how he solved this problem or that, how he replaced this piece with that other one, how he saved time by this process and money by that one. As he talks, he hoists the mast until it drops into its block, attaches a yardarm, and hooks various wires around the gunnels. He slips the rudder into a holding thingy at the stern and does some complicated tying and tugging with ropes and sails. Then stands for a moment, surveying his perfect creation.

"Where's my crew?" he calls. Saskia and Jane start forward. He waves them back. "The others first. Quentin! Mim! Austin! Shannon!" Boing, boing, boing, boing. The four heads pop up in order, the bodies come running. Saskia had no idea what a tight crew was. Thomas hands them in. "Are we ready?"

"Aye aye!"

He pulls from an inner pocket a bottle that sparkles in the light. He kneels next to Mim in the bow. "Spring water," he explains to the enthralled crowd. He leans out over the bow, intoning, "I rechristen you *Lila*," and pours the pure bubbly onto the eco-green. "Cast off!"

Jane and Saskia undo the ropes and throw them aboard, Thomas pushes off and waggles the rudder, *Lila* noses away from the dock. Thomas hauls on a rope and with a slithering shiver the mainsail rises like a finger pointing heavenward, Look! It catches the north wind and presto! is impregnated by it. The yardarm swings, *Lila* heels and accelerates. On the dock, the girls applaud.

Lauren turns to go back to the garden. "There's some squash I absolutely have to get in. You'll call me when he comes back to get us?"

"Sure."

Jane and Saskia watch her go. "She's mellowed out a lot," Saskia observes.

"You think so? I think she's gotten worse."

"You're just jealous."

Jane guffaws. "Of what?"

"If you don't know, I'm certainly not going to tell you."

Of course they are still friends. But it is strange having a friend you can't think of much to say to. That particular problem has not improved one iota since "the morning after" by the river of ichor. If anything, it has gotten worse, since Jane is now cheating on Lauren. Saskia's moral disapproval hangs between them like a silent black cloud.

They sit in the grass. Jane pulls a tall blade and chews on it. They both watch *Lila* in the distance. When Jane comes to Wholeworld for the weekend, Friday afternoon is taken up with homework and Saturday is filled first with the Farmers' Market and then with various cleaning assignments. On Sunday an awkward time or two is unavoidable, but Thomas invariably rescues the girls by taking them together into the barn, where they sit in the hay and listen to him. Saskia watches his hands, hums with his voice. When she leaves she usually helps Lauren in the garden. "Where's Jane?" Lauren asks.

"Taking a nap."

Lauren smirks. "Again?"

"I see you hanging around with Monica and Marie," Jane says, breaking the silence. She works the blade of grass around in her mouth. I'm oral, she said once. I'm terrible!

"Yeah."

"So . . ." Jane tries to speak nonchalantly. "How are they?"

"OK." They go back to watching *Lila*. She has turned and appears to be heading back toward the dock.

"So do you talk about me? With Monica and Marie?"

Would Jane rather hear "yes" or "no"? "No," Saskia guesses.

"Good." Jane spits out the blade and pulls another, begins to chomp on it. "They don't like me."

"You think?"

"I know. They think I'm a scag."

"No." A dweeb, actually.

"And you really like them? What do you talk about?"

Saskia shrugs. "Just things."

Jane throws away the blade and gets up, buries her hands in her pockets, returns to the dock. You can see how awkward it is.

Lila is coasting in, the sail dropping to be hugged by Austin and Shannon, Mim jumping from the bow to the dock to secure the rope. "Next!" Thomas calls.

"I steered!" Quentin says to Saskia as she comes onto the dock.

"And he did a great job," Thomas adds.

"Why couldn't I steer?" Austin asks.

"Next time." Thomas waves Saskia and Jane forward. "Where's Lauren?"

"She went back to the garden." Jane says. "I don't know why."

"She told me to get her," Saskia says.

"She can't wait around for ten minutes?"

"I guess not."

Thomas frowns. "The best way to appreciate a well-made boat is to watch her sail. I wish *I* could stay on the dock and watch her."

"Yeah, *Lila* looked really nice," Saskia says.

"We stayed right here," Jane chimes in.

"Someone go get Lauren, then," Thomas grumbles. Saskia turns. "No, forget her. We'll go without her."

"I think she wants to go, though."

"If she won't wait for me, why should I twiddle my thumbs waiting for her? Come on, get in." He waves them forward. "Sit there. Jane, you sit there." He shoves off. "What is she doing in the garden?"

"She said she had to get some squash in," Saskia says.

"Oh, the squash!" He bounces a palm off his forehead. "Well that explains it. Everyone knows the sky falls if you don't get the squash in." He throws a lever next to the centerboard trunk amidships and the centerboard drops like a guillotine. He yanks on a rope and hauls the sail up by its neck. It bloats like a corpse in the breeze. They head toward the opposite shore in gelatinous silence. "Can you tell how well she's sailing?" Thomas says abruptly.

"Sure," Saskia says.

"Can you? Do you know anything about sailing?"

"A little, I guess."

"How can you tell?" *Lila* is so different from the Captain's boats. She has no poop, no waist, no foremast or mizzenmast or topsails or topgallants or royals. The Captain talks about an overloaded boat feeling sluggish. It's very bad if a cargo shifts. Or if the cargo is rice and it gets wet. Lee shores are also a major problem.

"What about you, Jane? Do you know anything about sailing?"

He didn't give Saskia enough time! "Not really," Jane says, copping out.

"So as far as you girls are concerned, we could be out here in a bathtub, am I right?"

"A bathtub would sink," Saskia says.

"Would it?"

"It's made out of metal."

"And an oil tanker isn't?"

"Um . . ."

"Forget it."

"I think she rides in the water really well," Saskia ventures.

"Where did you pick up that phrase?"

Why isn't Jane saying anything? Why is Jane sitting like a bump on a log letting Saskia get in all the trouble? "She's . . . you know . . . she's got the wind in her face and she's not slipping back." Oh brother! How stupid can you get?

"As it happens, you're right."

Relief. Saskia doesn't make the mistake of saying any more.

"Boom coming over," Thomas says. Saskia is busy wondering what that means when she looks up to see the yardarm zeroing in on her forehead. Thomas catches it. "Duck!" She ducks. "You say you know something about sailing and you don't even know what a boom is."

The farther *Lila* gets from shore the faster she goes, and as Thomas pulls on a rope she heels farther and farther over. Saskia is on the downward side and the water rushes by inches from her shoulders. "Lean out!" Thomas says to Jane. Jane leans out. "Farther!" Jane sits on the gunnel and hooks her toes under the lip of the trunk. They ride like that for a while, Saskia getting wet below, Jane fluttering like a flag above.

"For a boat with this draft and beam to be able to sail so close to the wind is remarkable!" Thomas yells above the rush of water. "It shows very fine construction! And we haven't even put up the jib yet!" Saskia nods appreciatively, but doesn't say anything. "We're going to go over to the starboard tack," Thomas predicts. The girls look at each other. Does either one of them know what that means? Larboard is left, starboard is right. Saskia is on the right —

Lila rights herself. Jane almost falls in the water. "Coming about," Thomas says. He does something with ropes and the rudder. *Lila* swivels. The yardarm hits Saskia in the back of the head. Thomas pushes her head down and hauls it over. The sail flaps leathery wings. Is she seeing stars? She will not cry, she will *not* . . .

Lila picks up speed. Now Saskia is on the up side. Should she lean out? She looks at Thomas, but he gives no sign. He is staring at the horizon, wrestling with a vision. This is all Lauren's fault. Why couldn't she wait ten lousy minutes on the dock?

"Jane, put up the jib."

"The what?"

Thomas closes his eyes for a moment. "The jib," he says, controlling himself.

"Uh . . ."

"The other sail."

Jane jumps and gathers it in her arms. "Sure," she says, crouching. She looks at him, waiting, wide-eyed.

"Get in the bow."

"Uh . . ."

Duh, gee, Jane, even stupid Saskia knows what "bow" means! "The front of the boat!" Saskia says impatiently.

Jane scuttles into the bow.

"Attach the jib to the stay," Thomas says.

Jane fumbles, flustered, with the sail. "Right," she says vaguely. Mere filler. A pathetic attempt to buy time.

"I don't believe this!" Thomas announces to the air around them. The stay must be that wire going to the top of the mast. Saskia wonders if Jane is too dumb to figure it out. "Can't you girls do anything?"

That's not fair! *Jane* is the one bumbling around in the bow! "The wire, Jane," Saskia says, rolling her eyes. "Jeez!"

"For chrissake, help her out, will you Saskia?"

Saskia goes forward. "Give it here!" She grabs the jib.

"I can do it!" Jane says, pulling it back.

"Obviously, you can't." Saskia tugs on it.

"Yes I can!" Jane gets her long arms around the bundle and hugs it to herself.

"Forget it!" Thomas yells from the stern. He pushes the tiller away from him and *Lila* turns, ropes slither like snakes, the boom swings out over the water. The wind comes around behind, puts a hand in the middle of *Lila*'s back and shoves. "I'm taking you both back to the dock."

"No!" the girls wail.

"This is ridiculous!"

"It's because Saskia —"

"If Jane didn't —"

"I want to share something, and Lauren can't be bothered, and all you girls can do is fight with each other!" He shakes his head, pondering deeply in his great-hearted spirit.

"It's all Jane's fault!" Saskia says in the Old Speech. "I can do it! We can leave Jane at the dock."

The liquid Old Speech flows over Thomas like a balm, and he answers less angrily. "It's not you, Saskia," he concedes.

"Speak in English!" Jane pleads.

"It's not Jane, either. It's my fault. I don't know what's the matter with me. I just need some time alone."

Jane is glancing from one face to the other. "What are you saying about me?" She looks so stupid, not understanding the simplest words. "Speak English!"

"Learn Danish!" Thomas snaps at her. "Until then, shut up!"

For a couple of seconds she just looks at him. The corners of her mouth slacken as if she were suffering a stroke and her eyes perform this curious flattening-out maneuver, like marbles floating to the surface of a liquid. Then the liquid spills over. Saskia watches with interest. Such a tall, grown-up girl, the big one-four, and yet here she is, liquefying just the way Saskia sometimes does, when she hides in her room. "Oh God," Thomas groans. "There she goes again."

"I can't help it!"

The shore is looming. Thomas raises the centerboard and pulls down the sail. Saskia quite competently gathers it at the boom. *Lila* bumps against the dock. "So the two of us are going back out?" Saskia asks Thomas in the Old Speech.

"No." He looks at Jane, reddening. "I want you to do something about her."

"What?"

He heaves an impatient sigh. "Cheer her up."

Saskia wilts. "Aye aye." She takes Jane's hand and steps her out of the boat. Thomas pushes off again, fans the rudder, raises the sail. The water creams in his wake, and he does not look back.

Lauren is striding down the slope. "Saskia! Why didn't you come get me?"

"Thomas wouldn't let me."

"You little idiot."

"He came back right after you left, you should have just — "

"Thomas!" Lauren is calling out over the water. Saskia pulls Jane up the slope. "Saskia! Saskia, answer me when I speak to you!"

Saskia whips around. "*What?*"

"What did Thomas say?"

"About what?"

"When he wouldn't let you come get me?"

"He said you were right, it was important to get the squash in. He said he'd take you out later." That seems to calm Lauren enough so that Saskia and Jane can make their escape.

9

Saskia tries to be patient. "So what's the problem?"

"Lauren's the problem."

"How do you figure that?" Jane just stares off into space like a zombie. It's really kind of irritating. "Have you noticed we never talk about anything anymore?"

"So what am I supposed to talk to you about? You want to hear the gruesome details?"

"Why can't we be friends like we were before?"

"It's different now. Thomas and I are in love."

Saskia snorts. "He doesn't love you."

"He's told me he loves me a bunch of times!"

"If he loves you so much, why was he yelling at you in the boat?"

"It's because of Lauren, I already told you." Actually, Saskia can sort of remember thinking it was Lauren's fault, too. "He's under a lot of pressure. Lauren hangs on him too much."

"*She* hangs on him too much!"

"He says he can't just leave her. He's too kind-hearted. Why is she part of this, anyway? I thought she wouldn't let him in the house."

"You believed that? God, you're gullible."

"She trapped him! The first thing he knew, she'd thrown out Bill and was telling him she couldn't live without him and there he was, trying to figure out how to let her down easy."

"That's what he told you?"

"He's afraid if he leaves her she'll do something to herself. You know . . ."

"That's ridiculous!"

"That's what I tried to tell him! She's just using him! But soon we're going to go away together, and then everything will be all right."

Saskia sputters. "You're totally deluded!"

Jane grips her ankles and her face sets. "I know what I know."

"So, what, are you going to run away and play house somewhere? Thomas and Jane and the kiddies?"

Jane lifts her chin. "Maybe."

This is like dealing with a child. You can't have Thomas! you say, and take him away like a toy. No, give him back! waah! waah! Saskia looks for a long time at this girl who is so wrapped in herself, refusing to believe. She really thinks she is the only one. Saskia has been remembering a few things: Thomas, in Wonderland, leaving the garden with this one or that one, those face-smacking glimpses through the high grass. For so long, for years and years, she didn't understand. Nakedness meant nothing, everyone was naked then. She thought he was taking the older girls away to hug them, to shower them with approval. Why didn't he ever take her? Wasn't she a good girl? It was too painful even to think about. How stupid she was! It was only his Need. He used them according to his pleasure and cast them aside, six at once, like Kubilai Khan. Grass to his scythe. He returned refreshed to Lauren and Saskia, his two true loves, to the bosom of his family, flexing his fingers, shaking his head to throw off cobwebs. None of those others misunderstood, so why does Jane? Because she had him to herself for a few days by the river? There are so many things Saskia could tell her, to prick her balloon. But she hasn't the heart.

Saskia looks at Jane huddled on the bed, holding on to her ankles for dear life, and actually feels sorry for her. Of course she loves

Thomas, as any woman must. It is the lot of the Wanderer to leave a trail of broken hearts behind him. "We just want to go away, that's all, and have a normal life together," Jane says. "What's wrong with that?"

"Nothing, I guess."

Jane leans forward and looks earnestly into Saskia's eyes. "I'm good for him. He's told me so." You have to hand it to her, she's a good-hearted person. For the rest of the day, the air is clearer between them.

After dinner Thomas gathers the crew under his arms, Lauren hogs the armchair, Saskia takes the rocker, Jane sits at Thomas's feet. Saskia scrutinizes Jane, who stares at Lauren, who gazes at Thomas, who tells his story. Then to bed. Funny, you would think all these weekends when they didn't have much to say to each other the nights would be the most awkward. Retiring to Saskia's chamber as is expected of them, they would lie, you would think, stone-faced side by side, staring up at the stars and their own thoughts. But if the truth be told, on the first weekend back in Novamundus, with the light off, they kissed more than ever. No talking, no giggling, no witches getting their pretties, just deadly silent, deadly serious kissing. Did Jane start it? Did Saskia? In the morning they will not remember this, as Mim never remembers her nightmares.

10

She ascends the stairs into darkness, groping. She folds back the protective copper sheets. Starlight pours in. The metal tepee becomes an open platform with a view of the whole island and the sea of ice beyond. Her breath pluming in the cold air, she swivels the six-foot sextant and slides a sight along the arc until she has pinpointed a new star. With the other sight she locates a star whose position is already known and records the angle between it and the new star. She climbs down to the library, where Tycho's Great Globe glows in the candlelight. On it are inscribed with incredible exactness the positions of thousands upon thousands of stars. Though huge, the Globe rotates easily, at the lightest touch. Saskia turns it until the correct spot comes beneath her hands. With a golden compass she engraves the new star on the brass with a diamond-tipped stylus. Next to it, she writes in microscopic figures, "Stella Saskiae 20,413." Only 6,237,459 stars to go.

Tycho fills the door of the library. "You should take a break, Albescus."

"In a while," she answers, pinching the bridge of her nose.

"No." He steps into the room, his cloak billowing. "Now. Come." He takes her by the wrist in his strong grip and pulls her out of the library. They repair to the refectory. The other Adepts are there and they look up, eyes brightening. Everyone shifts on the bench to make a space for her, but she sits at Tycho's right hand. He and Saskia nod to either side. The silver basin is passed and each Adept takes from it a pinch of Stone. At a sign from Tycho they eat. Mercury fumes plume from their mouths and sulfur burns behind their eyes.

On this simple fare they have lived for thousands of years. The platters heaped steaming with fat beef loin are not for them but for Jeppe the dwarf, who sits under the table by Tycho's feet. When Tycho throws him a greasy morsel, he grabs it greedily, tears the tendons with his razor-sharp canines. Jeppe was once an Adept. In fact, he was Tycho's favorite. But one night he stole the Stone and ate of it when he was not ready. Instead of giving him eternal life, the Stone shrank him, twisted his bones, addled his brains. He can be seen occasionally in the dark halls of Uraniborg, hurrying on some nonsensical errand of his own imagining, muttering to himself. Or as now, under Tycho's table, slobbering over his meat and humming contentedly.

The peasants whisper there is method to his madness. They say he can tell when a sick person will die. When the milk will not turn to butter in their churns, they mutter it is Jeppe's doing. When a cow gave birth to a two-headed calf, it was said that one of the calf's heads was seen to nod and wink at the mention of his name.

Perhaps. But the peasants will believe anything. Tycho regularly makes fools of them. When a peasant comes to Uraniborg to complain about something, Tycho sits at his oak desk and turns the crank on his automaton, and the peasant gapes at the suns and planets and moons twirling around each other as if the thing were alive. It might be a male, trying to shirk a Tychonic construction project in order to get his potatoes in, or it might be his wife, a few days later, hoping to get her husband out of the dungeon. But the words falter at the sight of Tycho, lordly in his cloak, behind his huge desk, calmly watching the suns and moons go round and round. What could their concerns matter to him?

The nobles who come to Ven from time to time are not so easy to deal with. They are decadent inbred ignoramuses, but Tycho must be polite. He bows stiffly to acknowledge their asinine compliments and restrains himself from snapping his fingers to summon his English mastiffs. He confines himself to a Tycho-trick or two, inviting them to admire some statuette of cunning artistry, a naked boy it might be, piping and prancing. A nobleman leans close, Tycho turns a hidden knob, the boy twirls on his pedestal, and water squirts from his you-know-what, hitting the nobleman right between the eyes. The man is humiliated, angry, but he cannot show it, he must laugh and say, "'Tis a merry jest!" while a sycophant from his retinue hands him a perfumed hankie to mop his face.

When the visitors finally leave Tycho locks the door behind them and explodes, shouting imprecations at the coffered ceilings. Jeppe dances around him, making grotesque faces until Tycho says, "Sing, Jeppe, sing!" and the deformed creature cackles out some nonsense or other in his reedy voice.

> Ping pong goes the stones
> and bones roll in tones of moans
> jibber jabber, ho!

He attempts a cartwheel but falls in a heap, and looks so ridiculous with his pointed hat askew, a hurt look on his monkey face, that Tycho laughs, restored to good humor.

When the meal in the refectory is finished, Tycho leads Saskia out the front door. He whistles for his beloved English mastiffs, and the pack flows to him like a dog-brown sea to lap against the mound on which Uraniborg stands. He likes nothing better than to stand among them and raise an eyebrow or incline a finger to send them streaming away, baying like a carillon of bells, to chase down field mice or ignorant peasants, but now he harnesses them to his sled and lifts Saskia on. He climbs aboard after her, and the dogs pull them through the north gate, out across the snowy fields of Ven. The warm castle lights dwindle behind them. Her cheeks are apple red.

They ride down to the island's edge and continue out over the ice. It is so peaceful out there: the sparkle of stars, the panting of the dogs, the hiss of the runners. They ride all the way to the edge of the Circle and get out hand in hand to contemplate the water beyond, while the dogs flop down to rest. A pod of whales is out there, passing and repassing, blowing approval. Tycho fingers the Whale around his neck and calls, and the mother of the pod comes to nose against the lip of the ice and lift her huge head out of the water to regard them kindly. Saskia gives her a hug as wide as two arms can reach.

Paradise.

11

The sunlamp is what started it. Jane didn't have enough money for one and Lauren laughed obnoxiously when Saskia resorted to asking her: after the expense of putting *Lila* back on the water, they hardly had money for Betsy's gas, so Saskia could put such ridiculous ideas out of her head. But Saskia's tan was nearly gone, and clearly something had to be done. Terry is quite the sleazeball, he even *looks* greasy with his glossy black hair and the blackheads on his nose, but he is a reasonable businessman. His last operative went on to high school this year and Terry was slow about getting a replacement. In the meantime he was still coming through Tyler only once a week, and staying well off the property, because of his conspicuousness (with his red Trans Am, the tåbe might as well be flying a shield charged with joint fumant). He was losing business to competitors. He took Saskia for a drive and a job interview and she impressed him with her unflinching Eye and obvious head for figures. Maybe her bare feet and legs in the sunlight on the dashboard had something to do with it, too, he certainly looked at them enough.

Her predecessor was dumb, and kept the stuff in his locker. Saskia, in prudent contrast, packs it neatly into an airtight canister and stores it in the tank of one of the toilets in the opium den. An added benefit of the arrangement is that it saves water every time someone flushes. The traditional marketplace is behind the fence at the back of the fieldhouse, and Saskia hangs out her shield with the others during her lunch break. She carries the day's wares down her shirt because she wouldn't put it past the V.P. to slam them all into a wall and jam his hands in their pockets. Not that he would ever smell it on her, she isn't stupid enough to smoke the stuff herself, not like Jay, another merchant who practically gives you a free high if you just sniff his clothes. Jay and his older brother grow their own on a plot in the state forest. The other regular is Max, who gets his Ithacan Gold from some frat jerk at Huge Red. The three of them get along pretty well. Max examined Saskia's stuff her first day out and said it looked pretty good. "What kind is it?" he asked.

"Trans Am Red," she said, and he nodded knowledgeably.

Saskia looks on the business as serving two purposes at once: giving her the money she needs for a few essentials, and weakening the moral fiber of the native population, softening them up for the invasion. But as far as the latter goes, she runs a small operation. Most of her clients are boys (Monica and Marie, regular smokers, say they have never had to buy the stuff in their lives), and they like to see her reach into her shirt. "Hey Saskia, it's still warm," Greg Ludikov says, fondling his bag, and Saskia shoots right back, "Rub your face in it and dream on, Greg." The boys lap up that sort of thing and crawl back for more.

At the end of the fiscal week she does her brief business with Terry, who meets her at the top of the road up from Wholeworld. Despite his sleazeballitude he does have a certain integrity. After he punches everything into his pocket calculator, he gives her her cut down to the penny, pumping a change machine on his belt. He invited her once to come with him for a park and a smoke of his best stuff — limited edition, superbo excello — but how dumb does he think she is? She keeps the main stash in her room and carries the day's stock into school in a lunch bag, bold as you please.

There is the logistical problem of how to spend the money, since Saskia has to take the bus back to Wholeworld every day after school. That's where Jane comes in. "And get a little something for yourself," she adds graciously as she pours the filthy lucre into Jane's palms.

"It rots people's brains," Jane suggests.

"You're parroting Thomas. He's the ventriloquist, you're the dummy."

"He wouldn't like what you're doing."

"So you're going to rat on me?"

"No."

"If he knew why I was doing it, he would understand."

In her room she strips and suns. The warmth is delicious, a steady, ardent gaze admiring her all over. She feels at last like the full Moon, basking entire in the light of the sun, and as the warmth seeps deeper and a star of heat coalesces in her abdomen, she does a languorous Deed under the ardent eye. She turns to take the heat along her backside and reaches for her headphones, slips in a cassette of Satanic Silk, and turns up the volume until Andy's "Death Is for Children" pounds in her ears.

> death is for children
> torture for queers
> I haven't had
> so much fun in years!

An agent's research is never done. A pile of tapes at her bedside awaits her perusal. She presents her flank to the lamp and props herself on an elbow to work on her definitive discography of Anathema, a group she founded herself. Yesterday she designed the group's logo — "Anathema" in dagger letters, dripping blood — and the boys loved it. "The boys" are Ben Sinister, vocals and keyboard; Marco de Bestia, lead guitar and backup vocals; Johnny Starcross, electric bass; and Bob "Bong" Bolo, bongos.

ENTRY #SW-4438:
Album, DR2-36445, *Get Off*, copyright Dis Records, 13 Road to
 Dis, Stygian Fields, New Jersey 54321. All rites reserved.
All songs by Ben Sinister
Recorded on the Island of Insanity
Produced by S. Lee Zball and ANATHEMA
Engineering: Timur de Lane
Recording and Mixing: Juana Maria Fumanto
Cover and Layout: Ishakta Wise

Publishing under an anagram is one of the customs of her people; Tycho sometimes signs his papers Heyth Cobra.

— SIDE ONE —
Geta Holda This (3:42)
White as Poison (4:16)
Foreign Devil (3:10)
666 (6:66)

— SIDE TWO —
Flagrante Delicto (3:50)
House Afire (4:21)
I of the Storm (3:10)
Dwarf Love (5:05)

Here are some sample lyrics from the hit single "Dwarf Love":

> under the table
> you just take what I give you
> and take it smiling

I don't have to go
anywhere I just sit here
and get my dwarf love

Ben Sinister is the only songwriter in the industry to compose exclusively in haiku. In this month's lead article, *Pulse* hails his style as "a refreshing coupling of hard-driving sexuality with a refined, one might almost say delicate, rhythmic sensibility."

Saskia turns to expose her other flank. Since getting the lamp, she has been careful to use it only when Thomas is down in Ithaca or out on the lake in *Lila*, since he never knocks on her door but comes right in, in midsentence. The concern is not that he would see her without any clothes on but that he would realize how often she suns. Of course he deduced what she was doing as soon as she started to darken again, and he frowned, pointing out that sunlamps use a lot of electricity. She sort of implied she wouldn't use it more than once a week, and they left it at that. Actually, she was surprised how easily he let her off the hook. Perhaps he had had enough of her looking like a poisonous mushroom. He likes his girls dark, we've already established that.

Yes, she's frying up nicely, becoming coppery. In alchemy, copper is the color of Venus. An intriguing idea. Except that if you're Venus you can't be a maiden anymore. No, Saskia would rather keep her faithful dogs and her humming bow, thank you, and hunt men the old-fashioned way. Perhaps it would be more correct to say that she is becoming the dark side of the Moon. She turns onto her back again and luxuriates in the heat on her stomach. She is lightly sweating, and she slides her hands over the moist film. Her old bras are too big now, so she had Jane buy her some new ones, nice lacy things in red and black. Lauren has been poking her nose into the purchase of such essentials, wondering where Saskia is getting the money. That's one of the great things about Thomas, he isn't obsessed with money the way Lauren is, he didn't mention money once during the whole hiking trip. Lauren pinches every penny until there is nothing left to pinch. Saskia put her off with a story about a magazine contest her English teacher encouraged her to enter where you were supposed to write a 500-word essay on why it's important to protect the environment. Saskia won first prize and $150. It was a good story, tricked out in convincing detail. Storytelling is a custom of her people.

"And it never occurred to you, I suppose," Lauren said, "to think that money might be needed by the rest of us."

"No, it didn't."

"How do you think it would be if I spent all the money I earned on things for myself?"

Saskia shrugged. "Maybe you'd have nicer clothes."

She wondered what the opposite of baring your breasts to the moonlight might be, and clearly it is this. She has flat places over her hipbones now, and her ribs lend a pleasing texture to her dark slender back. Soon her breasts will be positively Amazonian in their undeniable not-getting-in-the-wayness. Saskia suns, and sweats, and shrinks.

No, she is not anorexic. Sue Walsh is anorexic, and talks about how fat she is even as she skeletonizes. Saskia doesn't bake all night, or dream all day of food, or scarf and barf. That's sick, like the decadent Romans. Saskia just wants to be dark and whip-thin, without grossness or excess, the essence of herself, a rod of apple wood stained with walnut juice and polished with beeswax, a scourge of the unrighteous. Is that so much to ask? It says right in her alchemy book, You will know the true Adept by this sign, that she no longer needs food. Everyone is an organism, and the less you consume, the less you secrete, and the less you secrete, the less you end up lying in your own muck. We must learn to tread lightly on this Earth, like the phantom walkers of Tasmania. Such a satisfying image! She would skim like a swallow over the rare lichens, she would look back and not even see footprints, nothing but nature, boundless to the horizons. No one would ever know she had been there.

12

If you go out at midnight in midautumn on a clear night you will see Perseus straight overhead. One of his legs points to the Pleiades, and if you continue in that direction through the Pleiades you will come to the southwestern quadrant of the sky. Chances are you never looked much here, because the whole area is conspicuously lacking in bright stars. Heh heh. It was designed that way. Take Thomas's binoculars and look again. Start with Perseus' leg and go through the Pleiades. About fifteen degrees farther on you will run into an oval of six stars. You are now in the constellation of Cetus, the Whale. The oval is the Whale's head. Continue southwest along the neck, one, two stars.

Stop. The star you are looking at is called Mira. It is classed as a variable, because over a period of 332 days its brightness varies from ninth to third magnitude and back again. In other words, Mira is usually invisible to the naked eye. Nonetheless, it happens to be the most important star in the galaxy. It has only one planet, and an unusual feature of the Miran system is that the planet remains motionless while the star revolves around it. In fact, the entire galactic disk revolves around this planet. Have you figured it out yet? The planet is Hyperbores.

Don't bother trying: you can't possibly see it, not even with the most powerful terrestrial telescope. But if you could, you would surely exclaim at how intensely blue it appeared in your eyepiece, like a marble of lapis lazuli. That, in fact, is why the Hyperboreans are also called Lapps. All of them carry the sign of their origin in their eyes, which twinkle from their sockets like hard blue stones.

Hyperbores shines so blue in the jet black of space because its surface is entirely covered by water. The only solid area to be found lies inside its Arctic Circle: right at the line, the water freezes. At the North Pole of Hyperbores, in the exact middle of this vast circle of ice, stands the only building on the planet, a castle as white as the pure ice, as green as ecology, and as pink as perfect love: the Ty-chonic Astronomical Observatory. No one except the Grandmaster of the TAO knows how long the castle has been there, or who built it, but all Hyperboreans drink in with their mothers' rich milk the knowledge of its sacred charge as Guardian of the Way. The TAO monitors every one of the 32,544 inhabited planets in the galaxy, applying corrective measures when necessary. Mira, in fact, is not a star at all but a vast and sophisticated generator of a communications beam that sweeps the galaxy like a lighthouse light, completing one circuit every 332 Earth days. TAO agents on the various planets compose messages with the aid of complex formulas and transmit them along the beam by means of special spermacetic chambers in their foreheads. Mira then relays them to the golden Cetus exhalant on the top of the Observatory, which focuses the beam and directs it downward to the specially designed golden nose of the Grandmaster, who hears the messages as voices in his head.

It was in this way that he heard one night a desperate message from his agents on a little planet circling a star called Sol, out toward the edge of the galaxy: "Then Man, rapacious, wild, insatiable, came upon Earth and upset the Balance of all things, and it did come to pass —" The Grandmaster sat bolt upright. "Man!" he groaned, bouncing a palm off his sleek forehead. "Not him again!"

When trouble is afoot on a planet, special agents have to be sent to do the undercover work that the regular agents cannot perform. Only the best and brightest Hyperboreans are selected for this work, and they undergo a grueling course of training at the Observatory to enable them to fit into the subject population. "You will be disguised as Men," Tycho said, "and for the entire period of this project I too will be disguised as a Man. I do this because, as you will shortly discover, it is an intensely unpleasant experience, and I cannot have my men thinking I would ask them to do something I would not do myself." Alas, he was right, the disguises were pure torment: the dry skin, as suffocating as a rubber glove, the coarse body hair, the clumsy mode of locomotion. Worst of all were the shit-brown contact lenses.

There were four of them. They would be known to each other on the target planet as the Four Unknown Superiors, and they would be sent not only to different continents but to different time periods. Their mission, however, would be the same: to learn as much as they could about the ways of these Balance-upsetting Men, to weaken them in whatever fashion feasible, and to act as advisers for the invasion force when it landed later to decimate the race. "Of the five billion Men that currently infest the place, we might allow a billion to live," Tycho said. "But I'm being generous." They picked their roles out of a hat. Albescus landed the hardest one, that of "Saskia White," a second-class citizen of Novamundus in the last quarter of the twentieth century. "What did you get?" she asked Haven, a male whale and a good friend.

"Odysseus," he said, reading the card. "A warrior and wanderer in the eastern Mediterranean, circa 1200 B.C."

"Oh!" she flapped her flippers. "Do you want to trade?"

But trading was not allowed. Her two other friends became Marco Polo, a merchant and traveler of the Far East in the thirteenth century, and Horatio Hornblower, a captain in His Majesty's Navy during the Napoleonic Wars. Tycho wisely gave them the ability to travel in time so that they could enjoy each other's company now and then, and thus avoid being driven crazy by loneliness. She, Odysseus, Marco, and the Captain get together just like old times on Hyperbores (except that they have to keep their darn skins on), to relax, to get away from the cares of business: they play whist, or shoot arrows through axes, or mix wine in the silver basin and go out in search of willing wenches. Sometimes they just sit around and shoot the breeze. They complain about teachers, or the Admiralty, or Poseidon's enmity, and usually end up laughing uproariously at what fools these Earthlings be. They all look forward to the invasion, after which they will be able to go home. Home! They are reminded of the warm consoling waters of Hyperbores by the tears that spill from their eyes whenever they speak of it.

And what about Jeppe? They sometimes talk about him. What *really* happened when he was the head agent in that Cassiopeian system that got into a horrible nuclear war, making its own sun go supernova? Such a beautiful star it was in the Hyperborean sky, marking the place where billions and billions of Way-following creatures had died.

13

With her contacts popped out to let in more starlight she can make out shapes even in the barn. She wishes she could shuck her skin off, too, but she doesn't dare. She slips across the rough wooden planks and stops at the black pit of the stall. She can feel the steam rising against her face. She squats and inches forward, feeling ahead with her hand until she touches bristle. The large mass suddenly butts up. She can just make out the dim gleam of Marilyn's eyes.

"It's me." She runs her hand along Marilyn's neck. "Go back to sleep." Marilyn drops her head to the floor and lets out a groan. Saskia continues to stroke her as she crawls to the place where Marilyn's rounded side is closest to the wall. There is some dry hay here, and just enough room for Saskia to sit. The knobby ridge of Marilyn's spine is at the perfect height for Saskia to rest her weary head. She throws an arm up the mountain of Marilyn and puts her cheek against the hot fur and breathes in the lulling fumes of straw and milk.

God how she misses this, when she is walking down the halls with her lavender hair, her perfumed wrists. Thomas smelled it when she came home and scowled, coughed. "I'm suffocating," he managed to choke out. "Is my Saskia in there somewhere?"

She had tried to wash it off before getting on the bus. She told Thomas that Monica insisted she try it. Of course Thomas would sniff out the decadence of it, the graveyard whiff of thousands of rabbits tortured to death in LD-50 tests. Yet Earthlings find this pleasing. Marilyn's smell is honest. It reminds Saskia of home. Her people, too, are great milk producers, and their milk is richer than cream, creamier than the swarm of stars at which they gaze up in wonder whenever they break the surface to blow an oar upright of steam. Funny, what this strange planet does to you. Now even Marilyn's relatively thin milk is too rich for Saskia. It seems to coat her throat like paint and lies heavily in her stomach. The waters of home always buoyed her up. The terrestrial substitute is coffee, which floats you up onto your toes and gives you the illusion of lightness for a while.

Autumn is the season in which Marilyn's milk production tapers off. She will be having a calf in a couple of months and Mim milked her yesterday for the last time. Now she will have a rest so she can go ahead and make her baby. The milking won't ever start again. Thomas let the girls finish the cycle so that Marilyn's rhythms would not be upset, but next year will be different. The calf will grow and will not be sold and Marilyn will eventually dry up, naturally. She and the calf will grow old together, peacefully in the meadow, un-meddled with by Man. "I'm just freeing the slaves," Thomas said.

Marilyn, a slave? But she stands so patiently for the milking. She lows when Saskia is late. Each spring, on the first day they let her into the meadow she runs skipping, her tail high. "De happy slave," Thomas said. "A typical slaveholder's fantasy." But Jane and Saskia worshiped her! She presided maternally over the bonding of their eternal friendship! "The fat black mammy. Another fantasy. Look at Aunt Jemima." But Marilyn does love Saskia! Doesn't she? In the darkness Marilyn sleeps, radiating warmth on this cold November night, accepting Saskia into her bed.

"Cows wouldn't survive one week without Man," Thomas said. "And just as well. There are too many of them, desertifying the world." He told Saskia to stop closing the door of the chicken coop at night. "They're grown animals, aren't they? Can't they take care of themselves?" On the third night something came in and killed four of them. Thomas guessed it was a raccoon. Whatever it was, it ate only their heads. "The fattiest tissue," he explained. "The delicacy." Saskia could hardly force herself to touch the mutilated bodies, and she cried weakly. "Try to let go of this sentimental idea about nature," he said gently, throwing the bodies into a wheelbarrow. "Chickens aren't a real species." Two nights later the raccoon, or whatever it was, came back and ate the heads of the last three hens.

Now when Saskia looks at the empty chicken coop she sees Thomasness. When she sees the straightened porch with the new floor she sees Thomasness. The elements of Wholeworld are one by one falling into place, orienting themselves along the axis of Thomasness like ions in a magnetic field. As each molecule locks into position the Wholeworld crystal becomes more pure, and as it becomes more pure it hums more and more like a goblet with Thomas's finger running along the rim.

14

Years ago Saskia brought home a doll that she had found in the grass at the Farmers' Market. The remarkable thing about this doll was that if you pulled on her champagne-blond hair it would get longer, and when you turned a knob on her back it would get shorter again. Saskia quickly tired of the gimmick and gave the doll to Mim, but the idea it inspired — experimentally pulling on the crew's hair to see if it promoted growth — lasted longer.

Now she stands in front of her mirror and brushes her hair, tugging furiously downward, fifty, sixty strokes. Hope springs eternal. But the hair merely recoils, curling again like something shriveling in pain. She detaches a cloud from the brush and dumps it in the waste-basket, resprinkles what's left, starts again. At times like this she wonders if she should just cut it all off and be done with it. Lauren says she feels much freer and lighter now that she has a crew cut. But if the truth be told, Saskia thinks she made a big mistake. She looks like a lamp without its shade, and her ears, surprisingly small, seem to cling for dear life. Worst of all, the deed was done while Saskia was at school, and by the time she got home Thomas had thrown the armfuls of glorious hair, which she had dreamed for so many years of having for herself, onto the compost heap, and emptied a garbage pail after them.

Saskia comes down to find Thomas and Jo cleaning up in the kitchen. "Look at you," Jo rasps. What? Saskia lifts a hand toward her hair. How hopeless is it? Is there a paper bag in the house? Jo shakes her head ruefully, as if Saskia were pulling a fast one. "You're starting to get pretty on us." Oh, just what she needs. The Jo Flynn Seal of Approval. You're looking great, Saskia, you look like a halibut. "But you should pencil your eyebrows. They look funny when they get blond like that."

"The way to solve that is to stop using the sunlamp," Thomas says.

"I wish I could get a tan like that," Jo asserts.

"You'll have the last laugh when she dies of skin cancer." He massages a dishtowel. "Are you ready?"

"Yeah," Saskia says, hanging her head.

"Get your coat on."

"I don't need a coat."

"It's cold out."

"We're going in Betsy, aren't we?"

"Your coat isn't sexy enough, I suppose."

"It's not that."

"Next time I'm in Ithaca I'll buy you a leopardskin, so you'll have something to wear." Saskia puts on her hideous old coat. They drive up the dirt road in silence. On the county road Thomas observes, "You're not wearing a bra. Why not?"

Saskia looks at him. Nothing occurs to her.

"I'm just curious. Why are you wearing a clinging knit dress without a bra? Do you want to look sexy?"

"No."

"Then you shouldn't wear it."

Betsy hums along through the dark.

"There's nothing wrong with wanting to look sexy, Saskia. You can admit it. You're getting interested in boys?"

"Not much."

"Then why are you going to this party?"

"Monica and Marie are going to be there."

"So the sexy dress is for them?"

"I'm just trying to look nice." So it's impossible. So shoot her.

"Are you going to put makeup on after I let you off?"

"No."

"You look better without it, you know. Your skin is good. Makeup will coarsen it. Lauren and Jane don't wear makeup."

"They can get away with it."

"All women look better without it. It amazes me how much money and time women spend making themselves uglier. Don't listen to Jo. You want to look like her?"

"No."

"A made-up woman looks like a corpse, ready for the open casket and the viewing line. Perfume is for corpses, too. And your hair looks better when you leave it alone. It's thin hair, you just have to accept that. It's *my* hair. You've got something against my hair?"

"You're a man."

"Being a woman doesn't mean you have to be a Barbie doll."

"I guess."

"You say 'I guess' when you're ignoring me."

"I'm not ignoring you."

"When you don't want to hear what I'm saying. Why do you want to attract these boys?"

"I said I didn't."

"But you're not telling the truth. You're tanning yourself and you're wearing sexy clothes and makeup because you want some boy to notice you. There's nothing wrong with that, but at least you can admit it."

"I just want to look nice!"

"Nice and sexy, you mean."

"OK! Nice and sexy, or whatever."

"Don't say 'or whatever.' Say, 'I want to look nice and sexy.'"

Saskia looks away from him, out the window. "I want to look nice and sexy," she says quietly. When she looks back, he is smiling.

"You do. You look very nice and very sexy."

He rests his right arm along the back of the seat, which is the signal for Saskia to slide across. She does. He gives her a manly squeeze. A few minutes later, he turns down the street where Sue Walsh lives. Rusty low-riding gas guzzlers line both curbs. "Don't let one of these high school boys drive you home, they're dangerous even when they're sober. Call me." He holds her head and gives her a kiss. She slides across to the passenger door. "You can leave the coat here. So you don't have to hide it in the bushes." She is so grateful to him for knowing everything. She shrugs off the coat. He tilts the rearview mirror toward her and turns on the dome light. "You can use this to make yourself up."

"But —"

"Go on. I know you've got the stuff in your bag."

She hesitates. "I couldn't," she says at last. Not in front of him.

"All right. Be careful with those high school boys."

"Sure."

"Are you wearing underpants?"

"Oh my gosh! Of course!"

"Well that's something, anyway. We need to talk about birth control."

Saskia is shocked. "No we don't!"

Thomas looks amused. "You'd be surprised. Here, give me another kiss. All right. Call me." He drives away.

Saskia hurries out of the cold through the garage door into the humid kitchen warmth of crowded boys and cigarette smoke. "Hey Saskia!" somebody says, and she throws a "Hey" over her shoulder as she hurries through, thinking only, Don't look don't look, down a hall stepping over legs and under arms braced from wall to wall until she finds the bathroom and locks herself in. The hair of the Saskia in the mirror has sproinged back into hideousness and she's still brushing it out again when someone knocks on the door. "Busy!"

"Is that you, Saskia? Let me in!" Marie is carried in on a wave of shouts and music. Saskia locks the door behind her. "I thought maybe you weren't coming this time, either," Marie says.

"My old man finally let me. We had a humongous fight about last week."

"So what's his problem?"

"Oh you know. Daddy's little girl out in the big bad world, blah blah. He's living in fantasyland. I accidentally mentioned birth control and he practically crapped in his pants."

"Birth control?" So pleasant to see Marie taken aback. "I mean . . . You don't have a boyfriend, do you? I mean, right now?"

"Nah. I just said it to pop his balloon."

Actually, the reason Saskia couldn't go to Bob Roszak's party last week was because Jane was at Wholeworld and there was the problem of what to do with her. She probably could have tagged along, but she would have moped and hung around Saskia, and the last thing Saskia needed was Jane messing up her maneuvers. She couldn't really leave Jane home, either, because that sort of blew the whole cover for why Jane was at Wholeworld in the first place. This inexorable logic made it look like Saskia wouldn't ever be able to go to a party, and she was pretty mad at Jane about that, but then Sing Sing came to the rescue. They wanted to visit friends in Boston this weekend and Mr. Sing has a thing about presenting a united front. The Happy Family Show, Jane calls it.

"Danny is here," Marie is saying. "He's not with Lori anymore." Danny Rizzuto is a high school dreng with raven curls and a sickly pallor, all the rage these days. "God, he's cute."

"Down, girl."

Marie sucks in her lower lip, juts her tiny chin toward the mirror. "Yuck." Her fingers probe around a point.

"Leave it alone." Saskia puts a drop of color on the end of her finger and strokes it back from an eye. As if the contact lenses weren't enough, now she has to plaster on this skin-coarsening stuff. It probably causes zits, too. "You'll just make it worse."

Too late. Marie hasn't popped it, she's only managed to squeeze it into a red cone, ten times more obvious. She tries to drown it in flesh-tone but it keeps poking out like Mount Ararat. "Oh God.

Danny's going to puke." Saskia darkens her funny-looking blond eyebrows. "You know what? Paul Potyondy has a crush on you."

"Yeah, I know." She puts the final touches of maroon on her eyelids and stands back. She resists the temptation to look along her thumb.

"So what do you think of him?"

"Dweeb. Real dweeb." Black, clingy knit dress, check; tan, check; dark eyebrows, maroon eyelids, check; reasonably blond, reasonably straight hair, check. She slips off her shoes. Tan bare feet, check. Every agent has to design his or her own disguise, just like the clowns at the Barnum & Bailey Clown College. Saskia couldn't say with certainty that she doesn't look like a clown, but somebody said she looked nice and sexy. "Besides, he's too young." Her mission is to capture the ringleaders, who are the only ones worth taking back for experimentation. She caps her vials. "I'm ready. Are you ready?"

"Yeah," Marie sighs, making a last couple of stabs at her hair. "I guess."

"Let's get us some high school boys."

"You're bad!"

Saskia switches on her gravitational field as she steps through the door into the shouts and music. Very nice and very sexy. The hum of the generators warms her stomach as the field slowly builds to full power. She moves, and the clingy knit dress rubs her skin like a hundred hands. The feeling is especially delicious where her bra usually is. She shifts her shoulders and the two sensitive points tingle. Her bare toes grip the troll's hair.

She follows Marie into the living room. A crush of bodies, couples grappling on the sofa, gloom and din. A boy swings into her orbit, turning to meet her, and she lasers him as she walks past, swiveling her head to keep contact for an extra second before turning away with a half-smile and leaving him to spin helplessly. "What's your name? I must know who you are! Please . . . !" His voice fades behind her.

A thin, fast-talking dreng in T-shirt and bow tie is refilling a punch bowl on a sideboard with ginger ale, strawberry juice, and an inch out of every bottle from the liquor cabinet. "Wait a minute, ladies, wait a minute while I adjust the mixture with just the precise quantity of, what is this, ah, B and B, that stands for Booze and more Booze, and then a finger, well, maybe two fingers of the finest vodka, what the hell, I'll put in a whole hand . . ." Saskia and Marie trade an eye roll. Clearly the court jester. Good for a couple of cartwheels but then back under the table with him. Saskia holds her glass up to a lamp swaddled in red cloth and studies the thick swirl of particles, the dim puce glow deep within.

"Bottoms up," Marie says, holding her nose and draining the glass. "Yuck." She giggles. "That should get me started."

Saskia sips. Sweet, revoltingly so, with something rotten beneath, the bitter tang of putrefaction. She studies the surface. Is it bubbling? Beware! This is alcohol, mind-muddling, the darkling mirror image of ichor. The Earthlings drink it not to find the essence of themselves but precisely the opposite. Saskia leaves the glass on the first table she sees.

"Hey Saskia!" It's Steve, one of her customers. "You selling tonight?"

She looks up at the gangly doofball, spreading her arms to let him see the whole of her clingy dress, her bare legs and feet. "Take a good look, Steve. Where do you think I'd be carrying it?" He clutches his beer and drools. "See me on Monday and I'll take care of you."

They locate Monica in Bob's lap in an armchair, her legs around his waist. She places a butt maternally between his lips for a long suck and then between hers. They touch forehead to forehead and intergaze speechlessly, their exhalations intermingling, until Monica tilts her head and moves in with lower lip outdrooped for Bob to bite. No conversation to be had here. "Maybe Danny's in the kitchen," Marie says forlornly, and they thread that way, passing through a swampy area of the shag and a spill of pretzels sharp as shards of glass. Saskia wipes her feet on the regained high ground. "Where are Sue's parents?" she asks, risking uncoolness.

"Her mom's on a honeymoon."

"Number?"

"Three, I think."

"They say that's the lucky one."

"Yeah? I should tell my mother that, maybe she'll finally get rid of number two."

Nobody is in the kitchen except Sue and Rachel, another eighty-pounder. The Captain has cannonballs that weigh more than these two. "— and I was standing there thinking about Paul," Sue is saying in a swift dark monotone, "just thinking about how shitty life is and my hand started turning the knife against my stomach and it started pressing it in and it was like I *couldn't stop it* —"

"You want a beer?" Marie is holding two.

"Sure," Saskia says.

Marie pops her top. "Hey Sue, have you seen Danny?"

"No."

"You haven't seen him anywhere?" She holds her nose and swigs.

"I *said* no."

"Oh yeah, I forgot, fuck you, too."

"Let's look in the basement."

As they descend the stairs, the gloom deepens, the music loudens. Into the beast! Fake wood paneling like Jane's basement. Are they all this way? A few couples are dancing while the rest crowd the pretzel tables and look on enviously, nursing drinks. In the dim corners Saskia can make out limbs intertwining. The girls find themselves pressed up against another punch bowl of devilish brew, and since there is only one glass, Saskia has to share it, keeping pace with Marie to maintain her reputation. It's a darn good thing she was trained to hold on to herself. Marie scans the room for the elusive Danny while Saskia watches the dancers and decides — and for some reason this doesn't surprise her — that boys can't dance to save their lives. They seem to have only two modes: clutch-and-stagger for the slow tunes and a stiff stepping and arm-pumping routine for the faster ones that looks like a workout with dumbbells. Saskia sighs. Just how hopeless is this species?

Marie happens to know one of a pair of boys. They close in at the start of a slow dance and that is the last Saskia sees of Marie. Only now that she is alone does she realize how strong her field is tonight. She is practically a black hole. The guy she is dancing with — Brad? Tad? — is so unmanned by her power, he is basically hanging from her neck by his lips, like a leech. She looks out past his chest to laser another boy, who immediately turns from his partner to gape at her. You'll get your turn, heh heh. At the end of the song Brad or Tad tries to kiss her but she turns away, "Thanks," and moves through the crush, the eyes of every boy following her until she chooses another one, walking right up to him. "You want to dance?" What can he say? He is but a man; he can do no other. He moves into her arms. Onto my rocks, sailor. Is he a ringleader? Could be. He's high school, anyway. Leather jacketed, brew on his breath. If she could tie him up and bundle him into the beam, they would have him on the marble slab in a jiffy. One experiment she has been longing to try is to tear a boy's heart out and hand it to him on a silver platter. But this one's girlfriend, coming back from the bathroom, goes on a slow steam, and he declines a second dance to follow her upstairs: "Hey! Come on!" Good-looking but weak. She dances with two other guys and gets into a situation where she has to drink some more. She gets a firmer grip on herself. Each time she says something, she pauses to examine what she just said and decides she's doing fine. She ingeniously plays the two guys against each other and destroys a lifelong friendship. Coming back up the stairs, she runs into Danny Rizzuto. "Marie is looking for you."

"Who?" He speaks in a half snarl. A raven curl as carefully trained as a grapevine hangs on his porcelain brow.

"Marie McDonald."

"Yeah? So what?"

"So nothing. I'm just telling you." What a røvhul.

"And who are you?"

Your dream come true, your worst nightmare. "Saskia."

"Yeah? Saskia what?"

What does Marie see in this lug? His dead-white face, his weak eyes, his six-word vocabulary. "Exactly. Saskia What. How did you know?"

And so, after this and that, they kind of end up upstairs, lying at the end of a dark hall. He is the first boy Saskia has ever kissed, if you can call it that, when he is basically holding her down and mining her mouth with the blunt instrument he calls his tongue. When he first tipped her back she was light-headed with desire, she wondered as his mouth opened to hers how far the explosion would carry them, but now she lies there, her despair deepening. Can't dance, can't kiss. Who *are* these people? The aching tingle of gentle strong palms lightly rubbing her breasts? Make her laugh. Danny is squeezing and pinching as if they might produce milk, except if he handled Marilyn this clumsily she would kick him clear through the barn wall. Saskia tries to roll him off her, but she is so frustrated, so disappointed, she only manages to lift his shoulders a little. His response is to clamp down harder. It hadn't occurred to her that having a gravitational field meant a dreng might fall on you like a ton of bricks. She is terrified she will start crying. Nothing leaches out coolness like an acid shower of tears.

But Danny saves the day. He leaves her breast for dead to grab her hand and starts to pull it down to his you-know-what. The utter crassness of this maneuver, the effrontery, steadies her. The revolting thought of getting within a hundred miles of Danny Rizzuto's you-know-what gives her strength. She resists. He tugs harder. Guards! With one steady pull — she is a cow milker, remember, she pushed the dial on the machine at the Ithacan Carnival up to "Bonecrusher" — she reverses his direction and breaks his grip. He is so surprised he lifts his head to look at her.

"You think I don't know where it is?" she asks him.

He gives her a look of vacant hostility. "What's your problem?"

"I can't breathe. Get off me."

She pushes him off and gets up. Her underpants are wedged up in her crack. "You're a terrible kisser, that's the problem." She means the remark to be devastating, unmanning. But it comes out sounding childish.

He smirks, one side of his mouth rising to show his pearly teeth, his eyes leering with malice. "How would you know? No one's probably ever kissed a dog like you before. I was taking pity on you."

"That's what you —"

"Anh, shut up!" He is on his feet. "Fuck you, bitch." He pushes her into the wall and heads for the stairs.

"You can't just — !"

But he doesn't turn. He is gone.

Saskia stares at the empty hall in disbelief. How did he do that? Few times in her life has she been so absolutely, blazingly in the right. Her vocabulary is ten times larger than his, her quiver is bursting with skewering dead-on remarks. There should be no way she could possibly fail to get satisfaction. Except that he left. So easy! So unanswerable!

Fuck you, bitch!

The doors off the hall are closed. There are couples in there, in the bedrooms, doing God knows what. The only open door is to the bathroom. She locks herself in. The hair in the mirror is a horrible mess, a fright wig. She raises her dress to unwedge her underpants. Lacy red silky things. She feels ridiculous. Her makeup is smudged. She has the distinct impression she is wearing too much anyway. How did she fail to see this in the other bathroom? No wonder the boys stared at her. She tries to wash some off but it only smudges more, mixing into mud on her face. She can't find any cold cream in the cabinet or under the sink. When she bends to get toilet paper she sees that the toilet is brimming with vomit and realizes only then that the room is filled with a sickening smell. She flushes, but the toilet is clogged and the vomit rises over the lip and dribbles greasily to the floor. Fuck you, bitch!

Dabbing furiously at her face with wetted paper, she manages to get most of the makeup off, her skin emerging blotchy and already noticeably coarser. Goodbye, clown. Hello, dog. Black particles cling like dead aphids to her lashes. What do I hear for this pitiable object? Do I hear ten cents? Do I hear five?

She descends dejectedly to the bottom of the stairs and hangs back in the dark by the front door. A couple sitting where Monica and Bob used to be are really going at it. So where are Monica and Bob? Upstairs, going all the way? What happened to Marie? She spots the court jester, who is, in fact, under a table, talking to a teddy bear and giggling in an asinine fashion. The phone is in the kitchen, but she will not run this gauntlet. Instead, she goes outside and in again through the garage door. Mercifully the kitchen, for the moment, is empty, and the phone reaches into the broom closet. Thomas says he'll come right away, and the trip takes fifteen minutes, so Saskia waits in the dark in the closet.

Very nice and very sexy. This is what finally makes her cry: the thought of how kind Thomas is. How he looked down with pity on his ugly daughter and racked his brains for something to say, and finally said she looked nice just to make her feel better. And how he is coming to get her, to save her from the high school boys who drive dangerously.

She can hear people coming and going in the kitchen. When a lull occurs she sneaks out, and down the driveway to the street. Frost glitters on the pavement under the street light. Her bare feet burn. All is quiet except for the hum of laughter and wild sex coming from the house behind her. The Moon is down. She hugs herself, but continues to dissolve through every loop in the knit dress. Minutes pass. By the time Betsy's lights swing onto the street and dazzle her eyes, her brain is slow from the cold, her feet dead. "Why were you outside?" Her teeth are chattering. She looks stupidly into the cab, at her old coat lying on the seat for her. Thomas slides across and pulls her in. "You're ice cold!" he says angrily. "What happened to your shoes?"

"I . . . I guess I lost them."

He unzips his jacket and takes her under his arm, pulling the jacket around her. She clutches him and buries her face in wool. "Here, this is better." He unbuttons his wool shirt, lifts his undershirt up and stretches it over her head and down, and suddenly she has her ice-cold arms around his warm waist, her body pressed against his in the man-smelling dark inside his shirt. He lifts her knees into his lap and his big warm hands close over her feet. "What happened, honey?" Honey! She starts crying again. "Did somebody — ?"

"No," she cries. "Nobody."

"Then what?"

"Nothing. It's just me." He is massaging her feet. She grips him harder and melts on him, the tears pooling above her lips where she has pressed them into his skin. "I love you," she says.

She is still cold when they get home, and since she has no shoes he carries her inside and up the stairs, pulls back the covers on her bed and deposits her. She clings to him. She buries her face in him. He strokes her hair and kisses the top of her head. "What did happen?"

"A boy kissed me."

"Is that so bad?"

"It was terrible."

He is rubbing her back. "Are you still cold?"

"I'm better."

She feels his lips on her forehead. He starts to get up. She clings to him. "What do you want?"

"I want you to stay."

"You want to talk?"

"No."

"You want me to sleep here?"

"Yes."

"I'll stay for a bit." He takes off his shoes and brings his legs up, throwing the blanket over them both. She clings to him. He says, "I'm hot."

"I'm still cold," she says. He removes his wool shirt and undershirt. She presses her face against his warm chest. She can feel nothing but his strong shoulders, the mountainous warmth of his body, smell nothing but him.

After a while she laughs, "Now I'm hot!"

THE SASKIAD

"Good."

"Should I take off my dress?"

He doesn't answer. He strokes her hair, kisses the top of her head. "If you want."

She releases him and shimmies, pulling the dress past her hips and arching her back to get it to her shoulders. He lifts her with one hand in the middle of her back so that she can slip it over her head. As she hugs herself to him he shifts his hand down, lifting her lower, and his hand keeps moving strongly down her legs, pulling her underpants down to her knees. He changes his grip and pulls them farther, and she kicks and they catch on her ankles, she kicks again and her legs are free. She lets her knees fall open. He is now half on top of her. She presses her face into his chest and waits for him to do what he does. He is gripping her tightly, his thigh between her legs. She closes her eyes and lifts her face and feels him kissing her. She opens her mouth and he kisses her like in her dreams, like Jane but with the bristly beard, and she presses herself against his kiss as though she might crawl into him, but he pulls away and holds her head firmly against his neck. She kisses his beard. Long seconds go by. He doesn't move. She knows where it is. Is she supposed to grab it? Just reach for his belt and he'll do the rest. But she couldn't possibly, not in a zillion years. She despondently kisses his beard and does nothing.

Suddenly he is getting up. She holds on desperately. "No," he says gently, pulling her hands away. "No, no." She goes limp. He folds her arms in front of her and wraps the blanket tightly around her up to her neck and holds it under her chin in a hard grip. She would never escape from this cocoon. "No." He kisses her forehead, then presses her firmly down into the mattress. He is heaving himself up. He is gone.

She lies for a long time in the cocoon, not moving.

Later, she has a dream. She is locked in a room. She is dressed skimpily, and her captors are slavering over her. "Get your fucking hands off me!" she screams at them. A rage like she has never felt before fills her, her head will explode if she doesn't vent the pressure by screaming. She fights them off while parts of her voluptuous body reveal themselves through the skimpy clothes. They are in agony they want her so badly, but they can't have her, or any of her secrets, either! She grabs a whip with which to whip them. But then she sees it's a you-know-what, right in her hand.

The talk at school on Monday is that Marie drank so much at the party she had to have her stomach pumped while Sue Walsh gave Danny Rizzuto a blowjob in the bathroom where Marie and Saskia made themselves up.

15

On Wednesday the schools close at noon and everyone goes home for Thanksgiving. That afternoon Thomas finishes installing the solar panels and climbs down from the roof. In the basement he oils and stores the tools. Then Saskia spies him in the common room, where he sits tugging at his beard, his face gone spookily blank again.

Is it her fault?

On Monday John came to Wholeworld while Saskia was in school, and when she got off the bus that afternoon Thomas was in the common room saying to Lauren, "I've been a gold mine for the White Corporation, they ought to be thanking me for all the Kruger-rands I've put in their coffers. But they just can't stand it that *I* did it, it drove them up the wall when they shunted the crazy hippies over here and waited for the whole thing to collapse and we made it work. John doesn't even have the guts to show up when I'm here."

"He's afraid of you."

"That's insulting."

"But what are we going to do about the money?"

"The charges are in your name, they'll bail you out. I'm saving them money in the long run."

On Tuesday Thomas announced that Wholeworld would not be

celebrating Thanksgiving, and everyone let him down. They gaped stupidly at each other, with "does not compute" blinking on their faces. To be fair, since Christmas has never been celebrated at Wholeworld (on the grounds that it is hollow, commercial, and narrowly Western), Thanksgiving has always been their biggest holiday. Lauren has traditionally baked a delicious casserole of maize, yams, onions, buttermilk, and sage, blanketed with cheddar cheese. Saskia can't remember a time when Lauren did not do this, and she always got an indescribably hyggelig feeling at the contemplation of that casserole. Since Lauren made it only once a year, it became a marker of time passing. Saskia can distinctly remember sitting at the two-ton oak table and saying to herself, as the casserole grandly steamed: "Now I'm six years old. Next year I'll be seven." Imagine! So few things, so very few things, have been more or less constant at Wonderland/Godhead/White-on-the-Water/Wholeworld.

Perhaps it's no wonder, then, that Lauren and Saskia gaped at each other. "It's a harvest holiday," Lauren said. You could practically hear her gears grinding. "Everybody has them."

"As a matter of fact," Thomas pointed out, "it's not a harvest holiday. You're a farmer — have you harvested anything lately? Real harvest holidays are in October." He was so earnest he went up on his toes, endeavoring to get closer to Lauren's face so that he could more effectively pour the truth into it. "The timing of Thanksgiving is the proof! The Pilgrims were late! They suckered the Indians into helping them survive the first winter. So thanks! Thanks be to Christ, and pass the smallpox blankets. No, I don't feel like celebrating that."

Once Saskia thought about it, she remembered that the much-vaunted casserole included cheese, and since they don't eat cheese anymore, the casserole is irrevocably a thing of the past whether they celebrate Thanksgiving or not. And anyway, Thomas does all the cooking, so if he says there isn't going to be a Thanksgiving, there isn't going to be a Thanksgiving, and arguing about it is as silly as telling the sun not to come up in the morning.

Thursday dawns cold and dark, with chalk-dust flurries of snow blowing in from the lake and whitening the seedpods of the high dead grass. Across the country millions of Novamundians are beheading and eviscerating birds to symbolize their thankfulness for nature. Saskia stands at her window, wrapped tight in a blanket, and silently watches the snow swirl against the pane and retreat, swirl and retreat. She hears Mim go down to the bathroom. Why doesn't she wake Mim anymore? She doesn't know. No, she does know. When Mim took over the milking for the summer she learned to get up on her own, and she still does it, even though the milking is a thing of the past. After all, Mim is in seventh grade now. Seventh grade! Saskia sees her occasionally in the gloomy halls of Tyler Junior, seemingly thriving in her ecological niche. She still has her two friends, she still carries her books adorably in front of her. But one must admit she is older, a different person. Saskia is not sure Mim would be her boatswain again, even if Saskia wanted her to be.

And why doesn't Saskia wake the crew anymore? Because Thomas wakes them. His and Lauren's bedroom is next to their quarters, so it only makes sense. And Thomas in three months has succeeded where Saskia in five years had not: Quentin has stopped wetting his bed. When was the last time she sopped up his slobbery chin? She can't remember. When was the last time Austin or Shannon did a single simple thing Saskia asked them to do?

She dresses and descends. In the deep gloom of the kitchen she finds Thomas brewing coffee. She raises her hand to the light chain, but he says, "Don't." She cringes. No, no.

They sit at the oak table for a few minutes all to themselves. They cup their coffees, dip their faces to the fumes. Speak! She doesn't speak. "Better enjoy this," he says. God how she loves that twinkle in his eye.

He rouses the crew and allows each member a cup of sweet herb tea and a piece of toast slathered with whatever they want. Then he tells everyone to go get blankets. She comes back down to find him out on the porch, where he's moved the couch. "Have a seat." Lauren is already there. The crew straggle down one by one, and he has them dump their blankets before climbing on. He spreads a blanket across laps. Then another, and another, and a quilt, and more blankets, until they are all buried to the chin. He puts his head under and crawls in. The mountain shifts. The crew shriek. He emerges in the middle, with crew under each arm. "There!" he says, looking around. "*Hvor hyggeligt!*"

All agree. Saskia burrows deeper. Thomas hushes the twins, and everyone holds their breath, waiting for him to speak. But he doesn't speak. He stares at the thin blowing snow, across the driveway to the trees. After his hush, no one would dare say a word.

"Do you hear that?" he says at last, quietly.

Saskia cocks an ear. The hush of snow, the tickle of an old leaf turning over the driveway gravel.

"What?" Austin asks.

"Silence," Thomas says. "Beautiful, isn't it?"

None of the crew answers. "Yeah," Saskia breathes. It's probably too sophisticated a thought for them.

For a long minute they all listen to silence.

"Today we're going to do something that Man never does," he says. "We're going to do nothing. Everywhere else today, the furnaces are going full blast and all the lights are on, so the cold and dark of a real November will be safely outside. When people look at their windows all they see is reflections of themselves. Thanks for this blindness. Thanks for this womb.

"Well, no thanks. We have a responsibility to understand where we are, what we are. Someone has to. So we here, on this porch, we aren't going to eat, we aren't going to turn on lights or heat, we aren't going to impose ourselves on the world today. We are going to let the world enter us. We are going to feel the cold on our faces, the snow on our hands. In our bellies we'll feel hunger, the hunger of winter.

"Silence is the hardest thing to learn. Look around you. See things you've never seen before, right here, where you've been a million times. Don't blot out the world with words."

With that, he stops speaking. Minutes go by. The grass by the driveway slowly whitens, while the gravel remains dark. A mist hovers over the gray lake. Everyone is quiet. Shannon fidgeted a moment ago, but is now still. Saskia steals a glance at Thomas and drinks in his profile, his blue eyes accepting the world. He waited for her, not imposing himself. Snowflakes blow onto the porch and bounce on the quilt before rolling smooth as pinheads into the creases. When a flake strikes her hand she glimpses for a split second the smashed crystal, replaced a moment later by a droplet of water. If only she could be like that snowflake, abandoning herself to the winds of the world, ready to melt into whatever home the winds blew her to.

The minutes melt and run together like the snowflakes. Saskia watches the snow gather against the bottom of the garage door and dozes. She wakes to see a chipmunk crossing the driveway, stopping and starting, raising its nose to twitch at smells humans never smell. "A chipmunk," she blurts out. She bites her tongue.

But Thomas is not angry. "Is it?" he says.

"Isn't it?"

"What does that mean, 'chipmunk'? Does the word mean we know what that life is? Or does it separate us from that life?"

"Um . . ."

"Chipmunk implies not-chipmunk. If you are not-chipmunk you don't know chipmunk, do you?"

"Um . . ."

"Of course not," Lauren butts in.

"What do you know?" Saskia says.

"Let's be quiet," Thomas says.

Shannon is half asleep. Austin is looking down under the blankets. He is probably twiddling his thumbs under there. He yawns. None of this would mean anything to him, of course, but he knows better than to cause trouble. Saskia looks back at the driveway. The chipmunk, or whatever it was, is gone.

Jo comes out of her trailer and circles to the back of the house, to enter at the kitchen and secrete in the bathroom. She looks toward the porch, but doesn't speak or wave, and keeps walking. When she comes out again around lunchtime she doesn't even look. Thomas must have warned her to leave them alone. The snow slacks off and the wind picks up. The lake darkens into ripples, and almond eyes of cornflower blue open and close in the sky. Lauren's unprotected ears commune with the cold, turning scarlet, until she gives up rubbing them and raises the quilt over her head. Mim has to go secrete, but Saskia doesn't, she wisely did that when she went up to get her blankets. A couple of lives that Saskia would usually call "squirrels" chase each other with a frantic scratching sound around a tree trunk, up and down like a double helix, and then disappear upward into the needles. Branches dip and shake off snow as the two lives jump to another tree. Gorgon appears on the porch, thinner now that she is a barn cat, jumps up on the quilt and stalks from face to face, waking Shannon with her cold fur, stopping at Thomas and settling down on his chest with a self-encircling curl of her tail. Saskia spends a long time looking at her, until she falls asleep. Gorgon, that is, not Saskia.

Shannon gets permission to go secrete. When she crawls back under the blankets she announces, "I'm hungry."

"So am I," Thomas says. "Isn't it wonderful?"

Saskia is hungry, too. It is easier for her than for the crew to see how wonderful it is, since she has often gone for a day, eating little. And prepared by all the silent and holy meals on Ven, she is much more able to meditate. Wasn't she just minutes ago feeling at one with the two lives on the tree? Didn't she feel that the blue eyes in the clouds were her own eyes, contactless? Saskia thought she wanted the casserole. She was like a cow wanting to go to the same field each morning because it is all she knows. But Thomas knew better, and here they are, hyggelig on the couch, blanketed, their breath grandly steaming. They are themselves the casserole. They have become that which they desired, they have entered into the object of their covetousness.

The afternoon goes on forever. The crew start to fidget more and more, and finally Thomas says, "Anyone who can't stand it anymore can go." That settles them down. But he goes on, "This isn't a test. It

really is all right if you want to go. I know it's hard to sit still so long."
After a few minutes, Mim and the twins creep out, shamefaced. You
can hear them in the kitchen. A light goes on upstairs. Quentin stays,
murmuring quietly to his diplodocus. Thomas strokes his hair. Saskia
makes a long waking dream about Tycho. When she opens her eyes
again it is dusk. So soon? She watches the garage door fade away.

It is night.

Out of the darkness comes Thomas's voice, mesmerizing after so
much silence.

"When I was fourteen years old, we were taught dissection in
school. They gave us dead frogs, and we were shown how to cut them
open, how to identify and remove the organs. I didn't like the fact that
the frogs were dead. They had been stored in formaldehyde, and
their whole bodies, all their organs, were gray. I thought, What's the
point of this? You learn to do dissections so you can fix something,
don't you? A dead frog doesn't need anything except a decent burial.
I wanted to be a veterinarian. I imagined myself setting birds' bones
in my backyard. Animals would come to me with thorns in their
paws. I caught a frog and anesthetized it by wedging chloroform-
soaked cotton in the neck of a funnel and holding the funnel over the
frog's head. It was easy. When the frog was knocked out, I spread it on
its back on a board and dissected it as I had done in school. I did a
careful job, folding back the skin and the chest muscles and tacking
them to the board. It was like opening a watch, taking the cover off,
removing the gears. I exposed the heart, and watched it beat. Just like
the spring of a watch. This was what I would do as a vet, I thought. I
pretended that there had been something wrong with that heart,
and I pretended that I had just fixed it. You're all better! Time to close
you up."

The voice pauses. It is pitch black. "It was only then that I realized.
They had shown us how to dissect a frog, but they hadn't shown us
how to put one back together.

"I stared at that little frog where it lay on the board, its insides open
to me, its heart beating. This wasn't a watch with a cover I could snap

back on. This was a living creature that I had mutilated. And there was nothing I could do for it. I soaked more cotton in chloroform and put the funnel over the frog's head. It would be easy to tell when it died, since the heart was visible. Here in the dark, right now, in front of me, I can see that heart, the size of a shirt button, slowing . . . slowing . . ."

The voice stops. On the other side of the lake a train is trundling toward the salt mine, sounding clumsy and sad. Then it gets where it is going, and the whole universe seems to be expressed by the whisper of falling snow.

16

The next morning, Saskia luxuriates over her coffee and a slice of toast. Outside the window the weather is warmer, the day glistening with rivulets in the driveway and sunlight sparkling the drops tasseling from the roof. Thomas comes in and says in the Old Speech, "That was good, wasn't it?"

"Let's do it every week!"

He smiles and rubs her neck, saying nothing.

But wouldn't you know it, just when the crystal is beginning to hum nicely, the impurity comes over. "It's not even ten," Saskia protests at the front door. But the car is already gone.

"Where's Thomas?" Jane tilts to one side and the other to look over Saskia's shoulders.

"I haven't the slightest idea. Maybe he's in town."

"Betsy's in the driveway."

"So maybe he flew."

"Just tell me where he is."

Thomas is approaching from the garage. Saskia sighs. "He's right behind you."

Thomas mounts the porch, scowling. "You're here early."

"I already tried to tell her," Saskia says.

"I just thought, there's nothing to do at my house and it's such a nice day —"

"We had a nicer day yesterday, without you."

"I don't want to get into this," Thomas says.

"We had a great day, sitting on the porch and meditating, while you were stuffing your face."

Jane turns to Thomas. "Couldn't we —"

"I said I didn't want to get into this!" he says sharply.

"You could drive her home," Saskia says in the Old Speech.

"Why should I?" he grumbles. "It's not my fault she's here."

Jane always gets upset when they talk in the Old Speech. "I could go read for a while, or something. I just thought . . . But if you're busy. It's no big deal."

"Don't let her stay," Saskia pleads, still in the Old Speech.

"It's none of my concern! I'm going sailing."

"Can I go, too?" It is a measure of how much Jane's untimely arrival has discombobulated Saskia that she blurts out the request at all.

"Not this time."

"Are you going sailing?" Jane asks.

"How did you guess?" Saskia says sarcastically.

"Can I come?"

"For pete's sake, Jane! He goes on his own, don't you know anything? Leave him alone!"

"You're not my mother, Saskia," Thomas says, his face turning deep red. "So shut up."

Air goes out through Saskia's mouth.

"Finally," Jane gloats. "A little peace and quiet around here."

"Both of you! Christ, this is embarrassing! Who is the adult here? I am! Don't you have lives of your own? I feel like I'm drowning in women!" He stalks off the porch.

Saskia watches him go, sparkling and dancing like a sun-mirage. "Boy, you really pissed him off."

"Me?"

"He only gets that way when you're around. I don't know what it is, you just rub him the wrong way somehow."

"Just fuck you, Saskia. OK? Just fuck you!"

When did Jane turn so ugly, so hard and nasty? Her pinched mouth, her calculating eyes. She has no friends at school, she never goes to parties, she wants only to follow Thomas, yes master yes master, grab him and cling to him like a drowning little girl, pull him under with her arms in a vise-like grip around his neck, drowning him, too.

Saskia follows her inside. "This isn't your house!"

Jane slings her knapsack over her shoulder. "I don't want to stay in your fucking house. And Thomas doesn't either. He's sick of this place."

Saskia follows her back out on the porch. "Who says?"

Jane continues off the porch and up the driveway.

"Who says?" Saskia repeats, right behind her. Jane doesn't answer. "Nobody says," she concludes derisively.

"That's right. Nobody," Jane says over her shoulder. "You'll find out."

"Where are you going?"

"To the garden."

"Oh, little nature girl! I suppose the squirrels will come and talk to you!"

Jane stops and turns, heaves a long-suffering sigh. "Saskia, why don't you just leave me alone?"

The horrible thought washes over Saskia that she is being a jerk. Not only a jerk, but a childish jerk. Jane is fourteen, and Saskia is thirteen, and Jane is a woman who has had sex with Thomas and Saskia is a little girl who is scared even to touch you-know-whats.

Jane walks away.

Saskia stares dully down at the house, at the fixed-up porch and new gutters, the lovingly fitted new shingles sprinkled here and there like a cuneiform inscription saying, "Thomas was here." She can see the barn below the house, and the lake below the barn, and *Lila* leaving the dock. Note how much he takes her out on weekends. Why? Because the weekends are when Jane comes over.

But he takes *Lila* out on weekdays, too. Out on the lake, *Lila* tacks. So what does it matter if he has to get away? He is sensitive. He starts to hum too much. He goes out on the water so his crystal won't shatter. *Lila* tacks and retacks like someone pacing, lost in thought, not to be disturbed.

Saskia makes her way up to the garden. "I'll find out what?"

"I thought you were going to leave me alone."

"Please tell me," she says, with all the reasonableness she can muster.

"We're going away together, OK?"

"Yeah, you said that before and you're still around."

"We've got the money now."

"Dream on!"

"Thanks, I will. Can I be left alone now?"

Saskia wants to hit her, smash her face with a rock, anything to wipe off that smug, sure expression. Instead she goes to find Lauren.

17

She should have told her a long time ago. What was she so worried about? Jane is just a plaything, no more important than the ones Thomas led out of the garden in Wonderland days, and Lauren understood that then, so surely she will understand it now. Saskia was giving Jane far too much credit in imagining that her little fling with Thomas was some deep dark secret.

She finds Lauren in the storage shed, going through the produce crates. "It's you," Lauren says in a friendly enough manner, turning a crate this way and that.

"What are you doing?"

"Thomas thought it would be a good idea to fix up some of the crates."

"Can I help?"

Lauren shrugs. With her crew cut and the baggy khaki pants with the pockets low on the thighs she looks like a soldier. Saskia still isn't used to it. "If you want. You can check those."

They work in silence. All Saskia's crates look fine. In fact, she can see places where Thomas has recently fixed them. She would recognize those three perfectly staggered tacks anywhere. Finally she discerns a small crack. "Is that bad enough to fix?"

Lauren presses a dirty thumb against it. "I'll ask Thomas. Put it in that pile."

"I was just thinking."

"Not again."

"Jane and I were talking just a minute ago, up in the field."

"I thought she was taking a nap."

"Why'd you think that?"

"Because you usually only help me when Jane is taking a nap."

"Really?"

"Mm-hmm." Lauren inspects her crate minutely. "Not that I expect much help out of you even then." She transfers her gaze to Saskia. "Like now. Are you going to help or are you going to just stand there like a dumb bunny?"

"About Jane . . ."

"I'm not interested in talking about Jane."

"Well, about her taking a nap, or whatever."

Lauren cocks an eyebrow. "Yes?"

"I mean, she's not really . . ." Oh boy, here we go. "I mean . . ." But she just peters out, her face burning.

"Spare yourself the trouble, Saskia. I don't care about that."

"About what?" Saskia can't even look at her.

"Why do you want to tell me now? What's going on? You're trying to get back at Jane for something? You're feeling sorry for your stupid mother?"

"You already know?"

Lauren lets out air. A sigh? A summoning of patience? "Of course I know." Saskia peeks at her doubtfully. "I'm not as stupid as you think I am. If I were possessive about Thomas I would have gone crazy ten years ago."

Funny, this is exactly what Saskia imagined. That Lauren would know and would not care. That she would rise above the fray and take her satisfaction in the knowledge that she was Thomas's true love. But the funny thing is, now that Saskia is faced with exactly what she imagined, it seems all wrong. But what's wrong with it? Isn't it magnanimous? On her part, to share Thomas, and on his, to share himself? "But isn't Jane kind of . . . *young?*"

"If she wants to have sex, she's not too young. At least she wants it, she's lucky."

"But she says she's going to go away with him."

Lauren looks uncomfortable. "Wherever did she get that idea? The poor thing."

"So Thomas isn't going away, then."

"Not with her. I couldn't imagine that."

"But he's not going away at all, right?"

"I don't know what you mean. We can't keep him here forever."

"When is he going?"

She shrugs. "When he wants to."

"But what about us?"

"Saskia, you can't tie Thomas down."

God, that condescending look is irritating! "If you're so independent, you seemed pretty darned glad I got him to come back."

Lauren smirks. "You?" This is the way she talks to the aphids. *You?* she says, spraying them with the soap that will dissolve them, what are *you* doing here? "You didn't get him to come back."

"I talked him into it. He didn't want to come."

"Don't have such a high opinion of yourself. He told me he was planning to come from the time he first asked us on the trip."

"Gee, that's funny. You said at the time he was really only asking me." Ha! Touché!

"He saw *you* all summer. So he must have come back to see me, right?" Actually, Saskia can sort of remember thinking that at the time. "Or maybe he came to see Quentin."

"Quentin?"

"What?" Lauren asks mockingly. "You mean you haven't figured it out about Quentin? Saskia, *all these years* you never noticed? Look at the two of you in the mirror sometime!"

"But — but — but —"

"You sound like a motorboat."

"But Quentin is Jo's!"

On Lauren's face a hateful little smile is curling up.

"Isn't he?"

"You get a gold star."

Being an only child was good enough for me, he said. It's good enough for you, right?

"Don't take *my* word for it!" Lauren spreads her hands, exasperated. "Why should you, you never do. Ask Jo."

Jo Flynn? Halibut Jo? "Impossible," Saskia says. She pours conviction over the ridiculous idea like wet cement, burying it.

Lauren hisses and turns away. She picks up a crate. "You're just . . . you're just too stubborn for words."

Saskia stands in the doorway of the shed and stares at the fuzz on Lauren's nape. Lauren goes back to checking the crates, as if Saskia did not exist, as if they hadn't been talking about anything in the slightest bit important. It occurs to Saskia to wonder if she understands Lauren at all. Strange question! She never framed it before. But surely it's natural not to understand adults. Thomas and Lauren are the adults here! And Jo!

And Jane? Is Jane enough of an adult that she understands Lauren? Are your eyes opened the moment you have sex with Thomas? Do they all — Thomas, Lauren, Jane, and Jo — get together and marvel at what a child Saskia still is?

She turns up toward the house, but stops. She starts down toward the lake, but stops again. Jane is in the garden. Thomas is on the lake. Lauren is in the shed. An equilateral triangle. But why stop there? Jo is in her trailer. And Quentin is in the house, in front of a mirror, bemoaning what an ugly runt he is.

Where does Saskia belong? She wanted to leave with him when he left the first time, she followed him up the driveway amid the flashing lights, the howling of the dog. But they pushed her out of the way and closed the door.

She runs. Where?

18

But even Marilyn's stall is not safe. Soon Thomas and Jane waltz in and ascend to the loft, without noticing her. She flees down to the dock. She huddles in *Lila*, holding the tiller until it gets dark and too cold. Trudging at last up to the house, she tries to slip up the stairs but Thomas appears silhouetted in the door of the warm lighted kitchen and steps into the hall. "Aren't you going to have dinner?"

"No."

"What's the matter?"

"I'm not hungry."

He comes forward. They stare at each other for a couple of seconds, Thomas massaging the dishtowel in his hands.

"You're not going to leave us, are you?" A second later she realizes she actually said it this time.

He is frowning. "Why do you ask that?"

"Nothing. No reason." She runs upstairs.

In her room she can hear them at table, the cantus firmus of Thomas's voice, Jane's laugh lilting above, the background static of crew noise. When Jane is here it's fun and games for everyone. Except for Jo, who probably left early, and Lauren, silent as usual, no doubt sitting straight-backed and watching Jane and Thomas eat and laugh with who knows what thoughts. Healthy, probably, and unpossessive, pitying Jane for being deluded about Thomas running away with her.

Kitchen noises, cleaning. Lauren's voice now, directing Jane how best to help Thomas. The crew disperses through the house, Mim comes up the stairs and passes Saskia's door to reach her own. What is she doing in her room? Does she ever think about Saskia anymore? Why doesn't Saskia *after all these years* know anything about Mim, about what she thinks about things, about what she dreams about? Is it because Mim is too pure for Saskia, too innocent? And in the quarters below, Austin and Shannon, wild and alike, noisy and unruly. They make Saskia inwardly cringe and quail, now that she has lost control of them. Does she understand them any better? And finally Quentin, most mysterious of all, his only real friends his dinosaurs, to whom he talks. When did she betray him?

"Story!" Thomas calls from below, and all the ions align themselves and flow down the stairs to him. This is the hardest part, not to hear a Thomas tale. But if she went, she would look at Jane and think of her filthy lucre. Or she would look at Lauren and think of Jane. Or she would look at Quentin and think: high forehead, check; round face, check . . . Lauren only said it to throw her off balance, but it has its own skewed logic. Thomas apparently knew Jo in the Wonderland days and her epitome of anti-Thomasness does seem to intrigue him, in a perverse way. And Saskia and Quentin do look, purely coincidentally — now that Saskia thinks about it — not entirely dissimilar.

Sounds of the crew ascending, replete with story, Thomas making the rounds of goodnight kisses. He opens her door. "You still alive?"

"Yeah."

He sits on the edge of her bed, his beautiful hands hidden in his folded arms. "Are you going to tell me what's the matter?"

"Nothing's the matter."

"Is it about you and me last weekend?"

"No."

"Are you sure?"

"Yes."

He nods, filing that away. His arms are still folded. "I can't stay forever, you know." Just what Lauren said. They all meet in the barn, to compare notes. What should we tell child Saskia?

"Why not?"

He makes a gesture of obviousness. "My life isn't here."

That hurts so much, she can't think of anything to say.

"There's work I have to do. You understand that."

"Yes," she says humbly.

"I'm nothing here."

"You're everything!"

"No!" He is suddenly angry. "I'm a ghost. I should have died here. But instead I seem to have come back, to haunt the place."

She so much wants him to kiss her. She reaches for him. With a defensive gesture almost of panic he gets up. "Please," she pleads. "Give me another chance. I'll be good!"

He retreats to the door. "The last thing we need is another chance."

He is gone.

She lies awake and listens to movements in the house. Thomas is in the bedroom with Lauren, then on the stairs, then in the bathroom. Then back with Lauren? She is not sure.

Utter quiet. Where is Thomas? She goes to her window, but sees nothing in the field outside. And where is Jane? She never came up to Saskia's room. A plot! Perhaps Lauren is the deluded one, not Jane. Jane knew what she was doing all along. She mixed a potion for him in a golden cup and with evil thoughts in her dark heart she added the drug to it. She lurks in the garage, getting out the ladder that he put away when he was done with the solar panels. She will toss pebbles against his window and he will throw open the sash and they will climb down the ladder together and walk up the road to the car waiting around the first bend. Saskia will follow and catch them just as they reach the getaway car and say, "Thomas, what are you doing outside?" and he will turn to her with eyes spookily blank and answer, "Outside?"

She turns on her lamp. Funny that Saskia, seller, has never rolled a joint before. Does she even have any paper? Rummaging, she finds a few squares she and Jane left behind when they went away for the summer. She rolls something abysmal. She recycles it into something only bad, which burns unevenly. Leaning back on piled pillows, she smokes it down to a confetto. She rolls a second.

What is Saskia doing?

She is preparing for battle, if you must know. She realized a long time ago that the antidote to Circe's bewitching brew, the mysterious moly that Hermes gave to Odysseus, was in fact the Stone, but the eternal question remained: "But the Stone, in fact, is what?" Well, the sages were right: after long searching, you will ultimately discover it right under your nose. "Black at the root, with a milky flower," the *Odyssey* says. Black ash and its curling bloom of smoke. Safely Stoned, Saskia will toss aside the poisoned cup and rush at Jane, drawing from her side her sharp sword.

To kill her, yes. Alas, she has no choice. Sulfur burns in her lungs and mercury fumes make her eyes water. The other clue was provided by Marco, but not even recognized as such, until now: how many times has he told her about the Sheik of the Mountain and his team of Assassins, or — as they style themselves in the Saracen tongue — the *Hashshashin*: the eaters of hashish? Mortally feared they were, as they fearlessly closed in on their target, the ecstatic trance on them, their eyes fixed on the Paradise they knew would soon be theirs. When right is on your side, you will surely prevail.

Saskia stubs out the second confetto. The time has come.

She rises from her bed and glides down the stairs. Thomas's door is closed and quiet. She continues down, into deeper and darker realms. The common room is empty. Where are they? Fumbling animalistically in some dark corner? She glides ghostlike to the kitchen, the darkest and deepest of realms.

Don't turn on the light, he said. Of course not. From the racks on the walls she extracts jars of powders, unguents, essences. From a cupboard, an agate mortar and pestle. She fires up the athanor and the blue light quivers on the shelves above. She takes down a crucible and places it over the fire.

The secret fire is the slow flame, the generative heat that provides gentle coction for forty days, while the natural fire is the dual salt of aqua fortis and aqua regia. She tips red powder, the dried blood of children, into the bubbling, whose subtle nitre has matured into that peerless salt, Virgin's Milk. Now the action of Mars is desired, and Saskia pounds iron filings in an agate mortar and steeps them in aqua vitae until the resurrected substance — which Adepts call the Knight with the Lance — is added to the Scaly Dragon, piercing it and drawing out the Virgin's Milk. The whole is poured off and cohobated until the desired consistency is achieved. Thus is created the female element, mercuric and volatile.

Separately, Saskia prepares the male element, fiery and catalytic, composed of philosophic sulfur and the prime substance. She spoons nuggets of Prime Substance out of a glass jar and presses them with her fingers around the sides of the mortar, then pours the sulfur to pool inside, making the Golden Egg, laid by the Philosophic Goose. The Egg is returned to the crucible and incubated through the action of the slow fire until it hatches and the spirit of the Goose is released to fly either northward (daylight, advancing, male) or southward (darkness, retreating, female). The broken Egg is mixed into a paste and then reduced over the fire to a calx. What is thus obtained is a well-calcined gold oxide, to which added black earth, which sets it to bubbling so that an oil rises to the surface. Saskia skims off this tincture with a pigeon's feather and sets it aside.

Now comes the crucial moment when the two primal elements, male and female, are brought together. Saskia stirs the mixture with a bamboo stake hardened in the eye of the athanor, and the compound commences immediately to bubble. An excellent sign! The compound foams obscenely, popping with small explosions that throw off a foul smell. Success! Saskia has achieved the resolution of two opposing principles! The perfect Synthesis!

In such a manner does the Adept produce the Elixir of Life. But — ha ha! — Saskia has performed it all backward! And now as she decants the frothing liquid, thick with scum and stinking horribly, into the golden cup she intones, "Gnis Enaj! Dne yht teem!"

Pinching her nose, she holds the cup straight-armed out in front of her and reascends the stairs. In her chamber, in her own bed, the usurper Jane lies sleeping, and Saskia pauses for a moment to watch the dark girl breathe. Then she jabs her in the stomach and she starts awake, wha — ?, her head rising from the pillow, her mouth opening upward, and Saskia tips the golden cup and pours the scalding poison down her throat. Jane splutters and chokes. She scrabbles at her throat, the tendons on her neck standing out, and falls naked out of the bed to the floor. She tries to crawl to the door, but Saskia blocks her. It should take a few seconds. Ah, there. She is going into convulsions. Her back keeps arching backward, farther and farther, impossibly far (that would be the strychnine), and from her mouth billow clouds reeking of bitter almonds (that's the cyanide kicking in). With a last wrenching spasm that draws her lips back from her milk-white teeth into a textbook case of the *rictus sardonicus*, Jane swallows her tongue, vomits, and dies.

Finally, a little peace and quiet around here.

Saskia strips the sheet from the bed and winds Jane's body in it. Boy, is she heavy! Saskia staggers to the window and throws open the sash. Grunting, she lifts Jane's legs over the sill and rocks her to her waist, at which point her own weight pulls her torso and arms slithering through. Saskia looks out to make sure she cleared the greenhouse.

Chancing to glance up, she notices peasants coming across the fields, carrying torches and pitchforks. She tries to draw her head back in, but her hair, which reaches down to the ground outside, is caught on something. She pulls at it, but like a fouled anchor it will not budge. Someone is climbing it. A face appears over the parapet, a peasant with blackened stumps for teeth, leering and pulling himself along her hair, hand over hand. With all her strength she yanks her head back into the room and brings the sash slashing down like a guillotine blade, cutting her hair off. She runs to warn Tycho, banging on all the doors in the garret to wake the other Adepts and racing down the stone steps to slide — in the nick of time — the oaken beam across the front gate. Tycho is below on the marble slab, and as she bursts in he throws back his coverlet, "What is it?," leaping up. She glimpses for a second his anatomical incorrectness, the Ken-doll smoothness between his legs, but that is simply the Whale in him, and he reaches for his skin hanging on a peg and shrugs it on, leg and leg, centering with his hand the stiff man-thing, pulling the manhood over his sleek head and fastening it with the gold and silver nose.

"We're under attack!" Saskia says.

He grabs his sword off the wall and runs with Saskia up the stairs to look out a loophole. "Christian's men!" he growls.

The enemies of the TAO! Hyperbores has been invaded!

"But — but — but —" Saskia splutters, "*we're* the ones who were supposed to invade! Weren't we?" Tycho bounds up the stairs, not answering. She runs after him. "Weren't we?" She finds him among the Adepts, furiously directing them to parapets, battlements, barbicans. She tugs at his sleeve. "They couldn't actually win, could they?" He runs farther upward.

She catches him again in the belvedere, where cauldrons of molten lead are bubbling. "Help me with this!" he commands, and the two of them drag a cauldron to one of the windows and tip it forward, pouring the molten lead down the walls. Lauren is scaling the wall, a knife in her teeth, and Saskia directs a river of the molten metal right into her upturned face, scouring her from the wall.

The peasants are falling back! Out across the expanses of snow and ice, Saskia can make out Christian, towering miles high, his leathery wings fanning the winds, beginning to scowl at the failure of his forces.

"Jeppe!" Tycho bellows, leaning over the parapet. "Jeppe, no!"

Down below Jeppe is removing the oaken beam from the front gate and throwing the doors wide. The peasants turn from their headlong flight and pour, cheering, past him as Christian begins to laugh and his wings beat faster and the icy winds mount to a gale, a driving blizzard. The windows of the belvedere blow out, forcing Saskia and Tycho to seek shelter below, and in an instant they are in the thick of the fighting, laying about to right and left. The Adepts have been overwhelmed and slaughtered, the marble slab overturned, the pipes torn from the walls. Tycho and Saskia fight back to back, holding off the murderous horde while inching toward the inner sanctum. Tycho lunges and opens the door, pulls Saskia through, and barricades it behind them.

Safe!

They turn from the door. Jeppe is sitting behind Tycho's desk.

"Oh!" he squeaks, jumping up and grinning in a feces-consuming fashion. "Hee hee! Hello, boss." He does a cartwheel. "I'm sure glad you're OK! Say, did you hear the one about — ?"

Tycho grabs the dwarf by the hair and throws him on the floor. Unbuckling his sword belt, he twists the stunted arms and legs back and cinches them tightly, throws the free end of the belt over the roofbeam, and hauls Jeppe to a convenient height.

"Hey boss, this kind of hurts," Jeppe says. "I mean, I like a little rough stuff, too, everybody does, that's natural, but —"

Tycho swings his bright sword and lops off Jeppe's nose.

"I bead, I lige a liddle rubb stubb doo, dads dadural —"

The sword flashes again. Saskia turns away. She always hated this part. She goes to the window. The Moon is full, and across her face, forming V's like laughter lines, the geese are flying.

She sits up in her bed. Daylight. She has slept in her clothes. It's late. Where is Jane? What day is it?

Thomas has left.

The knowledge comes to her in a flash. She looks out the window, toward the dock. *Lila* is gone.

19

But Saskia was wrong. Seconds after she looked out the window, she heard Thomas's voice, somewhere in the house. Jane had been too angry at Saskia to come upstairs, and had slept on the common room couch. Thomas had taken *Lila* out of the water early that morning because it was getting too cold for sailing.

Simple, reasonable, obvious. When will Saskia ever learn that life doesn't so neatly follow portents and dreams? Isn't that an indication of what a hopeless child she is?

She gets another chance to learn her lesson four days later — four inconclusive days, during which she sees a bit of both Thomas and Jane, and wants to talk to both of them about hugely important things, but doesn't — when she wakes in the morning after a night of ordinary dreams she can hardly remember and finds a note tacked to her door: "Saskia — I don't see the point of goodbyes. What could I say that would mean anything? Nothing would help. Forgive me."

20

So that's life! So grow up!

That was Wednesday, approximately a million years ago. Tomorrow will be Monday, and there is a rumor going around that Saskia will be going to school in the morning, but she doesn't set much store by that. It's only a theory. Amazing how her things all sit stupidly around as if nothing ever changes. Her spears would be perfectly happy to fight a Khanate war again, the charts still think they show the way to treasure that was unearthed, worn out, and thrown away years ago.

Twenty words. Twenty-one, if you count "Saskia." But why should she count "Saskia"? She doesn't even know what it means. Why didn't she ever ask Thomas what it meant? She pestered him about everything else under the sun, but never that simple question. She was afraid there was a simple answer. She was afraid he would shrug his shoulders and say, "It doesn't mean anything. I just liked the sound of it." That would put her in the same boat with Lila, who is fated to die every few years, or with *Lila*, who must periodically have her hull staved in, by *Green* or by Thomas himself. Although the pattern remained incomplete this time. *Lila* was still in her cradle in the garage, under a tarp, untouched. Why? But there she goes again, looking for patterns. Grow up!

Lauren was right about one thing: he didn't take Jane with him. At first Jane refused to believe the obvious. Some unforeseen problem, she speculated, some minor glitch, but he would be back to get her, because he'd said, he'd said, blah blah blah. Really, now. His pack was gone, his clothes, everything. Eventually the you-know-what really hit the fan.

But that is how humans react. Arrows snag in the so-called "protective" body hair and are deflected inward, just as a splinter catches in the woof of your sock and is driven up into your foot, whereas Hyperboreans take some Stone, and the slings and harpoons of outrageous fortune merely glance off their sleek backs.

Jane will probably take her hurty feelings out on everybody by telling her parents. Who knows? Maybe she has already told them. Saskia can't imagine what the response would be. Something pyrotechnical, no doubt. But what can they do? Thomas is gone, and as far as Jane knows, Lauren never knew. Saskia recognizes now the necessity of the arrangement, this whole charade of secrecy when Lauren actually knew all the time. Thomas's departure would be part of it. He knew the thing with Jane couldn't go on forever, but he also knew he couldn't break it off without her spilling the beans. So he had to leave without notice. He had to go. He had no choice.

Meanwhile, Lauren has been reprising her Post-Thomas role. She stays in her room. Saskia has had to go back to keeping an eye on the crew, who don't seem to quite appreciate what has happened. "Where's Thomas?" they asked at the first breakfast.

"I have no idea."

"That isn't the way Thomas makes pancakes."

"Do I look like Thomas? Sit down and shut up."

Seeing Lauren retreat into her cocoon has reminded Saskia of the First Post-Thomas Age, of things she hasn't thought about in a long time. Of both doors: Lauren's, which Lauren wouldn't open, and

Saskia's, which Lauren wouldn't open, either. She remembers fanta-
sizing about a rescue. Not the usual little-girl fantasy of the white
knight coming to carry the princess away. No, when her knight came
through the window he threw her a sword, and together they broke
down the door and slew the witch, and when they rode away Saskia
wasn't behind him on his horse like a spoil of war, she had her own
horse, and she could gallop as fast as he could. He was Thomas, of
course, her brother-in-chains, her twin. She had been locked in her
tower, he in his.

They tore his heart out and handed it to him on a platter. That's
why he came out of his tower the way he did, his gaunt face in
torment, his hands clutching at the sheet. The blue antenna twitches
of the police car, the red cauldron bubbles of the ambulance. Saskia
followed him over the gravel, with the dog's howls in her ears, but
they pushed her away and lifted him in. In also went the umbilicus
and the bottle of ichor, which one of the white-clad men hung on the
oar upright by his shoulder.

Who were these men? White and silent, strong. Agents of the
TAO? Thomas was in trouble and they whisked him away. Perhaps in
the ambulance he threw off the coverlet and sat up on the slab,
unhurt. "Good work, men." He would have glanced around. "But
where's Saskia?" And the two white-clad men would have looked at
each other with dismay surfacing on their loyal but somewhat stupid
faces. "Saskia?"

Too late. Lauren had locked her away.

And later, she lied to her. Why did she want Saskia to believe that
Raymond had been the guru? To diminish Thomas in her eyes?
Fortunately, it never worked. Surely Saskia always knew somewhere
deep inside that Thomas was Truth. How else could the realization
have come washing over her all by itself, while she stood alone in the
driveway at the intersection of Lauren-in-the-Shed, Jane-in-the-Gar-
den, and Thomas-on-the-Water?

It explains why, in the photograph of everyone on the porch, he is
the only person who is sitting. It explains why Lauren could never tell
Saskia what Thomas's commune name was, and it also explains why

Saskia had no commune name, because the commune names came from Truth, and Truth had already named her Saskia. (But what did it mean? What did it mean?) Above all, it explains how and why he left. As Thomas modestly put it, he went a little nuts, but a truer way to say it is, he sat in his tower counting the stars and communing with the crystal spheres until his own crystal vibrated so much it shattered. He was too sensitive.

But why did Thomas back up Lauren in saying that Raymond was the guru? Perhaps, being generous, he did not want to contradict her story and thus show what a liar she was. Or perhaps he knew that if he identified with his old self too much, his crystal might again start vibrating too much.

Did he leave this second time because he felt that he was approaching the shattering point? What must it feel like when the wall of the bubble of consciousness splinters and the sea roars in? Only the great souls know, the seekers who go to the limit, who probe the outer edges of themselves to find out what they are shaped like. Alchemists went crazy all the time, driven by the urge to become perfect, which this sinful world will not allow. The ultimate martyrdom. Saskia has imagined she could endure any torture for the Way. Let them break her body, she has always said. But her mind? Could she bear to go crazy? A frightening thought.

And a more frightening thought: how do you *know* if you're going crazy? After all, if you are going crazy, then there is no sane "you" to say, "Hey! Aren't I going crazy?" Perhaps Saskia is going crazy right now. She looks around her room and tries to think of a definitive test. How does she know she is in her bed? What if she is really on the marble slab? But she can feel the bed, she can smell it. But that might just mean that she is thoroughly crazy, instead of just marginally crazy.

How does she know she is Saskia? How does she know all the memories of her entire life as "Saskia" are not false? In fact, hasn't she sort of thought before that all her memories are false? What if she has "gone native"? What if she was never meant by the technicians of the TAO to actually believe she was born on Earth? How does she know that she isn't, right now, actually on the marble slab in the cellar of Uraniborg, staring vacantly into space and drooling, and Tycho is turning away with tears in his eyes and saying to another Adept, "I'm afraid we've lost her"?

And the most frightening thought of all: can worrying about whether or not you are going crazy drive you crazy? But how, in fact, do you stop worrying? Because you're worrying about your worrying, aren't you? Isn't this, in fact, proof that she is crazy, that she has been sitting in bed worrying about worrying about worrying? Why can't she be like Mim? There is something sick, isn't there, about Saskia's thinking, questioning, figuring, calculating, plotting, observing. A net with which she chases the world, falling farther and farther behind. Mim just opens her big eyes wide and the whole world slips right in, as easy as you please.

Saskia sweeps the scattered chips of Stone back into the bag and returns it to her drawer. Throwing on her nightgown, she crosses the hall to Mim's room. Dark and quiet. "Mim!" she whispers, shaking her.

Mim burrows deeper.

"Mim!"

She opens her eyes. "What?"

"Come into my room!"

"Why?"

"I had a bad dream."

"I have to bring horsey."

Saskia leads her across the hall. Her adorable nightgown, her adorable little feet. Little? Funny, Mim is taller than Saskia. How long has *that* been going on? Saskia coaxes Mim into her bed.

"I need giraffey and elephanty." Saskia goes back to Mim's room and finds them in the pile, carries them across. "And alligatory and hippopotamusy." Saskia brings them all, in armloads. Mim disposes them around her, burrows deeper. She sighs twice. She is asleep.

Just like Jane. They fall asleep and leave Saskia behind. It's like having someone die on you. She huddles against Mim and puts her lips to her ear. "Home," she whispers. "Warm kitchen. Kittens."

Cowy and calfy have rolled down to Saskia's side of the bed and she reaches out and rights them, pressing calfy's velcro nose into cowy's udder. There is something so nice about that, it makes her cry.

Wong-king.

The geese are flying across the face of the Moon.

Wong-king, king, wong-king.

A cold wind keens through the broken windows. Saskia turns away and goes down the stairs, her feet crunching on shards of glass, splinters of wood. She parts cobwebs with her hands. "Hello!"

Hello. Hello.

The rooms are empty. Saskia follows a sound but finds only the drip drip of a broken pipe, a pool of scum on the stone floor.

King, king, wong-king.

The geese are flying south, and Tycho has been carried with them, into captivity, into the camp of his enemies. Prague, the heart of Christendom. Exile.

There are no fields of snow and ice in Prague, no limitless sea, no endless night of swarming stars. Only open sewers and bubonic plague. Tycho wakes one morning to the gray light and realizes he can no longer take his skin off. Was he ever a whale? Was he the Grandmaster? The low skies press down on him, suffocating him like the skin that he cannot remove. Where are his instruments? Where are his Adepts? "I am here," Saskia says. She can no longer take her skin off, either. She did this for him, the ultimate martyrdom, to be by him in his exile.

He is at table with his guests. "More coffee!" he shouts, pounding the table with his fist. Saskia prefers to see him this way, full of life, instead of moping around and dreaming of his lost island. She brings in the brimming tankards and sets them down, leaning far over the table so that the Captain can see down her laced bodice.

"You're looking very décolletée today, my dear," he says gallantly, blushing.

"Thank you, sar." Marco pinches her. "Oh, sar!"

"I'll say this, you're doing fairly well, boys," Tycho is conceding. "But it won't be long now. Drink up!"

The men clank tankards and chugalug. Tycho wipes his foaming mouth with his sleeve. "You see, the more you consume the more you secrete. Isn't that right, Saskia?"

"Aye aye, sar."

"But that's only true for humans," Odysseus points out.

"We'll see who's human! Bring in a double portion, Saskia."

When she returns, groaning under the weight of all that coffee, Tycho is saying, "Now, for example, I don't feel any pressure at all. Not a thing! I feel as empty as if I'd just taken a fine long piss, I mean one of those drumming streams that really foam up the bowl —" The Captain's face turns scarlet. A pool is spreading beneath his chair. "Oops! There goes the first one!" Tycho laughs.

"What a lightweight," Marco sneers.

The Captain disappears into thin air.

"Thank God that dweeb is gone, eh boys? Drink up! Another round, Saskia." He gives her a significant look.

They have arranged this ahead of time. She is supposed to creep secretly under the table, take a hold of Tycho's stiff man-thing, and milk it into a golden pitcher. She goes off to get more coffee.

When she returns, Tycho is saying cheerily, "Getting uncomfortable, boys? You look a little on edge, Marco. Are you trying not to think about running water? Isn't it funny how hard it is *not* to think about something once you've started? Damned if those images of streams and rivers flowing, the sound of water gushing down over the rocks, just keeps coming back to you, no matter —" Marco turns cramoisy. "Oops! There goes another one!" Marco disappears.

Odysseus looks impassively at the two pools, the empty chairs.

"Now it's just between me and you, Odysseus. Now we're down to the real men." Tycho gives Saskia a long significant look.

She goes off to get more coffee.

When she returns, Odysseus takes a tankard from her tray and drains it straight off. He gazes expressionlessly at Tycho.

Tycho sips from his tankard. "I've got to hand it to you, Odysseus, you're doing well. Very well indeed." He lasers Saskia with a long and intensely significant look.

She goes to get more coffee.

When she comes back, Tycho is talking through clenched teeth. "It won't be long now! You can't possibly hold out much longer!"

Odysseus gathers the handles of two tankards in one huge hand and pours the contents of them both with a gushing gurgling sound down his throat. Tycho turns to Saskia, his eyes beseeching. "Saskia . . ." His face turns pale. "Ohh," he moans. His eyes turn up in his head. He collapses. There is no pool below his chair. His bladder has burst inside him.

Pandemonium. Saskia screams, dropping the tray. Tycho rolls out of his chair and hits the floor with a sodden sound. Odysseus calmly drains the last tankard and rises, unhooks the tube from his leg and empties the can strapped to his ankle into the sink. The sink overflows with a gurgling rushing foaming sound and Saskia finds herself in up to her ankles, then up to her thighs. The two-ton table rises off its feet, and Saskia with it, and they and the tankards, trays, and pitchers are swept toward the door, where they jostle each other in the warm froth before rushing out onto a plain. "Interesting," Saskia thinks as she bobs and twirls in the bubbling liquid, "this means I need to go to the bathroom. A textbook case."

And with that thought she realizes she is asleep, and with that realization she asserts control with the magisterial ease that comes of long practice. She pulls the plug on the mighty river. She dries her clothes and inserts herself effortlessly into Wholeworld's bathroom. Now that she has gotten rid of all that unconscious Freudian imagery she can feel quite distinctly that she needs to relieve herself. The toilet is right here, and the lid is up. How easy!

But wait a minute. She is still asleep. In reality, she must be in bed with Mim. She needs to wake up and go down to the bathroom for real.

She wakes up, gets out of bed, goes downstairs and settles herself with a sigh of relief on the toilet.

But wait a minute. She is still asleep. She must still be in bed with Mim.

Wake up!

She opens her eyes. Mim is lying next to her. Yes, this time she is awake. She gets out of bed and hurries downstairs. She settles herself with a big sigh of relief on the toilet and starts to let go.

Hold it. She is still asleep. For pete's sake! She flies out through the window, reenters through the one above. There she is, asleep with Mim. She feels the beginnings of fright. How, exactly, do you wake from a waking dream? Why hasn't she ever thought about this problem before? She can do anything she wants to in this universe: she can fly above the rooftops, travel between galaxies, give herself orgasms. She can do everything in this universe except leave it. She commands, Wake! But the answer comes back, with incontrovertible logic: I *am* awake.

When she goes to sleep, she draws her bubble down. She must make the bubble go back up. Surely she can do that. She closes her eyes and concentrates. She is at the bottom of the ocean. She starts to swim upward. That's the way! She claws her way up and up out of the pit. She must have been incredibly far down. She can feel the medium (water? air?) lightening around her as she pulls herself upward and upward. The feeling of blankets and mattress begins to coalesce around her. Yes, that's it! Higher! She can feel that she is lying on her side. Her palms are pressed between her drawn-up legs. She *really* needs to go to the bathroom. Open your eyes, now. Come on, eyes, open up. Open!

She is only raising her eyebrows. She is lying in bed next to Mim, desperately needing to go to the bathroom, and all she can do is arch her eyebrows. The lids! Open the lids!

Her eyes fly open. Her room is around her, clear and solid. She tries telekinesis on the door. It doesn't work.

She is really awake.

She jumps out of bed and runs downstairs, lifts the lid of the toilet and settles on it in the nick of time, just as the stream bursts from between her legs, ahhhh, thank God. The painful pressure in her bladder pleasurably subsides.

She wakes. Her nightgown is soaking wet. Horrified, she sits up and turns on the light. The sheets are wet. The cow and calf are wet. Saskia touches Mim's nightgown. Wet.

Like brother, like sister.

21

The morning is still dark and cold, but the walk up the dirt road warms her. The county route is quiet. She turns south toward Ithaca, walking along the shoulder. This must have been what Thomas did, walking in the predawn dark under the stars, turning with his thumb out to face the occasional headlights that sprang up behind him. What did he feel? Disgust? Disappointment?

She runs her hand over the short brush of hair on her head. It feels good to have released that ballast. Bombs away! A balloon, she surged higher. Lighter and lighter. Where will she go? Wherever the winds take her. She is getting out just in time, lifting away from the taffrail as it disappears into the water beneath her. There is a note on Lauren's door: "You never told me anything so I won't tell you anything either."

Cars are few and far between. The fourth one stops. "Ithaca?" the driver says.

"Fine." She throws in her pack.

He scrutinizes her in the rising light as he drives. "How old are you?"

"Eighteen."

He laughs. "No one's going to believe that."

"Seventeen?"

"Fifteen is more like it."

She gives him an impressed look. "Pretty good! Actually, I just turned sixteen."

He rubs a war-drum belly, pleased with himself. As they come into town he observes, "You're crazy to be hitchhiking, a little thing like you. It only takes one wrong number and you're gone, left in a ditch somewhere."

"I'm just going to the bus station." She only says it so she won't have to argue with him. Ten minutes, and he's already playing the father figure. But it turns out the bus station is on his way, so he drops her off. She decides that while she is there she might as well look at the schedule, and as it happens, the next bus is leaving in only half an hour, and as it happens, it's going to the City. What the hell. Wherever the winds carry her.

She buys a ticket, realizing now why she got into the hemp business, so she would have the money to fly away. The sky has lightened to teal, and a persimmon haze in the southeast shows where the sun is about to rise. A triad of gongs shimmers in the gelid air and she looks over the roofs of the orderly Ithacan houses, up to the ridge, where the stone clock tower of Huge Red stands sentinel, asking, "What's the password?" She has no idea. The bus arrives, blotting out the view. She ascends into the gloom, now you see her, now you

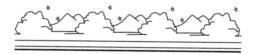

PART 5

SASKIA

And if you find her poor, Ithaca has not defrauded you.
With the great wisdom you have gained, with so much experience,
you must surely have understood by then what Ithacas mean.

— Cavafy, "Ithaca"

1

"IS THIS SEAT FREE?"

Curly dark hair, slight frame, soiled windbreaker. She shrugs. "Looks that way." She returns to staring out the window, at a train yard, at fading paint on old brick: Senate Brand Fancy Canned Foods. "This is Brmbledm," the driver said when they left the highway.

"Where are you headed?"

Her gaze drifts back to him. Small dark eyes, wispy mustache. Eighteen? Nineteen? "The City."

"Me too. I'm Russell." He holds out his hand.

"Hello Russell." Shaking it, she throws in a little bonecrushing action for the hell of it.

He smiles uncertainly, showing little gaps between little teeth. It doesn't look good. "Do you have a name, too?"

"Yeah." She lets him wait.

"Do you . . . tell people what it is?"

Ishakta Wise? Estasha Kiwi? Thea Iwaskis? "Jane," she says.

"Hello, Jane." He puts his hand out for her to shake again. It's meant to be a joke, this repetition of the handshake, but also, of course, a chance to touch her again. She decides to give him an alluring smile as she treats his hand to some more bonecrushing action. Then she goes back to looking out the window.

"Do you have a last name?" A conversational whiz.

"Jane isn't enough?"

"Jane's fine."

"No," she assures him in a fatigued tone. "It's boring. Plain Jane."

He looks puzzled. She can see crossing his face the decision not to pursue this. "My last name is Tierney," is all he can think to say.

"Hello, Russell Tierney." This time she holds out her hand first and he eagerly inserts his into it for some more bonecrushing.

"Dark," she concedes.

"Excuse me?"

"My last name."

"Is Dark? Dee ay are kay?"

"Yeah."

"Well that's not boring. I never heard of anyone named Dark."

"Funny, everyone in my family is named that."

He laughs, drawing his upper lip behind his mustache and revealing those unfortunate gaps.

"Or was," she adds. "They're all dead."

The smile drains away. "That's too bad. I mean, that's terrible, I guess. I'm sorry." In fact, he does a fairly good imitation of regret.

She gives a shake of her head, a dismissive frown. "It was a long time ago."

He waits a decent interval before asking, in a voice conscientiously emptied of morbid curiosity, "Was it an accident?"

"I really don't want to talk about it."

"Sure." He colors. "That was rude of me to ask, huh?"

"No," she smiles sadly. "People always do." She turns back to the window, to be alone with her thoughts. Car crash? Fire? Boating accident? Execution-style slaying?

She turns from the window. "And you?" she asks briskly, changing to a lighter subject.

"Me?"

"What about your family?"

"They're fine, I guess."

"Big, happy?"

"Excuse me?"

"Big happy family?"

"Pretty big. My aunt's a cool lady. I'm coming from her place right now. I was up for Thanksgiving. Had a whole week off. Man, it was great."

"Did you eat a turkey?"

"Sure."

"Sounds nice."

"Didn't you have Thanksgiving?"

"No. Let's see . . . That was the day it was snowing, wasn't it? I think I spent most of the day in a haystack. Good place to stay warm."

He gapes. "Don't you . . . you know, have some relatives or something you go to?"

Jane Dark considers the matter. "No. I've been on the road ever since my family died." She counts the seasons on the ceiling. "About three years, now."

"How old are you?"

"Sixteen."

"You've been on the road since you were thirteen?"

"Is that surprising?"

"It's amazing!"

"It's no big deal."

"Where have you been?"

"Easier to say where I haven't been."

"I mean . . . I don't know, like Europe?"

"Europe, India, Tasmania, you name it."

"How do you pay for food and stuff?"

"I deal some. I steal some. But only from the rich. I usually hitch-hike, I'm only on a bus today because I met this guy who had a return ticket he didn't need and I saw it was for the City and thought, What the hell? It'll be good to see the old City again."

"Have you ever had any trouble, hitching?"

Jane Dark laughs. "I'm trained in self-defense."

"You do have kind of a strong grip."

"That's nothing. Imagine five times that around your testicles." He looks blank, then guffaws. "It works."

"I bet it does!"

"I could also put my thumbs on your eyeballs and jam them into your head. Incredibly painful."

"Man!"

"You wouldn't be able to see for days."

"Stop!" He cups his palms over his crotch, then over his eyes, then over his crotch again, as if he needed four hands. "I guess I've been warned."

"Tell me about your Thanksgiving, Russell," she says dreamily.

"What about it?"

"Tell me some cozy things. What's your aunt's place like?"

"It's nice."

"Give me some details."

"I don't know, it's just a nice place. She makes you take your shoes off when you come in."

"Carpeting?"

"Wall-to-wall."

"Tell me what you had for Thanksgiving dinner." She settles back in her seat, closing her eyes.

"Well . . . turkey . . ."

"Golden brown?"

"Yeah."

"Who else was at the table?"

"My aunt and uncle and Ryan. He's my cousin."

"How old is he?"

"Seven."

"Cherubic?"

"Excuse me?"

"Blond, beautiful?"

"He's got dark hair."

"He looks up to you?"

"I guess. Sure."

"So what else is for dinner?"

"String beans, mash potatoes."

"Stuffing?"

"Sure."

"Heaped high on your plate, steaming?"

"Yeah, I guess."

"What's for dessert?"

"Apple pie à la mode."

"What flavor ice cream?"

"French vanilla."

"Mmm."

"I know what you mean, it makes me hungry just talking about it."

"And then you went to bed?"

"No, we saw the football highlights. Then I played ping-pong with my uncle."

"In the wood-paneled basement."

"In the game room."

"Wood-paneled."

"Wallpaper. I'm pretty sure."

"You won."

"My uncle kicked my butt."

"I'm sorry."

"Nah, it was OK. He gets kinda pissed off when he loses."

"And then you went to bed."

"Yeah, eventually."

"Where?"

"In Ryan's room."

"Where did Ryan sleep?"

"Same room. They have this foldout cot."

"You slept on the cot."

"Yeah."

"Under a thick quilt."

"Just a sheet."

"And you slept deeply."

"Sure."

"Naked."

"Excuse me?"

"You slept without clothes on."

"I . . ." There is a pause, and he goes "huh."

"You sound like a steam engine when you do that. Did you sleep without clothes or didn't you?"

"I sleep in my underwear. I can't believe we're talking about this."

"Mm." Jane opens her eyes and wriggles sensually in her seat, stretching in a feline manner. "Thank you, Russell, that was nice. Now I've had Thanksgiving, too. I'm going to take a nap now." She brings up her weather-beaten feet and turns toward the window, closing her eyes.

2

A man is but a man; he can do no other. In the City bus station, Russell asks, "Where are you staying?"

"No idea. Something will come up, it always does."

It's kind of funny, really, watching him count off the seconds before saying it, so he won't seem too pantingly eager. "You can stay where I'm staying, if you want. I'm sure my friend won't mind."

Jane Dark gives him a frank scrutinizing smile. "All right."

"Great! Here, let me take your pack."

"No, don't."

On the shrieking subway he wedges his knapsack between his feet, looping one shoulder strap around a sneaker. "Keep an eye on your pack," he says. "What am I saying, you already know that." He performs an odd bobbling of his eyes and shoots himself in the temple. They walk up into daylight. A steel shutter is spray painted with "Magnolia" in berserk letters, black and orange. An electronics store suffocates in fluorescent signs. "You can go that way and live to tell the tale," he points left. "One block this way," he points right, "puts you in Zululand."

They walk past stoops divided by spear-tipped iron fences which give the impression that dirt and wind-blown trash will be stolen if they're not protected. Glancing up and down the street, Russell mounts to a metal grate, unlocks it and the door behind, draws her through. "I lived in North Dakota with my grandparents for a year," he says as they ascend the dark stairs. "In winter you'd hear about some bozo who didn't have his keys ready when he came home and they'd find him the next day, frozen solid on the doorstep. That's what it's like around here. You got to present at least a moving target."

On the top floor he wrestles with the bolts on a metal-clad door and calls into the apartment as he opens it, "James?"

"Yo!"

"I'm back! I brought someone with me."

In the kitchen, James looks up from a plate of waffles drowning in Log Cabin. "Who's this?"

"Jane Dark. I met her on the bus."

He stands in a mock courtly manner and holds out a clammy hand. He is built like a padded door, with that thin film of fat all over that you first notice in the way it rounds chin and shoulders. If humans tasted any good, he would be the one the lions would lick their lips over. "Is she staying here?" he asks Russell, returning to his lunch.

"I said you wouldn't mind."

"You could try asking me first. No offense, Jane. I would have said yes. But it's the principle of the thing."

"I figured —" Russell says, casting an embarrassed look at Jane.

"Forget it. Look, I've got a gig in Astoria tonight, so I gotta eat and get ready. We'll talk. Good meeting you, Jane, make yourself at home." He disappears behind the plate as he raises it to slurp the syrup.

The apartment is as gloomy as the tiled halls of Tyler Junior. The view from the soot-streaked windows is a wall of yellow brick. The common room is empty except for a television on the floor, a plastic couch, and a pile of boxes that turn out to hold Tab. "You'll sleep on the couch, I guess," Russell says sadly. He indicates a closed door. "That's James's room. Here's mine."

He has to be kidding. Jane has never seen a room so small. No, she remembers a train compartment she once shared with someone on one of her journeys. But at least that one had a window. "It's a walk-in closet. James cleared it out for me." The mattress completely fills the floor. Socks and shirts are draped over a line strung at chest height, personal items are heaped in the corners. Russell upends his knapsack and crumpled clothes rain on the crumpled sheets. "It was lucky I had my friend James here. I only have to pay three-fifty a month. This apartment is eight hundred, if you can believe it. That's cheap, unless you want to live with the Zulus. You hungry?"

"No. I want a smoke in the worst way. Let's share a joint."

"I don't know, I'm supposed to be at work in half an hour."

"Just one." Jane closes the door and sits Native American style on the mattress, patting the spot next to her. He doesn't stand a snowball's chance in hell.

The room makes a fine opium den, filling quickly with the cozy fumes. "Man!" Russell exclaims. "This is good stuff."

"Straight from Al-Transam," Jane assures him. "Near Marrakesh. I made the run myself, just to stay in practice."

Handing him the joint, she flops back on the mattress, letting her arms fall above her head. "You know, this closet is all right! I approve."

James knocks and speaks through the door. "I'm taking off, lovebirds."

"Shit," Russell says, looking at his watch. "I have to go to work, too." He glances between his watch and Jane. "I wonder if I could call in sick or something."

"You mean, lie?" Jane frowns.

"You're right, that's pretty sleazy, huh? And since I just had a week off —" He opens the door and swings his feet out into the hall to put on his sneakers. "I just thought — I mean, now, of all times. Man!"

Jane rises from the mattress, heads for the kitchen. "What's so special about now?" James is gone.

"Nothing, I guess." He follows her, hurriedly filling his pockets. "Are you going to stay here? While I'm out?"

"I thought I might."

"I can get an extra key made tomorrow. There might be something in the fridge, I don't know. The stuff in the freezer is James's, maybe you shouldn't eat that." He hovers by the door. Will she be here when he gets back? Or will he return to an empty apartment, to his empty life, and wonder for the rest of his days if she was just a vision, a figment of his overheated imagination?

"You're going to be late."

"Right, right." He turns on his heel. "Lock the door behind me." But he pushes his way back into the room and crosses to the windows. "Are these locked?" He stops for the second time on his way out the door. "Turn the knob on the deadbolt twice, like this."

"I think I can handle it, Russell."

"See you tonight. I'll be back around midnight."

"What a shame, that's when I turn into a pumpkin."

"Excuse me? Oh, yeah." He laughs appreciatively, and finally disappears.

Jane Dark spends the evening wandering silently around the apartment. No wonder the common room and kitchen are so gloomy, the light has been reserved for James's room, which looks out on the street and a sunset. James's only furniture are a futon, a desk, and a music stand. A small telescope by the window. The bottom desk drawer contains printed music. The middle drawer, handwritten music. In the top drawer she finds photographs of what must be James's band, in the corners of various subterranean lounges, or next to a row of warming trays with the smiling bride and groom — drums, bongos, electric guitars, and a vibraphone behind which James stands with his arms crossed, two mallets sprouting from each fist. There's also a photo of a cheerleader type, probably some airhead girlfriend. Phone bills, checkbook, lubed condoms. A closet full of fancy clothes and shoes. A couple of intriguing boxes on the shelf above, but they contain only tax forms and receipts. Jane returns everything to its place, as if she had never been there.

A suspiciously humped corner of Russell's mattress turns out to conceal porno magazines, and the pile above includes hand lotion and toilet paper. All a man needs. Why do they even bother to pull your hand to their things, when their own hands so obviously suffice? Jane flips through the photographs of upended women, their dagger-like fingernails prying open their own pulpy interiors as if about to cut themselves for the delectation of men, biting their own tongues in anticipation of pain.

Under another mattress corner she finds a sheaf of letters, all from Mrs. Michael Foley, at an address in the city that must be Brmbledm. The postmarks are consecutive, a letter for every day and two on Mondays, each beginning "Dear Russell, Ted, Susan, Julie, Mark, and Andrew," with the "Russell" circled in pen. Every letter fills one page with typescript, ending with "Aunt Patty" written in pen, beneath which is typed "Aunt Patty."

November 19

Dear Russell, Ted, Susan, Julie, Mark, and Andrew:

Yesterday was considerably warmer than it has been for weeks, and I finally got MF to cut back the forsythia which has been threatening to grow clear across the front walk. He grumbled and groaned, but did a good thorough job, and then got the wheelbarrow out of the basement and moved the clippings out to the sidewalk where the city is supposed to pick them up. I called the Department of Public Works to inquire about this, and a woman there directed me to the Sanitation Department, where a polite young man explained that as long as the clippings were tied together in bundles and no bundle exceeded thirty-five pounds, the trash crew would pick them up along with the regular trash. As there has been some uncertainty before about the rules and regulations vis a vis trash pick-ups I will feel better when I see a clear sidewalk tomorrow morning. MF spent the rest of yesterday out in the back working on the Dodge, while I worked on Susan's pillow, and made good progress.

God's love and mine to you all,
Aunt Patty
Aunt Patty

Dear Russell, Ted, Susan, Julie, Mark, and Andrew:

MF still hasn't figured out what is ailing the Dodge, however. It continues to lose coolant even though he ran a pressure check and tightened up the hoses. Now he thinks it might be the heater core, so yesterday evening he came home with a tool that he needed for the appropriate operation. (Here I am trying to sound like an expert, but Russell, Ted, Mark, and Andrew are probably laughing as they read this!) I was hoping to finish Susan's pillow yesterday, but instead I was pleased to have an unexpected visit from Sally. She reports that hers are all hale and doing well, especially Liz, who so far has received only the highest marks in her first semester at B.C.C. Sally said that she had spoken to Liz on the phone last weekend and that Liz had asked after Russell. I said Russell would be with us for Thanksgiving, so perhaps the two young people can "catch up" over the holidays.

By the time I looked out the front window this morning, the clippings had already been picked up. Kudos to the Sanitation Department!

> God's love and mine to you all,
> *Aunt Patty*
> Aunt Patty

Jane skims one or two more before returning the rest to their place unread. She never imagined she would be doing this — passing up the opportunity to read someone else's mail — but the letters defeat her. Further searching turns up nothing of interest.

He gave her a chance, but she failed him, and he never came back. Or maybe he decided she was too ugly. Or both. Hell, why not both? Failed him, and ugly. Scaredy-cat. Those hands . . . Where are they now? On what tiller, on what oar? Humming Phaiakian songs on the limitless sea, fore regardant with fortitude, rere regardant with regret. She had potential, he grants her that. How could she not, being his? But unaccountably, a scaredy-cat. And so *ugly*. What a pity. The sail bellies out, the craft surges forward. Will a postcard come? "Lauren and my Quentin . . ."

She strips in Russell's Hole and aims her sunlamp at herself, rolls and lights a joint. Jane Dark, meet Jane Darker. One of this sinful world's many paradoxes: by coming under the bright lamp she dims, as if she were stepping away from the golden lamp in a Rembrandt painting, shedding layers of chiaro to reveal her true scuro nature underneath. We have penetrated your disguise, now tell us! Who are you working for?

I'll never tell!

But what if they discover her major design flaw? She could disappear into the darkness, but she would leave a trail of blood behind and the dogs would be after her, baying. She draws the smoke deep into her lungs. Hemping stops mooniness, he said.

A million years ago, she thought this stick was the Stone. What childishness! What melodrama! Does she mean to say that *all this time* she never noticed what it looked like? A styptic pencil. So simple! You apply it to bleeding emotions, and *voilà!* Shameless Helen knew all about it. She called it hearts-ease, and she mixed it with the wine to make the men forget their sorrows, to make them forget what a manipulative bitch she was. With hearts-ease in your veins, no tear would roll down your face, not if your mother and father died, not if men murdered your brother or beloved son in your very presence with the pitiless bronze. Surely there can be no greater happiness.

She squints into the lamp's glare, shading her eyes.

Tell us!

Fuck you!

She can barely make them out beyond the lamp, dark silhouettes slavering and moaning over her naked body. How do you like *this?* She spreads her knees and touches a finger to the object of their slavish desires. But she is as far away from feeling like the true Deed as are those women in the photographs, who must be wondering, as they stick their soft parts in the air and bite their tongues, when it will all be over and they can go home.

Voices in the common room. The lamp is off, the Hole pitch black. She must have been dozing.

"— must be sleeping."

"Or she made off with the silverware."

"Her pack is here. James, it's amazing, she travels on her own, everywhere. She sleeps outside. So I just thought — you know, it would be, I don't know, good hospitality to offer her a roof over her head for once."

"And a bed, naturally. You stud."

"I wasn't thinking about that."

"Of course not. How old is she?"

"Sixteen."

"She looks younger. I'd ask to see some ID before I reamed her, you could end up getting reamed yourself by some lifer in the joint."

"She only looks young because she's so small."

"The waif look. Sucked you right in. So if she isn't going to sleep with you, where is she going to sleep?"

"I thought maybe on the couch."

"I don't want the living room turned into the waif's boudoir. I have to put on a bathrobe to come through? What if she sleeps late? We tiptoe around?"

"I'll sleep on the couch. She can sleep in my room."

"I don't want anybody sleeping on the couch. This isn't a flophouse. Maybe that sounds hardassed, I'm sorry."

Russell cracks the door. "Are you asleep?"

"No."

He turns on the light. Jane has pulled the covers chastely to her chin. "We have a problem. About the sleeping arrangements."

"Why?" she asks innocently. "This mattress looks big enough for both of us."

She drinks in the extraordinary transformation his face undergoes. Fatigue and unease are instantly blotted out and in their place bloom surprise and delight and gratitude, the bloom only deepened by his hopeless attempt to suppress it. "Fine, fine, that's fine!" He calls back into the common room, "Everything's fine, James!"

"Glad to hear it, stud."

Russell sprints to the bathroom to make himself presentable, sprints back and looks down at her, at the mattress filling the room, at his own feet standing on his own mattress. He takes off his sneakers. "What, uh . . . what should I . . ."

"You said you always sleep in your underwear."

"Did I?"

"Yes."

"I guess I do."

"Whatever you're used to."

"OK."

"Me, I always sleep naked." She arranges the sheet around her in such a way as to give him a split-second glimpse of her breasts. "I hope you don't mind."

"Whatever you're used to," he squeaks.

He turns out the light, and in the darkness she hears the rustle of his clothes. What is he doing about his underwear? Is he a man of honor? He slips in next to her, leaving a couple of inches of mattress between them. From the light coming in around the door she can see him now, perched on his elbow and staring at her, wondering what he can get away with. "Good night, Russell," she says, turning away.

"Good night, Jane."

She lets him marinate for a while in his bitter disappointment. Then she turns back. "You can give me a goodnight kiss if you want."

"I guess I do want." His lips descend and plant themselves on hers. Of course it isn't long before that old blunt instrument comes knocking.

She draws away. "Am I going to have to put my thumbs in your eyes?"

His face deflates. "No." His voice is hollow, crushed. "Not if you don't want . . ."

"If I want," she says, raising her hand to kindly touch his cheek, "you'll know." She lets her hand fall, and in doing so allows it to brush against his front, just for a second, but enough to tell her two things. He does still have his underwear on, this man of honor. And inside is one of Them, called into existence by none other than Jane Dark. Imagine! She turns away, putting another foot between them, and contemplates the thing dying for want of her, as the hope in his face did. Poor boy! Maybe she'll make it up to him.

Maybe not.

Scaredy-cat.

3

Perhaps it is the windowless room that never lightens, or the dead air, or the white noise of traffic, but each night Jane sleeps deeper and longer than ever before and wakes without remembering her dreams. Stupid and heavy, she goes to the kitchen to make coffee and sees by the clock that it is always late morning, very late, really rather unbelievably late. But she can't hold a candle to Russell and James. They stagger from their mattresses at noon or one with faces puffy as if beaten mercilessly by their pillows, squinting at the ashen light like the risen dead. James worried about her sleeping too long. Ha! His concern regarding bathrobes was equally baseless. Headed for the toilet on the first day, he passed through the kitchen naked, scratching the bush above his thing so that it jiggled in an undignified manner, still so zonked that he didn't notice her at the table, where she was drinking her coffee and enjoying a smoke until she drawled, "Morning, James," and he started and cupped himself like a cartoon character. But while draining the thing into the toilet he apparently decided he liked the idea of her sitting at the table unfazed by his exhibitionism, so when he came back out he didn't bother to hide anything and actually joined her at the table for a cup of coffee, his hair askew and his slightly flabby body exuding a stale bed smell.

There is nothing in the refrigerator except beer and Tab, nothing in the freezer except James's frozen waffles, fish sticks, and ice cream.

Jane doesn't mind, but boys will be boys and want to stuff their faces, so in the afternoon they go out for breakfast a block away, where Russell's two eggs and toast are 99 cents, and James's two eggs, toast, and stack of pancakes smothered in syrup are $1.69. Jane drinks her coffee and listens to the guttural language spoken by the cook and the cashier, which she is sure she could learn if the boys would just shut up and let her listen.

Back in the apartment James jams on his vibraphone while Jane suns like a cat on his windowsill, smoking and letting her thoughts drift, watching people on the street below hurrying with such comical seriousness toward trivial appointments and meaningless errands. She applauds languorously with the joint dangling from her lips when James ends a tune by dribbling the mallet up the scale and dying out on a four-mallet roll. He and his band want to play jazz, but they can't make money at it, so they spend their evenings cranking out schlocky Latino and Hawaiian numbers at weddings and receptions. "Thank you, thank you," he says, bowing to her applause and pausing before the next tune to chugalug from a two-quart container of Tab. Meanwhile Russell watches TV, laughing and calling out, "Hey, Jane, you should come see this!" She wanders in to stand behind the couch and lets her hand fall on his shoulder while she looks on for a few minutes, until Russell, who laughs less now that she is standing behind him, watching languidly, not laughing, says, "It was better before." When Russell locks himself in his Hole James knocks on the door as he passes and asks cheerfully, "How's it going in there, stud?" and Russell's voice comes out, aggrieved, "Will you shut up?" By contrast, when Jane suns naked in the Hole, leaving the door ever so slightly open, the Deed feels approximately a million miles away. She flips instead through the repulsive porno pictures and wonders which inflamed vulva Russell was panting over when he gave himself his lube job.

Every day a letter arrives from Aunt Patty, which Russell looks at incuriously. "Aren't you going to read it?" Jane asks.

"You can, if you want." He tosses it to her.

"What if it's personal?"

"It isn't."

December 3

Dear Russell, Ted, Susan, Julie, Mark, and Andrew:

The storm last night kept MF awake worrying that the silver maple out front would drop a limb on the power line, but when morning came we saw that all was well . . .

"Why does she write these?"

Russell sighs. "My Aunt Patty's a great lady. She thinks if she can make it like me and my brothers and sisters are all living with her and Uncle Mike, having, you know, a regular family life, then maybe we won't get in trouble. She started these letters when we found out my sister was a heroin addict."

"Which one is that?"

"Julie. I'm the youngest. You know, the baby. That's why I get the original. Everyone else gets a xerox."

"So your parents are dead?"

"No. But my mother's kind of whacked out. A religious nut."

"Eastern stuff?"

"Nah, charismatic. She's a real pain in the butt, I have to say. I was the only one still living with her, and Mark was always saying, When are you gonna get out of there? But, you know, I thought, She's my mother. Then she came into my room one night and dumped about fifty pounds of ice cubes on me while I was sleeping. That was supposed to drive the devil out. It sure did, only I went with him." He thinks about that for a second before a throttled laugh breaks out of him and his eyes bobble.

For some obscure reason Russell wants Jane to visit him where he works, so one night she agrees to come at the end of his shift. "Then we can go do something," Russell says.

"Like what?"

Clearly, he has no idea. "You've spent a lot of time here, what do you do?"

She smiles gently, trying to let him down easy. "The things I like to do here, I have to do alone."

He wants her to take a taxi since the subways are so dangerous, but she tells him not to be ridiculous. So he goes out and buys her a can of Mace and describes to her how to carry it and where to aim it and how she has to remember to do this and never do that or else this happens, until she cuts him off with a reminder that she knew how to handle herself long before she met Russell Tierney.

When she goes to the address she finds a diner on a big avenue, and she sits at the counter and orders coffee from a Jo look-alike. It's near closing time, and the place is mostly empty. Looking through the open square where the waitresses hang up the orders, she can see the cook cleaning off the grill for the night, and off to the side, bobbing into view now and then, Russell stacking white dishes as thick as books. He doesn't see her, and she watches the intent hurry he brings to his task, white towel over his arm, retreating farther back to roll a tray of dishes into a hold, pull down the metal shutter and slap the button.

"More coffee, honey?" It's Jo, holding the glass bubble forward with crooked arm as though she were one big coffee pot and this her spout.

"Thank you."

"You're waiting for Russ?"

"Yeah."

"She's here, Russ!"

After Niko, the owner, flips the sign on the door, Russell fills ketchup bottles, straightens menus in their metal holders, mops the floor, all with the same seriousness and speed. "You been getting enough coffee? Holly, is there more coffee?"

Niko says, "Good enough, Russ. Go have some fun." Russell picks up a bag of leftover marble cake — "For James" — and Niko unlocks the door for them and waves them through with a smile for Jane, "Nice meeting you," even though she didn't exchange a word with him, and they set off in search of something to do.

Unfortunately, all Russell can think of is to go to a bar and have a beer, but none of them will let Jane in. The cafés, on inspection, prove to be too expensive. "Three fifty for a beer! Look at all those suckers in there."

"Why don't we just take a walk?"

They walk a few blocks up the bright avenue past the caged stores until the porn shops begin, at which point he insists they turn around. Back down the blocks, on the other side of the avenue. "Maybe we could see a movie or something," he says. But the only moviehouses on this stretch of the avenue are the porn ones, and he doesn't know where to find others.

Doesn't he ever go to movies?

To be honest, no. Ridiculously expensive. Only suckers go.

"It's probably too late to do anything," Jane says.

"No, this is the city that never sleeps. You can buy a kumquat at three A.M."

They end up in a diner not unlike the one he works in. Over his hamburger Russell talks about his job — about Niko, who "has a good head on his shoulders," who "saw an opportunity and acted on it," and about a couple of his coworkers, "bozos," who "wouldn't have the initiative to take their pants off if they were on fire." "I'd deal with those bozos in a second. I'd say, 'Hey, Jack! If you don't want to work, take a hike.' People are always trying to buck the system. You work with the system, and let it work for you. I want to learn the business."

"Dishwashing?"

"Food service."

Listening to him, Jane wonders fleetingly about his interior life — i.e., whether he has one. Does he dream at night? Or is he the source of that black hole of dreamlessness into which her own dreams are sucked? Last night she turned on the light while he slept and he lay there like a ton of bricks. "Russell," she said. Nothing. She's surprised the ice cubes woke him. Maybe his mother was just trying to get his attention.

Back in the apartment they smoke a joint in the Hole, and when the goodnight kiss comes she finds herself opening her mouth. She notes clinically that he is a better kisser than Danny Rizzuto. Soon he is mouthing her breasts. She pushes him up and unlike Danny he rises, stopping. "Don't," she says. But she has called another into existence. She can feel it against her thigh. "Do you think I'm sexy?" she asks curiously.

"Oh baby, do I."

What, exactly, is stopping her? Just another part of the body. Perfectly natural. *After all this time,* is she still not ready to put away childish things? Pathetic. She pulls down the front of his underwear and takes the top of it in her hand. All right, there it is. Are you satisfied now? A few days too late, a million years too late. "Oh baby."

"Don't call me that." *He* is the baby, with his simple need. All he wants, and so much better if Mommy does it. And the equipment right by, the tissues like diapers and the cream like lotion for his little bottom. She takes the lotion in her hand and does it. He turns his head to mouth at her breast and she would give him milk if she had any, but she lost that long ago, when she could no longer take off her skin. Instead she has this formula bottle, which keeps slipping out of her hand. He squirms. "Shh," she says, holding him tighter. He quivers, and whimpers, the milk spills from the bottle, and she holds him until he falls asleep.

4

"Hello?"

"Jo? It's me."

"Where in hell are you?"

"In the City."

"What the fuck are you doing there? Are you OK?"

"I'm fine."

"Who are you with? Are you in trouble?"

"I'm fine."

"Lauren is worried to death."

"Yeah, sure."

"Did you call Lauren?"

"No."

"Well what are you talking to me for?"

"I don't want to talk to Lauren, I want to talk to you."

"All I want to hear from you, you little nitwit, is that you're coming home."

"Forget it."

"Where are you staying? Are you in a hostel?"

"I want to talk about Thomas."

" . . . "

"Jo? Hello?"

"What about Thomas?"

"You know things about him, don't you?"

"Not much."

"I'm not coming home until I get some answers."

"That's very melodramatic."

"But true."

"You're going to have to ask Lauren."

"I know he was the guru."

"All right, so what, so he was the fucking guru."

"Why has Lauren always lied about that?"

"It's complicated."

"For pete's sake, Jo. It's my life, too. You and Lauren act as if it has nothing to do with me. He's my father!"

" . . . "

"Jo? . . . Jo, he *is* my father, isn't he?"

"Yeah, he's your father."

"And he's Quentin's father, too?"

"So you know about that, too, huh?"

"No thanks to you."

"You never asked me."

"Are any of the other kids at the place his?"

"No."

"Does he have kids someplace else?"

"How should I know?"

"Did he have others at the old commune?"

"I wasn't a part of the commune."

"How did you know Thomas?"

"None of your business."

"OK, fair enough. But don't you think some of this is my business?"

". . ."

"Don't you think I have a right to know a few basic facts about my own family? I mean, I do exist, don't I? Or is that something else no one has gotten around to telling me? Did I die locked up in my room and am I just a ghost? Is there a gravestone hidden out in the high grass with my name on it?"

"Don't be silly."

"Well that's what it feels like! Come on, Jo! Don't you think it's unfair? Don't you?"

"Yeah, I suppose. Life's unfair."

"So are you going to be unfair, too?"

"Like I said, you never asked me. You were always too snooty to talk to me."

"Well I'm asking now. I'm groveling."

"So what do you want to know?"

"Why did Lauren lie all those years about Thomas not being the guru?"

"Thomas told her to."

"Why?"

"Look, he ended up chewing razor blades and banging his head against the wall. I don't think he was exactly proud of it."

"He was too sensitive."

"Pff. That's what Lauren always said. Me, I just think he's a border-line nutcase."

"So Lauren was just doing what Thomas told her to do."

"Lauren has always done what Thomas tells her to do. Christ, when she was his favorite dish she used to wash all his clothes in the stream for him and make the fire in his prayer hut and sweep his fucking floor for him. And she had to do it while he was out of the hut, because he didn't like seeing menial work. It was fucking revolting."

"How do you know all this?"

"I've known Lauren since I was a kid."

"Yeah?"

"My mother cleaned her parents' house, if you have to know. To tell you the truth, I thought she was a real snotnose too, until I figured out she was kind of fucked up."

"Thomas said she was abused."

"You don't want to hear about it."

"I'm a big girl now."

"Unlike Thomas, I don't think it's my place to talk about it."

"So if you don't like Thomas, how come you slept with him?"

"None of your goddamn business. Look, just because you ran away doesn't mean you can be obnoxious. I can just hang up."

"I'm sorry! I just don't understand."

"Some big girl."

"OK! I'm groveling again."

"And now you're being a wiseass."

"No, I'm serious, Jo. I don't mean to be obnoxious, I really don't. There are all these things I want to know, and you're the only person who's ever told me anything. I really appreciate that."

"So what else do you want to know? Who's paying for this call? This is going to cost a bundle."

"I'm staying with a guy."

"What guy?"

"Someone I met on the bus."

"For sweet Jesus' sake! He's probably a pimp!"

"Russell? I don't think so."

"I saw something on TV about this. They hang around the bus station looking for runaways."

"No, I met him before that, on the bus, I already told you."

"Are there other girls there?"

"Not that I've noticed."

"If he tries to hook you on drugs, you get out of there."

"Sure thing. Can we talk about Thomas now?"

"Why don't you come home. I'll tell you everything you want to know when you get home."

"No way, Renée. If Thomas was the guru, who was Raymond?"

"He was just one of the disciples. I think he was the favorite for a while. Maybe when Thomas was staring at his navel up in the tower."

"So there were several favorites?"

"Oh, yeah."

"Lauren was just the first."

"No, there was some skinny chick, I forget her name."

"But then why did the commune start right off at Lauren's place?"

"Every commune needs a rich girl. For the land."

"And Raymond killed himself?"

"Did he?"

"I'm asking."

"As far as I know, he's still living in Ithaca. He got rich making tofu."

"Thomas said he killed himself."

"That doesn't mean a thing."

" . . . "

"No more questions?"

"So the ambulance took Thomas away because he was chewing on razor blades?"

"No."

"What, then?"

" . . . "

"Please tell me, Jo?"

"If you really must know, there was some Jap nutcase writer who committed harry-carry —"

"Hara-kiri."

"Where I come from, we say harry-carry, we don't know any better."

"Sorry."

"So this Jap nutcase did it, and Thomas got, you know, obsessed with the guy."

"Thomas committed hara-kiri?"

"He tried to. I mean, this isn't my specialty, but I think you're supposed to have your disciples around you and they're supposed to finish you off. You know, cut off your head."

"You're kidding."

"No, those were wild times, life's been kinda boring since then. But instead, they called an ambulance. He was fucking pissed. Lauren still feels guilty about it."

"Let me get this straight. Lauren feels guilty because she didn't chop Thomas's head off?"

"It sounds pretty funny, doesn't it?"

"Lauren is my mother, isn't she?"

"Of course."

"She doesn't have any other kids?"

"Not that I know of."

"So why does she hate me?"

"She doesn't hate you. Look, Lauren's not . . . You know . . . What am I trying to say . . . Lauren's not exactly . . ."

"Gee, that explains everything."

"That's your whole fucking problem. You want everything explained."

"Yeah."

"Well it doesn't work that way, kid."

"Yeah, well, I gotta go."

"So are you coming home?"

"No."

"Look . . . You know, you can call collect if you need to. Don't run out of money! You start running out of money, you get the fuck home. Before the pimps get you."

"Rightio, Jo."

5

Simple and trivial. Appalling to contemplate how long she was a scaredy-cat regarding this utterly mechanical operation. Every night it's the same: they kiss, she removes his underwear, he groans and quivers, she wipes up the spilled milk. Somehow, ages ago, she got the idea that learning to do the Deed was a descent only to the first circle, only one step on the way to more personal horrors which would culminate in something that, by necessity, involved a boy. What a childish conception! With Russell she remains light-years away from the state of surrender required by the Deed. "What about you?" he asks. "Don't you want anything?"

"No, nothing."

Of course, there is the intercourse issue. "Are you a virgin?" he asks tentatively.

She gives him a withering look. "Of course not."

"Then why can't we?"

"It's not enough for you that I don't want to?"

"No, of course. If you don't want to —"

"You seem to enjoy what we do."

"Of course, it's great —"

"Have you heard of Artemis Syndrome?"

"No."

"It's a medical condition. It means sex is intensely painful for me."

"That's terrible!"

"Not if I don't have sex."

"Is there a cure?"

"Not yet. But I'll find one. That's why I'm going to go to medical school. As soon as I cure it I'm going to fuck everything in sight." She enjoys watching the deep chagrin that steals over his face when she says things like this. "Let's get to work," she says, taking hold of it, calling it into existence for its brief strut upon the stage.

Yes, appalling, how trivial. Now she can even look at it while she does it, she can even say to herself the words: I, Jane Dark, am holding a penis in my hand. Which shows how fatally childish she has been in shying away not only from doing but even thinking about certain things. Like the sounds from Thomas's tent when they were on the hike. She told herself he was polishing his stove! God! How screamingly funny! If she had been less of a blind baby she would have sent that other Jane over much earlier, and Thomas would have gotten tired of her and dumped her long before they returned to Novamundus, and she wouldn't have ruined everything.

Jane Dark takes a long hot shower every morning. But Russell goes for days without changing his underwear. James lets his hair get so greasy that a dark spot on the wall above his bed marks the place where he rests his head when he lounges in his dirty bathrobe and lubes himself. (Yes, he does it too, behind his closed door, she is sure of it. Don't they all?) She smokes at the kitchen table and contemplates, clinically, her disappointment with boys, or men, or whatever. Males. She has a vague memory that Thomas made a prediction about this. Or did she dream it? Thank God for hearts-ease. No tear rolls down your face even as you mull over your "boyfriend." Because that's what Russell is, isn't he? Say it: Russell is her boyfriend.

No wonder he and James can't get any girls. No wonder he resorts to picking up runaways on buses and is absurdly, slavishly grateful when they give him hand jobs. The photo in James's drawer is no doubt of some girl he got fixated on in high school, and he probably pestered her, never taking no for an answer. No wonder Russell and James resort to looking through their telescope into a curtainless window across the street where a buxom black-haired woman nightly undresses for bed.

"Oh baby, come on."

"All right!"

"Boomba-boomba."

"Oh man."

Jane finds herself strangely comforted by her disgust, since it proves she is only here by accident, she could as easily be with some pimp or, who knows, some jaded Park Avenue couple who both want her for their degenerate games. She simply went home with the first person she met, and here she is, and this revolting display only confirms what she already knew about boys, or men, or males, or whatever. So she encourages them, for the comfort it gives her. Having overheard the telescope talk through James's closed door, she later said, "So what's that woman doing tonight?" and while Russell and James traded a glance she swiveled the scope until she found the window and lo, the raven beauty was there. Now the boys crow and slaver while she looks on, feeling proprietary, a vegetarian throwing meat to her dogs.

Boys will be boys! Before she came they hardly knew how to feed themselves: James with his frozen fish sticks and waffles, Russell with the burger, fries, and six-pack he picks up on his way home from work. Jane has brought a little variety into their constricted culinary lives. She bakes them butter cookies, cream pies, cakes with thick sugar frostings — the classic White Work. She pours cup after cup of pure white sugar into the mixing bowl. Come and get it, boys! She steals just a taste of the finished product, a gob of frosting on her finger, or the coconut filling of a frosted éclair, and declares, "It really is sickeningly sweet, isn't it?" or "I really overdid it this time, didn't I?" while the boys shovel it in.

For dessert she brings out the hearts-ease, generous with her provisions, and time floats by on dreamless sleep and tearless waking. Lotus eaters, forgetful of their returning, they lie cradled in the web of the done. While the boys work in the evenings she wanders out and lets the web carry her along, turning her down avenues and even those streets about which Russell worries so pointlessly because, of course, nothing happens. No longer able to take a vow of chastity, she can at least go into silence, as Thomas did, and she walks taking no notice of those around her, and when the occasional nutcase or molester speaks to her she doesn't answer. Even her thoughts are webbed, every random image tugging with it strands of other images that return, return. Thomas went into silence and tried to tear out his own heart and hand it to someone else on a platter. How Christ-like can you get? Or perhaps Antichrist-like. Because it was the wrong path, he said later, which is why he told Lauren not to talk of it, to turn from it, to let it go. He learned his lesson. But poor Lauren! She didn't. First too weak to chop off his head and then too weak to see that the guru-disciple relationship is inherently unhealthy. She stayed her hand, but for the wrong reasons. He could have guided her hand but he didn't, instead he gnashed his teeth and left, disappointed in her. And the others? The skinny chick, the Young Things? Did they all disappoint him, or did he take some with him? Where are they now? Where are his other children? How many are there? Were his postcards so brief because every time he sat down to write he had to reel off dozens? "Corine and my Ian"; "Claudia and my Erika"; "Liz and my Liam." Do any of this race of half-siblings live near Ithaca? Has Jane seen any short, moon-faced, thin-haired kids haunting the stacks of the Ithacan library, or speaking several languages at the Farmers' Market?

She wanders in the City, where no nature is. One shouldn't tread on the rare lichens, but what about tipped trash cans and gummy sidewalks? Is care ordained in such a place? Or can she simply drop this wrapper and walk on, unburdened? If she can walk silently past people collapsed in doorways, laid out in malnourished stupors on cardboard, surely she can drop this wrapper.

In the Hole Russell gazes for long moments at her, brushing his palm over the fuzz on her head. "I love girls with short hair."

"Maybe you're a closet homosexual."

"Huh." She has almost grown fond of that sound, half shock, half amusement, and the shake of his head, the long-breathed "Man!" "I'm about as far from being a fag as anyone I know."

"I'd kind of like to be a lesbian, I think."

"Why?"

"I wouldn't have to have anything to do with men."

His mouth turns down, his eyes look away. "Don't be like that."

She has a dream: she is walking down the dirt road to Wholeworld with her pack on her back. The house below her proudly wears its new shingles and straightened porch, its sparkling solar panels. Proud, too, is Lauren, who opens the door, coyly turning sideways for Jane to see that her classical line is broken. "I thought his tubes were tied!" Jane exclaims.

"That can be reversed."

Jo steps heavily onto the porch, groaning. "But he said his tubes were tied!" Jane wails.

"That doesn't mean a thing, kid."

Mim and Shannon crowd close, yelling, "Welcome home!" They press their swelling bellies against her.

Waking, she contemplates her flat brown stomach in the bathroom mirror, her small mahogany breasts. She shrugs on a white T-shirt and tucks it tightly into her loose pants so that it hugs her torso, showing the shape and color of her nipples. "Oh, baby," Russell groans, "you look so good." She no longer tells him not to call her baby. She imagines herself at the other end of the telescope, stripping by the lighted window, oh baby oh baby oh baby, while across the street James and Russell lube themselves, or maybe each other, and she upends herself and presents her soft parts to the pane, how do you like *this*? and she can hear all the way across the street, though dimly, as from another dimension, the ghostly moans, the splatter of ectoplasm against the glass.

"What have I ever done that compares with all the things you've done?" Russell says. "Nothing! I mean, all the adventures you've had. Man! Smuggling drugs, going to this ashram in India, working on this anti-whaling boat. And you're a girl! I mean . . . You know what I mean. All I did when I left home was go to my grandparents in North Dakota and work on a farm. Next to you, I haven't even lived. I don't know, am I a coward or something?"

"Not necessarily," she says, squinting as she languidly inhales and holds.

"I feel like I've been living in a cage all my life and never even knew it. You're this wild, beautiful thing that's flown into my life, like a bird. You're this beautiful thing that nobody owns, this free spirit, and I'm afraid if I blink you'll fly away. But maybe I'll fly away with you, or, who knows, maybe you'll stay, and then I'll feel so incredibly lucky that this wild thing came to stay with me, you know, to find its home and be protected."

"That's a bit much, Russell."

"You don't know how special you are. To you, you're just you."

"I can't argue with that."

"Like you don't realize how beautiful you are."

"Come on."

"That's just what I mean. 'Come on!' You've got this gorgeous skin, this incredibly sexy body —"

"What about my face?"

"It's an intelligent face."

"Thanks a lot."

"No, I mean it. I knew as soon as I saw you on the bus. I thought maybe you were on your way back to college."

"As young as I look?"

"I've heard of real smart types going to college at sixteen."

"But don't you think I look even younger than my age? James says so. Sometimes I look in the mirror and think I look like I'm about thirteen years old."

"No way. You're too mature. You know, I can see us, with you being a doctor, and me being a restaurant manager somewhere. Man, we'd be doing all right! Doctors make a shitload, and managers don't do so bad, either. Or what the hell, if you were really raking it in, I could raise the kids. You know, after you found the cure for this syndrome. Or we could adopt. I like kids. I get along real well with Ryan. I can see it on the mailbox: 'Dr. and Mr. Jane Dark.'"

"Whoa, there."

"You're an amazing person, Jane. Maybe not enough people have told you that, I don't know. But I took one look at you on the bus, and I knew. I said, this is the girl I've been looking for my whole life. And I was right, baby."

And he goes off to work while baby wanders through the streets. On a wide busy avenue with snow drifting down out of the darkness she stops to look at Christmas displays in department store windows: motorized Santas jerking bells, smirking elves on toboggans, plastic trees dusted with confectioners' sugar. A vision rises before her of the crew and Lauren cutting this year's plot of seven-year-olds, wrapping them and loading them in Betsy. How is Lauren managing without her there to keep the crew under control? She always loved the smell of the trees. Is she really going to pass it up this year? Is there anyplace in this city of stinking sidewalks and trash cans where you can close your eyes and breathe in the scent of pine? She kind of doubts it.

On the solstice Lauren and her astrology group build a fire circle on a hillside and chant and go in the sweat lodge, and greet the rising sun with hymns to light and hallelujahs, while Jane always stayed at home with the crew to supervise the version she designed for them. They had popcorn in the evening, followed by a hunt for a hidden gem (representing light, get it?), and in the morning she waked them before dawn with a big tray of mugs of hot chocolate, which they sipped while seated by the east windows, watching for the first splinter of sun, at the appearance of which they were allowed to attack their presents.

Jane stares at the plastic tree in the window with the presents piled underneath and thinks for some reason of a gob of frosting on her finger. "It really is sickeningly sweet, isn't it?" And all of a sudden she remembers something: a cake with white frosting, trimmed with hard sugar holly leaves and berries, green and pink. A Christmas present, and the box it came in, with her name on it. Her cake. And someone throwing it away. Thomas, in fact. Or Truth. "It's nothing but sugar," he is telling her angrily as she wails. "You don't want it." But she did want it. A present for her, a cake in a box, white and green and pink.

She turns away from the window. Why is she still remembering things? Why can't she just remember everything at once, instead of dribbling it out like this? Admit it, she wanted the cake. It was all sugar, all teeth-rotting poison, but it was for her, it had her name on it. Buttressed with boughs and crenelated with berries, a beautiful castle. Who would send her such a cake? All the communards ate granola bars, honey-miso-nut chews, molasses–brown rice cookies. Who would send something like that?

When Russell comes back from work he pleads with her to undress in front of him while he lies back on the mattress nursing his beer, and she does so, looking sexily up past dropped lids and shimmying as she pulls off her clothes. The next day she suns after Russell goes to work, and afterward puts on her white overalls without underwear or any shirt at all and goes to James's room to see what he is doing, and he drools and says what he has been saying from the first day, whenever Russell is out of the apartment: "Come on! What Russell doesn't know won't hurt him." Yes, like the rent, which Russell doesn't know, but which Jane does, because she found the lease one day when she was poking through James's papers. The rent which is only four hundred dollars a month. "Why should Russell get it all?"

6

"Hello?"

"I thought of some more questions."

"Haven't you run out of money yet?"

"No."

"Has he tried to have sex with you?"

"He's been a perfect gentleman."

"So you're all right."

"I'm fine."

"Lauren'll be happy to hear that. Why don't I go get her?"

"I don't want to talk to her."

"You know, it kinda hurts her feelings that you don't want to talk to her."

"That's really pretty screamingly funny."

"Listen, it seems to me like you got a choice. You can keep being mad at Lauren, or you can get on with your life. You say you're a big girl, OK, be a big girl."

"I just want some information."

"Like what?"

"You said Thomas tried to commit hara-kiri."

"Right."

"So is that why he has that scar on his stomach?"

"Pretty nasty, huh? I'll say this for him, I don't think I'd be able to get that far."

"He told me he was cut by a harpoon line while he was trying to save a whale."

"He's probably told other people it was an assassination attempt when he was King of the Moon."

"But he did fight whalers, didn't he?"

"Yeah, it's an interesting question. I think most of Tom's stories do have some truth mixed in."

"I mean . . . he did have a boat named *Lila*, right?"

"You mean the sailboat?"

"No I mean the big boat, the one that rammed the pirate whaler and sank."

"Boy, he was really telling you some humdingers, wasn't he?"

"*Didn't* he?"

"I think he worked for a while on one of those eco boats. But it wasn't *Lila*. It was *Green*, I think."

"No, *Green* was the name of the pirate whaler that they sank."

"If that's what he said, that's typical. He was really pissed off at the people who ran the *Green*, or owned it, or what have you. I got the impression he was being his usual pain-in-the-ass self and they finally got fed up with him. They gave him some kind of severance pay, or settlement, which is why he had some money for once. He usually just sponges off everyone else."

"You're always putting him down."

"If I don't do it, who will?"

"I think you're just jealous."

"Of what?"

"Of him! Of all the things he's done."

"Sure thing, kid."

"While you've just been sitting in a trailer your whole life watching TV."

"Where I come from, we don't know any better, we don't know how to read or anything."

"I mean, why should I believe you?"

"I don't give a flying fuck if you believe me or not. You're the one asking questions."

"There was this pirate whaling ship that no one would do anything about, so he filled the bow of his own ship with concrete and rammed it."

"It sounds familiar."

"Yeah?"

"I think I saw something on TV about it."

"There!"

"But that doesn't mean anything, it was just TV. I didn't read it in a fucking encyclopedia or anything."

"But it does mean he did do it."

"Nah. He probably saw it on TV, too. Look, if you're really interested in finding out anything, why don't you look in old newspapers or something about that whaler thing? If not, just keep your fingers in your fucking ears the way you've been doing this whole phone call."

"So long, Jo."

7

The irony is that most of Jane's classmates would not be able to find anything in a library except the bathroom, whereas Jane, with all her precocious knowledge of catalogues and reference materials, has no trouble unearthing documentary evidence that Thomas does not tell the truth. There it is on microfilm: in 1979 the *Sea Shepherd*, its bow reinforced with concrete, rammed and disabled the pirate whaler *Sierra* outside a Portuguese port.

And who was the captain of the *Sea Shepherd?*

Paul Watson.

A pseudonym?

Perhaps. But that does not explain the photograph of Watson and his crew, none of whom are Thomas.

Is the *Sierra* the only whaler in the sea? Why couldn't Thomas have rammed a pirate whaler, too?

If he did, it never got in the papers.

Didn't Thomas, in fact, say something once about somebody else getting all the press?

He said Greenpeace did. But he also said, "I name all my dogs Lila," to which that other Jane said, "And all your boats," to which he answered, "Only one boat." That is, the boat Jane has seen with her own eyes, the wooden sailboat.

But he didn't call the metal *Lila* a boat, he called it a ship.

Aren't you grasping at straws?

Well how about the *Green?* Is there any mention in the literature of a ship of that name?

In fact, yes. In a source book of ecological activism Jane has found the *Green* listed among several boats — or ships, if you insist — that took part in a flotilla protesting ocean dumping of nuclear wastes. In other words, the *Green* was not a pirate whaler. Once you think about it, it *was* named *Green*, after all. Doesn't that kind of tell you something?

But Thomas said it was a mocking name.

And even at the time you thought that was a little far-fetched.

No, you didn't.

Yes, you did.

8

Surely Thomas's biggest lie was "Everything you do matters." Nothing matters, we've already established that. Truth, trust, caring, hand jobs: all meaningless. Unfortunately, the more clearly she sees this, the more Russell imagines Significance everywhere. "I was going to take the bus the day before, but at the last minute I decided not to," he marvels.

"If anything, that shows how random it was, Russell."

He elaborates on the Fate theme until she wants to scream. But that also means nothing. Or nothing more than that she forgot to take her hearts-ease medication.

But no. Even saying "Nothing matters" is imposing too much coherence. A few things apparently do matter. She is running out of hearts-ease. She is also running out of money. What then? Grow her own? Where is Bluffaroo when she needs him? Get a job? With Russell? She would have to listen to his lunatic theories all day long. In James's band, singing Hawaiian love songs? She would have to fight off his advances in some dark corner during every break.

Because it has progressed to that. James touches her whenever Russell is not looking. He laughs as he tweaks her, and laughs again, unpleasantly, when she tells him to stop. When all of them are sitting on the couch irradiating themselves in the blue light he reaches along the back of the couch right behind Russell and massages her neck. Well, so what? Russell doesn't own her. James repels her, but does he repel her any more than Russell does? It's a tough call. Maybe she should give James a hand job, too, if he wants it so badly. It doesn't matter.

But something stops her. James is not asking politely. Sunning in the Hole while Russell is at work, hearing James pause in the hall outside the door, Jane is suddenly vouchsafed a clear vision, like a shaft of sunlight parting the haze of hemp: James could come into the Hole anytime and fall on her like a ton of bricks. What could she do? The stacks of pancakes and waffles he stuffs into himself every day suddenly seem sinister. He is padding himself, so that when he gets around to raping her, her punches will just bounce off him. Couldn't she plunge her thumbs into his eyes? But that is merely something she read. It probably wouldn't work.

She locks herself in the bathroom and takes Russell's shaving razor out of the medicine cabinet. She turns on the water in the sink.

When Russell comes home from work he finds her lying in the Hole and exclaims, shocked, "What did you *do?*" He drops to his knees to examine her.

"Hair as a concept is vastly overrated," she says. Russell runs his hands over her gleaming pate. "Since you liked my hair, you must hate this."

"No," he says after a long moment. "I love it."

She shrugs, defeated. It figures.

Like when he noticed her haiku. "What are these?"

"Nothing. I don't know why I even carry them around. Don't read them, I'm going to throw them away."

"But I like these."

"They're stupid."

"I never liked a poem before, but I really like these."

"I call them 'moment essences,'" she said bitterly, trying to put him off.

But she forgot that he likes it when she uses fancy words. "They're so small, like you. That's why I like them."

"You must be a closet child molester."

"Just because you're small?"

"Because I'm thirteen."

"You don't look thirteen, I already told you. I swear on a stack of Bibles."

But age is irrelevant, now that her hair is gone. She looks neither thirteen nor sixteen. In the mirror she sees a coffee-colored doll with too large glittering eyes and too small ears. Only as old as the factory date. But Russell can negotiate any curve. "I love you. Don't you love me?"

"I like you as a friend."

"Is that all? Isn't there anything about me that you love?"

"Sure."

"What?"

"I like . . ." She ponders wearily. "God, I don't know. I like the way you're a hard worker."

"Like, not love?"

"Aren't they the same?"

"Love is strong. You don't feel anything strong for me?"

"I like you, Russell."

"But why don't you love me? Tell me what you don't love and I'll change it. I can read more."

"I don't want you to read more."

"You probably want to talk about more intellectual things."

"Intellectual things make me want to barf."

"What do you want?"

"I want to talk about something else."

But he circles back incessantly. His visions of their future life together are branching, sending down roots. Dr. and Mr. Jane Dark, with their kids of yet-to-be-determined parentage. They could live in Virginia, since land prices are low there. But after looking into it (yes, he looks into it) he discovers Virginia has a personal property tax, so perhaps North Carolina would be better. Somewhere warm, anyway, where Jane can sun as much as she wants, and where the economy is growing, where hard workers have a future unencumbered by unions, which protect only bozos. Near a city, so Jane can commute to the big hospital where she will have her brilliant career. He talks about the stone house they will live in. Stone is best because it lasts the longest and doesn't require the maintenance of wood or brick. It's the only sensible thing. It costs more up front, but in the long run it saves you money. You have to plan ahead. If he did read more, he would know about moats, and he would talk about the fat deep one they would get dug around their stone house, although he would suspect that the moat-building contractor would probably take advantage of them. "Better to dig it ourselves," he would say. "It might take longer, but we would know the job was done right. And we should train the moat monsters ourselves, otherwise there's no telling . . ."

And she thought Russell had no interior life. She is the empty one, this doll with glittering eyes and smoke coming out of her mouth. His visions fill her until she catches herself wondering what the stone house will be like, whether the North Carolinian summers will be too hot, how difficult it might be to find a cure for her syndrome. "I don't want to live in North Carolina," she struggles to say.

"Fine," he says, negotiating the curve. "We can live wherever you want to live. You're the one who'll have the more important career."

"I don't want an important career."

"Fine. I don't mind making most of the money. We won't have as much, but that's OK. And you'll have more time for your research."

"I don't want to do research."

"Or whatever! You can do whatever you want! Whatever you do, baby, I'm sure it will be great. I'll support you all the way."

Whatever she does. How about *this?* The doll gets into bed with Russell, taking off her underwear. He gulps and stares and for once can't choke out how much he loves it. "I do sort of feel like a child molester this way."

"Finally," she says, jerking him off.

Now it doesn't matter if she can't get her skin off, since she is as hairless as if she could. And it doesn't matter that he is uneasy, because he sleeps like a log, anyway. He'll figure out how to love it. By the morning he'll be saying, "You're like a little, wild whale! That's what I love about you." The next logical step on the road to anatomical incorrectness is to ensure that her period doesn't come, so she smokes another joint.

9

But her period comes, just as if she were human, and with it, as inexorably, comes the realization that she is leaving. Normally she would have no trouble getting out the door without waking the boys, but of course on this particular morning the bloodhounds are hot on her trail. Russell appears in the kitchen in his underwear, squinting at the light, just as she is zipping the last zipper, and it takes several exchanges on the order of "What are you doing? / I'm leaving," before he wakes up enough to become alarmed, but by that point Jane has her hand on the door.

He doesn't grab her or block the door or throw himself in front of her like a protester before a bulldozer. She'll hand that to him. Instead he runs toward his Hole, pleading "Wait!" and follows her down the stairs, having got his pants on, clutching a shirt which he shrugs on at the landing. By the metal grate he hops, pulling on his sneakers, and chases her down the stoop. "This is crazy!"

"Maybe *I'm* crazy, Russell," she says, hurrying away from him with her fingers in her fucking ears.

"Just talk to me! Tell me why!"

"It's complicated."

"But it's so out of the blue! What about all our plans?"

"*Our* plans?" Jane stops to face him. "You never listened to me. I kept telling you you were dreaming."

"One second we're talking about marriage, and the next —"

"We never talked about marriage." Jane walks away from the very idea.

"Dr. and Mr. Jane Dark!" he says, trailing her.

"Oh yeah, on the mailbox."

"Maybe I said something. Did I do something stupid? What did I do?"

"It has nothing to do with you."

"We've got something fantastic here, baby, the two of us together."

"For pete's sake! Don't call me baby! That's exactly what I'm talking about. I've asked you a hundred times not to call me baby and you keep doing it!"

"Is that why you're leaving? Heck, I can stop calling you baby."

"That's not why."

"But our relationship is so — so —"

"One-sided."

"— so special! I never felt so sure about anything in my life! I've never been so happy!"

"I'm sorry I make you happy, Russell. I didn't mean to make you happy."

"Look. I'm thinking . . ." He hugs himself in his thin cotton shirt. She can see the unappetizing boniness of his chest and arms. "Why don't we get married? Let's just do it and get rid of this uncertainty. We can go to city hall. James can be our witness."

And fondle Jane through the whole ceremony, what a great idea. "You don't even know me, Russell."

"I knew everything I needed to know in the first five minutes."

"Yeah? How come you don't know I'm not old enough to get married?"

His brow furrows in puzzlement. "I thought sixteen was old enough."

Jane shrieks, "How many times do I have to tell you I'm not sixteen?"

"OK, what are you, fifteen? We can go to some other state. I think in the South you can get married even when you're fourteen."

"Wow, that young, huh?" Jane stops at the subway stairs. "My family isn't dead, you know. I actually haven't traveled much. I don't have Artemis Syndrome. I lied about all that."

Russell is blushing deeply. "So what? I lie about some things, too."

"I shave my head and my pubic hair. Don't you think that's strange?"

"This is New York City."

"You should get together with this Liz person. She sounds like a normal person."

"Liz?"

"The girl your Aunt Patty likes. The first night I was in your apartment I looked through all your things. I'm not only a liar, I'm also a snoop."

"I don't care about any of that," he says in a strangled tone. "I know what's important."

"Yeah? I'd love to know. What's important?"

"You."

Jane throws up her hands.

"You and me." He speaks with grinding insistence. "We're important."

"God, you're gullible." She turns down the stairs.

"So you're not perfect," he says, following her. "We'll help each other, that's what it's all about." She needs a machete, a yataghan, a snickersnee. Anything to cut the jungle vines twining around her arms and legs, reaching for her throat. "Please," Russell says at the turnstile. "Let's talk. Just give me an hour. If you still want to go after that, I'll let you go."

"'Let me go.' You see? Don't you see?"

"I can follow you."

She puts a token in the turnstile and pushes through. "You can't even come on the subway, you don't have any money." He starts to climb over. "Don't!" He leans forward to jump, but she pushes him back. "*Don't!* I'll start screaming. I'm a good liar, I'll say you raped me."

For the first time, instead of being insistent, groveling, or just plain deaf, he is surprised. "You wouldn't."

"Try me."

He falters, and in those seconds she can see in his face that he is switching directions, dimly realizing that he can't, in fact, count on her not to make a horrible scene. Like a drowning man, he flails and gets his hands on a piece of flotsam. "You can go away, but it won't change anything. I'll wait for you."

"That's a real bad idea."

"I'll find you, wherever you go."

"You don't know where I live."

"I know your name. There can't be too many Jane Darks in the world."

A train is coming. "I'm going to get on this train, Russell. Are you going to let me go, or do I have to get someone to cut you off?"

The enraged roaring of the approaching train. Russell shakes his head, slack-mouthed: "If you want to go, I won't stop you."

But when it comes right down to it, Jane can't stand to leave him there looking so desperately unhappy, so uncomprehending. "Look," she says, mentally bouncing a palm off her forehead and bellowing to herself No! No!, "I'll give you my address."

"Yes!" he says, hugging this lifesaver. "I promise, I won't bother you. I'll let you think things through on your own. Just send the word, and I'll be there on the next bus."

The train blasts into the station on a tide of warm air, a whirlwind of gum wrappers and tissues, as Jane scribbles her address on a page ripped from the haiku notebook and thrusts it at him. The blessed doors are open, beckoning. She runs through them and as they slice shut behind her, cutting him off, she feels the release, a sensation so strong it seems physical — like the Discipline she used to practice down by the lake when she cupped the plasma of Sky in her palm — as if real vines coiled around her chest loosened and fell dead to the floor. Perhaps this is the Essence of Freedom: the taste of oxygen in her lungs.

10

So half of her problem is solved, and with only thirty dollars to her name and not a shred of hearts-ease, she wanders around the bus station, wondering about the other half. She has to admit, she is kind of reluctant to stay in the City, where, it seems, her only options are the pimps or the degenerate Park Avenue couple. She is also reluctant to hitchhike out, when it would take only one wrong number for her to end up in a ditch somewhere. There are always the buses, but here, too, danger lurks, in the person of the man who will sit next to her and become slavishly dependent on her.

But she cannot dawdle, looking so obviously low on money and at a loss, since any minute the pimps might get her. Although the station is huge, with signs pointing toward trains, subways, shuttles, airport buses, and limos, she finds herself inexorably drawn to the counter of the only company she knows. Can the embarrassing truth be told? Jane Dark buys a ticket for Ithaca. Some wanderer! We each get the road we deserve, and hers has turned out to be a dark alley, and she too much of a scaredy-cat even to stay in it.

To give her the benefit of the doubt, perhaps the ticket price had something to do with it. Twenty-nine dollars. Fated? Russell would have said so. But Russell is dead. She cut out his heart and handed it to him on a silver platter. No, her return to Ithaca is not fated, it is merely a case of the dog returning to her vomit. What a disgusting image. She tries to put it out of her mind. Will she ever be able to think delicious thoughts again? Will she ever deserve a warm kitchen on a cold snowy day, baking bread and buttering the fresh, steaming slices for the crew?

In the bowels of the station she climbs into the bus and puts her pack on the seat next to her to keep the lunatics at bay. But the bus is nearly empty. It rises out of the ground into light snow, into traffic like cold treacle, the driver intoning points north.

Going home. Is that what she should call this? Is home where you feel needed, wanted? That seems too restricted a meaning to be of much use. Perhaps "home" merely means the place you could walk around in with your eyes closed, the place you know best. But since she doesn't even know what to call it anymore, how can she know it? "White-on-the-Water" is childish, self-important. "Wholeworld" is wherever Thomas is. Maybe Lauren has been right all these years, simply saying "the Old Place."

Perhaps it was called that by her family, seeing as they owned it since the glaciers retreated. She can see the Whites sitting around the gleaming forty-foot dinner table in White Mansion, spooning oxtail soup from Wedgwood bowls. "The Old Place has a hole in the roof," the Chairman of the Board would sigh, dabbing linen against the corners of his mouth. "What are we going to do about it?"

"We could take it off our taxes," one son says.

"We could depreciate it over five years," says another.

"We could torch it and claim a deduction," says a third.

"We could fix it and call it a capital gain," says a fourth.

"But it's so far away, no one would want to live there," sighs a fifth.

"Beulah, take this mayonnaise sandwich up to Lauren, here's the key," says the sixth.

The White men exchange glances.

So Lauren wasn't raised by loving parents, and she dropped out of college to go to India. When she arrived at the ashram, was Thomas already there? Was he the guru's favorite because he smacked his lips the loudest when drinking the guru's urine? One sure way to reduce the waste stream is to connect the outflow pipe with the intake valve.

When the second Lila was killed by the motorcyclist, Lauren came to his hut. Did he, having just lost his true love, take up with Lauren on the rebound? But no, Jo said Lauren wasn't his favorite until after they had moved to Wonderland.

But who says Thomas only had sex with his favorites? Perhaps Thomas's favorite in India was the skinny chick, but he also had Lauren on the side. When the guru deputized him to go out and spread the Word, he vaguely remembered that woman who came to him after Lila died, the one who casually mentioned her family's huge land-holdings while they were having wild sex, what was her name?

And so they came: Thomas, the skinny chick, a few other women, and Lauren. Thomas bused in some other men so that he wouldn't drown in all those women, but he reserved the right to have sex with all of them and to make any woman his favorite at any time, which meant she would sweep his hut and clean his clothes in the stream.

And join him in the brass bed? Perhaps the brass bed was reserved for the favorite, while all the other women and girls had to content themselves with the high grass, or the barn loft. Perhaps the brass bed in those days was in Thomas's hut, and it was only moved into Lauren's bedroom after the commune fell apart. She would have been ecstatic to have this symbol of divine favor all to herself, and she would have cunningly moved it to the soft pinewood floor so that the legs would dig into the planks and the bed would be hard to take away from her.

And Thomas's children came along. Was Saskia at least the first? Which of the strangers in the photos underneath her bed are her half-brothers and half-sisters? Perhaps all of Thomas's daughters were named Saskia. Perhaps "Saskia" means "series."

And then Thomas's crystal began to hum too much. Everything he looked at shined Thomasness back at him. No matter what he did, his disciples inched forward, saying, "Yes? Yes?" And so he beat them, and then tried to hand his heart to them on a platter, and finally ran away, searching for some faraway land where no one would recognize Thomasness. But before he left, he gathered his women around his hospital bed and told them to lie for him, and they did. "That Thomas is dead," he told them, having learned his lesson. "If my various Saskias ever ask . . ." And all those eight long years, Lauren never wavered in her promise to him that she would not tell Saskia he was the guru. Did Thomas himself pick Raymond as the false guru? Or did Lauren pick him on the spur of the moment, when Saskia first asked about the photo of everyone on the porch? Raymond was near the middle, and therefore he was the guru, and after that Lauren would say no more because anything she might say would be a lie. And Lauren, Saskia has a feeling, doesn't lie if she can avoid it, she just refuses to tell the truth. And in her heart, failing to negotiate the curve, she still revered Thomas *qua* guru, and felt guilty for not having chopped his head off when he asked her to.

Wild times.

And she locked Saskia in her room, but eventually forgave her —

for what? for staying behind? — and let her out. Two years later, Jo Flynn showed up with four kids but no husband, because Mack or Mick had taken off as soon as he had figured out that Jo was pregnant by Thomas (which must have been obvious, since Mack or Mick's tubes were really tied, unlike Thomas's, which were either never tied, or tied and then untied). Perhaps Lauren took Jo and the children in, letting all of them live rent free, because she felt guilty about the fact that Thomas had broken up Jo's marriage, and because Lauren is a martyr, unlike people who are raised by loving parents.

What was Thomas doing for eight years? Those wonderful stories! How true were they? An interesting question, Jo said. Was he, indeed, working on the *Green?* Was Bent working there too, and was McBride the captain? Did Thomas burn something, or sink something, or kill somebody, and did McBride wax wroth, bellowing, "I'll have you arrested, by God!" and did Bent intervene, in his stolid manner, saying, "Perhaps it would be better just to pay him a settlement"?

But if there was no *Lila,* and she did not sink, what happened to the third Lila? She was a puppy when Saskia was two, so she would have been ten or eleven when Thomas suddenly wrote to Saskia and Lauren, suggesting a summer trip. Did she just die of old age? Did Thomas think that was too boring to admit to? Why did Thomas suddenly want to see Saskia after eight years? He told her in the veggie café that he had waited until she was old enough to come to him on her own. But was he telling the truth? Lila had just died, naturally or not. He wrote and invited both Lauren and Saskia. Lauren said he didn't really mean her, but she was still feeling guilty and unworthy of him because she had failed to chop his head off. Maybe he did want her to come. Maybe the death of the third Lila reminded him of the death of the second, after which he took up with Lauren on the rebound. "I felt so lonely when she died," he said, speaking of the first Lila.

Isn't it time to face something? Long ago, back in the laughable days when Saskia thought she was an only child, she imagined

Thomas's two true loves amid all the other negligible women: Saskia and Lauren. Ha! Dream on! Surely Thomas had three true loves: the three Lilas. On the rebound, Thomas asked for Lauren, and got Jane instead. And although he had had sex with Young Things before, perhaps Jane was a little too young, since she didn't even have breasts. So instead he masturbated every night in his tent until Saskia handed Jane to him on a silver platter. Why did he come home with the girls? Was he already tired of Jane and wanted to trade up to Lauren? Or did he merely want to go back to the old days when he had had several at once?

Anyway, they all came back, and Thomas lasted as long as he could stand it, until he had to run away from Thomasness again. Last time he shattered first, but this time, having learned his lesson, he left before he started beating people up. Saskia thought he had left because she disappointed him, but maybe when he closed the front door that morning, escaping cleanly, what he felt was the loosening of vines around his chest. Will a card arrive at the Old Place in six months, saying, "Lauren and my Saskia and Quentin"? Will there be a photo enclosed of Thomas and a black and white puppy?

Where does Saskia fit in all this? Does Thomas think at all about his various Saskias when he's not with them, or does he merely whistle for his dog and thank his lucky stars that he doesn't have any albatrosses for the moment around his neck? Can she honestly expect any more from him? Why should he care about her? She is no perfect companion. Look at the wreckage she has caused. She boxed Quinny's ears and made him piss on the floor, and then abandoned him and left him blubbering. She plotted to get Bluffaroo booted, and on the day he left he was crying in his trailer and he turned and saw her at the door and sobbed, "Are you satisfied?" and yes, in fact, she was, she was so satisfied she didn't give another thought to him, she disappeared him the way Mrs. Sing disappeared the can opener. She pushed Jane into Thomas's arms, all the while surely knowing that Jane would fall madly in love with him, as any woman must, but that Thomas would assuredly want to trade up to Lauren, or at least diversify, and in any case he would eventually escape, and Jane would be devastated. And for her next trick, she went down to the City and tore out the heart of the first person she met, and in the very act of ripping his heart out, she managed to twist the blade, being merciful enough to give him her address but not merciful enough to give him her real one, but instead the address of her record company:

13 Road to Dis
Stygian Fields, New Jersey
54321

It probably wasn't even mercy, but merely squeamishness.

How did all this happen? How did she cause so much trouble, so much suffering? She wondered once if she would ever be the heroine of her own story. It never occurred to her that she might end up being the villainess.

Everything is more complicated than she thought. Are cows motherly saints who fit into their spaces better than any of God's creatures, or are they stupid creations of evil Man who are desertifying the world? If you protect the chickens and eat their eggs you're not a true vegetarian, but if you let a raccoon eat the chickens' heads, then you are? You can't really let a thousand babies die, can you? But what about ten thousand babies the next time around? Is Saskia human if she can't understand humans? If she isn't human, why is she menstruating like one? Why is she menstruating after smoking so much hemp? Or was that another of Thomas's lies? Why does Thomas lie? Was Thomas lying about the whales? If Man's brain is too big, why are whales' brains, which are bigger, not too big?

Saskia leans her head against the glass. Her brain hurts. What does she know? Does she know any more than that this window is cold? *Cogito ergo sum.*

An image keeps returning to her. She and Jane and Thomas are drinking champagne in the tent by the river of ichor, knee to knee to knee: an equilateral triangle. It felt incomplete at the time, so why does it look complete now? Surely that was the true Paradise, that one brief hour. And she didn't even recognize it. She sinned, wanting more. She thought Jane and Thomas could be yin and yang, and she the eely line between them. She didn't realize she was the snake in Paradise.

The web is torn, and Saskia is falling. In the City, the web had felt like a trap, carrying her down dark streets where she was afraid to go, forcing her to do things with Russell she didn't want to do. So is she free now, as she falls? Perhaps this, and not the other, is the Essence of Freedom: vertigo, terror.

11

Down into Ithaca's glacial ditch, past clapboard houses, the Masonic temple, the center for homeless women. Once she would have imagined herself disguised, coming secretly to pass tests (but which?) and save someone (but whom?), but she is just Saskia, returning to her vomit.

She doesn't even know who to call from the station, but settles finally, guiltily, on Jo, quailing at the prospect of Lauren asking why she never called her. As it turns out, Lauren isn't even at the Old Place, but "off jigging around a fire somewhere," as Jo puts it. So tonight is the solstice, then.

Did Jo sound relieved on the phone? Happy? Who knows? She didn't say, "Glad you're back, honey," if that's what you are wondering. As her Honda pulls into the lot, she cranes her head out the window, gaping. "What did you do to your hair?" Saskia gets in. "Is that the style in New York?"

"Yeah, they have these big shaving salons."

"No kidding. You look like a lightbulb."

"Thanks."

"And Lauren with such short hair now, too. Maybe I should get cropped."

"It's a mistake. It's cold."

On the way to Tyler, Saskia gets the latest. Bill is back.

"Already?" So he crawled back for more.

Saskia tries to reformulate Jo during the drive home, but doesn't get very far. She is chain-smoking, filling the Honda with a fog of nicotine, driving fast, muttering at drivers who get in her way but not bothering to get angry at them. Why should she? They are hardly obstacles, as she swerves past them on blind curves and hills. Thomas had sex with this woman. Is that drooping lower lip fun to kiss? Is she a wildcat in bed?

Construction paper signs festoon the front door of the Old Place: a big "Welcome Home, Saskia!" above and, below, drawings of kids crying tears as big as cherries, and exhaling cartoon balloons: "Don't go away again!" The one with shading must be Shannon's, the cute bugs saying "We love you!" are vintage Mim, while the crude crowd of stick figures could only come from the pen of Quentin. Even Austin contributed, as he makes sure she realizes: the block letters of the welcome banner are all his. Perhaps it would have been a touching reunion, but her looks frighten them. Mim bursts into tears.

"I think it looks cool," Austin says. "Can I shave my head, too?"

Studying them, she wonders if they could have grown up so much just in the weeks she was away. Mim will be wearing a bra soon, and Saskia makes a mental note to teach her about tampons and, more importantly, to shield her from the dread mensis meal. She looks hardest at Quentin. Almost eight, in second grade, no longer slobbering much. Are those water-blue eyes weak, or watchful? Doesn't his love for his dinosaurs indicate a sensitive streak?

"So what did you guys think of Thomas?" she asks curiously.

"He was super!" Mim says.

"Anh, he was OK," Austin demurs. "Kind of a slave driver. Is he coming back?"

"I don't think so."

"So hopefully we can have a normal Thanksgiving next time. That couch thing was really dumb."

Gorgon is back to being a house cat, and already getting fatter, as she no doubt pigs out to console herself for her absent god. And Bill? Some things never change. "Hey, Sas!"

"I don't answer to 'Sas.'"

"Whoa, Jo told me about the haircut." He makes a frame with his two hands and peers through it. "I like it, I like it!"

"That makes one of us."

"Lauren was really worried about you," he says, dropping the banter. "She even had a psychic spend a night in your bed."

"Yeah? What did the psychic say?"

"She said you were among a lot of people, and you were near water."

"Since I told Jo I was in New York, that's not too amazing."

Saskia unpacks in her room, wondering how she feels about being back. She can only conclude it has been a confusing year. In Tycho's day, they used to annually devise a motto that captured the spirit of the past twelve months. The trick was, all the letters in the motto that were Roman numerals had to add up to the year. To get through the last hour of the bus ride, Saskia slaved over one, which she now tacks on the outside of her door:

SASKIA CAPTURES JANE, LURES BUT LOSES THOMAS,
LEAVES LAUREN, EXPERIENCES EXILE,
RETURNS STUPIDER THAN EVER.

Not very comforting. But she remembers having read a book once that predicted this would be an awful year.

At dinner, Bill appears in the doorway holding a bottle of sparkling cider and leads the whole table in a rendition of "For She's a Prodigal Daughter." She remembers what she was thinking on the bus about her inability to understand people, and she looks hard at him — yes, even at him — trying to reformulate him. Pudgy, pretentious, clownish. But does he mean badly? When she brings her plate into the kitchen, she pauses by him at the sink. "Thanks for the cider. That was nice."

He looks at her, the nostrils of his tiny blob of a nose flaring faintly in surprise. "You're welcome."

All this time, she has bitten back the big question, because she has been afraid to ask, but Jo is in the kitchen, too, and she and Bill will be going to their trailers soon, so this may be Saskia's last chance until tomorrow. "Do either of you know what happened to Jane?"

Bill gazes uncomfortably into the dishwater. Jo waggles her head, a sour expression curdling her face. "That poor kid," she says.

"She's dead, isn't she?" Saskia feels hands closing around her throat. "You can tell me."

"What?" Bill says. "Nothing like that."

"If I'd known he was fooling with her, I woulda kicked him in the nuts," Jo says.

"So what happened to her?" Saskia persists.

"Her parents sent her away," Bill says.

"Because she's pregnant! I knew it!"

"No," Jo says. "They sent her to some boarding school with lots of shrinks."

Jane once told Saskia that if she was ever sent to a boarding school again, it would be one with searchlights on towers, and slavering German shepherds. Saskia will have to swing down on a rope with a Tarzan yell to rescue her. But will Jane want to be rescued by Saskia? Will Jane ever forgive her?

Outside, it is snowing.

She feels better when she wakes in the morning darkness. How comforting to wake in her own bed, with her mind clear! Opening her door, she finds a note attached below hers. Doodah green rag-paper, four pile-driven thumbtacks:

WELCOME BACK, SASKIA! I HOPE NEXT YEAR
WE WILL BE FRIENDS.
XX,
BILL

Her first thought is, he blew it, it adds up to one too much. But then she realizes, no, he means next year. He even says next year, stupido.

As she goes downstairs to get to work, she wonders how they can ever be friends if she is always so willing to think the worst of him.

She pops the corn, and wakes the crew, and together they watch the light bleed back into the world. "Happy winter solstice!" she says to them when her meteorological table tells her the sun has risen behind the clouds. Since she had no presents to give them, she made extra popcorn, and as they wish each other a happy solstice, they throw it in the air like confetti, and pelt each other, and stuff it down each other's shirts. So it's childish. So shoot her.

The morning light has revealed that it snowed heavily during the night, and Saskia wonders what kind of awful, uncomfortable night Lauren spent. At 10 A.M. Betsy comes creeping down the road, turning gingerly at the switchback and almost getting stuck in front of the garage. Saskia is sitting alone in the kitchen when the back hall door opens, letting in a blast of arctic air before Lauren slams it shut. She turns to take off her coat.

When Thomas came, Saskia was deprived, because of her own blabbiness, of the sight of calm Lauren looking surprised for once in her life. Maybe there was method to her madness, because missing it before makes the sight now of Lauren's jaw dropping, her hands stopping in mid-unbutton, doubly sweet. "Saskia!"

"Hi."

"You're back!"

"I guess so," she giggles.

"Your hair!"

"Oh. Yeah. I —" Saskia wonders how to explain, but before she can think of anything, she finds herself getting hugged.

"I was so worried!"

"That's what everyone's been saying," Saskia says, thoroughly delighted.

"I had a psychic sleep in your bed."

"Bill told me."

"She said you were all right, so I didn't worry as much after that."

Premature death of delight. "Oh, great. And what if the psychic was wrong?"

"She's a very good psychic."

So all the danger lying in wait for Saskia — the pimps in the station, the molesters on the street, Russell in his Hole, and James in the hall — all of them mean nothing because of a lousy psychic? Saskia is already irritated. But Lauren is still hugging her, so Saskia holds on tight, using her Discipline to expand these few seconds into hours, and supplies her own running text: I missed you so much, honey! I'm so glad you're back, sweetheart! I love you so much! Don't ever leave me again!

"You had a rough night," Saskia says.

"You're not kidding. I'm exhausted!"

"Why don't I make us some coffee?"

"That would be nice." Lauren takes off her coat and collapses in a chair while Saskia goes about getting the coffee ready. "So what did you do to your hair?" And for a couple of minutes they cover the basics, catching up, until Lauren asks the biggie, with anger in her voice: "Why did you run away?"

"I don't know," Saskia says honestly. "Why did Thomas run away?"

"Thomas didn't run away. He had things to do."

"When people don't say goodbye, I call it running away."

Lauren is silent.

"He told you he was going, didn't he?" Saskia says, trying not to sound accusing.

"Only the night before. We knew he had to leave sometime, what does the timing matter?"

"What did he say?"

Lauren shrugs. "He said he had to go."

"He had no choice, right?"

"What?"

"And what would he think about Bill being back?" Saskia can't resist this. Lauren's bovine acceptance of everything Thomas does irks her so.

But Lauren merely raises her eyebrows, surprised at Saskia's obtuseness. "He told me to take Bill back."

The coffee machine is hissing. Saskia pours a cup and sets it by Lauren's cradled chin. Lauren sniffs it, sits up, sips, sighs.

"Why does Thomas lie?"

"What are you talking about?"

"All this stuff about the guru, when he was the guru."

"That was to protect you."

"Seems like it was more to protect himself."

"You were four at the time, Saskia, and bound to ask all sorts of questions later. What could we have told you that you would have been able to understand? Thomas was right."

"How about the other things? He told me stories about things he did that weren't true."

"All teachers tell stories. They're guides to understanding. Saskia, this is the simplest thing! You'll understand later. And a few things, no, maybe you'll never understand. There are some things I don't understand. But you learn not to judge what you don't understand."

"Ours not to reason why?"

"You can put it snidely if you want to, but yes, that's right."

"I'm sorry, I think I deserve a few explanations."

"Obviously, you've been talking too much to Jo. She's never forgiven Thomas for Mitch leaving her. I wouldn't believe much of what she says."

Saskia's not sure she can take any more for the moment. But there's one last thing: "Do you remember a cake that came for me around Christmastime, when I was maybe three or four?"

"Sure. They came every Christmas."

"Who were they from?"

"Thomas's parents. A sweet thought, but they really were awful things, all sugar. Thomas never told them he threw them away."

"This was before his parents died?"

Lauren looks curiously through the rising steam of her cup. "Who said they died?"

"Forget it."

Lauren is quite revived from her sleepless night, and will no doubt work hard all day. "Thanks for making this." And glancing up at Saskia, she says seriously, "I'm glad you're back." Honey. She looks away, to take the curse off the question. "And you're glad to be back?"

Saskia thinks about how even now and probably for years to come she will be tripping over little items that Thomas lied about, for no apparent reason, merely for the love of tricking people. She thinks about the twinkle in his blue eyes, and the beautiful hands. She thinks about the first thing she will do now that she is back, which will be to walk barefoot in the snow to the boarding school with the searchlights and the slavering German shepherds, and to kneel outside the gate with her head bowed in shame until the gatekeeper asks her for the password, and to cry past him, up to the windows of the towers in which the homeless girls are locked away, "Friend! Friend!" She thinks about her own name, whose meaning she still does not know, and she thinks of all the years she waited to ask him, then never asking him when she had the chance, and how it is just as well, because even if he had said something other than "I just liked the sound of it," it probably would have been a lie. She thinks about Lauren, who all these years has never betrayed Thomas, and how hard and thankless a job that was, when Saskia was pestering her for information when she felt she could give none, and she thinks about Thomas, who betrayed Lauren at every turn, saying, among so many other things, when she was thousands of miles away and could not defend herself, that it was her fault that he had left Godhead and subsequently stayed away. She thinks about him telling Lauren to go back to Bill, which was just one more order in a long string of orders, and this makes her think about the note he left for her, which, now that she thinks about it, was also an order: not "I'm sorry," but "Forgive me." Who says he's sorry? She thinks about the one thing she can do, the last scrap of power he left her, which is to refuse to forgive him. "Yeah," she says. "I'm glad I'm back."

And thinks: I think.

THE SASKIAD

AUTHOR'S NOTE

The books that Saskia has read and reread are real books, and bits of their texts have lodged themselves in her mind. Since her unconscious borrowings could hardly be flagged with quotation marks, I should acknowledge my debts here. The biography of Tycho Brahe that Saskia picked up in the Round Tower is by J. L. E. Dreyer. Her favorite book on alchemy is Jacques Sadoul's *Alchemists and Gold*. Many of her naval and Napoleonic turns of phrase hail from C. S. Forester. Marco Polo and the various Tartar Khans sometimes speak in the words of Ronald Latham, translator for the Penguin edition of *The Travels*.

My most important debt by far is to Richmond Lattimore, whose magnificent translation of the *Odyssey* crops up in gemlike fragments throughout the *Saskiad*. I would love to be able to say that the grave and beautiful description of the island of Ithaca that opens this book — "low and away, last of all on the water toward the dark" — was my own. It is Lattimore's.